What Others Are Saying About Sharlene MacLaren and *Heart of Mercy*

Mercy me, what a love story! Sharlene MacLaren has done it again—swept me away with a tender tale that has stolen both my breath and my sleep. Rich with historical detail, small-town magic, and the wonder of hearth and home, *Heart of Mercy* will coax tears from your eyes and hope from your soul.

—*Julie Lessman*
Author, The Daughters of Boston and the Winds of Change series

This Tennessee mountain Romeo and Juliet story is a roller coaster ride of a tale—and it's MacLaren's best yet. Of course, I think that about each of her books!

—*Lena Nelson Dooley*
Author, *Love Finds You in Golden, New Mexico,*
and the McKenna's Daughters series

Three words come to mind when I think of Sharlene MacLaren's amazing novel, *Heart of Mercy*: Lovely, lovely, lovely! Truly, one of the best inspirational historicals I've read in ages, with the ideal mix of romance and intrigue. Highly recommended!

—*Janice Thompson*
Author, *Queen of the Waves*

Feuding families. Forbidden romance. A first real kiss that leaves you breathless. With nail-biting excitement, a heart-tugging marriage of convenience, and a powerful message of faith and forgiveness, *Heart of Mercy* is Shar MacLaren's best book to date. I loved it!

—*Vickie McDonough*
Author, *Whispers on the Prairie* and *Call of the Prairie*

HEART OF Mercy

HEART OF
Mercy

—A Novel By SHARLENE
MACLAREN

WHITAKER
HOUSE

Heart of Mercy
Tennessee Dreams ~ Book 1

Sharlene MacLaren
www.sharlenemaclaren.com
sharlenemaclaren@yahoo.com

ISBN: 978-1-60374-963-3
eBook ISBN: 978-1-60374-987-9
Printed in the United States of America
© 2014 by Sharlene MacLaren

Whitaker House
1030 Hunt Valley Circle
New Kensington, PA 15068
www.whitakerhouse.com

Library of Congress Cataloging-in-Publication Data (Pending)

1 2 3 4 5 6 7 8 9 10 11 ᴡ 21 20 19 18 17 16 15 14

Dedication

To Charity, my wonderful sister-in-law and forever friend. I am so thankful and blessed that Dick chose *you*. When I think how tirelessly you cared for our mother, my heart fills to overflowing. Thank you for being the generous, caring, fun, and loving individual that you are. You have lived up to your name many times over.
I love you.

Evans Family Tree

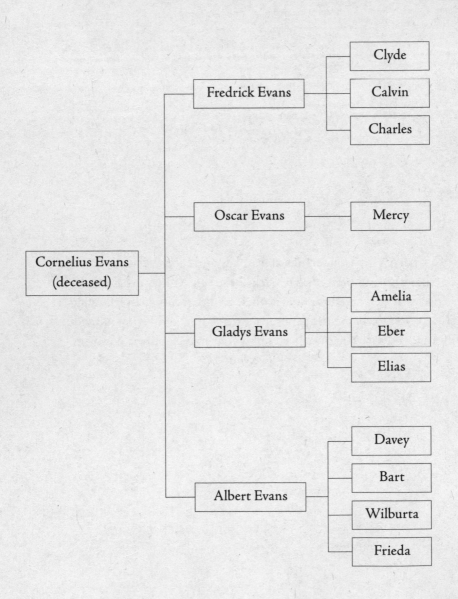

Connors Family Tree

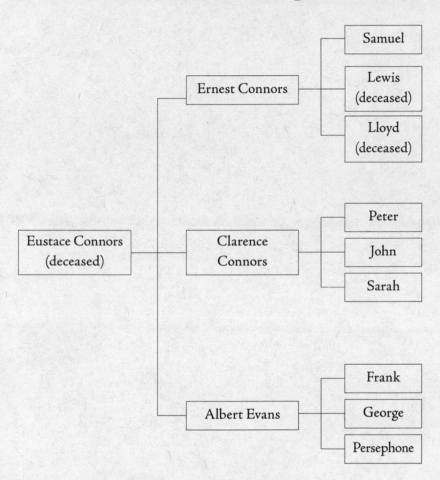

1

1890 · *Paris, Tennessee*

ire!"

The single word had the power to force a body to drop to his knees and call out to his Maker for leniency. But most took time for neither, instead racing to the scene of terror with the bucket they kept stored close to the door, and joining the contingent of citizens determined to battle the flames of death and destruction. Such was the case tonight, when, washing the dinner dishes in the kitchen sink, Mercy Evans heard the dreaded screams coming from all directions, even began to smell the sickening fumes of blazing timber seeping through her open windows. She ran through her house and burst through the screen door onto the front porch.

"Where's the fire?" she shouted at the people running up Wood Street carrying buckets of water.

Without so much as a glance at her, one man hollered on the run, "Looks to be the Watson place over on Caldwell."

Her heart thudded to a shattering halt. *God, no!* "Surely, you don't mean Herb and Millie Watson!"

Mercy Evans and Millie Watson, formerly Gifford, had been fast friends at school and had stuck together like glue in the dimmest of circumstances,

11

as well as the brightest. Millie had walked with Mercy through the loss of both her parents, and Mercy had watched Millie fall wildly in love with Herb Watson in the twelfth grade. She'd been the maid of honor in their wedding the following summer. And she'd rejoiced with the couple at the birth of each of their sons, now ages five and six.

But her voice was lost to the footsteps thundering past. Whirling on her heel, she ran back inside, hurried to extinguish all but one kerosene lamp, snatched her wrap from its hook by the door, and darted back outside and up the rutted street toward her best friends' home, dodging horses and a stampede of citizens. "Lord, please don't let it be," she pleaded aloud. "Oh, God, keep them safe. Jesus, Jesus…." But her cries vanished in the scramble of bodies crowding her off the street as they made the turn onto Caldwell in their quest to reach the flaming house, which already looked beyond saving.

Tongues of fire shot like dragons' breath out windows and up through a hole in the roof. Like hungry serpents, flames lapped up the sides of the house, eating walls and shattering panes, while men heaved their pathetic little buckets of water at the volcanic monster.

"Back off, everybody. Step back!" ordered Sheriff Phil Marshall. He and a couple of deputies on horseback spread their arms wide at the crowd, trying to push them to safety.

Ignoring his orders, Mercy pressed through the gathering mob until the heat so overwhelmed her that she had no choice but to stop. At the same time, a giant arm reached out to halt her progress. She shook it off. "Where are they?" she gasped, breathless. "Where's the family?"

The sheriff moved his bald head from side to side, his sad, defeated eyes telling the story. "Don't know, Miss Evans. No one's seen 'em yet. We been scourin' the crowd"—he gave another shake of the head—"and it don't appear anybody got out of that inferno."

"That can't be." A sob caught at the back of her throat and choked her next words. "They were at my place earlier. I made supper."

"Sorry, miss."

"Someone's comin' out!" A man's ear-splitting shout rose above the crowd.

Dense smoke enveloped a large figure emerging from the open door and staggering like a drunkard onto the porch, his arms full with two wriggling bundles wrapped in blankets and screaming in terror. Mercy sucked in a cavernous breath and held it till weakness overtook her and she forced herself to let it out. Could it be? Had little John Roy and Joseph survived the fire thanks to this man?

"Who is it?" someone asked.

All stood in rapt silence as he passed through the cloud of smoke. "Looks to be Sam Connors, the blacksmith," said the sheriff, scratching his head and stepping forward.

"Sure 'nough is," someone confirmed.

Mercy stared in wonder as the man, looking dazed and almost ethereal, strode down the steps, then wavered and stumbled before falling flat on his face in a heap of dust, bringing the howling bundles with him.

Excited chatter erupted as Mercy and several others ran to their aid. Mercy yanked the blankets off the boys and heaved a sigh of relief to find them both alert and apparently unharmed, albeit still screeching louder than a couple of banshees. Through their avalanche of tears, they recognized her, and they hurled themselves into her arms, knocking her backward, so that she wound up on her back at a right angle to Mr. Connors, with both of the boys lying prone across her body. In all the chaos, she felt a hand grasp her arm and help her up to a sitting position.

"Come on, Miz. You bes' git yo'self an' them chillin's out of the way o' them flames fo' you all gets burned." She had the presence of mind to look up at Solomon Turner, a former slave now in the employ of Mrs. Iris Brockwell, a prominent Paris citizen who'd donated a good deal of money to the hospital fund.

Mercy took the man's callused hand and allowed him to help her to stand. By the lines etched in his face from years of hard work in the sweltering sun, Mercy figured he had to be in his seventies, yet he lifted her with no apparent effort. "Thank you, Mr. Turner."

Five-year-old John Roy stretched his arms upward, pleading with wet eyes to be held, while Joseph, six, took a fistful of her skirt and clung with all his might. "Come," she said, hoisting John Roy up into her arms. "We'd best do as Mr. Turner says, honey. Follow me."

"But…Mama and Papa…." Joseph turned and gave his perishing house a long perusal, tears still spilling down his face. John Roy buried his wrenching sobs in Mercy's shoulder, and it was all she could do to keep from bolting into the house herself to search for Herb and Millie, even though she knew she'd never come out alive. If the fire and smoke didn't kill her, the heat would. Besides, before her eyes, the flames had devoured the very sides of the house, leaving a skeletal frame with a staircase only somewhat intact and a freestanding brick fireplace looking like a graveyard monument. Her heart throbbed in her chest and thundered in her ears, and she wanted to scream, but the ever-thickening smoke and acrid fumes burned to the bottom of her lungs.

With her free hand, she hugged Joseph close to her. "I know, sweetheart, and I'm so, so sorry." Her words drowned in her own sobs as the truth slammed against her. Millie and Herb, her most loyal friends. Gone.

Sheriff Marshall and his deputies ordered the crowd to move away from the blazing house, so she forced herself to obey, dragging a reluctant Joseph with her. At the same time, she observed three men carrying a yet unconscious Sam Connors across the street to a grassy patch of ground. Several others gathered around, trying to decide what sort of care he needed. Of course, he required medical attention, but Mercy felt too weak and dizzy to tend to him. Best to let the men put him on a cart and drive him over to Doc Trumble's. Besides, she highly doubted he'd welcome her help. He was a Connors, after all, and she an Evans—two families who had been fighting since as far back as anyone could remember.

She'd heard only bits and pieces of how the feud had started, with a dispute between Cornelius Evans, Mercy's grandfather, and Eustace Connors over property lines and livestock grazing in the early 1830s. There had been numerous thefts of horses and cattle, and incidents of barn burnings, committed by both families, until a judge had stepped in and defined the property lines—in favor of Eustace Connors. Mercy's grandfather had gotten so agitated over the matter that his heart had given out. Mercy's grandmother, Margaret, had blamed the Connors family, fueling the feud by passing her hatred for the entire clan on to her own children; and so the next generation had carried the grudge, mostly forgetting its origins but not the bad blood. The animosity had reached a peak six years ago, when Ernest Connors had killed Oscar Evans—Mercy's father.

"That man's a angel," Joseph mumbled into her skirts.

"What, honey?"

"John Roy was wailin' real loud, 'cause he saw somethin' orange comin' from upstairs, so he got in bed with me, and after a while that angel man comed in and took us out of ar bed."

She set John Roy on the ground, then got down on her knees to meet Joseph's eyes straight on. His were still red, his cheeks blotchy. She thought very carefully about her next words. "Where were your parents?"

Joseph sniffed. "They tucked us in and went upstairs to their bedroom. John Roy an' me talked a long time about scary monsters an' stuff, but then, after a while, he went to sleep, but I couldn't, so I got up t' get a drink o' water, and that's when I heard a noise upstairs. I looked around the corner, and I seed a big round ball o' orange up there, and smoke comin' out of it, and I thought it was a dragon come to eat us up. I runned back and jumped in bed with Joseph and tol' him a mean monster was comin' t' get us, and I started cryin' real loud."

John Roy picked up the story from there. "And so we waited and waited for the monster to come after us, but instead the angel saved us. I think Mama and Papa is prolly still sleepin'. Do you think they waked up yet?"

Mercy's throat burned as powerfully as if she'd swallowed a tablespoonful of acid. Her own eyes begged to cut loose a river of tears, but she warded them off with a shake of her head while gathering both boys tightly to her. "No, darlings, I don't believe they woke up in bed. I believe with all my heart they awoke in heaven and are right now asking Jesus to keep you safe."

"And so Jesus tol' that angel to come in the house and get us?" Joseph pointed a shaky finger at Sam Connors. The big fellow lay motionless on his back, with several men bent over him, calling his name and fanning his face.

Mercy smiled. "He's not an angel, my sweet, but that's not to say that God didn't have something to do with sending him in to rescue you."

"Is he gonna die?" John Roy asked between frantic sobs.

"Oh, honey, I don't know."

She overheard Lyle Phelps suggest they take him over to Doc Trumble's house, but then Harold Crew said he'd spotted the doctor about an hour ago, driving out to the DeLass farm to deliver baby number seven.

A few sets of eyes glanced around until they landed on Mercy. She knew what folks were thinking. She worked for Doc Trumble, she had more medical training and experience than the average person, and her house was closest to the scene. But their gazes also indicated they understood the awkwardness of the situation, considering the ongoing feud between the two families. Although the idea of caring for him didn't appeal, she'd taken an oath to always do her best to preserve life. Besides, the Lord commanded her to love her neighbor as herself, making it a sin to walk away from someone in need, regardless of his family name.

She dropped her shoulders, even as the boys snuggled close. "Put him on a cart and take him to my place," she stated.

As if relieved that his care would fall to someone other than themselves, several men hurried to pick him up and then carried him to Harold Crew's nearby buggy.

"What about us?" Joseph asked.

The sheriff stepped forward and made a quick study of each boy. "You can stay out at my sister's farm. She won't mind adding a couple o' more young'uns to her brood."

Joseph burst into loud howls upon the sheriff's announcement. Mercy hugged him and John Roy possessively. "Their parents were my closest friends, Sheriff Marshall. I'd like to assume their care."

He frowned and scratched the back of his head. "Don't know as that's the best solution, you bein' unwed an' all."

"That should have no bearing whatever on where they go. They're like family, and they're coming home with me." She took both boys by the hands, turned, and led them back down Caldwell Street, away from the still-smoldering house and the sheriff's disapproving gaze. Overhead, black smoke filled the skies, obliterating the night's first stars and the crescent moon.

2

Sam Connors fought his way to consciousness like a mouse trying to work its way through a maze. Everywhere he turned, he hit a dead end, his mind clogged with thick fog and his head pounding like a hammer striking an anvil. His lungs burned, and he desperately needed to take a long, deep breath. Voices he couldn't distinguish called his name and spoke in broken sentences; he couldn't piece together what they wanted, let alone lift his heavy eyelids to see which voice belonged to whom. Now and then, he heard a woman order everyone to hush up or leave. Presumably, the voice belonged to the woman whose gentle ministrations he sensed—a cold cloth dabbing his forehead; a chilly metal instrument pressed to his chest. He found comfort in the voice, even though he didn't recognize it. He liked its no-nonsense quality.

He had the strongest urge to learn his whereabouts. Nothing felt familiar, least of all the firm, narrow surface he lay upon. Somebody's sofa, perhaps.

Little by little, his head started clearing as waves of remembrance rolled over in his mind—scorching flames extending out at him like a thousand vicious snake tongues; the tortured cries of children. Yes, there had been a massive fire. He recalled it now—the two-story structure on the corner of Caldwell and Washington, with orange flames spewing from its upstairs windows.

Without a moment's hesitation, he slammed the weight of his body against the front door and stormed inside. He took the steps two at a time, rounded the corner at the top, and came face-to-face with fiery, hissing balls of orange and yellow that churned out blinding black clouds. He couldn't fight his way through the raging wave of red-hot flame, so he turned away. Smoke, thick and rancid, invaded his lungs, rapidly stealing his breath. He tried not to suck in the poisonous fumes, but his head soon went dizzy from lack of air. Hot, so hot. Was this what hell was like? Flames licking at one's feet, scorching the face and neck, and reaching out to steal the last second of life? Frantic, he felt his way back to the stairs, blackness encasing him like a tomb. Then came the heart-wrenching screams—from the first floor, it seemed—which gave him a new sense of purpose. He stretched out his hand and found the railing, eyes mostly shut, save for a tiny slit, to ward off the searing sting of smoke. Grasping hold, he gingerly took the first step, then the next, and the next. About halfway down, a board gave way with a loud crack. Instinctively he leaped forward, losing his footing; he tumbled until his body landed in a crumpled heap at the bottom of the staircase. He gathered his senses, found a bit of air to suck in, and determined he hadn't broken anything. Another wolfish howl drove him to his feet again. Staggering through the pungent smoke, he turned a corner and passed through the kitchen, then found a closed door and flung it wide. In the room, he found two small boys huddled together on a single bed. Thank God, the smoke had not yet found them. He scooped them up, tossed a blanket over each of their screaming heads, and then wasted a few seconds looking for a back door. When he couldn't locate one in the smoke, he raced back through the kitchen and into a room now engulfed in flames. "Oh, Lord," he cried, "if You hear me, please get us through this nightmare." Dodging flames and falling planks, he found the open front door and, putting his head to his chest, dashed through it.

And that was as far as his memory took him. What of the boys? Had they survived? Had someone else managed to find their parents?

"Mr. Connors, can you hear me?" The female voice pulled at him, and he felt like that mouse again, careening off the walls toward a dim shaft of light. His brow muscles worked hard, but to no avail.

"I think he's comin' around," said a man with a deep, raspy voice. "Look! He's tryin' to open 'is eyes."

A cough building in his chest burst out of its own accord and brought him to partial consciousness. He opened his burning eyes a crack and looked into a pair of dark brown ones with golden flecks belonging to…belonging to…. He recognized her, but his fuzzy brain couldn't call up her name. Another cough barreled out of him, one he was sure would make his heart stop. He had no control over the spasm, no ability to hold it at bay. His head continued to pound, his throat burned, and his scorched lungs still couldn't seem to take in enough air.

"Here, Mr. Connors, try a sip of water. It will soothe your throat."

He felt a cool hand come around his neck and lift his head. He tried to help but hadn't the strength, although the need for water urged him to give it his all. Another hand came around his shoulder—a stronger, firmer one—and gave him the boost he needed. The rim of a cup touched his lips, and then the taste of cool water met his tongue. He started to gulp, but the woman stopped him.

"Mustn't drink too fast, sir, or you'll give way to another of those spasms—not that it's a bad thing you're coughing. It's important you get all that soot out of your lungs."

His head hammered so hard and loud, he could barely make out the voice, but he did know it to be calm and controlled. "My head's killin' me," he managed in a hoarse whisper.

"Hey, did y' hear that? He spoke!" some fellow shouted. "That's a good sign, ain't it, Miz Evans?"

Evans? Sam's mind whirled. *Mercy Evans?* He wanted to get another look at those deep-set, chestnut eyes. He could envision her face now, a perfect oval, delicately carved, and with a mesmerizing smile that had the power to knock a man off his feet. She always wore her dark hair pulled up in a proper bun, but anytime he ever happened upon her, it seemed several stubborn strands wanted to fall around her cheeks. Probably went with her personality. After all, weren't the Evanses all a hardheaded bunch? Granted, he didn't pay much mind to his relatives' rants against them. In fact, he rather took pride in distancing himself from all the bickering.

"Yes, it's a very good sign." He felt her breath on his face, cool and wispy. "You took in a lot of smoke, Mr. Connors. That's why you've got that awful headache."

He tried to respond, but then a swell of blackness engulfed him, and he drifted into another dizzying slumber.

Unbelievably, Samuel Connors showed few outward signs of burns, with the exception of some minor blisters on his arms and whiskered cheeks. They would heal, of course. Mercy's biggest concern was his lungs, which whistled and hissed whenever she put the stethoscope to his broad chest. He needed to cough, but he didn't stay awake long enough for her to instruct him, and she wished Doc Trumble would hurry up and deliver that DeLass baby so he could take over Mr. Connors' care.

She glanced across the room at John Roy and Joseph, huddled together on a single chair, their eyes as big as saucepans and as red as cherries. The weight of the world plunked down hard upon her shoulders, and she wanted nothing more than to escape the awful reality threatening to squeeze the breath right out of her. How could everything change so dramatically in a matter of moments—sitting around her supper table, enjoying the company of her friends, only to find out a few hours later they'd perished in a house fire? Moreover, how would she ever find the strength or the right words to comfort their children?

A pounding at the door commanded the attention of everyone in the room. Mercy glanced at Abner Stockton, who worked for the local lumberyard, and he made for the entryway.

"I want my son removed from the premises at once!" came the shrill female voice that could belong to only one person—Flora Connors. "What on earth possessed you to bring him here? He should be at Dr. Trumble's clinic. Where is he? Where is Samuel?"

"He's thataway, ma'am, but he shouldn't be moved till Doc Trumble arrives to assess the situation," Abner Stockton explained. "He's out at the DeLass farm deliverin' a baby."

"Humph! I'm taking my son home this minute. You will instruct Dr. Trumble to come to my place when he returns to town. George, Frank, kindly retrieve your cousin."

"Yes, Aunt Flora."

Thunderous footfall like that of a band of soldiers on a mission drew ever nearer, until the stern-faced, gray-haired woman came around the corner, her equally solemn nephews in tow. "Ah, there he is." She marched into the room, her eyes gleaming with cold, hard purpose, and gave her son a quick appraisal, then cast Mercy a hateful glare. "I trust you haven't done him any further harm."

Mercy might have lashed out, were it not for the hand of God clamping down on her mouth. Flora Connors had despised her for as long as Mercy could recall, even though it had been her husband who'd killed Mercy's father. By all accounts, Mercy should have been the one carrying the grudge, but she'd decided long ago to leave the bad blood to her relatives. "As Mr. Stockton suggested, your son should stay put till Doc Trumble arrives," Mercy replied politely. "You'll notice his breathing is a bit labored."

The woman sniffed. "My son will breathe much better once he's removed from this…this stale abode."

Ire chased up her spine, but she held it in check. "You should be quite proud of your son, ma'am. He rescued those two fine boys over there." She nodded at little John Roy and Joseph, whose watery eyes had widened at the woman's daunting presence.

Mercy detected the slightest thaw in her icy demeanor. "Yes, I heard." But then she lifted one corner of the sheet covering her son's shirtless body, and the cold chill returned, along with a loud gasp. "Who disrobed my son?"

"We did, ma'am," said Mr. Stockton, leaning forward. "Weren't Miz Evans, here, although she is a nurse, and she's no doubt seen a good share of men." With his chin, he indicated two other fellows whose faces looked only vaguely familiar to Mercy. She figured them to be barkeeps, as both wore aprons and carried the smell of ale. "We had to see if Sam had any burns needin' tendin'. He's a right lucky fellow. Seems the Man Upstairs had His eye on 'im."

Flora Connors pursed her thin, crinkly lips and fixed Mercy with another frigid stare. "He oughtn't suffer much if we move him, then. Frank, George, carry Samuel to the carriage out front."

The men stepped forward, prepared to lift their cousin, but then a coughing fit overtook Sam with such force that his face went as purple as a cluster of grapes as he flailed and gasped for air.

Stepping in front of his cousins, Mercy put her hands under her patient's shoulders to heft him up. "Lend me a hand, Mr. Stockton." The man moved forward to help sit him up, and Mercy gave Mr. Connors a few good pounds on the back to loosen the mucus in his lungs, causing him to spew forth a black, tar-like substance.

Flora Connors gave a sharp gasp and jumped back, her nose crinkled in a show of revulsion. "Good gracious! Is that soot he's coughing up?"

Had the situation not been so perilous, Mercy might have laughed at the woman's weak stomach. One would think she'd never cleaned up after a sick person—much less her own flesh and blood. "Indeed it is, ma'am." Once the coughing quieted, she and Mr. Stockton lowered him to the pillow again, and she reached for a nearby towel to dab around his mouth and throat. The poor man hadn't a clue of his whereabouts, having awakened for only a short moment before slipping back into a deep sleep. "I'm afraid burned particles have deposited themselves in his lungs and trachea," Mercy explained. "The coughing, while it sounds quite terrible, is actually a healthy thing. The more he expels, the better off he'll be. He's very sick, though, and it would be dangerous to move him before the doctor has a chance to evaluate him. He appears to be unconscious, probably due to his lack of proper oxygen while he was in that burning house."

"Yes, yes, I can see he's sick," his mother sputtered, "but I will not have him staying here, regardless of what the doctor says. In light of who you are, it wouldn't be…appropriate."

Mercy's ire shot up another notch. Folks like Flora Connors made living the Christian life a real chore. She cleared her throat, carefully considering her next words. "It's not as if I asked to have him delivered to my house, ma'am. I have no more desire to care for your son than I do a grizzly bear. But, being a nurse, I make it a point to give care where care is needed. You would do well to lay aside your ill feelings, even if just for one evening."

The woman raised her chin and looked down her nose at Mercy, eyes glowing like two hot coals. She had once been an attractive woman, to Mercy's recollection, but years of bitterness had done quite a number on her face. The men at her sides stood waiting like territorial militia ready to do her bidding. "And you would do well not to lecture your elders."

Cantankerous meddler, she wanted to spout.

Thankfully, Sheriff Marshall intervened. "It might be best if you left, Mrs. Connors. Seems to me your presence is causin' some dissension. I'll send one of my deputies over to let you know what Doc Trumble says pertainin' to Sam's condition."

Several heads nodded in agreement, but Flora Connors didn't budge; she just stood there stubbornly, chin jutting out, shoulders drawn back. "I will not leave my son in this woman's care."

"This isn't your house, you know," said Wayne Lamar, one of Mercy's neighbors. "Miss Mercy, here, could tell you to leave, and you'd have no choice."

"That's right," said his wife, Rhoda. "She's merely trying to help your son. Seems you ought to show a little gratitude."

Most knew Flora Connors as a hardened soul, demanding and difficult to like, so it came as no surprise to Mercy that she didn't soften at Rhoda's words. If anything, she gathered more resolve. "I am removing my son from the premises."

"Is he goin' t' die?" came a tiny voice from behind.

Mercy recognized John Roy's shaky speech. Keeping her eyes trained on the coldhearted woman, she said, "Not if we can help it, dearest."

Flora Connors gave the boy a fleeting glance. Could she not even acknowledge the child whose life her son had saved?

"He'll be okay," Joseph piped up with confidence. "Angels don't die."

3

A shrill voice like a bothersome parrot kept thumping at Sam's senses, calling him back to consciousness. "I'm not wasting another minute here. Frank, help Sam to a sitting position!" the parrot squawked. A scuffling sound erupted. As if crawling up the sides of a deep, dark well, Sam mentally searched for something to grasp hold of and continued the ascent, clawing to the surface, determined not to give in to the blackness again. *Gotta hang on this time*, he told himself. *Gotta find my way back.* Confusion clogged his throbbing head, and, once more, air seemed hard to find. A coughing fit wracked his body, stole his breath, and rattled his brain. *God, help me*, he prayed. At long last, the spasm ended, and a small voice near his ear drew him closer to the surface.

"Wake up, angel man."

Angel man? Surely, he hadn't passed on into glory. He wasn't quite ready for that, nor did he expect to find God's welcoming arms at the gate. Lately, he hadn't been leading what one would term a holy life. Oh, he'd invited the Lord into his heart as a boy, but as a man, he'd grown lax in his commitment. He'd stopped attending church a few years back, often let his temper get the better of him, enjoyed a little imbibing on occasion, and cut loose a colorful word on more occasions than he should. No, he had serious doubts that God was any too eager to see him.

"Like the sheriff said, Mrs. Connors, it'd be best all around if you left." The female voice held a definite edge.

"I'm not leaving my son with an Evans, least of all you."

Mother? He clawed faster, desperate to awaken.

"What are you implying, Mrs. Connors? That I will inflict further injury?"

"I'm implying nothing. What I'm stating plainly, young lady, is that I don't trust you."

"Now, settle down there, Flora." The frenzied male voice was unfamiliar. "Nobody's said anything about leaving Sam alone with Mercy."

"And they'd better not." He caught the rising fury in Mercy Evans' tone and decided his mother had met her match. "I didn't ask to take care of your son, but Doc Trumble would expect me to do everything in my power to help him."

"Humph. Isn't that nice. I'm still taking him home."

"Now, Flora, let's be reasonable."

"Sheriff, you know good and well Connors and Evans blood don't mix."

Although his eyes burned like the flames he'd dodged earlier, Sam managed to open them just wide enough to see through. "Mother." Instant quiet seized the room as he tried to make sense of his own voice, so hoarse and gravelly. "What're…you…doin'?"

"Samuel?" His mother lowered her face to within inches of his, then brushed several strands of hair from his eyes. "I'm taking you home. You don't want to stay here."

What he wanted was to push her hand away, but with all the eyes looking on, he had no desire to make an even bigger scene. He cared for his mother, but she had a knack for pulling on his last nerve, especially when she treated him like a helpless youngster. Not only that, but her loathing for the Evans clan had long been a thorn to his side, and his father's recent passing in prison had only intensified her hatred. He couldn't count the number of times he'd told her to just let it go.

She cleared her throat. "I've brought your cousins. They're going to help you to the carriage."

He feebly raised a hand. "I don't need help."

"Nonsense! Of course you do."

With effort, he craned his neck to glance around. Standing in the doorway was Abner Stockton, as well as Jeb Finnegan and Gil Stone from Finnegan's Tavern. All three eyed him with obvious concern. At the foot of his bed were Tom Edwards, Charles Shears, and a man and woman he didn't know. To his left, his nuisance of a mother and his cousins Frank and George hovered, and at his right stood Sheriff Phil Marshall and the beautiful Mercy Evans. He could hardly wait to find out how he'd wound up under her roof. Clinging to Mercy's side were two little sooty-faced boys with saucer-shaped blue eyes and disheveled brown hair. "Are these…the boys?" he asked, ignoring his mother and cousins.

The taller of the two boys nodded. "You comed into ar room and saved us from the fire." He noticed how Mercy drew them possessively to her side, and wondered about her connection to them. Had she known their parents?

"My brother says you're a angel," piped the younger one. "Are you a real angel?"

His throat stung with a mix of smoke and emotion, and he shook his head. "'Fraid not." He looked at the sheriff. "Was…was there anyone else…?"

"Yes, the boys' parents. I'm afraid they didn't…."

Sam's heart sank. If he had gotten there sooner, they might have made it out.

The sheriff shifted his weight and rubbed the back of his neck. "Glad you came out alive, Sam, and with them boys intact. That took a great deal of courage."

Several people nodded in agreement, and somebody across the room said, "Amen!"

Sam couldn't abide the attention, especially since he was hardly a hero. And he didn't want people putting him on some kind of pedestal. He'd merely acted on impulse, nothing more. Someone truly courageous would have gone through the flames and rescued the parents. He clamped his eyes shut against the awful burning and tried to concentrate on breathing through his rattly lungs.

"Would you like to try another sip of water, Mr. Connors?" Mercy's voice rang with a tone more like obligation than compassion, and he realized someone had probably coerced her into bringing him into her home. In fact, he thought he recalled her saying she never asked to take care of him in the first place. He did need to get out of here, not because she was an Evans, but because he didn't want to inconvenience her. Plus, he wanted to escape all these eyes boring into him.

"Help me up, Frank."

Sheriff Marshall stepped forward. "I think you should wait till Doc Trumble gets here."

"Yeah," said Abner. "You just came back to the land of the livin', Sam."

"I'll be fine." He sat up and gathered his bearings.

"Yes, he'll be quite fine," his mother echoed, as if his words weren't convincing enough.

Meeting Mercy's gaze, he managed to paste a slight grin on his mouth. "I thank you for the use of your couch, Miss Evans. Sorry I can't stay." Her momentary blush gave him a small satisfaction. She sure was a pretty thing, with that sleek, dark hair and those chocolate-brown eyes hooded by thick black lashes.

Rather than say anything else to the boys, he merely nodded and gave them each a gentle pat on the head, not having the heart to linger on their hangdog expressions. Frank seized hold of one arm and helped him to a standing position, and then George took the other arm, and together they guided him to the door. A coughing spasm threatened, but he managed to hold off the worst of it till he got outside. When they reached the carriage, he grasped hold of a handle and hauled himself up onto the rear seat, then reclined as best he could. The walk, though short, had so exhausted him, he wondered if he'd find his next breath.

"Well!" His mother situated herself in the front, next to George. Sam could envision her pressing the wrinkles out of her skirt and picking at invisible lint balls. "That was awkward, to say the least. I hope never to cross paths with that woman again."

"It's a small town, Mother," Sam muttered. "I guarantee you'll be seein' her for years to come."

"Can't you make that horse move a little faster, George?" she asked, ignoring his remark.

As the carriage wended its way up Wood Street, Sam clamped his lips and tried to control the burning tickle in his parched throat, but it gave way to a coughing episode that seemed to go on forever.

"There goes Doc Trumble now," George said, and Sam heard a horse gallop by. "Looks like he's headin' to his place."

"Turn around," Sam said. "I want you to drop me off there."

His mother whirled her head around. "But he's coming to the house to check on you. You'll be more comfortable in your own bed."

He rolled his stinging eyes skyward. Thirty years old, and he was still living under his mother's roof—and taking her orders. Too long she'd manipulated him into believing she couldn't fend for herself. When his father had gone off to jail six years ago, he'd felt obligated to stay with her at the family's big farmhouse. But lately—especially after her embarrassing tirade tonight—he'd been contemplating his escape from under her clutches. Shoot, he'd move into the barn if he couldn't find a place to suit him. His mother would survive just fine on her own. Even if she didn't, he couldn't let her continue governing his life. The hatred she spewed for the Evans family was worse than poison, and he'd grown downright sick of swallowing it.

George turned around to look at him, and when he saw that Sam was dead serious, he turned the carriage around. Frank and George assisted him up the beaten pathway to Doc Trumble's house, his mother following behind, sputtering that she couldn't understand why he didn't just go home and let the doctor come to him. Arriving at the same time were Abner Stockton and Jeb Finnegan.

"What're ye doin' here?" Jeb asked in his typical Irish brogue. "We come to tell the doc to go out to yer farm."

"He has no common sense," his mother chirped.

"He wanted to see Doc Trumble in his office," Frank said, taking one of Sam's arms to help him up the front steps.

Doc met them at the door. He knew just about every breathing soul in the area, having delivered almost every person in Henry County age thirty and under—Sam included. "Well, what've we here?" He pushed wide his screen and stepped aside to allow their entry.

"My son entered a blazing house fire, Doctor, and he needs your immediate attention."

With nary a question about the fire, the full-bearded gentleman scurried down the dimly lit hallway to one of his patient rooms, and by the time they reached it, Sam fairly collapsed on the narrow cot, his body drenched in sweat from all the effort, his ears ringing as loud as the bells at First Methodist Church. Rattly lungs were a constant reminder of the smoke he'd inhaled and the effort it took to catch one good breath. Sickening dizziness came over him again, and as Doc peered down at him through worried eyes, he lost his will to stay awake, once more slipping into the oblivion of unconsciousness.

⌒

After a mostly wakeful night, Mercy pushed the cotton blanket off her and dragged herself up, her first thoughts of the two boys asleep in the big bed in the room across the hall. It'd been past midnight when she'd finally tucked them in, their little bodies spent and their emotions drained. She'd tried to find the words to comfort them, but none had come—probably because she was in need of comfort, herself. So, she'd prayed with them instead; but each plea had sounded bleak and empty. Little boys didn't understand phrases such as "Mama and Papa are with Jesus now," or "We must trust the Lord, for He has reasons in allowing such things."

A long, jagged sigh issued out of her as she shuffled across the cool wood floor to her bureau and riffled through the drawer for her underclothes. In methodical fashion, she shed her nightdress, donned her pantalets and camisole, and then went to her wardrobe and passed over each cheerful, floral print until she found a simple, drab-colored cotton dress. She slipped on a pair of dark stockings, followed by her practical brown oxfords. Then, in routine fashion, she walked to her dresser to retrieve a horsehair brush and whisked it through her long locks, sweeping them up in their usual knot at the back of her head and fastening it with a bronze comb. She gave her face a quick glance, frowning at the sight of her puffy eyes.

On her way downstairs, she looked in on the brothers and found them sleeping soundly. Relief washed through her at not having to start her day dealing with their fresh tears. As it was, she could barely deal with her own tears, the depth of her loss only now beginning to register. How would she ever manage without Millie and Herb? They'd been the best of friends for years, sharing the same church pew on Sunday mornings, partaking of meals at each other's homes, playing games and working jigsaw puzzles, laughing and romping with the children, and enjoying picnics together on warm summer days. For years, it'd been the five of them, and now, in the blink of an eye, the number had whittled down to three.

After a quick trip to the outhouse, she found herself at the sink, filling a teakettle from the faucet. She stared numbly at the gushing water, which put her in mind of the bucket of tears she'd shed through the night. The sun had risen in the eastern sky, giving way to a cloudless morning, and birds, oblivious to the ravages of the night before, sang a new song to welcome the day. Before, she would have delighted in the masterful morning, but today her world had taken on a grey and mournful hue, and she couldn't see past the clouds that shadowed her usually sunny disposition.

I will refresh you, My child. Keep your eyes on Me, your Maker and Provider.

The words ran sweetly through her mind, bringing a sense of reassurance.

"Oh, God," she prayed with uplifted face, "I don't know what tomorrow holds or how I'll manage with these boys, but I know You have all the answers. Help me to trust You so I can make the right decisions for my future—for *our* future. I'm responsible for three of us now, and my heart weighs heavy. Please confirm to me Your promise to never leave us or forsake us. Help me to trust You." She reminded herself of her many blessings—a secure job with Doc Trumble, a mortgage-free home, thanks to the inheritance her father had left her, food aplenty, and, most important, her faith. No husband, of course, but then what did she need with one when she'd always managed fine without? Besides, at twenty-six, she'd passed the age of marriageability and now wore the badge of spinster.

Around nine o'clock, Mercy was seated in the dining room, sipping tea and reading from her mother's Bible, when the boys ambled downstairs. They each wore one of her father's old work shirts, having lost all their clothes and other possessions in the fire. They also wore bedraggled faces, their eyes full of unspoken pain, and their hair mussed and standing on end. No tears fell, but she knew it wouldn't take much to get a steady stream going again. She grinned. "Well, look who finally woke up. Are you two hungry?" Both shook their heads. "But of course you are. How do bacon and eggs sound?"

They shrugged their narrow shoulders. Taking that as a yes, she pushed back her chair.

"Did the angel man live?"

Joseph's question put a halt to her standing. She'd barely thought about the tough, tall, rawboned man with the longish sandy hair that curled around his damp forehead. "I'm sure he did, darling." She could only hope she hadn't misjudged his condition, and that Doc Trumble hadn't discovered anything beyond the symptoms of smoke inhalation and the burns on his forearms and cheeks.

"Can we go see him?"

"Oh! No, I think not."

Both added disappointment to their already sorrowful expressions. How could she possibly explain the words *animosity* and *hatred* to two children who'd never dealt with such emotions?

"But we want to thank 'im."

"I understand, but there's really no need. He already knows how very grateful you are." He had no idea how far her gratitude stretched, though. "I suppose we could write him a letter today. How would that be?"

Joseph's eyes brightened for the first time. "Yeah! I can write it if you tell me the letters."

With resolve, she stood and walked to the stove, putting on a cheerful demeanor, although it took great effort. "We'll work as a team, then."

She reached for the frying pan hanging on a nail above the big cookstove, then moved to the icebox to retrieve some eggs, her long skirt swishing with each step. Just as she started to fire up the stove, a loud rap sounded on her door. "I'll get that. Would you boys mind setting the table? You know where I keep the utensils." She wiped her hands on her apron and headed for the front of the house to see to her early-morning visitor.

Through the sheer curtain, she spied Sheriff Marshall standing on the porch. She swung wide the door. Something in his expression caused a knot to settle at the pit of her stomach. "Good morning, Sheriff. Is there a problem?"

He held his hat in both hands and shot her a cursory nod, then glanced past her. "Are the Watson boys about?"

"They're in the kitchen. Is there something I can do for you?"

"I thought you'd want to know we found the bodies of Herb and Millie Watson."

Her heart gave a hard wallop against her chest. Rather than invite the sheriff inside, she stepped onto the porch and closed the door behind her. Swallowing down a bitter taste, she gathered her resolve and asked, "And the fire...do you know how it started?"

"Looks to be an overturned lantern next to their bed."

"Oh, no. Millie said Frank liked to read in bed. Perhaps he drifted off before extinguishing the lamp."

He nodded, keeping his eyes on his shoes. "We figure he must've bumped it turnin' over in bed."

Her heart shattered as the impact of the truth slammed hard. What a cruel conclusion to life for two people so in love with each other and their children, not to mention their Lord and Savior. She couldn't help but ask how He could allow such devastation. Of course, she knew that Christians were not exempt from the awful consequences of a fallen world. Right now, however, that knowledge didn't offer much comfort.

"Would you like to come in for a cup of coffee, Sheriff?"

"No, no. I actually came to talk to you about something else." He started turning his hat in his hands and shifting nervously.

"Oh?"

"I met with Judge Corbett this mornin', and it's his belief that since the Watson boys have no known relatives, they need to go to a married couple. I'll be returnin' for them at the end of the day. That should give you time to talk to—"

"What? Absolutely not! I won't have it. I may as well be their next of kin. They need to be with someone familiar—someone who understands their anguish and who loves them."

"There's plenty o' compassionate folks in Paris."

"I don't doubt that, Sheriff, but no one knows them as well as I do."

"The Watsons have other friends, Miss Evans—married friends equipped to care for two growing boys. You work full-time for Doc Trumble. How do you expect to keep that up with two kids underfoot?"

"I know a few widows with younger children, and they seem to handle things just fine."

"And they have families willin' to help. Who do you have?"

"I have friends and several relatives. I'm not a recluse, Sheriff."

He huffed out a loud, whistling breath, a result of his having smoked stogies for as long as she'd known him. "Well, it's the judge's decision, so you're arguin' with the wrong person."

"Then I shall take this up with him just as soon as I've fed the boys their breakfast."

"Ain't Doc expectin' you to report to work?"

"He won't mind my leaving for a while."

"And the boys? You plannin' to take them with you to see the judge?"

She hadn't thought about that. The last thing they needed was to worry about the possibility of having to go to someone they didn't know. "Doc won't mind if they sit in his parlor."

"Ah, so that's how it's goin' to be, is it? When you don't know what else to do with them, you'll haul them to Doc's office."

"I'm working on a plan, Sheriff. If I have to hire someone to watch them at my house, I will. Sweet lightning, you've barely given me a second to grieve the loss of my friends, and already you're here to steal their boys out from under me?"

He showed only a hint of remorse. "It's not me makin' the decisions here, Miss Evans. Judge Corbett is adamant the Watson boys need two parents."

Indignation sizzled in her chest. No way would she let anyone—not even the judge—take those children. Why, she'd get married herself before she let that happen!

The notion struck her like a boulder to the head, nearly knocking her sideways. Such a preposterous solution, but it just might work.

That is, if she could find somebody willing to marry a self-proclaimed— and self-sufficient—spinster. And quick!

4

It had been a long three days at the clinic, but, thanks to Mercy's ministrations under Doc's supervision, Sam had recovered his appetite and a good deal of strength. He never had succeeded in striking up any kind of conversation with Miss Evans, though. Seemed to him she'd built herself a strong shield to hide behind. It shouldn't have mattered one iota that he couldn't break through it, but she had the prettiest face in town, and he had a stubborn streak long enough to make it impossible not to try. Of course, his mother and several cousins had made regular visits to Doc's office, continually berating him for allowing an Evans to see to his care, but he hadn't paid them any heed. He hadn't said it to their faces, but in his head, he'd told them to mind their own blasted business.

Mercy had brought the Watson boys to Doc's office to visit him earlier today—apparently at their dogged insistence—and he'd taken the opportunity to assure them he wasn't going to die. For some reason, they'd latched onto him and persisted in calling him an angel, which, of course, he was about as far away from being as a horse was from being a hog. It did put a tender spot in his heart when he saw them, though, knowing he'd had the wherewithal to save them from that fiery pit and that God—yes, God—had led him to that tiny bedroom on the other side of the kitchen where the flames had not yet stretched their deadly fingers. The real miracle, of course, was that not a hair on their heads had been touched. He'd heard that folks all around town agreed.

Doc strolled into his room while he sat propped up with a pillow behind him, eating his supper of chicken noodle soup and corn bread. He'd been coughing a lot less, and, while his lungs still had a bit of a wheeze to them, Doc said he was confident the threat of pneumonia had passed. He hadn't known till afterward how concerned Doc actually had been for his life. "You're a lucky fellow, Sam. I'd say Somebody up there had His eyes on you."

"You might be right, Doc," he said. Inwardly, he wasn't so sure. He was plain sick of his hypocritical relatives, who wouldn't dream of missing a Sunday service but also spewed their hatred on the Evans clan. If that was a representation of God and Christianity, he wanted no part of it. The only relative whose faith seemed halfway genuine was his uncle Clarence, who worked with him at the family's blacksmith shop. Not a strong case for attending church. Still, he did believe God had led him to save the boys.

Doc dragged a stool over to Sam's cot and sat, pulling on his long white beard, which put Sam in mind of St. Nick's woolly whiskers. He also had twinkling eyes and a friendly smile, which endeared him to all who met him. "You're looking quite good this afternoon, Sam. How are you feeling?" For a change, the fellow didn't haul out his stethoscope.

"I'm ready to go back to work, Doc."

He chuckled. "I'll let you go home today, if you want. Your mother said a driver would be by within the hour. But I'd say take at least another week off, to rest those lungs."

His mother. He had yet to inform her he'd soon be moving out, and he could about imagine the fight she'd put up.

Doc must have read something in his expression, for he quirked a white eyebrow. "You don't look too pleased."

"Oh, I'm happy to be goin', Doc, don't get me wrong, and I appreciate you and Mercy nursin' me back to health. But puttin' up with my mother's fussin' will be another story. You wouldn't happen to know of a small house for sale in town, would you? Or anybody with a room to let?"

A light dawned in the elder fellow's face. "You're planning to leave Flora to her own defenses?"

"It's about time, don't you think?"

He chuckled. "Perhaps past time. She's healthy as a hog."

"You'd never know it to talk to her. She's managed to convince any number of people she's dyin' of one disorder or another. I used to think the same, but now I know it's her way of keepin' me around."

"Flora Connors will do just fine on her own. She has a nice little nest egg and plenty of other family members to dote on her, not to mention Virgil Perry running the farm. High time you lit out, Sam. I'm sorry I haven't any suggestions as to where you might hang your hat, however…unless you'd consider Mercy Evans' present dilemma."

"Mercy Evans' dilemma?"

"I guess you haven't heard."

"You've kept me cooped up in this little ten-by-ten room for the past few days, and it pains Miss Evans to speak more than three consecutive words to me at one sittin'. Far be it from her to clue me in on any sort of pickle she's gotten herself into."

"It's not exactly a pickle, and maybe 'dilemma' wasn't the best choice of word. I'd say it's more like a crisis, and it involves those two Watson youngsters whose lives you saved."

His spine straightened like a rod, and he set his plate of food on the bedside table. "What's happened to those boys? I just saw them this mornin'."

Doc put a hand to his shoulder. "Slow down. Nothing's happened to them…yet."

"What do you mean, 'yet'?"

"Apparently, Judge Corbett doesn't believe it's in their best interest to stay with Mercy, being as she's unwed, plus she works full-time. So, he's ruled that they've got to go to a married couple. I took it upon myself to pay Joe Corbett a visit on her behalf, told him I'd lessen her hours, if need be, and keep her pay the same, but he insists they need a two-parent family. I'm not saying Mercy would have accepted my offer, anyway—she's one proud woman, I tell you—but I had to see if Joe would soften at my suggestion. Best he could do was give her thirty days to find a husband. And she's agreed to his terms. If she doesn't find herself a man, the boys will go to a worthy couple."

"Thirty days? That doesn't sound very reasonable. Corbett's an old grouch, if you ask me. Always has been."

"He wants those boys settled in a stable environment."

"Yes, but who knows them better than Miss Evans? I understand she and their parents were good friends."

"The best of friends."

"Well then, tearin' them away from her would be downright cruel. Don't they have any close relatives?"

"None that I'm aware of. Herb's dad ran off with another woman when Herb was but a boy, and his mother raised him and his sister to adulthood, then died of diphtheria. Herb's sister married and moved out west somewhere. Word is they haven't even been able to reach her with news of her brother's death. As for Millie, she was an only child, and her parents died two years back, in much the way she and Herb passed, except that they were lodged in a Chicago hotel that went up in flames." He gave his head a slow shake. "It's a world of devastation we live in."

Sam grunted. "I'm sorry about the situation, but I don't see where I could do a single thing to help."

Doc narrowed his gray eyes at Sam. "I hear she's placed an ad in the *Paris Post-Intelligencer*."

Sam's gasp generated a coughing spasm.

"You okay, son? I didn't mean to set you off like that." Doc gave his shoulder a light squeeze.

"I'm fine." He recovered and let Doc's proclamation absorb for a bit. "She'd actually go to such an extreme just to keep those boys?"

"She loves them a great deal."

"Guess so. I just hope she knows what she's doin', puttin' herself out there like that. Somebody could easily take advantage of her, not carin' one hoot about those boys."

"Hmm. You sure are right about that. Well"—Doc put his hands on his knees and stood up—"I best drive out to Bertha Neville's place and check on her boy's rash. You come back and see me in three days so I can give those lungs a good listen, you hear?"

He was tempted to fish for a few more details about Miss Evans' quest for a husband, but he didn't want Doc getting the wrong idea. He couldn't have him thinking he'd ever consider such a wild notion. Imagine the commotion if a Connors married up with an Evans. Why, he nearly laughed out loud at the very thought, and might have, if another coughing spell hadn't started.

⌒

On Saturday morning, Mercy and her two little waifs crossed Poplar Street at Washington to make their way to May's General Store, her written list of necessary items tucked deep in her dress pocket, Joseph and John Roy holding tight to her hands. She had to remind herself to walk at a slower pace than usual, to accommodate their short legs, which weren't capable of keeping up with her long, hurried strides. Shoot, she had to remind herself on a continual basis that it wasn't just she but three now.

Joseph did his best to kick every stone and stick in his path. "Whatcha need at the store?" he asked.

"I have quite a list."

"Are we gonna have to carry it all back?" John Roy asked, speaking for the first time on their jaunt east toward the center of town.

She smiled. "No, honey. Mr. May will have one of his clerks deliver my order later today."

Joseph paused to aim his toe at a large rock and sent it sailing across the dusty road. It just missed a passing rider on horseback, but Mercy refrained from scolding him just yet. "Can we get some candy sticks?" he asked. "Mama always buys ar favorite colors."

She noted how he mentioned her in the present tense, and her heart developed an instant ache. "Then we shall have to carry on the tradition."

John Roy squinted up at her. "What's that?"

"I guess you could say it's something people continue doing out of habit."

"You mean, like Mama and Papa sayin' prayers with us every night?"

"Yes, just like that."

Joseph stopped in the middle of the sidewalk to pick up a stick. "But now they ain't goin' to, 'cause they went up to heaven. Leastways that's what the preacher said at that cemetery before those guys put them big boxes down in the ground. What were those for, anyway?"

John Roy had grown unusually quiet. She felt his gaze land on her, so she said a silent prayer before answering, fighting back the tears. It had been eight days since the deadly fire, and the boys had remained mostly quiet about all that had transpired in their lives. She resumed walking, towing the boys along with her. "The boxes carried your mama and papa. Don't worry; they are warm and comfortable as can be in there. Besides, it's just their bodies. Their souls are with Jesus."

Land sakes, Mercy. How are they supposed to grasp that concept?

"Miss Evans! Miss Evans!"

She breathed a sigh of relief, then glanced behind her. There was Wilma Whintley, a middle-aged widow whose yard backed up to hers, waving her white handkerchief. She paused on the wooden sidewalk to give the woman a chance to scurry across the road, her hefted skirts revealing black, high-top, button shoes. Although the bustle was on its way out, the woman still insisted on wearing the hideous contraption that fastened around her waist under her skirts to give her a big-bottomed look—rather humorous in itself, considering Mrs. Whintley had a hefty enough frame without the help of a bustle. She also insisted on wearing big, feathery hats, no matter the occasion or the sweltering temperatures.

Mercy put on her usual smile. Although she'd rather chat with someone other than the somewhat meddlesome woman, the interruption was an opportune excuse to cease discussing the morose subject of caskets with John Roy and Joseph. "Good morning, ma'am."

"And a fine mornin' to you, Miss Evans." Winded as if she'd just run a full mile, the woman offered a diminutive smile to the boys. "My, my, you two are lookin' mighty handsome," she puffed. "Looks like Miss Evans done went out shoppin' for you." She raised the handkerchief to her face and dabbed at her damp forehead.

Joseph raised his chin to engage the woman, but he didn't appear to have a remnant of a smile in him. It had been awhile since he or his brother had shown even a hint of one. "A whole lot of folks been stoppin' by with clothes an' such, 'cause ar house burned down."

She shifted her position and frowned. "I know, and I'm ever so sorry about that."

John Roy looked up at the woman. "Yeah, and we ain't seen ar mama and papa since. Mercy says their souls is with Jesus. Do you gots a soul?"

"Why, I—" A strained and pallid expression washed over the woman's sun-crimped face. She produced an accordion fan from her skirt pocket and set to waving it, then cast a hurried glance at Mercy. "I suppose I do, yes." The inquiry certainly seemed to have unsettled her. Most people hadn't a clue what to say to the newly orphaned boys, and many of those who thought they did would have been better to keep their mouths shut. Why, just yesterday, Mrs. Mortimer, the Watsons' neighbor, had told the boys, "I certainly will miss your parents. The Lord must have something more important for them to do up there on them golden streets than raise you two boys." Mercy had wanted to kick the woman right in the shin for saying such a rude thing. Why couldn't people think before they spoke? Thankfully, neither boy had brought up the remark again, and Mercy hoped that meant it had sailed straight over their heads.

Mrs. Whintley's gaze lifted from the boys to Mercy. "And how are you doing, Miss Evans?"

"I'm managing at the moment."

"Ah, yes, 'at the moment.' I heard about the judge's decision." She chewed her lower lip, and Mercy could about imagine the stirrings going on inside that feather-topped head of silver hair. "Also heard tell you're lookin' for a husband. I didn't read your advertisement, mind you, but I've heard plenty of talk. Why, you're the main topic of conversation about town."

Mercy didn't doubt her for a minute. Ever since she'd placed the ad in the *Paris Post-Intelligencer*, her ears hadn't stopped itching, nor had folks stopped staring at her like she'd lost her last scrap of common sense. She suppressed a sigh.

"Any, uh…"—the woman leaned in close and lifted her graying eyebrows so high, they disappeared under her hat, her greenish eyes twinkling like twin stars—"promisin' prospects?"

Having grown fidgety in their waiting, the boys let go of Mercy's hands and went in search of sticks. Keeping a close watch on them out of the corner of her eye, she muttered under her breath, "I don't know that you'd call them promising, no."

Oh, she'd gotten plenty of calls—in fact, her door knocker had taken quite a beating of late—but her options were limited. Paris plain lacked eligible bachelors, and the ones who did qualify were either missing a front tooth or two, had a gnat-sized brain, or, sorry to say, hadn't learned the finer skills of bathing. Granted, there were some not so hard on the eye, but they were lacking in either personality or proper motives, drawn in by the appeal of a nice house over their heads and caring not one smidgeon about the boys. Worst were the clowns who got the wrong idea about their sleeping arrangements, assuming she'd welcome them straight into her bed.

"So, you're sayin' you've had no luck?"

She really didn't care to discuss her private life with Mrs. Whintley, the woman dubbed "town crier" by many. Still, giving her a few crumbs would make her feel important, as if she had an edge, and keep her busy sharing her privileged information—for the next few days, at least.

"Well, if you promise not to say anything...."

Mrs. Whintley's eyes went round as pennies, as she bobbed her head up and down several times.

"I will tell you that I do have a few possibly good prospects. One is"—the poor woman held her breath and looked ready to fall over—"oh, I best not say his name, but he's a professional about town—a fine Christian man who's never married. He would probably do quite well. And then, there is Mr.—oh! Again, I mustn't let the name slip. Let's just say he's a widower who lives outside of town. I doubt you know him. Let's see...." She scratched her temple, feigning deep thought. "Oh, yes! Another man I don't know, whose sister wrote to tell him of my plight, will be arriving on the afternoon train tomorrow to meet me."

Mrs. Whintley's jaw dropped. "Gracious me! Really?"

Mercy nodded. What she'd said was true enough, except for the part about them being "good prospects." Perhaps Harold Beauchamp, the forty-something postmaster, who would remain nameless to Wilma Whintley, came the closest in terms of decent possibilities, but only because he understood her immediate need, had always treated her with utmost respect, and hadn't seemed to object when she'd explained the rule of separate bedrooms. If anything, he'd blushed profusely at the mention of it. Best, he professed to know the Lord, which, of course, rated of utmost importance.

Unfortunately, the poor fellow had a pudgy belly, thinning hairline, and crooked teeth that hampered his smile—which also hampered her spirits.

Of course, she had yet to meet Caroline Hammerstrom's brother. He could be her perfect match, for all she knew. After all, she'd been praying unceasingly ever since paying Judge Corbett a visit and learning she must find a husband. Surely, God would answer her prayer, sooner than later.

A horse whinnied, and a deep-throated "Whoa" turned both women's heads. Sam Connors, riding high and straight and looking fully recovered from his brush with death, pulled back on the reins of his shining black steed, bringing it to a halt at the side of the road. He gave the women a cursory nod and lifted his hat an inch from his curly head before replacing it, but the boys received his full attention. At first sight of him, they both dropped their sticks and ran to meet him.

Mrs. Whintley bumped against Mercy and murmured under her breath, "My mother's milk cow, Miss Evans. Now, there's a man for you. It's a cryin' shame your families don't get along."

A shame indeed, Mercy thought. But, the family feud aside, she couldn't marry the man whose father had murdered her pa. No sir, never in a million years. Not even if God wrote the command in the sand with a stick.

5

*S*am looped the reins over Tucker's saddle horn. The worn leather of the stirrups creaked as he raised himself up, swung one big leg over the horse's rear, and jumped down, making the dust fly. He brushed off his pants and smiled down at the boys, patting them both on their sandy heads and taking care not to gawk at Mercy Evans, who looked mighty pretty today in her pale blue skirt and fitted floral blouse with low, rounded neckline and shiny buttons climbing up her front. She had her black-as-midnight hair pulled back in a loose bun, as usual, the strings of the ribbon woven around it and tied in a bow dangling to her neckline, and a few homespun curls framing her face. She was a scrumptious sight, if he did say so—but, again, quite untouchable.

"You never came to see us," said the older of the two boys—Joseph, if he recalled correctly. He had just a wisp of a grin on his face, making Sam wonder what, if anything, would make him smile these days. Sam would just about give away his left arm to finagle a giggle out of either one of them.

"No, I don't guess I did. I've gone back to work, so I've been pretty busy. That don't mean I haven't thought plenty about you, though. You doin' okay?"

Neither boy responded; they merely lifted their slim little shoulders in a slight shrug. The gesture tugged at his heart, and he turned his eyes on Miss Evans—the "husband hunter," as he'd been mentally referring to her—and the older woman standing beside her. The unknown woman stepped forward and extended a hand. "Good mornin', sir. I'm Wilma Whintley. My Wilfred, rest his soul, surely did appreciate your blacksmithin' services."

Oh yes, the infamous Widow Whintley. Poor woman. He'd often heard others refer to her as Wilma "Windbag" Whintley, due to her extreme love for gossip. He tipped his hat at her. "Nice meetin' you, ma'am. You let me know if you have need of any metalwork."

"Yes, indeed I shall. Well, I'll be goin' now. I'm to meet Mrs. Rutherford and a few other members of the Paris Women's Club to discuss our annual city picnic in late August. Perhaps I'll see you there, Mr. Connors." To Mercy, she added, "And you be sure to come as well, Miss Evans, and bring those boys—that is, if you still…you know…."

"Yes, yes, I will. Thank you. Good-bye, ma'am."

Sam watched the woman skedaddle across the street, her bustle bouncing behind her like a jumpy dog.

Mercy let out a noticeable sigh.

He chuckled. "Good friend of yours?"

She glanced across the street. "A neighbor." Then, blowing out a loud breath, she surveyed him hastily. "So, you've returned to work, have you? I take it you're feeling much better, then."

"A whale of a lot better than I did a week ago. Doc says I shouldn't have gone back to work yet, but I'm no good just sittin' around. Thanks for askin' after me, nurse. I wasn't aware you cared."

She slapped at a fly, then shielded her eyes from the sun. "I was asking as a professional courtesy, of course."

He grinned. "Of course. By the way, not sure I ever did thank you for takin' me in that night."

"I assure you, I didn't take you in—willingly, that is—and you certainly weren't around long enough for me to do you much good. Your mother saw to that."

Did he detect a bit of antagonism? "My mother can be somewhat of a nuisance, I'll give you that. I don't know what she said to you when she and my cousins came bargin' into your house, but whatever it was, let me just apologize for her rudeness."

"You certainly don't have to do that, but I appreciate it." She drew the boys close and looked at him. "We want to thank you again for running into that blazing house. I don't know how…or why…."

He flicked a wrist. "Never mind that. I'm just glad I acted when I did. There wasn't another soul around at the time, so I didn't have a second to waste." He set his eyes on the boys now. "By the way, which one of you wrote that fine thank-you letter I got in the mail the other day?"

Joseph raised his hand as if he were sitting in a schoolroom. A lively grin popped out on his handsome young face, and Sam wondered if it was the first time since the fire. "Mercy helped me. She spelled the words, and I writed all the letters."

"And so did I!" John Roy piped up. "Help, I mean."

"You didn't write it," Joseph said.

"No, but I tol' you some of the words t' write!"

Mercy applied a bit of pressure to their shoulders. "Boys."

Sam looked at her, searching his memory for a prettier face but coming up empty. Giving himself a mental rebuke, he turned his attention back to the boys, bending at the waist and touching both their noses. "It was mighty fine o' *both* of you to send the letter. I folded it up and put it back in the envelope for safekeepin'."

Mercy cleared her throat. "Well, we must be on our way, as we have a number of errands to run. Nice to see you, Mr. Connors." She made an attempt to turn the boys in the opposite direction.

"Likewise. Oh, one more thing, Miss Evans." He raised his index finger. "Just curious how that, uh, advertisement scheme of yours is workin' out."

She blinked and promptly blushed. "I wasn't aware you'd heard about it."

He couldn't help but throw back his head and laugh. "Heard about it?" He removed his Stetson, ran a hand through his tangled hair, then plopped the hat back in place. "Is there anyone in all of Henry County who hasn't? You've made quite a stir."

She pulled back her shoulders and sniffed. "I figured folks would find my public notice a bit out of the ordinary—desperate, even—but I hardly expected anyone to find it humorous, Mr. Connors. In fact, I would expect you to cheer me on, seeing as you are the one who saved these boys from perishing in the fire."

Well, she did have a way of wiping the grin right off his face. He collected himself and glanced down at the boys, both of whom stared up at him with looks of confusion. He doubted they were aware of her plan. "Do you have any serious contenders?"

She lifted her chin. "Perhaps. Actually, yes." With her curt reply, she turned the boys around, took their hands in hers, and proceeded up the street without so much as a "Good day."

"Wait!" He clicked at Tucker, who lifted his head and ambled toward them. "Who are they—your prospective...you know?"

She whirled. "It is none of your concern. Now, if you'll excuse me, the boys and I have errands to run." Again, she turned and set off.

He snagged her by the arm, not hard, but enough to bring a halt to her steps. Tucker snorted, as if to say, *Make up your mind. Are we coming or going?* "Darn tootin' it's my concern. You just said yourself I ought to be cheerin' you on." He spread his arms. "Well, here I am, cheerin' you on. Now, tell me who you've picked."

"I haven't picked anyone—yet. But with all the callers I've had, I wouldn't expect it to take much longer."

He rocked back on his boot heels and ignored the annoying stirring in his chest. What was it? Mere curiosity? Or, worse, jealousy? "You've had a lot of interest, then?"

"Let's just say I'll need to repaint my porch steps for all the traffic they've had."

Although he knew she'd meant the remark in jest, she didn't break a grin—more like a smirk. Oh, she was an imp, and it irked him that she attracted him. Somehow, he knew that given the chance to dig, he'd find a sense of humor buried beneath that thick shield she wore so snugly around her. This was a strong woman who'd known pain but had learned the art of mastering it.

"So, you have how much time left to make this...this decision?"

"A couple of weeks. But I'll be making it sooner than that, as there's the wed—the ceremony to plan."

"Performed by a preacher, I presume. And what if he doesn't approve of this little plot you've cooked up?"

She bristled. "I'll have you know I haven't 'cooked up' anything. I'm being forced into it. And for your information, I've spoken to Reverend Younker, and he understands my predicament. As long as I marry a fine Christian man"—was it his imagination, or did she throw him a scornful glance?—"he's agreed to perform the nuptials and bless the union."

Joseph's head jerked up. "You're gettin' married?"

Mercy snarled, and with a scowl to scare away a skunk, she looked Sam square in the eyes. "Now look what you've made me do." She turned on her heel. "Come on, boys." And with that, she set off again, this time at a much faster pace, so that the boys had to run to keep up.

"Huh? I didn't *make* you do anything, lady!" He tagged along behind, Tucker clip-clopping after. "It was your tongue that slipped, not mine. And, just so you know, they were bound to find out anyway. Why the big secret?"

Without turning, she let go of Joseph's hand and gave a backward wave. "Good-bye, Mr. Connors!" Then, taking Joseph's hand again, she whisked the boys across the street, her long skirts blowing in the wind. The last thing Sam heard was little John Roy's pleading voice. "Ouch! My side hurts. Why're we runnin'? Who's gettin' married?"

He watched until the threesome had vanished from view, and then he climbed back in the saddle, sputtering to himself. "What in tarnation do I care who she marries?"

6

The next few days went by in a storm of male callers. Apparently, news of Mercy's infamous ad had spread beyond Henry County. Oh, how she'd beseeched the Lord to lend her wisdom. The biblical command *"Pray without ceasing"* had taken on a literal meaning. She knelt at her bedside each night; prayed while she dutifully performed her job in the doctor's office, with the boys playing next door at the home of Etta Parsons, a grandmotherly type with a world of energy and love; and pleaded to the Father as she went about her household chores, both kids talking and sometimes bickering in the background. She needed a whole wagonload of wisdom, but, so far, God had not shed one particle of light on what she should do or whom she should choose as a life mate. About the only words she got from Him were gentle reminders to wait and trust. *Wait and trust?* Really? When the clock kept ticking?

A flicker of attraction to at least one of her callers would've helped, but none quite measured up to the standards she'd set for her future husband: (1) Must love God, (2) Must love children, (3) Must have a sense of humor and enjoy life. It went without saying that "Must have front teeth intact" ranked rather high. Her list went on, even as she questioned whether her extreme pickiness had slowed the process. Her mind kept skipping back to Harold Beauchamp, the kindhearted, highly respected, even godly, Paris postmaster. Surely, she could grow fond of him over time, despite his being so much older than she. Perhaps she might even encourage him—tactfully, of course—to lose the bulge that hung over his belt.

As it turned out, Mercy and the boys had waited exactly one hour at the train station the day after her encounter with Sam Connors, only to be stood up by the one man she'd hung her last hopes on. According to Caroline Hammerstrom, her brother had lost his nerve in the final minutes before boarding his train in Chicago, claiming he simply wasn't ready to make such a commitment. Well, fine. Mercy didn't want to marry a coward, anyway, so it was best he hadn't come. Still, it had been a deep disappointment not to at least meet him. Surely, he would have loved the boys and immediately sensed their deep need for a father's care. On the other hand, perhaps he had an even bigger breadbasket than Mr. Beauchamp.

She had decided to tell the boys about the judge's decree. With all the talk around town, not to mention the stream of male callers, they'd figure it out soon enough, anyway. Best they hear it from her, even though their young minds wouldn't fully grasp it. Of course, they'd bellowed to the tree-tops and cried rivers at the thought of having to live with anyone other than her, and nothing she'd said had consoled them, until she'd finally promised it wouldn't come to that. And she wasn't about to break her promise. Even if it meant that she had to marry her least appealing candidate—Festus Morton, a toothless farmer who'd traveled seven miles by mule to offer his hand that very day in exchange for lodging at her house and all the food he cared to eat. He'd even promised he'd give up farming and spend all his time with the boys so she could keep on working full-time, or even overtime, if she had a mind to. In a word, he wanted room and board for life.

She'd shooed him out the door as quick as she could, but now she told herself that if it came down to it—if marrying Festus Morton was the only way to keep the boys for good—she would go crawling to him on her hands and knees.

Her cousins Frieda Yeager and Wilburta Crockett, daughters of Uncle Albert and Aunt Gertie, paid her a visit to tell her how sorry they were to hear of her plight. "Marriage ain't always what it's cracked up t' be," Frieda said. "I shore hope y' don't get y'rself into a fix you'll regret f'r the rest o' your life." Frieda and her husband and kids had moved back to Paris just a few months ago, after spending five years in East Tennessee. In that time, she'd picked up a stronger accent, and Mercy suspected it came from living up in the hills.

She knew she had a southern drawl, herself—who in Tennessee didn't?—but her mother had been a real stickler for proper English, so she'd spent a good share of her life reading grammar books and working on polished speech.

"Indeed!" Wilburta agreed. "You might hitch up with some half-wit, and then where would you be, Cousin?"

Had Mercy's conscience not pricked her ahead of time, she might have told her cousins that their husbands were nothing to brag about. Land of Lincoln, Wilburta's husband, Ellis, had Festus Morton beat in looks and smarts by only a hair or two.

"I'm lookin' for someone with some brains," she said, hoping to earn a smile from them. "And it wouldn't hurt if he were halfway decent to look at."

Both remained solemn-faced while they all sat around the table sipping on sweet tea. Frieda plunked down her glass and stared off. "Cain't say I could name a single eligible bachelor in all of Paris that fits them traits.... unless y'r talkin' the likes o' Samuel Connors."

Mercy's spine stiffened. "Which I am not."

"I should say not, Frieda Yeager. He's a Connors, anyway. No Evans would ever consider hookin' up with a Connors. Why, it'd be downright sinful."

Mercy would've liked to ask Wilburta how she'd come to that conclusion, but since she had no interest in Samuel Connors, she kept the question tucked away.

"Still, it don't hurt t' ask what he's like," said Frieda, her green eyes flashing with interest and a speck of mischief. "He is right fine-lookin'. Don't know why nobody's ever snatched him up. Did he have much to say to you whilst you helped Doc take care o' him?"

Mercy recalled how he'd tried his darnedest to make conversation with her, even attempting to flirt, and how she'd kept her words to a minimum. She'd probably come across as just short of boorish, but she preferred to think she'd acted professionally. "Nothing out of the ordinary. We were civil with each other."

Frieda's shoulders slumped. "Well, I s'pose it's f'r the best. He might be good-lookin', but he comes from devil's stock."

At that, Mercy bristled from the top of her head clear down to her toes. "Why on earth would you say that?"

"Mercy Evans, you need to ask?" Wilburta's voice rose to a pitch that rivaled the highest piano key. "His father killed your pa!"

"That doesn't make Samuel Connors responsible. Have you forgotten he walked into a burning house, with no thought for his own well-being, to save the lives of John Roy and Joseph?"

Wilburta, the more garish of the two, turned her mouth down and sniffed. "O' course, I hain't forgot that, but that don't erase the fact he's a Connors. Everybody knows the Connors clan is bad."

"Not everybody, Burtie. To my knowledge, it's only Evans folk who feel that way."

"Well, no matter. Evans and Connors blood don't mix."

Rather than argue, Mercy changed the subject to something safer, inquiring after her cousins' latest quilting and sewing projects. When the boys came bounding down the stairs, asking what she planned to fix for supper, the two ladies gathered up their things and said good-bye—and none too soon for Mercy.

When she'd finished washing the supper dishes, Mercy reined in her thoughts and gazed out the kitchen window at her neglected garden, where the boys climbed an old apple tree in need of a good pruning. At least they'd found something to while away their minutes before bedtime.

"Mercy Beauchamp." She tested the name on her lips. Wrinkling her nose, she stepped away from the window, passed through the dining room, and entered the front parlor. "Good evening, Mrs. Beauchamp." She plopped down into the old settee that had been sitting against the same wall since before her father passed. "How do you do, Mrs. Beauchamp?" she said in a singsong voice, mimicking Thelma Younker, the reverend's wife. "Lovely day, isn't it? My, my, I do declare, the longer you and Harold have been married, the more you two look alike." That thought snapped her back to the present and made her groan.

Resting her head on the back of the sofa, she stared at the ceiling. "Oh, Lord," she vented in sheer frustration, "is Mr. Beauchamp really Your best choice for me?"

Wait and trust.

She groaned. "Wait and trust, wait and trust. What does that mean, Father? Show me a sign."

But all she got in return was the constant, irksome ticking of the heirloom clock on the fireplace mantel in the front parlor.

⤙

Sam mopped the sweat from his brow with his shirtsleeve, ready to clean up after a long day of work. This time of year, Connors Blacksmith Shop grew uncomfortably warm. The fact that it had been built into a hillside, constructed of stone, with plenty of shade trees surrounding it, meant that it stayed cool in early summer, but these factors were no match for the relentless rays of the late July sun.

Across the room, his uncle, not quite ready to call an end to his labors, put the final touches on a garden gate he'd been crafting for one of their customers by attaching a forged hinge to it.

Sam took up the broom and started sweeping dust and shavings from under the table onto the dustpan, then dropped the debris into the nearby wastebasket.

"You find y'rself a place to live yet?" his uncle asked.

"Nope." Sam glanced at Uncle Clarence, who hadn't bothered to look up. "But I did learn Bessie Overmyer has a room to let at the boardinghouse."

Now Uncle Clarence shot him a quick glance, his gray eyebrows upturned. "You must be pretty desperate to get out from under your ma's clutches if you're thinkin' 'bout movin' there. Hear them rooms are about as big as Mother Goose's shoe. Ain't she mostly set up for travelers passin' through?"

"Yeah, but I talked to her, and she says she has a room at the back of the second floor that would accommodate a longer stay. 'Course, I'd have to share the single washroom with the other tenants."

His uncle wrinkled his nose. "Seems y'ought to be able to find somethin' better'n Bessie's Boardinghouse, son. Think I'd endure your ma's constant carryin' on for the comforts of that big ol' farmhouse 'fore I'd resort to livin' in a twelve by twelve room."

Uncle Clarence never had been one to mince words when it came to Sam's mother. He couldn't fight back the grin. "You don't live with her."

"Thank the good Lord for that!"

Truth was, Sam had been giving serious thought to approaching Mercy Evans about her need for a husband. As far as he could tell, he'd be her best bet. Just that morning, while sipping a tin mug of hot coffee over at Juanita's Café, a dingy little hangout where the local laborers liked to gather before heading to their job sites, he'd overheard a few men jawing at another table. "If I weren't married m'self, I'd offer up my services to that pretty little Evans dame. That one's a looker." This from the rough-and-tumble Bill Jarman, who worked over at the tanning factory. Several men had added their two cents on the matter, one middle-aged fellow joking that it might be worth a divorce, and one old codger saying, "Divorce nothin'. My wife died five years ago. I been thinkin' on startin' over with someone."

Juanita Mendez, the healthily plump owner of the establishment, had sauntered over with a tray of breakfast buns, her black hair done up in its usual braided knot at the nape of her neck, her long red skirts whooshing around her chubby ankles. "You boys don't stand a chance," she'd said in her machine-gun-fast Spanish accent. "Miss Evans, she already name her future husband."

All ears had perked, including Sam's, as she'd taken her time setting the tray of goods in the center of the big round table. "That so?" Bill had asked, stretching out his fat paw to snatch up a jelly roll. "Who's the lucky feller?"

Juanita had straightened, shifted to one side, and placed a hand on her round hip. One black eyebrow had jutted higher than the other. "Harold Beauchamp."

Sam had coughed, not so much from his continued bouts of congestion since the fire but from the fact that his coffee had gone down the wrong pipe at her response. A few surprised gasps had filtered through the room, followed by spurts of laughter. "The Paris postmaster?" someone had asked. "Are you sure?"

"Sí, señor. I hear it from the man who bring my mail to me."

"Well, ain't that somethin'?"

"What's he know about raisin' young'uns?"

"Who says it's them young'uns he's interested in?"

"What in all creation does she see in him?"

The questions and remarks had kept up until Sam had heard enough and pushed back in his chair, its legs screeching loudly across the grainy concrete floor. He'd tossed a few coins on the table, nodded his thanks at Juanita, then stalked out the door, his dander up for reasons he couldn't identify. Why should it matter one whit whom Mercy Evans chose to marry?

But even as he'd strode through the shop door that morning and fired up the forge, he'd mulled over the idea of offering her his hand. She'd probably chase him right out of her house, but it was worth a shot, even if she refused. He cared about the future of those little boys, and he frankly couldn't see Beauchamp having the energy or desire to invest a lot of time in them. Not that he wasn't a nice enough guy, but what did Mercy see in that balding, pudgy bachelor, who had to be nearing his mid-forties?

Now Sam decided to test his uncle's reaction to the notion of approaching her. "You hear about Mercy Evans and her search for a husband?"

"Yep." His uncle kept his eyes on his task, using a mallet to fix an angle, then laying it down and taking up a file to perfect the shape to his liking.

"You ever talk to her?"

"Nope." The filing motion made a *swish, swish* sound.

"She's a pretty thing."

"Yep."

"I been thinkin' 'bout…makin' her an offer, I guess you could say."

Uncle Clarence stilled his hands, and he looked up, his thin lips barely visible beneath his bushy mustache. Still, Sam swore he detected the faintest upturn of the corners of his mouth. However, his gray eyes refused to give away any emotion. "That so?"

"You think it's foolhardy o' me?"

"Depends on your motive, I guess."

"My motive?" Sam stood the ancient cornhusk broom in a corner and set the dustpan alongside it, then reached around to untie his apron and lifted it over his head.

"Sure. Are you lookin' for a permanent place to hang your hat? The fastest way to pull your mother's chain? Are you marryin' for love?"

"Love? Heck, no!" A tiny knot of guilt rolled around in his gut. "I won't deny it'd be nice to have my own place."

"It wouldn't be your place. It'd be hers."

"Yeah, but she's advertisin' for a husband. I would expect she'd be willin' to share her house with 'im."

"I wouldn't expect much more than that from her."

Sam caught his uncle's drift, and a wave of warmth stole into his cheeks. Made him glad for the shop's dimming light. "It'd be a purely legal arrangement, nothin' more."

"Uh-huh. And how long would you stand for that?"

"Uncle Clarence!"

"She's an Evans, son. I don't have to warn you what the outcry would be, from both families, if you two hitched up."

How quickly he'd breezed past the subject of keeping the union strictly platonic. "It's those boys I'm thinkin' about. I'm fond of them, and there's a sort of unseen bond between us. If Mercy doesn't find a husband soon, she'll be forced to give 'em up. It would tear those little guys to shreds."

"Ah. That part is understandable, your wantin' to help them out. Poor little fellers. I will give you credit for havin' a noble cause."

"So, you don't think it's entirely ludicrous?"

The man took a few more swipes with his file, then laid his project aside. "I didn't say that." He set to straightening his tools, clearly taking his sweet time to expound upon his answer. At last, he raised his head and looked Sam head-on. "Marryin' her would stir up a real storm. Don't be countin' on anybody's blessin'."

"Not even yours?" Sam ventured. "I wouldn't want to put up a wall between us."

"Pfff." His uncle tossed his head to the side and went back to sorting his tools. "Don't go worryin' your mind over that. I respect you enough to let you make your own decisions. I always have thought this feud a waste of time and energy. But it does have its roots, and roots go deep."

"I know." Sam sighed. "Well, I'm not expectin' anything to come o' my offer, anyway. I hear she's already leanin' toward Harold Beauchamp."

Uncle Clarence made a snuffling sound. "I would hardly put them two together. Ain't he 'bout old enough to be her father?"

"Darned close. Harold's a nice fellow, though."

"He may be, but that don't make him a good fit for Mercy. 'Course, he's also a fine Christian, and I 'magine that's a high priority for her."

"How would you know about her priorities?"

"Everybody knows Mercy Evans is a God-fearin' woman. She's not gonna marry someone who won't abide puttin' God first, going to church, sayin' his prayers, readin' his Bible, and teachin' those boys the ways of the Lord."

Sam studied his scuffed shoes and scratched his temple as a blanket of silence settled between them.

"It wouldn't hurt you to brush up on your faith, son," Clarence finally said. "It's been a while since you attended services."

He was right, of course. Mercy would be looking for somebody who shared her values and religious beliefs. Well, heck, it wouldn't kill him to go to church.

But something told him she'd expect a little bit more out of him than simple church attendance.

Wasn't he putting the cart ahead of the ox? Who knew but that she'd kick him straight off her porch before he even spoke the first word of his proposal?

7

After punctuating their bedtime prayer with a hasty "amen," Mercy leaned forward and planted a kiss on each boy's forehead, then tucked the light cotton blanket up snugly to their chins. Both offered up sleepy half smiles, having finally exhausted their seemingly endless questions about the evening with Harold Beauchamp: "Do you like him?" "How come he don't have much hair?" "Did he get tired of playin' with us?" "Why'd it sound like he swallowed a whistle?" "How come he tripped over that shoe? Can't he see very good?" And the one that beat all: "Why'd you pick *him* t' marry?"

She'd tried to answer each question as best she could, but the last one had purely stumped her. Why indeed? Because he best fit her criteria? It was a sad day when not one man who'd crossed over her threshold in the past ten days with eager eyes for marriage could get her heart to thumping. Was it possible she'd taken matters too much into her own hands, even though she'd bathed her days in prayer? Had she misread the Father's cues? Oh, why did it have to be so hard to determine His will? Could it be He didn't wish for her to marry Harold Beauchamp—or any man, for that matter— because the boys would be better off with someone else? The very notion produced tears she had no desire to suppress.

Weary, she extinguished the light, tiptoed out of the darkened room, and descended the wooden staircase with a loud, long sigh that blew upward and caused a few stray hairs to lift off her forehead. Mr. Beauchamp had thought it a good idea to spend the evening with her and the boys—to get acquainted, he'd said—and she'd thought it wise, as well, but he'd certainly worn a fatigued expression at the close of the night, the boys having run him ragged with their rounds of tag, hide-and-seek, and leapfrog. She figured he hadn't played much of anything of late, except for that newfangled gramophone he'd recently ordered from the Sears & Roebuck Catalog and couldn't stop talking about. The boys had winded him so badly that gigantic sweat circles formed under his armpits, inflicting havoc on his neatly pressed Sunday-go-to-meeting shirt. She tried to imagine washing his sweat-stained shirts, and felt her nose scrunch up all on its own.

While he'd treated them all with kindness, it had been clear he wasn't accustomed to being around children, and she worried he just might call off the whole arrangement, deciding their raucous play was more than his ticker could handle, not to mention his wheezing lungs. No wonder John Roy thought the poor man had swallowed a whistle. She would have to warn them that Mr. Beauchamp might not be up for that much activity going forward.

When he'd announced his leave-taking, around eight o'clock, the boys had bid him good-bye, then scampered off to the kitchen for their promised bedtime snack of cookies and milk. He'd hesitated by the door, chewing his lower lip, as if trying to figure out how to break the news that he'd rather live with a family of venomous rattlesnakes than take on two active young boys, but in the end, he'd just given her a tentative smile and nodded good night. Now that she thought about it, he hadn't given any indication that he'd had a nice time. She let go another heavy wad of air, trying to expel her worries, then shuffled into the kitchen and set the tea-kettle on the stove to heat water for a cup of tea.

As she lifted the kettle off the flame and prepared to fill her cup, a gentle knock sounded on the front door. Jolted to attention, she set the kettle down—too fast, causing the liquid to splash. Pricks of scorching heat singed her wrist.

"Ouch!"

The knock came again. Mr. Beauchamp, no doubt. She groaned. He couldn't have waited till tomorrow to tell her of his decision to back out of the arrangement? She scurried through the dimly lit house to the door. Through the glass, she could make out the silhouette of a figure—a silhouette that stretched much taller and wider than the frame of Mr. Beauchamp.

⌒

Sam prepared himself for a tongue-lashing. What sort of man came calling on a woman at nine thirty in the evening? Why, she might have readied herself for bed; but then, she wouldn't have come to the door. At least, that was his assumption. She stopped and stared at him through the glass, mouth agape.

He cleared his throat. "Good evenin'. May I come in?"

She swept a few stray hairs out of her face and straightened her shoulders, then slowly turned the lock and opened the door a crack. "I'm afraid I'm not a hospital, Mr. Connors. If you're still having medical problems, you'd best go see Doc Trumble."

He wedged the toe of his boot inside the door to keep it from closing, which prompted a tight little gasp from her throat. "I'm glad to see you, too, Miss Evans." He grinned and hoped she'd take his remark as playful. "I don't need medical care. I've come to talk to you."

Her face contorted in a mix of annoyance and confusion. "Have you no idea of the time?"

Even with that frown, you're flawless. "Yes, I know. Sorry about that, but it's urgent. May I?"

Rather than open the door so much as a hair further, she adjusted her stiff stance, as if prepared to slam it shut. "What could you possibly need to tell me at this hour?"

A mosquito buzzed around and lit on his forehead. He slapped it before it could start feasting. "I'd rather talk inside before I'm eaten alive. I promise not to overstay my welcome."

She arched a dark eyebrow. "You already have."

"I guess I asked for that one. Let me rephrase. I'll take just a few minutes o' your time." He batted at another mosquito, hoping she would relent.

Ever so slowly, the door inched open. "Say your piece, then."

Before she could change her mind, he scooted past her and removed his Stetson. He sure had a talent for stirring up her ire. In all the years of knowing her, even though only on a formal basis, he'd never managed to wrangle a smile from her, but it didn't dampen his determination to try.

While turning his hat in his hands, he gave a hurried glance around, remembering certain aspects of the expansive yet cozy house from the brief time he'd spent there after the fire: the wide oak staircase; the parlor; the wrought-iron coat tree, which he would bet money his uncle Clarence had crafted and sold to May's General Store for resale.

"Nice house," he said.

"What can I do for you, Mr. Connors?" she asked, not bothering to acknowledge the compliment.

"Um…could I come in?"

"You are in."

Feisty little mite.

"Oh, all right. Come into my parlor, if you must."

He nodded and entered the room. On the west wall hung a large painting of a little girl with big eyes and wispy hair sitting on a child-size chair, legs crossed at her ankles, and holding an open book in her lap. Under the canvas print stood a long sofa with side tables on either end, a vase of flowers on one and a small stack of books on the other. A floor lamp towered over the table with the books. On the inside wall was a brick fireplace, flanked by a pair of wing chairs upholstered in a dark burgundy brocade, and the wood floor was covered with an ornately patterned wool rug.

"Is this the room I was laid in after the fire?"

She gave a quick nod, minus any semblance of a smile. "Yes. Have a seat there." All business, she pointed at the sofa, where he must have lain mere weeks ago. He walked over and sat down. "Can I take your hat?" she asked.

He glanced absently at the tattered thing and realized holding it gave his hands something to do. "No, thanks. I'll keep it with me."

She remained firm as a starched collar staring down at him. "I was just making myself a cup of tea. Would you care for some?"

He let out a whiff of air. "Sounds great."

"Fine. Make yourself comfortable." Her long skirts ruffled as she left the room.

"Well, this is a little better than standin' on the porch gettin' gnawed to death by mosquitoes," he muttered to himself. He spread his knees, settled back, laid his hat beside him, and twiddled his thumbs in his lap. That kept him occupied for about a minute. He glanced around, his gaze falling on the side table with the stack of books. Reaching over, he plucked the book on the top of the pile. *The Christian's Secret of a Happy Life*, by Hannah Whitall Smith. The title struck him as odd. He'd never considered the Christian life a necessarily happy one. More like dutiful. Every so-called Christian he knew didn't come off as excessively joyful, his mother a prime example. While she wouldn't think of missing Sunday service, she was always grousing about one thing or another; more often than not, she wore a sour face, suggesting to him that living happily as a Christian didn't come naturally.

The sole exception was Uncle Clarence, who was always humming or whistling a hymn when he came to the shop in the mornings. Folks about town knew him to be friendly, kindhearted, generous, and fair. In fact, Sam couldn't recall him ever uttering a harsh word—quite the opposite of his brother Ernest. Sam's father.

"Are you a reader?"

Mercy's voice gave him a jolt. He hadn't heard her approach. "I like to read, yes." He quickly set the book back where he'd found it.

She handed him a dainty china cup and saucer, which he took clumsily in hand, his big, earthy fingers easily encircling the whole thing.

"What's your favorite genre?" she asked.

"My *what*?" He'd never heard the word before, and he was irked by his own ignorance. Old Beauchamp had probably read every book ever published—Christian, that is—and he no doubt knew his Bible from front to back, perhaps even had whole chapters memorized! What chance did he stand against someone like him, never mind his rather sagging appearance? She obviously saw deeper than the man's exterior. He took a swallow of tea and nearly scorched his tonsils.

"What is it you like to read?"

"Oh." *The newspaper.* "The Bible, o' course."

There went those lovely brows, forming two inverted Vs, and he knew by the spark in her chocolate eyes she didn't for a minute swallow it. "Is that so? Then I'm sure you won't mind sharing your favorite Scripture verse."

She had him there. "Uh, sure. It's, um...'Jesus wept.' My mother used to say it when I disobeyed. She'd say, 'Jesus wept—and I know why.'" He grinned. "I guess she thought it was funny."

Mercy didn't smile.

He sobered. "But it wasn't, of course."

She gave a slow shake of the head and narrowed her eyes to slits. "Are you going to tell me the reason for your visit?"

His heart took a dive, its fast tick pounding loud in his ears. He took another nervous swig of tea, this one slower. Where had his courage run off to, anyway? The lady's fine looks put him in a regular dither. "Are you gonna sit?"

With a shrug, she moved to one of the wing chairs next to the fireplace. It was then that he took note of her bare feet peeking out from beneath her skirt. How could he have missed them when she'd gone into the kitchen? No wonder he hadn't heard her return to the parlor. Small, pretty, and nicely shaped they were—and a pure distraction. As if he needed anything else to divert his poor, slow-thinking head.

She must have noticed him gawking, for she quickly drew her feet under the blue fabric of her skirt. "Now then, tell me what brought you to my house at this hour."

He swallowed more hot liquid, then set the cup in the saucer in a less than delicate manner, sounding a loud *clunk*. "I...well, I've come to make you a proposal." "*Make you a proposal*"?

She stared, saying nothing.

"That didn't come out quite right. What I meant to say is...well, I know you've been on this husband hunt, and I wondered if, well, I might throw my name in the hat...as a contender."

"You want to *what?*"

"Don't worry; I understand it wouldn't be a *real* marriage. I wouldn't put any demands on you, and I could help out with the boys and fix things around the house. There's always one thing or another that needs fixin', right?"

She blinked three times, but no other muscle as far as he could tell even flinched.

"So, what do you say? You want to get hitched?"

She scratched her temple and sat there, mouth slightly sagging, but as for answering, nothing came out.

"We could visit the preacher next weekend…unless that's rushin' you too much. But then, it's Judge Corbett that's rushin' you, not me."

She cocked her head and eyed him warily. "You're serious? You want to marry me?"

He was beginning to think she might say yes. "Sure. What do you think?"

As if a fire had just lit beneath her, she stood to her pretty little feet in record speed, causing a bit of tea in her dainty cup to spill out onto the saucer. She set them both on a side table and faced him. "What I think is that you've fallen off your rocker, Mr. Connors, and it's time you left."

"We'd make a good team," he hurried to say. "The boys already like me. Shoot, they think I'm an angel."

"I don't give a skunk's ear what they think about you. I am not marrying you." Her skirts billowed when she turned and crossed the room, as if a gust of wind had swept through and caught them up. She reached the door and threw it wide, shooting daggers from her brown eyes. "Good night and good-bye."

"Wait a minute." He stood and snatched up his hat but took his time walking toward the door. "Calm down. I didn't say it right."

"You said it fine, Mr. Connors. And don't tell me to calm down."

His chest constricted with the painful realization that he'd blown his chance. How to rectify it before she socked him on the nose? "You can call me Sam, you know."

She gripped the open door so hard, her fingers turned white. "I think you'd better leave."

"Just give me a minute to explain myself, and then I'll go." He kept his voice low, his demeanor collected.

She huffed a breath through her nostrils. "Talk fast."

"You said you don't care what those boys think about me. Actually, you said you didn't give a skunk's ear, but that's beside the point. I know you do care. You want what's best for them, don't you?"

She shifted her weight from one foot to the other and glanced at the floor.

"I heard you planned to marry Harold Beauchamp. To be honest, I don't think it's a good match."

A tiny muscle flinched along her jaw. "Who I choose to marry is none of your concern." This time, her voice lacked conviction.

"Like I said the other day, it is my concern. I saved those boys from a deadly fire, and we've had a connection ever since. I think I should have some say about their future."

Her shoulders dropped a smidgeon. "I couldn't possibly marry you."

"Because you've already promised your heart to Harold Beauchamp?"

"Not my heart, no, but we've made an arrangement to marry because he is my best option."

"An old guy who knows nothin' 'bout raisin' kids is your best option?"

"Forty-one is not old."

"Forty-one? He sure looks older than that. Acts older, too."

"Mr. Beauchamp is also a faithful Christian, which is, of course, my first priority."

She had him there. "I'm a Christian."

"When was the last time you attended church?"

"Just because I haven't made a habit of goin' to church every Sunday doesn't make me a heathen. I've been a believer since I was a boy. I'll admit I'm not up to your standards, but I'm not hell bound."

"You imbibe."

"I—how would you know that?"

"I've seen you walk into Finnegan's Tavern."

"Ah, you've been keepin' an eye on me, have you?"

Her cheeks flushed. "Certainly not!"

"I can change my habits, if that's what you want. I'm not a drunkard, by any means. Shoot, I'd survive fine if I never took another swallow of brew. I mostly go to Finnegan's just to jaw with the guys. And I don't smoke, which should take me up a few rungs on your ladder of approval."

She stood up straight and stared at him squarely. "You haven't even made it to the first rung, sir."

"Look, let's be reasonable," he pleaded. "I'm young and full of energy, I make a good livin', and I'm already in good standin' with the boys." *Not to mention I need a roof over my head.*

"Be that as it may, the whole notion is preposterous. Sorry to be so blunt, but you're the last man I want to marry."

She sure had a splendid way of cutting him down to size. "I'm not exactly in love with you, either, madam, but those kids deserve better than Harold Beauchamp. He's a fine man, I'll give you that, but he doesn't strike me as overly hearty—or handy, for that matter."

She bit her lower lip. "The boys did wear him to a frazzle tonight."

A pang of jealousy pinched his heart. "You've been courtin', then?"

"Not that it's any of your business, but he spent the evening with us, yes. The boys engaged him in play, and it plain exhausted him."

"There, you see? They're too much for him."

"They are a handful, even for me, but I'm sure we'll find a balance, and the boys will learn their boundaries."

"It'll take a lot to heal those boys' hearts, you know. Right now they're just pretendin' to be holdin' it together, just as you're doin'; but one day— and it could be soon—everything's gonna come tumblin' down. How do you suppose Beauchamp's gonna handle that? At least you and I know a thing or two about grief."

She opened her mouth and then clamped it shut again. Her eyes shimmered with dampness, and he feared he may have pushed her to the limit. He felt a twinge of regret. "I'm sorry. I didn't mean to stir things up. I know that the Watsons meant a lot to you, and your havin' to find a husband just so you can hang on to their boys must be takin' quite a toll."

She dabbed at a single tear, and he felt like a heel. Handling tearful women had never been his forte.

"They were my d-d-dearest friends," she whimpered, "and I miss them terribly."

"I know you do. And, like I said, I'm mighty sorry." The glow of burning lamps had been all the invitation needed for a number of mosquitoes and a few moths to flutter through the open door. "You're lettin' in a whole slew of bitin' insects, you know."

She cleared her throat, tipped her chin upward, and pulled back her narrow shoulders, regaining her composure in fast order. "All the more reason you should leave—so I can shut the door."

He knew he should respect her wishes, so he took one step forward before blurting out, "It's that blamed family feud, isn't it?"

⌒

Mercy's nerves were stretched tauter than fiddle strings. How to get this man to leave her premises? What on earth was he thinking by suggesting the two of them hook up? She could no more marry him than she could marry the toothless Festus Morton! Not that Mr. Connors didn't have the handsome looks she wished for in a man. Heavens, he went far and above the attraction factor. But she couldn't marry a Connors, no matter that she didn't share the rancor that sizzled between the two families. She loved her aunts and uncles, and she didn't wish to fall out of favor with them—a prospect that obviously didn't worry Mr. Connors.

"That's it, isn't it?" He stepped forward and closed the door, preventing any more pesky bugs from entering. Then he turned, towering over her, his shoulders broad as a barn door. "You're afraid takin' my name will ruin your fine reputation."

His size didn't intimidate her, because, in spite of it, she had an innate sense he wouldn't harm her. No, he struck her as different, perhaps even poles apart, from the rest of his family, but the fact remained he was a Connors—and, worse, his father had murdered her daddy. Marrying Sam Connors would not only shock her relatives; it would shame Oscar Evans' memory.

She tilted her head back to meet the man's summer-sky eyes beneath his sandy hair, pushing aside how attractive she found him. "I don't harbor any of the ill-will that flows between our families, but I do cherish the love of my kin. And my uncle Albert, Pa's oldest brother, would have a regular conniption if he heard I as much as talked to a Connors, let alone married one."

He arched an eyebrow. "Let me get this straight: It wouldn't bother your fine relatives if you married a man several decades your senior, but marryin' someone with the wrong last name, regardless of the fact that he's the one who saved the lives of the boys you're marryin' *for*, would irk the shirts off o' them."

Mercy shrugged. "I must respect their wishes, and I would think you'd feel the same toward your own family. Why, I can just about hear your mother now. She detests the very ground beneath my feet. Imagine if you married me. It was enough that you spent all of a half hour in my house before she swept in with your cousins and rescued you from my clutches."

"My mother is exceedin' dramatic."

She couldn't help laughing out loud. "Is that what you call it? She wanted to shoot poison through my veins that night. I saw it in her eyes."

He studied her, one corner of his lip twitching upward, whether to smile or smirk, she couldn't say. "Do you even know what the feud is about?"

"Not entirely, but I know it was strong enough to cause a horrible clash between our fathers. Glory sakes, your father killed mine. That fact alone ought to make you think twice about coming near me."

"You just said you don't harbor any of the hatred."

"I don't. Can't you see? It's awkward, to say the least. I can't—it wouldn't be right. No, I won't even think of it. Please leave, Mr. Connors."

"I care for those boys, you know. Don't know 'em well, but I can tell they're good kids. That night, when I first saw flames shootin' from the roof-top of the Watson house, I could hear their cries clear out in the street. Did I tell you that? If I'd been chained to a tree, I would've figured out a way to break free and get in there."

She blinked back tears, but one leaked out. She used the heel of her palm to wipe it dry. "I'm grateful, but...."

"I know—it's not enough. Tell you what. When you lay your head on your pillow tonight, you pray about it. Fine Christian woman that you are, I'm sure you've been askin' the Lord for guidance."

"Of course I have. And what about you? Fine Christian man that *you* are, did God instruct you to come knocking on my door and make this preposterous proposal? I think not."

Rather than retort, he smiled down at her, and the sight of his blond lashes, surprisingly thick and long, caused a strange flutter in her stomach. The only sounds were the crickets' song and the tree frogs' *vreep, vreep.*

"I suppose God speaks to each of us in different ways," he finally said. "That night when I went inside a burnin' house and saved those boys—did God audibly tell me to do it? Nope. But did He figure into the plan? Yep." With that, he pivoted, plunked that big Stetson on his head, turned the knob, and pulled the door open. He started forward, and then, with one foot on the porch, the other on the threshold, he turned to face her again. "I might be all wrong in askin' you to consider my proposal. I know you'd be takin' a big risk. Heck, I would be, too. But there's those boys to consider. You've got to ask yourself what's best for them."

She opened her mouth, but nothing came out. The blasted man had rendered her speechless with his common-sense way of looking at things, and it plain vexed her.

8

The next day glistened with sunshine so searing, it fairly melted the tarred shingles right off the roof of the blacksmith shop. Still, Sam and his uncle tried not to let the temperature dictate the speed at which they worked. There were far too many orders on the docket to let a little heat slow their progress. But it wasn't so much the heat wave that had Sam in a lather as it was the menacing memory of his flop of a meeting with Mercy Evans. Instead of convincing her to marry him, he'd convinced her he'd lost his mind. Hadn't she said as much?

Across the room, Uncle Clarence whistled "Come, Thou Fount of Every Blessing"; meanwhile, in Sam's head, "Nobody Knows the Trouble I've Seen" kept repeating itself.

As if reading his very thoughts, Uncle Clarence broke right into them. "You go out to see that Evans girl last night?"

Sam got all fumble-fingered and dropped his hammer with a loud clang. "What makes you ask that?"

"Well, you been awful quiet, and you did tell me yesterday you were thinkin' on it. I s'pect you don't have much time, seein' as the postmaster's already got dibs on her. I stopped in at Juanita's for a cup of coffee before work and overheard all the talk."

"I heard the same yesterday mornin', but I guess I told you that." Sam chortled. "You rascal. You rarely drink coffee. I'm guessin' you went in there just to get the latest blather."

"Ha! You know I'm not one to spread gossip."

"You might not spread it, but you listen to it, like anybody else. What'd you hear, anyway?"

"Not a lot, 'cept that Beauchamp spent a few hours over at her place yesterday. Somebody caught sight of the four of 'em in her yard, lookin' for all the world like a real family. You didn't go bargin' in on them, now, did you?"

"No, I got there around nine thirty. Beauchamp was gone by then."

"Nine thirty's pretty late for callin' on a woman."

"I know that, Uncle, but time's wastin'. I figured if I was gonna make my move, it may as well be sooner than later."

"You mean later than sooner."

"Whatever."

"Well? What did she have to say?"

Sam ran his fingers through his hair. "Nothing promisin'. Guess it was a long shot."

Uncle Clarence gave a sympathetic smile. "She stickin' with Beauchamp? I 'magine he's already blown her over with sweet promises for the future. No doubt he's put away a nice nest egg, too, seein' as he's been single all these years."

"My nest egg isn't exactly empty."

Uncle Clarence lifted his gray eyebrows and cocked his bearded head to the side. "That so?"

"What do I have to spend my earnings on, besides a drink now and then?"

"You'd have to give that up if you ever had a mind to impress Mercy Evans."

"That's already been determined."

"Oh? She already laid down the law to you, did she?" His eyes crinkled in the corners.

"Not in so many words." Sam frowned. "Whose side are you on, anyway?"

"I'm on the side that's right." Clarence shuffled to the door. "I'm goin' out to the johnny."

"What do you mean, 'the side that's right'?"

The older gentleman put a callused hand to the door latch, sighed, and then partially turned to regard Sam with eyes that had the ability to see straight through him. "When you go home tonight, you read from the Good Book. You've got a Bible, don't you?"

"Somewhere, yep."

"Well, I want you to dust it off and read the twenty-ninth chapter of Jeremiah, payin' special attention to verses eleven through thirteen. Then, get on those knees of yours and seek the Lord with all your heart. Ask Him who's the better choice for Mercy Evans and those boys."

"I already know I'm the better choice. Beauchamp's too old to want to pour his time and effort into two raucous little tykes."

Up went those gray eyebrows again. "If you're so sure about that, then you'd best also ask Him to give her a like mind. I overheard Juanita sayin' she heard from somebody or 'nother that someone else told 'im she was hitchin' up this comin' weekend."

"That's a lot of somebodies out there talkin' about stuff they know little about. For someone who doesn't cotton to gossip, I'd say you had your listenin' ears on this mornin', Uncle."

He gave a lopsided grin and sniffed. "Just lookin' out for my nephew, that's all."

"I appreciate that."

"Well...." The man shifted his weight to the other foot and pulled on his beard. "Gossip or not, one thing is clear: Judge Corbett gave that little lady thirty days to find a husband. Since she wants to hang on t' them boys, I'd say she's goin' to be hitchin' up with somebody right quick here, maybe this weekend. Question is, who?"

"She's already made that pretty clear."

"Humph. You're givin' up awful easy, aren't you? Sometimes, you've got to fight for a woman. You ever done that? No, didn't think so."

The man didn't give him a chance to respond.

"Might be you could have a little talk with Harold yourself," Uncle Clarence continued. "See where he stands, exactly."

"What? You mean, pay him a visit?"

His uncle chuckled under his breath and gave his head a little shake. "My, my, things could prove mighty interestin' if you two hitched up. Yep, mighty interestin', indeed."

Uncle Clarence stepped outside and shut the door, leaving Sam with a gaping mouth and a load of things to mull over. He could hear Clarence resume whistling the hymn, the tuneful melody merging with the song of the black-capped chickadees and whip-poor-wills.

⌣

In the morning, Mercy dropped the boys off at Mrs. Parsons' house. The older woman had been so helpful in caring for them since the fire, and so Mercy was dismayed when the woman announced her plans to spend the rest of the summer with her daughter in Nashville. "I figured my leavin' wouldn't matter much, since you'll be marryin' soon," she said. "I do hope you understand."

"I'll still need someone to watch the boys during the day while I work," Mercy explained.

The woman's brow crumpled like a stomped tin can. "I should think you'll be stayin' home once you marry Mr. Beauchamp. He makes a decent enough livin', don't he?"

Mercy was grateful the boys had gone straight to the backyard to explore, and were not within earshot of the conversation. She cleared her throat. "Who told you about my plans to marry the postmaster, if I may ask?"

"Oh, gracious, I don't know. It's all over town." Instant dread etched the woman's wrinkled countenance. "You ain't the last to find out, are you? Good grief, I hope folks hain't been spreadin' lies, but, you know, your situation is a rather peculiar one, so it has caught the attention of lots o' folks."

Mercy sighed and shook her head. "I understand that people are curious. And, no, it's not a lie. I wouldn't say it's exactly official, though. Mr. Beauchamp and I haven't come to a firm agreement."

"I see." The elderly woman found a hair on her chin and began twirling it between her thumb and index finger, her gray eyes seeming to size up the matter. "Mr. Beauchamp is a fine man, but…." She pursed her lips and drew her eyebrows down.

"Yes?"

"Well, I don't mean t' sound petty or anythin', but he ain't what you'd call the handsomest critter in Paris. Truth told, I've seen some stray mutts 'bout town with better looks than his."

At that, Mercy nearly choked because, doggone it, Mrs. Parsons spoke the truth. It was a shame her betrothed couldn't have been blessed with handsomer features. Still, he remained her best choice, no matter that Sam Connors had offered his hand mere hours ago, his visit having made for an almost sleepless night.

She thanked Mrs. Parsons for watching the boys, then trudged next door to Doc Trumble's. She climbed the porch steps, wiped her shoes on the rug, and entered the house, the entire main level of which consisted of Doc's medical practice, the front parlor being the waiting room, with ten or so sturdy wooden chairs surrounding a large brick fireplace. Down the hall, several rooms served as examining areas. There was a small pharmacy, with cabinets where Doc kept his medical supplies, a tiny kitchen and washroom, and four rooms furnished with cots for long-term patients. The second floor served as the residence of Doc Trumble and his wife, Nora.

As Mercy entered the vacant office, which would soon be bustling with patients eager to see the doctor, she reflected on attending to Sam Connors—bandaging his burn wounds, sticking a thermometer under his tongue, forcing water and broth down his parched throat, assisting him in walking around the room to keep his muscles active, and encouraging him to cough up as much black mucus as he could, to prevent him from falling victim to pneumonia. All the while, he'd tried to engage her in conversation, but she'd ignored him, telling him now was not the time for talking but for concentrating on his recovery.

Looking back, she realized she'd put up a wall thick enough to prevent herself from entertaining as much as a smidgeon of curiosity about him. He remained untouchable in her eyes—and certainly an impossible candidate for marriage, considering her family's certain reaction. On the other hand, they highly endorsed Harold Beauchamp for his strong religious values, not to mention his high standing in the community. How ironic that on the outside, they all wanted to be looked upon as virtuous, but on the inside, they seethed with bitterness at their enemies, placing the Connors clan on the same level as the devil himself. And from what she knew, the Connors did the same, attending Sunday services while harboring equal loathing for the Evanses. Would it ever end? Could she not do anything to help stop the hate and to heal the wounds of the past? She had great passion and even talent for helping to cure the physical body, but the inner soul? No, that was God's department.

Love is the key, My child. Step out in faith and do the unthinkable. Trust Me. The insight flashed across her mind so abruptly that she stopped short in the middle of the parlor, looked toward the ceiling, and then gazed about the room, as if to identify from which direction the Voice had come. *"Do the unthinkable"?* What did that mean? *Lord, are You speaking to me?*

The sound of Doc's heavy footsteps descending the stairs forced her to dismiss, for the time being, the wild notion that God just might be telling her to marry—of all people—Samuel Connors.

9

It had been one of those days when even taking a moment to breathe seemed a luxury. By the time four gongs chimed on the grandfather clock in the hallway, marking the final appointment of the day, Doc had admitted two patients for an overnight stay, sent several home with pills and tonics for stomach problems and coughs, bandaged up a few wounds, and even set a bone or two. Why, even Mrs. Trumble had come downstairs to help, as she did when the workload became more than Doc and Mercy could handle alone. She was happy to perform any task she was able—unless there was blood, the mere sight of which sent her into a dead faint.

Given her weak stomach and low tolerance for sickness and death, Mercy wondered how she and Doc Trumble had wound up together, even though their love for each other easily bridged the vast differences between them. Apparently, there was some truth to the adage "Opposites attract." It boded well for her and Harold Beauchamp, who, beyond a shared love for God, had very little in common. Of course, she probably had even less in common with Sam Connors, and why she persisted in even allowing his image to pop up in her mind's eye perturbed her something fierce.

Mrs. Trumble entered the waiting room, where Mercy was straightening chairs. "Isn't it time you went and retrieved those boys, Mercy? Let me finish cleaning up. You're looking mighty spent, if I may say so."

Mercy blew several strands of dark hair off her face. "Does it show that much?"

The woman folded her arms across her portly bosom. "You've taken on quite an assignment in caring for those youngsters, young lady. It would be too much for most people."

"I'll admit, it worries me some, but I know I'll manage fine."

"A husband will help share the burden."

"I'd have preferred it not come down to that, but the judge was adamant."

Mrs. Trumble offered her a half smile. "I understand, but he's only thinking of those boys' best interests. Mr. Beauchamp will make a fine father figure for them."

Mercy sighed. "Is there no one in town who hasn't heard Mr. Beauchamp is my primary contender?"

The older woman laughed. "Can't get much by the people of Paris. Your situation is big news around here."

"So I've gathered."

Mrs. Trumble's gaze traveled over Mercy's shoulder and out the window. "Speaking of the postmaster...."

Mercy whirled around. Sure enough, the roundish, balding man was making his way up the front walk. Her stomach clenched. What had brought him here? She didn't remember arranging to get together today. Had he come to pay her a spontaneous visit? Or had he taken ill and come in search of medical attention?

Mercy stepped out onto the porch and closed the door behind her. "Hello, Mr. Beauchamp."

Seeing her, he halted, removed his bowler hat, and took to turning it in his hands. "Miss Evans." He nodded. "I hope I haven't interrupted your workday."

"No, not at all. I was about to pick up the boys from Mrs. Parsons'. I must say I'm surprised to see you. Did you close the post office early?"

"No. Mr. Lawson, my clerk, is manning it for a while."

"I see. Is everything okay?"

"Uh…not exactly."

"Dear me, you don't look so good. Do you need to see the doctor?"

"No, nothing like that." Sweat beads had formed on his forehead and now dripped down his plump face. "I've come to talk to you about this…marriage deal."

"Oh." *Marriage deal?* Uncertainty made her pulse accelerate. "In that case, why don't you come up on the porch so we can talk?" The sweltering heat only exacerbated her sense of dread.

Next door, a screen door slammed shut, and the squeals of John Roy and Joseph traveled over. "Mercy! Are you comin' to git us now?" This from John Roy, who ran across the drive separating the two houses, Joseph close behind. After greeting her with a hug, they commenced skipping up and down the wooden steps.

Mrs. Parsons ambled out onto her front stoop and shielded her eyes against the sun. "Hullo there, Miss Evans! Them boys is plain anxious to see you. Guess they're tuckered out from all the jobs I gave 'em today."

Mercy smiled. "Thank you for watching them," she called back. "I appreciate it."

Mrs. Parsons flicked her wrist. "Think nothin' of it. My pleasure. They sure got energy, though." Turning to go back inside, she gave Mr. Beauchamp a quick appraisal. "Afternoon, Mr. Beauchamp. Lovely day, ain't it? Plenty hot, though."

He shuffled his feet. "Yes, ma'am. Quite so."

"Well, you have a good afternoon, both o' you." Her skirts flared as she disappeared inside her house, the screen door flapping against the frame.

"We helped Mrs. Parsons clean out 'er shed today," Joseph announced to Mercy.

"Did you now?"

The boy stretched to his full height, which wasn't saying much. "She gived us cookies and milk afterward, 'cause we done so good."

She ruffled his hair, noting that it needed a trim. Add that to the long list of things to think about with boys, along with clothing, shoes, toys, and games. Heavens, she needed a man just to help her sort out all their needs. She hoped Mr. Beauchamp was up for the task.

John Roy gazed down at him from the porch steps. "Are you comin' over for supper again, Mr. Bonechomp?"

Mercy almost laughed at the mispronunciation, but the postmaster merely cleared his throat and gave her a desperate glance, so she cleared her throat to cover her giggle. "Um…boys, why don't you go out back and play a bit? Mr. Beauchamp and I have some discussing to do."

"'Bout your weddin'?" asked Joseph.

"Uh, yes," she answered. "Go on, now."

They bounded off the steps and made for the backyard.

"Now then, Mr. Beauchamp—or perhaps I should begin calling you Harold—why don't you come up on the porch and make yourself comfortable?"

But something in his expression told her that making himself comfortable was the last thing he'd be doing. He lowered his gaze. "I'm not sure I'll be staying long."

Her heart bumped hard against her chest, and she took a deep breath, fighting down her dread. "I see."

"I'll just get on with it," he said, casting her a troubled glance. "I'm not so sure this marriage is a good idea, after all. I'm afraid I—"

"Please, Mr. Beauchamp, don't do this to me!" She flew off the porch. "You are my only hope for keeping those boys."

The outburst surprised Mercy almost as much as Mr. Beauchamp, who stepped back, his eyes wide with alarm.

Duly embarrassed, she straightened her shoulders and composed herself. "I'm sorry. What I mean to say is, if your hesitation is due to the boys and all their energy, I will see to it that they contain themselves when you come home from work. I'm sure they'll settle down; they're just young, is all. But I keep a neat house, and I'm a good cook, and I'll—"

"Please, Miss Evans." He raised both hands, palms out. "I'm simply not the man for the job. After giving this arrangement much thought and prayer, I've reached the conclusion that our marrying would not be in everyone's best interest. Don't get me wrong; you're a lovely woman—beautiful, even—but I'm a bachelor who prefers to remain as such. I'm sorry to have strung you along. I thought it could work between us. Were it not for those boys, perhaps it might have."

She jerked her chin up. "Were it not for those boys, I would not have asked you, Mr. Beauchamp."

He gave a soft smile. "Therein lies the problem."

"But—"

He shushed her with a gentle touch to the arm. "You're a fine Christian woman, Miss Evans, but you know as well as I we're no match for each other. God no more intended for us to be together than He intended for the sun and moon to collide. I think there must be somebody in this town far better suited to you."

"There isn't." She hated her mawkish tone. Good grief, did she have no dignity?

"I'm sure there is," Mr. Beauchamp said.

She studied his face. Kindness, pure and simple, filled his brown eyes, and for the first time, she thought she could learn to care for him—never love him, maybe, but care for him. Surely, that would be enough. Wouldn't it?

He nodded, then glanced over his shoulder. "In fact, I believe I see a suitable prospect coming up the street as we speak."

She followed his gaze, and her heart jostled.

Riding tall as a tree, his cowboy hat drawn low over his eyes, Sam Connors reined in his coal-black horse at the foot of Doc's drive and tipped his hat at them. "Afternoon, folks. Am I interruptin'?"

"Yes," said Mercy.

"No," said Mr. Beauchamp.

"I'll be going now, miss." The kindly postmaster leaned forward and added quietly, "I've been praying for you, and I think you'd do well to take Mr. Connors up on his offer."

"His offer? You know? But how—?"

With another crooked-toothed smile, he plopped his hat on his head, turned around, and started down the walkway to the street, where his horse and carriage waited. Confusion swirled in Mercy's head like a miniature typhoon as she watched him nod to Samuel Connors before climbing into his carriage and driving away.

There sat Samuel Connors, wearing a grin. Had he somehow convinced Mr. Beauchamp not to marry her? Why, that arrogant rat!

She marched down the walk, prepared to give the man what for, but when he climbed down off his steed and held out a bunch of flowers tied with a yellow ribbon, the steam drained right out of her, at least for a moment.

Had he completely lost his mind? Sam figured so when he saw her tramping down the walkway, the hem of her skirts in her hand, vengeance in her eyes. The sight of the flowers seemed to give her pause, but then that fiery look came back all the fiercer. For a Christian woman, she sure did have a streak in her.

"What do you think you're doing?" she demanded.

He glanced around to see if they had any company. It wouldn't have surprised him had he seen a few neighborhood doors fly open the way her voice shot to the treetops.

How to answer her with his throat suddenly closed up tighter than a bank safe? While gathering his wits, he mustered a small grin and thrust the flowers under her nose, but she made no move to take them. Heck, she didn't even give them so much as a peek.

Give me strength, Lord. As prayers went, this one ranked low, but it was a start. After digging up his Bible and reading from it last night, particularly the verses his uncle had recommended, he'd been seized with a hunger to figure out God's plans for his life. He had a strong suspicion they included Mercy Evans, but convincing her of that wouldn't be easy.

He dropped the flowers to his side and considered his next words. Might as well just come out with it. "Have you given any more thought to my proposal?"

"Mr. Connors, I thought I made it plain that—"

"And have you prayed about it?"

"What?"

He could hardly fault her for her disbelief. It wasn't often he did the preaching. Shoot, he hadn't even darkened a church door since last Christmas. "Because I have. Prayed and also read God's Word. Last night, I memorized Jeremiah twenty-nine, verse eleven: *'For I know the thoughts that I think toward you, saith the* LORD, *thoughts of peace, and not of evil, to give you hope in your latter end.'* I think my *'latter end'* involves marryin' you and helpin' raise those boys. Harold Beauchamp is not your man. He doesn't even like kids that much. He told me so, just this mornin'."

"You went to see Mr. Beauchamp?" She pressed her hands to her temples. "Mr. Connors, I—"

"Sam, just call me Sam."

A low growl came out of her. "I don't know what to make of you."

He smiled. "You'll learn over time."

"What? No. I've already told you, our families—"

"—will have to learn to mind their own business," he finished. "We shouldn't let a long-ago feud kept alive by our relatives rule the way we live our lives."

Her eyes rounded like two brown billiard balls. "Your father killed my daddy."

He closed his eyes and put his face to the sun. The truth stung. "I know." He lowered his face and met her gaze. "I doubt anyone from my family has ever apologized for that, so I'd like to do that now. Truly, *truly*, I am sorry for what my father did. We may never fully learn what transpired between them that day." He swallowed hard at the sight of her, several strands of hair framing her cheeks, her dark eyes filled with tears to the point of brimming over. The emotion seeping out of her made him want to draw her close, but he didn't even dare touch her arm, for fear of frightening her. He couldn't believe he'd had the nerve to broach the subject of marriage again, but he'd been compelled to at least try, spurred on by his uncle's remarks.

Maybe he'd been wrong to go see Harold Beauchamp this morning, but the man needed a little reality drilled into him if he thought marriage to Mercy was going to be easy. He didn't have a clue how much work it took to raise two boys. Granted, neither did Sam, but he'd had plenty of practice keeping up with his energetic young cousins. He almost grinned, remembering the gray pallor Harold's face had taken on when Sam had painted a picture of life with two young boys who were likely to live at home for at least fifteen years more.

By the time Sam had finished talking to him, the poor man had confessed that he wasn't Mercy's best choice, no matter that he liked her well enough. It was those kids and their seemingly inexhaustible energy that worried him. He didn't think he had what it took to work ten hours a day, then come home to a bustling household of rollicking boys—not when he'd grown accustomed to the simple solitude bachelorhood afforded. He'd admitted to long having admired Mercy Evans; that, when the opportunity to wed her had presented itself, he'd seized it—with no thought for the boys' welfare. Now he regretted it, he'd said, especially after speaking with Sam.

In the end, they'd shaken hands, and Beauchamp had actually thanked Sam for talking some sense into him. He'd told him he would visit Mercy mid-afternoon to announce his change of heart, so Sam had kept an eye out for the fellow driving past his shop, then planned his arrival right around Harold's delivery of the bad news. He could only hope his plan wouldn't backfire.

Unfortunately, it appeared to be doing just that, even as he tried to make her see things his way.

10

Gladys Froeling, her father's oldest sibling and only sister, had always been Mercy's favorite relative. She admired her lively spirit, her youthful demeanor, her dynamic personality, and her love for the Lord. Add to that her refusal to involve herself in the Evans-Connors feud, and Gladys had Mercy's deepest respect. Despite her rather unsophisticated, if not primitive, air and appearance, the woman didn't lack for wisdom, and Mercy often sought her out for advice on everything from the art of baking bread to stitching a quilt, from important financial decisions to the meaning of a Scripture passage. Today, however, she came to her for an altogether different reason. She'd spent the past two days praying good and hard over Sam Connors' marriage proposal, and now it boiled down to one thing: seek out Aunt Gladys's no-nonsense advice and follow it. It almost seemed as if her very future lay in the old woman's hands.

Mercy veered the buckboard to the far right side of the road to allow an oncoming carriage to pass on the narrow dirt track. She feared the front wheel might drop into the gully, but with careful manipulating of her horse, Sally, they managed fine. The drive up Thoroughfare 69 and then west on the winding Jones Bend Road had never been a short, easy jaunt, but today's perfect temperatures and gentle breezes made the drive to the farm pleasant, especially with the company of two youngsters sitting on either side of her on the buckboard, eager for conversation.

Overall, the boys had adjusted to their loss and all the changes it had brought far better than Mercy had expected. Of course, they had the resilience of youth on their side. If only her heart had the same durability. Not a day had passed since losing her best friends that Mercy hadn't shed a wheelbarrow's worth of tears—not in the boys' presence, of course, but certainly into her pillow. She always ended her crying sprees by giving thanks to God that the children had survived, and then opening her Bible and reading its words of comfort, always seeking strength, guidance, and wisdom from its feathery pages. In her mind, she always reached the same conclusion. God didn't *cause* tragic circumstances, but He did *allow* them—and for reasons she would probably never fully grasp. What she did grasp, though, was His absolute love and care for her and the boys. She also recognized her desperate need for His grace, and so she pressed on in her quest to honor and obey Him, even when she couldn't understand His purposes and plans.

The Froeling farm sprawled across a huge parcel of land, most of which had been left untended since the death of Mercy's uncle Chester some ten years prior. Plenty of people had offered to buy the property, but Aunt Gladys, sturdy, stubborn, and strong, refused to sell. "This here's my home, and ain't no amount of money on earth goin' to make me give it up," she'd say. Even her own children couldn't talk her into buying something smaller and closer to town.

Mercy didn't blame her for wanting to hold on to the farm. Though seventy-five, she still had all of her mental faculties and could work circles around most people half her age. Who was she to try to convince her aunt to leave the old homestead when it was all she'd known for the past fifty years or so, ever since her husband had inherited it, shortly after their wedding?

"Who lives here?" asked John Roy, pointing at the three-story house at the end of the long drive, nestled amid the vast, rolling hills of blue green.

"This is the home of my aunt. Her name is Gladys, but I like to call her Gladdie."

"We been here before," Joseph chimed in. "We comed with Mama and you one time."

"Yes, you did. I'm impressed you remember that. It was in the spring-time, strawberry-picking season. We went home that day with a few buckets full of luscious fruit, and your mama and I cooked up a mess of strawberry jam in my kitchen. I still have several jars in my pantry." The recollection stirred a semi-sweet tangle of emotions in her chest. "I bet you'll remember my aunt, as well. She'll step out on her porch almost any second to see who's coming up her drive."

As Mercy guided Sally toward the watering trough, both boys scooted forward on the seat to watch for the first peek at her aunt. True to Mercy's word, the screen door pushed open with a whine to reveal a short, round, white-haired woman, apron tied around her waist, hand shielding her eyes from the sun. She waved excitedly, then hefted her skirts above her chubby ankles and bustled down the steps like someone twenty years her junior.

"I remember her," Joseph said. "She gots a great big red cookie jar settin' on her counter, and she lets us have as many as we want."

Mercy laughed. That very cookie jar was a fond memory from her own childhood. "Indeed she does, but don't go thinking you can eat your fill. Two apiece should suffice."

No sooner had she set the brake on her rig than both boys leaped to the ground.

"Well, lookie here, would y'? Two handsome boys come t' pay me a visit. What on earth did I do t' deserve sech a fine surprise?" Gladys opened her arms and welcomed the boys into a big embrace, then raised her round face to Mercy, who smiled down from her perch.

"Hi, honey! You come on down and tell me what brings you clear out here."

Mercy set the reins over the brake handle, swiveled her body, and stepped down with as much decorum as she could manage. She had yet to figure out a ladylike system for climbing off a buckboard in ankle-length skirts. On the ground, she huffed a breath and dusted herself off. "Do I really need a reason to visit my favorite aunt?"

"Pshaw! Don't let Gertie or Aggie hear of my bein' y'r favorite, or they'll come at me with a broom handle." The boys stepped aside, and Gladys wrapped Mercy in a tight hug that nearly stole her breath. Then, quick as lightning, she set her back for a good looking over. "My mama's corset, you've been in the sun. Them cheeks are brown as oak leaves. Where's your hat, missy?"

Most women wore wide-brimmed bonnets to ward off the effects of the scorching Tennessee sun, but there was just no hope for Mercy. Somehow, the rays always managed to find their way to her olive skin, deepening its tint the more. Besides, some days, she set off in such a hurry, she forgot altogether about snatching up a bonnet from the hooks by the door.

She waved off her aunt's scolds and looped her other hand around the woman's arm. "The boys and I thought we'd drop in to find out what flavor cookies you're offering today."

Gladys clasped her hands at her waist and looked from one lad to the other, their eyes shining with hopeful glints. The woman chortled and hustled them all toward the steps leading up to the grand wraparound porch. "We best go lift the lid off that jar then and find out. Who's goin' to do the honors?"

"Me!" both children cried in unison.

Up the steps they raced, then waited at the door for permission to enter. *Such little gentlemen*, Mercy thought. *Why would Harold Beauchamp turn tail and run from the privileged opportunity to raise them?*

Moreover, what possible reason could she come up with now for turning down Samuel Connors' hand in marriage? Perhaps Aunt Gladys would have one for her.

It took a good hour before Mercy drummed up the courage to broach the subject, and, of course, she had to wait till John Roy and Joseph had scuttled outside to the tree swings in the backyard, where, even now, their voices carried over the breeze with gleeful shouts as Aunt Gladys's hired hand, Harley Gleason, pushed them to the heights.

The women watched through the open window over the sink, Gladys rinsing off the platter on which she'd set ham sandwiches, carrot sticks, and chocolate mound cookies, and Mercy clutching a cold glass of water in both hands, at one point pressing it against her sweaty forehead for a moment of relief.

"'Twas a mighty nice surprise, you comin' out to see me, dear."

"Yes, but…." She had to search for the right words.

"But somethin' else besides my bein' your favorite kin brought you here, right? Don't go thinkin' you can fool the likes o' me. You been fidgetin' ever since you climbed off that rig. You gettin' cold feet about marryin' Mr. Beauchamp?"

Mercy drank the rest of her water, then set the empty glass in the sink. "I never could put one over on you, Aunt Gladdie. Can we go sit in the living room?"

"I've a better idea—let's go perch ar hineys on the porch swing."

Outside, the birds and squirrels created quite a racket, whether in harmony or dissonance, only the most dedicated nature lover would have the ability to distinguish. The ladies plunked themselves into the aged swing, and for the hundredth time, Mercy marveled at its strength. It seemed destined to break one of these days. She gazed at the rusted chains suspended from corroded bolts, and wondered how they'd held for so many years with nary a complaint, save for the familiar screech at every back-and-forth sway. It surely had served its generations well, rocking many an elder and baby into peaceful slumber. She settled back and allowed her aunt to shove off, joining her efforts as they kept the swing in motion.

"Okay, girlie. Spill it. What's on y'r mind?"

"More than my little head can hold. Mr. Beauchamp changed his mind about marrying me."

Aunt Gladys let out a low whistle. "I had a feelin' he wasn't quite cut out for that job. But, boy, he won't have another opportunity as good as what you offered. Don't think you would've been happy with 'im, anyways, honey. Plus, he's too old for you. But I'll go give 'im a good-sized piece o' my mind, if you want me to."

"Auntie!" Mercy put a hand to her stomach to hold back her chuckles. "You are the berries, I tell you. I appreciate your concern, but no, it won't be necessary to give him any of your mind. At your age, you need every bit of it."

Gladys stepped right over her attempt at humor. "So, what are you goin' t' do? You got less'n a week to find yourself a husband. Might be you're goin' to have to go up in them hills and fetch that toothless feller. What was his name again? Fester?"

"Close, but not quite. Festus. Festus Morton. And I wouldn't marry him if my daddy raised himself out of the grave and ordered it."

At that, Aunt Gladys's face contorted with shock but quickly converted to amusement. She gave Mercy a friendly bump in the side. "Good gracious, girlie, the things you say!"

"Well, it's true, Aunt Gladdie. You didn't clap eyes on that—that malodorous critter."

"And I'm thankful I didn't. You explained him right good to me the followin' Sunday in the churchyard." Gladys gave the swing another push with her foot. "Well, what's y'r next move?"

Mercy gulped a big swallow of air before proceeding. "Someone else has stepped forward, but I don't know what you'll say to it."

Gladys brought the swing to a halt. "He ain't older than the postmaster, I hope."

"No. I think he's right around thirty, so not that much older than I."

"Well, what's the big secret? Who is it?"

She pursed her lips so tightly, they stung, but then she blurted out, "Sam Connors! I know, it's probably the most bizarre thing you've ever heard. Imagine—one of our family's archenemies, proposing marriage. I've already turned him down, repeatedly, but he did save the boys' lives, and he seems determined to help take care of them. I don't know what to think of it all, but I'm beginning to grow a little desperate. I know it would probably create an awful stink in the family if...."

Aunt Gladys put a hand to Mercy's knee and gave a gentle squeeze. "Well, if you'd shush your gabber for just a second or two, I might be able to get a word in edgewise."

"Oh." She clamped her lips shut, folded her hands in her lap, and stared down.

"Well, I got my reservations, o' course," she ventured. "You're right about your relatives, and his, for that matter—they'd have a regular conniption. It could go either of two ways: make things worse than ever or calm the waters. I guess only time is goin' to predict the outcome. My main concern is where Mr. Connors stands with the Lord."

"He's a Christian, I've no doubt about that. But he's a weak one, and he'll admit it."

"Ain't nothin' wrong with bein' weak. Lord knows we all come out of the womb frail and needy. Can't spend ar lives drinkin' milk, though. Gotta get into the Word of God, our true meat source, and let it feed and nurture us, so's we can grow and mature. I wouldn't want you marryin' someone that's gonna drag you down in the spiritual sense."

"He's been reading his Bible and praying, more or less to appease me."

"That's a step in the right direction. And now, for my next question: What's in this arrangement for Mr. Connors? Why exactly would he want to stir up a bees' nest by marryin' into the Evans clan?"

"I wondered the same. At first, I thought he was plumb loco—still do, to a point—but he made the comment that maybe our marrying would bring our families closer together, make them see how futile it is to continue this feud. Neither of us has ever fully understood it."

"And it makes no matter if you do. What's important is bringin' it to a screechin' halt. Your Mr. Connors may have a point."

"Aunt Gladdie, he's not 'my' Mr. Connors. Glory! We hardly even know each other, beyond saying hello and good-bye."

"And, thanks to Judge Corbett, you won't have the luxury of gettin' acquainted till after the weddin'."

Mercy gulped. "After the wedding? You mean…you think we should go through with it?"

"Humph." Aunt Gladys folded her arms across her ample bosom and scanned the side yard, where the clothesline was strung, several of her skirts, blouses, and undergarments billowing in the breeze. "I barely knew my Chester when we got married, and our union wound up bein' the best part of my life. Y' shouldn't put limits on what God can do when you fully trust His plans for you. It says in Jeremiah, *'For I know the thoughts that I think toward—'*"

"I know just what that verse says. Sam Connors recited it to me just the other day."

"Well, well. Right there's your sign that it's meant to be."

"What?" Could it be that marrying Mr. Connors wasn't as harebrained a notion as she'd once thought? She had asked the Lord to give her some sort of sign. Still…. "Oh, Auntie, I don't even love him."

The woman grinned. "I can't say I loved my Chester in the beginnin', either. I'll be dad-burned if I even liked him much."

At that, Mercy laughed. It was the first spurt of outright laughter she'd experienced since the fire—and it felt good.

"What's funny?" John Roy asked, running around the corner of the house, Joseph chasing after, both of them red in the face from exertion. Harley Gleason appeared, as well, shovel in hand. He dipped his head at Mercy. "Miss Evans. Good seein' y' again."

"Hello, Mr. Gleason. Thanks for taking time out of your busy day to push the boys on the swings. It warmed my heart to hear them laughing."

The man removed his hat and wiped his bald head with his sleeve. "'Tweren't nothin'. Them swings don't get near the use they once did. I been thinkin' 'bout takin' 'em down, but after hearin' your youngsters' happy squeals, I guess I'll leave 'em be."

Mercy's heart leaped at his referring to the boys as "her" youngsters.

"O' course you'll leave them swings be, Harley Gleason," Aunt Gladys said. "I got grandchildren, you know, and another one on the way. Besides, y' never can tell when I might get the hankerin' to go out there myself and swing to the treetops. I ain't too old for swingin'."

Harley gave a full-out grin, his teeth white as pearls against his cocoa skin. "No, ma'am, you ain't. Yo' jest seasoned."

The porch swing shook with Aunt Gladys's cackles. "If I'm seasoned, then you're well-done!" The two laughed heartily in unison. They'd been friends since Harley's first day at the Froeling farm, long before Mercy was born. She remembered him from her childhood, always hardworking and full of joy.

Harley returned to his work, and the boys bounded down the steps, then commenced spinning in circles in the front yard. Gladys pressed her hands to her knees and pushed up, then turned and offered a hand to Mercy, as if she were the one in need of assistance. Mercy took her wrinkled hand, finding the grip firm yet warm. "You best be on your way, child. I believe you have to pay a call on your betrothed."

Mercy's heart pounded with unprecedented panic. "Oh, Auntie, I don't know about this."

Still clenching her hand, Gladys pressed her other palm on top and gave a gentle squeeze. "It'll work out fine, dear. As for the family, don't pay them no mind. Gotta think of them boys first. My only request is this: Let me come and witness y'r vows. I want to put my blessin' on them."

Her blessing on their nuptials? It was more than she could have ever dreamed. Even if the earth beneath the graves of Oscar Evans and Ernest Connors would quake and rumble in protest.

11

You're going to *what?* Samuel David Connors, you can't possibly be serious. Marrying that woman would bring utter disgrace on our family! I demand you tell her to look elsewhere for a husband. I don't care if you did save those boys from that house fire; they are not your charges. You will drop this ridiculous plan immediately!"

Sam shrugged. "Sorry, Mother. We've already made arrangements with the reverend."

"Then you will unmake your arrangements."

Good grief, she could be an ear-piercer. But Sam started to load his belongings into the crates and valises he'd carried up to his room, determined not to let her get the better of him this time. She'd been ordering him around for thirty years, and he'd had his fill.

"What are you doing?"

"Movin' to Mercy's house."

"You—you're going to live with that woman outside of the bonds of marriage?"

"No, of course not. I'm just packin' my things so they're ready for Saturday."

"You're marrying her *this* Saturday? What on earth has gotten into you, Samuel? You used to have a level head." Suddenly she covered her mouth with her hand. "Oh, my. It's that fire, isn't it? All that smoke inhalation did permanent damage to your mind. Have you talked to Dr. Trumble about it?"

Without casting her a glance, he picked up a pair of socks and tossed them into a suitcase. "There's nothing wrong with my reasoning abilities. I'm merely doing the right thing."

"The right thing, you say? You think marrying that—that *Evans* woman is proper and right? She's a...a...."

He whirled around. "Be careful what you say, Mother. She's gonna be your daughter-in-law."

She made an awful rumbling noise deep in her throat that would have scared off a bear. "This is the most asinine thing you've ever done, Samuel. Whose idea was this, anyway? Hers, no doubt. She's probably had her eyes on you since the night of the fire when she brought you into her house—I never did approve of that, you know. And then, all those hours she spent with you at Dr. Trumble's clinic...."

He turned and gave her a wily grin. "You really think she's had her eyes on me? I rather like the sound o' that."

"Oh, stop it. This is no joking matter."

"No, it isn't." He went back to sorting through his dresser drawers.

"How did she go about convincing you to marry her, for heaven's sake? I suppose she turned on that Evans charm."

He stopped shuffling through the drawer. "Evans charm?"

"You know what I mean. Did she bait you? Bat her eyes at you? Coo into your ear and make ridiculous promises?"

He straightened and crinkled his brow at her. "Actually, Mother, she did none of those things. In truth, I wooed her...if you can call it that."

"Pssh!" She slapped the air and scowled. "I cannot believe you would pursue any woman with *that* last name."

"Why do you hate the Evanses so much?" He held up a holey undershirt, then tossed it into the trash pile.

"I don't understand how you could ask such a question. You know our families have been fighting for generations."

"Yes, but why, exactly? I know it started with our grandfathers, but why drag it on long after their deaths?"

She narrowed her eyes, her frown deepening. "I am in no mood for talking about this now."

"You're never in a mood for talkin' about it, which makes the feud all the more ridiculous in my mind. Nobody talks about it. My cousins go along with it, but they have no more understandin' of the muddle than I do. It's just that their parents instilled in them their hatred of the Evans clan—somethin' you failed to do, despite your best efforts. I'm not your puppet, Mother. Never have been."

"My puppet? Is that what you think I've tried to make you? I raised you to be an upstanding citizen, and to carry on your father's business. Of course, it would have suited me more had you decided to take over the farm, but there was no hope for that."

Sam knew he'd been a great disappointment to his mother when, at sixteen, he'd announced he had no interest in taking over the farm. He much preferred forging to farming, and he couldn't see himself doing both. They'd hired Virgil Perry and a band of hands to tend the land and raise the beef cattle.

"At any rate," his mother continued, "I've brought you up to be a good, honest, successful man. And this is the thanks I get? After all I've done for you!"

He'd known it was just a matter of time before she'd pull out the guilt card. She'd used it often enough, and it usually worked. But not today. At the same time, he wouldn't stoop to utter disrespect. He chose to soften his stance. He paused in his task and swiveled his body.

Her face was still contorted into a frown, reminding him of a topography map, with varied lines crossing every which direction on her forehead and over her countenance. He wished she would let go of the hate. The woman could be quite attractive when she put her mind to it, and in her day, she'd been quite beautiful. The proof was in the tintypes of her and his father, displayed on the stone mantel over the fireplace. Even today, she maintained a trim figure. Too bad her sour personality had added years and wrinkles to her formerly unblemished porcelain face.

He put his hands on her shoulders, felt the knots there, and tried to loosen them. She jerked away, another standard ploy. He huffed a sigh. "I'm thirty years old, Mother. It's high time I got my own place."

"Getting your own place is one thing; marrying *her* is another." She blew out a loud breath to match his. "And what am I to do without you? You know I'm growing weaker with age."

"I know no such thing. Doc Trumble says you're healthier than a filly."

"Pooh. He doesn't know."

He could argue with her, but why? He decided to take the high road. "It's not like you'll never see me again."

"I do not want you bringing that woman around."

"You mean Mercy, my future wife?"

Another low growl stirred in her chest, and she lifted her chin. "She will not be welcome in my house. Do you hear me?"

"Don't be so unreasonable."

"I won't allow it."

He groaned. "Do you even know the reason for all the bad blood? Why don't you explain it to me, once and for all?"

She stood at his bedroom window, her back to him. "It had to do with Oscar Evans," she said, her voice chilly with disdain. "Your father would not have killed him that day, had it not been for his vicious, venomous words."

A sick kind of interest built up in his mind. "What exactly *did* he say, Mother? I wasn't aware it ever came out in court."

"It didn't, exactly." She dropped the curtain, and he could feel her hemming. She turned and gave him a derisive stare. "Saturday, you say?"

"Yes. Two o'clock."

"Well, it's unfortunate that I shall be busy." She walked to the door, then turned and scanned the room. "See to it you tidy up before you retire for the evening."

"You won't come to my weddin', Mother?"

But she had already disappeared around the corner.

His stomach turned over at her refusal to soften toward Mercy, no matter that she'd never done her any harm. It made him all the more determined to marry her. Perhaps his motives weren't the best—picking a spouse just to spite his own mother—but he cared for those boys, and that had to count for something. At least he was partly motivated by selfless aims. Of course, he knew next to nothing about raising kids, but then, he doubted

Mercy did, either. They would figure it out together. Weren't two heads better than one when it came to matters such as these?

⁓

Saturday dawned with dark, heavy clouds and the promise of rain, a perfect accompaniment to Mercy's song of woe as she stared into the mirror of her vanity. How had it come to this—having to marry Sam Connors, a man she barely knew? "Having" was the operative word, as no one else had stepped forward in the final hours to offer a better solution. She could blame Judge Corbett, though she supposed he did have the boys' best interests in mind. She could point her finger at the fire itself, which, of course, made no sense; she could fault Herb Watson, for failing to extinguish his lantern before falling asleep that night.

Or, she could blame God. Didn't He usually get the blame when bad things happened to decent people? The Watsons had been some of the most God-fearing people Mercy had ever known. Why, oh, why hadn't God protected them in their hour of greatest need?

I protected their children. The voice knocked at her heart's door and brought tears to her eyes, which she quickly dabbed at, so as not to smear the bit of color she'd added to her face in preparation for the ceremony.

"Yes, Lord, I know You protected Joseph and John Roy, and I thank You for that. But why couldn't You have—"

"And we know that to them that love God all things work together for good, even to them that are called according to his purpose." The whisper of her favorite verse, Romans 8:28, brought a measure of comfort. She determined to drop the questions for now.

She leaned forward on her stool and studied herself in the mirror. For some reason, she wanted to look her best, regardless of the fact this wasn't the happiest day of her life. It was her wedding day, not the one she'd dreamed about since childhood, but "her day" nonetheless, and to show up at the church in rags with a tearstained face would only make the situation worse, giving her something to regret, if not today, then later. She would make the best of it, for the sake of the boys and no one else—certainly not her groom, who'd been all grins when she'd gone to him a few days ago and accepted his proposal of marriage. My, how she'd hated to admit—silently—that he was her best offer. At least she hadn't said it to his face. She simply had no other recourse for keeping the boys in her care. And so, she'd chosen to move forward with this pitiable plan, all to avoid giving them up—for she was convinced that no one else could love them near as much as she.

At one thirty in the afternoon, her neighbors, the Lamars, arrived in their fashionable barouche to escort Mercy and the boys to the church. Unlike the majority of folks in Paris, who scraped by on next to nothing, the Lamars were reasonably wealthy, thanks to the return on Wayne's investment in a successful pharmaceutical company. They were also among the kindest, most down-to-earth people Mercy knew. She had tried to decline Wayne's offer of transport, insisting that she could drive her own rig, with capable Sally leading the way, but he had emphatically overridden her argument. "No bride ought to even entertain such a notion," he'd told her. "The wife and I will escort you, and that is all there is to it!"

Now, Mr. Lamar was perched on the high box seat out front, top hat and all, directing his pair of high-quality horses up Wood Street toward the center of town. The half-hood served to protect Mercy from the falling mist. Despite this being far from the happiest day of her life, Mercy had to admit to feeling quite important as she and the boys snuggled in the rear seat, facing a chatty Rhoda Lamar. Her constant babble did help to settle Mercy's nerves, and, of course, the boys delighted in the fancy conveyance.

To her great dismay, upon arriving at the little white clapboard church known as Paris Evangelical, she saw members of both the Evans and Connors families standing outside, arguing in loud voices.

"Mercy, you mustn't go through with this sham of a weddin'," came the voice of her cousin Bart, son of Uncle Albert and Aunt Gertie. "You don't know what you're doin'. Do you want to start a war?"

"Yes, Mercy, consider what you're doin'," said Aunt Aggie, her father's sister-in-law. "Why, if Oscar were here, he'd have your hide. This is downright disgraceful."

"She ain't fit to marry a Connors," jabbed someone from the other side of the steps, no doubt one of Samuel's cousins.

"Watch yourself, Frank Connors," shouted Mercy's cousin Wilburta, who picked up her skirts and marched straight over to face him nose to nose. "You say one contrary word about ar Mercy, and there'll be a brawl right here on the church steps."

Mercy's heart took a deep dive. What were they doing here, this cluster of unwelcome family members? She and Mr. Connors had purposely intended this to be a quiet, unobtrusive affair, so they'd kept the number of invited guests to a minimum.

Mrs. Lamar swiveled on her seat to gaze at the gathering crowd. "Oh dear, what have we here?"

Mercy gave a grave sigh, put an arm around the boys, and drew them closer. "I'm afraid what we have here is a family feud of the worst making, Mrs. Lamar. Perhaps there is a back door we could enter through. Mr. Lamar, would you mind…?"

"Don't you worry your pretty little head, Miss Evans," he called over his shoulder. "We will get you inside that church if we have to go through the roof. And if that doesn't work, well, I'll go through the roof myself, and it won't be in the literal sense. These people have no business ruining your special day."

Special day? Mercy mused. *Hardly.*

12

The ceremony had been anything but lovely. "Tense" best described it, seeing as Sheriff Phil Marshall and his deputies had been called to the church to break up the dispute taking place on the front steps between the unhappy couple's cousins, a few aunts and uncles, and a smattering of curious onlookers who simply took pleasure in watching a good fight.

To Sam's great relief, his mother had stayed away, as promised. Uncle Clarence and Aunt Hester, and Mercy's aunt Gladys, had walked right past the melee without speaking to anyone, even though their relatives had berated them harshly. Sam had never witnessed such a skirmish, and he carried a good deal of the responsibility for its happening. Had he not been so persistent about this whole marriage matter, none of this would have occurred, and it worried him that he'd made an unfortunate mistake. Still, the alternative—giving the boys to another couple—would've been worse, so, truly, he amounted to nothing more than Mercy's best option.

The boys wound up being the highlight of the entire affair, leaping up from their seats with a cheer when the reverend had pronounced them husband and wife. But when he'd added, "You may kiss your bride," a lump the size of an apple had lodged in Sam's throat.

"What?" he'd asked.

Reverend Younker had smiled and urged him, "Kiss your bride."

Mercy's cheeks had flushed pinker than the rouge she'd applied before the service. "Oh, that's not necess—"

But Sam had taken her by the shoulders and drawn her close—awkwardly, to say the least, and not the slightest bit like a first kiss ought to have been—and pressed his lips against hers, probably harder than required. Mercy had stood as stiff as a pine post, her hands planted at her sides, her lips closed tight, and her eyes scrunched shut, as if she'd just tasted something bitter.

What a fine pair they made!

In attendance, in addition to Clarence, Hester, and Gladys, had been Doc Trumble and his wife, Nora; the reverend's wife, Thelma, who'd also played the wedding march on the piano; and, of course, Mercy's neighbors Wayne and Rhoda Lamar, who'd been kind enough to drive her to the church. Sam had offered to pick her up himself, but she'd declined, saying it wouldn't be at all proper for him to see her before the ceremony. He hadn't figured her for the mawkish type, being that there wasn't an ounce of love between them, but perhaps her reasons were more superstitious than anything else. Whatever they were, he'd given in to her wishes.

After the brief ceremony, Aunt Gladys had invited everyone back to her home for a small feast. And everyone had gone, for who among them hadn't heard about the woman's cooking abilities? In fact, Sam would have sworn he saw a drop of drool on Wayne Lamar's lower lip. With the service concluded and his nerves settled, even Sam found he'd developed an appetite, for not only had he acquired a wife; he had a place to call home—and it wasn't under his mother's roof.

Flora Connors scrubbed her wooden floor till it shone like glass, working every gritty stain and grimy smudge out of cracks, corners, and crevices till sweat rolled down her face like small rivers and dropped to the floor to merge with the mop water. The more she perspired, the harder she worked, figuring the labor did her stewing mind good. Glistening sunbeams filtered through the window and fell on her shoulders, but they did nothing to improve her spirits. *Imagine, a Connors hitching up with an Evans*, she mulled angrily. *And my own son, for heaven's sake. Why, it's nothing short of disgraceful!*

The screen door to the kitchen opened with a whine, then flopped shut, followed by the sounds of footsteps on the tile floor. "Who's there?" she called from her stooped position in the hallway. "You'd best not be dirtying my tile."

Within moments, her burly hired hand, Virgil Perry, appeared around the corner and leaned his bulk against the doorjamb. Oh, but this man was the bane of her existence. She would like to fire him for all the trouble he'd visited upon her, but she had no way of doing so. Ernest had hired him some fourteen years ago to run their farm—the farm he'd insisted they maintain, even though he was always busy at the blacksmith shop. His argument had hinged on having two sources of income.

Virgil held a half-eaten turkey drumstick, no doubt left over from last night's dinner with Flora's sister, Mable Hughes, and her husband, Henry. She'd expected Samuel to show up for the meal—had even set a place for him at the table—but he'd begged off, saying he had much to do to prepare for the wedding. Of course, he'd once more invited her to attend the ceremony, but she'd adamantly declined.

"What are you doing in my house?"

"Come to see what's in your icebox."

"Stay out of my icebox! You have no business in there."

He took a large bite of the drumstick, then chewed with an open grin, revealing his yellowed teeth. "Saw it on the platter," Virgil said with a shrug. "Sure is tasty." He snagged another bite, his eyes rolling with satisfaction.

"Why, you...you roach." She pushed herself up and dropped her soiled rag with a plop into the murky mop water, then stood to face off with the man who had brought her more trouble in the past several years than she knew what to do with.

"Bet you're none too happy 'bout Samuel marryin' up with that Evans woman, huh? That why you're workin' yourself into a regular stew?"

"That is none of your business, Virgil. Now, kindly leave the same way you came in, and next time, knock."

He lifted his thick, dark gray, scraggly eyebrows and looped a thumb over his belt, his larger-than-life belly spilling over it. "Are you sayin' I ain't welcome?"

"I'm saying you're my hired hand, and you presume too much."

"I would think, after all I've done for you, you'd treat me with more respect. Consider me one o' the family."

"Psh. All you've done is take my money, you greedy son of a sea serpent."

At that, he tossed back his grizzled head and snorted. Oh, but she detested the sardonic sound of his laughter. Always had.

"Now, Flora, you know I've always taken fine care o' this here farm. Ernest would be mighty pleased, if not proud. The cattle are well fed, the fields are tended, and the milk's flowin'. You can't deny that."

That much was true, but he'd milked her of most of her money, as well. And she hated the very earth he strode across. "No, but I pay you a far piece more than you're worth. I could hire someone else for a great deal less who would work circles around you."

He flicked his thick eyebrows, arching one higher than the other. "Ah, but your hands are tied now, aren't they? You know good an' well what would happen if you tried to fire me. I'd have to spew the truth about you."

Her stomach clenched into a tight, grueling knot. "Get out of my house. You have work to do."

He laughed and pushed himself off the doorframe, the turkey drumstick gnawed clean to the bone, remnants of meat still sticking to his greedy lips and clinging to his dense mustache. "I'm goin', I'm goin'. Now, don't you worry none, Miz Flora. Your secret's safe with me." He dipped his chin and flashed her a beady-eyed wink. "Long as you keep doin' y'r part, I'll hold up my side o' the bargain."

She growled. "Get out. Now."

He turned and ambled none too fast toward the exit, his low chortle resonating off the walls, till he threw open the screen door and sauntered back outside in the direction of the barn.

Sam recalled Gladys Froeling's farm from boyhood. He'd made deliveries there for his father on more than one occasion—tools, horseshoes, shovels, and other various garden implements. Gladys had always been a friendly sort, whereas her husband had always eyed him warily, never once offering a kind word, probably due to his opinion of the Connors clan. Still, theirs had been—and still was—the only blacksmith shop in town, and when folks needed metalwork done, they had no choice but to contract with them.

With Aunt Gladys's feast concluded, the small gathering of wedding guests, still rubbing their bellies in satisfaction, began to scatter in different directions—the women to the kitchen, the men to the living room or den. Sam held back, John Roy and Joseph clinging to his sides like little shadows. They'd become noticeably quieter since finishing off their slices of white cake with thick icing, and he wondered what was going through their minds. He knew his own head had set to swirling with all manner of thoughts, so he couldn't imagine how theirs must be spinning, not to mention Mercy's. Was she kicking herself up one side and down the other for marring him? During the meal, they'd barely exchanged more than two words, let alone looked at each other, even though they'd sat shoulder to shoulder at the long, extendable farm table, which had seated the entire party comfortably.

"Can you push us on the rope swings?"

Sam gazed down into John Roy's pleading eyes and rubbed the boy's head. Joseph didn't echo the plea, but he did shoot him a similar look. "The rope swings, eh? I seem to remember those from my own boyhood, but I never had the pleasure o' puttin' 'em to use."

"They's pretty fun," offered Joseph, though his voice didn't carry a great deal of enthusiasm.

Mercy entered the dining room from the kitchen, and they locked eyes at last. "The boys would like me to take them out back to the swings," Sam told her.

"I think that's a fine idea."

"You don't mind?"

She shook her head and shrugged. "Why should I?"

He gave a half smile, glad to be out of earshot of almost everyone. "It is our weddin' day."

She frowned. "Yes, and it should be treated as an ordinary day. We married in name only, and for that reason, you shouldn't feel beholden to me. I, for one, expect no special treatment, and you shouldn't, either."

She could be a cold one. "No regrets?" he asked.

"About what?"

He bristled like a rooster. "About marryin' me."

"No, of course not. What choice did I have?"

He stared at her for all of three seconds. "Right. What choice?"

She must have detected his slight indignation, for she quickly put in, "Don't get me wrong; I thoroughly appreciate the sacrifice you've made for us, and I'm thankful now that you were so assertive."

His ire shot up a full notch. Had he been that pushy? In retrospect, he supposed he had. After all, he'd been about as desperate as she. "Well then, we'll go on out back. Let me know when you're ready to head to your house."

"Yes, I'm sure you're quite anxious to get settled in your room." He noted the special emphasis she placed on the word "your." Should he tell her she need not worry her pretty little head over him demanding his husbandly dues?

He took both boys by the hand and led them to the side door off the big dining room. "Have fun, boys," she called after them. Neither reacted to her voice.

⌒

Aunt Gladys stood with Mercy as she bid the last of the guests goodbye. Sam was still outside with John Roy and Joseph, as he'd been for the past hour. Mercy suspected he didn't know how to act, so escape seemed his best recourse. Of course, she had no idea how to behave, either, so they made a fine pair. She walked to the kitchen window overlooking the swings but found them vacant, swaying in the soft breeze.

"Your husband has been noticeably absent." Aunt Gladys came up beside her and bumped shoulders with her. "And he was more than a little quiet during the meal, although I noted he didn't lack for an appetite."

Mercy chortled. "If that's a sign of things to come, then I'd better stock my pantry with a few more items."

"I'd say."

Mercy's slight mirth turned to conjecture. "He's probably filled with misgivings. I wouldn't blame him."

Gladys put an arm around her, drawing her close, and Mercy leaned into her embrace.

"I doubt that, dear. More likely, he's just tryin' to process everythin', and spendin' time outside with those boys is good for the mind and soul. Speakin' of John Roy and Joseph, I'll bet they got a whole lot of questions churnin' in their heads."

Mercy sighed. "It's going to be a big adjustment for all of us. What if it makes a bigger mess than the problem it was meant to solve?"

"Only God knows that. All you can do now is trust Him to lead the way. You and your husband need to be a team when it comes to raisin' those youngsters, and I've got no doubt you'll give it your best shot. Now, stop y'r worryin'. God will give you what you need at just the right moment. Have a little confidence in yourself and a whole lotta faith in Him."

She made it sound so simple. Mercy gazed at her through misty eyes. "You're always full of such good advice, Auntie. Too bad the rest of our relatives who showed up at the church today didn't share your view. All they could do was try to talk me out of making the 'biggest mistake of my life.'"

Gladys flicked her wrist. "Don't pay them no mind. Your nuptials were none o' their business, and they should've known better than to interfere. If you want the truth, I plan to visit each an' ev'ry one of 'em next week to tell 'em so."

"Oh, Auntie, don't do that. You'll just make trouble for yourself."

"Pfff. You think I care about that?"

"I've never understood this feud, but some have compared our families to the Hatfields and the McCoys. I hate the thought of going down in history alongside the likes of them."

The older woman pushed a few strands of white hair out of her eyes and gazed straight ahead, where the sunflowers bowed their yellow heads at the back of the garden. "Longstanding feuds have a way of dyin' slow deaths, honey. But, heaven sakes, let's not talk about that on your weddin' day. Matter o' fact, let's head outside and see if we can find Sam and those boys. What do you bet they've gone an' found Miss Tabitha and 'er batch o' kittens?"

At the back door, they saw Sam and the boys emerge from the barn. Indeed, John Roy and Joseph each carried a squalling ball of black-and-white fur. "What did I tell you?" Gladys asked, nudging her.

The women stepped onto the back stoop. Mercy crossed her arms, her heart hitching at the sight of her new family. Sam halted his strides when his eyes met Mercy's, and then he threw her an impish grin, followed by a broad-shouldered shrug.

"Looks like you'll be takin' home some kittens," Aunt Gladys whispered.

"Looks like it."

13

The improvised family made it through the first couple of weeks together without much incident. Even the two kittens, christened Roscoe and Barney, had made the adjustment, neither one objecting to being toted around by John Roy and Joseph.

Sam tried to make himself at home in the room Mercy had assigned him, located across the hall from her bedroom and just a few steps from the boys'. There was a washroom halfway down the long corridor, with a claw-foot tub, a two-faucet sink, and a toilet chair, the latter of which he refused to use; the outhouse served him just fine.

Only a few times had he encountered Mercy either coming or going, the most memorable occasion being at two in the morning. Mercy had emerged from the washroom and had let out a gasp to find herself face-to-face with him, bare-chested and wearing Levis, in the dimly lit space. "Didn't mean to scare you," he'd fumbled, arrested by the sight of her in that long, scoop-necked nightgown. It was the first time he'd seen her dressed in anything other than her daily attire, and the effect had done anomalous things to his innards. She'd recovered quickly, giving him a thin-lipped smile, and scooted back down the hall toward her bedroom, leaving him rubbing his whiskery jaw. Once she'd closed the door, he'd scampered down the stairs and made a beeline for the outhouse.

He still had trouble viewing himself as a married man, but the continual ribbing he took from the guys at Juanita's Café provided him all the reminder he needed, and he longed for the day when his marriage would become old news. Thank goodness Uncle Clarence hadn't made much of a to-do about it. At the shop on Monday following the wedding weekend, he'd merely cast Sam a teasing look and asked him how he liked married life.

"Haven't quite got the hang of it yet," Sam had confessed.

His uncle had tossed back his head and laughed. "I been married to your aunt for nigh onto forty years, and I still ain't got the whole business figured out. Women are hard creatures t' understand, an' hitchin' up with one... well, it turns your whole life into one giant puzzle."

Sam had not been encouraged.

At Doc Trumble's counsel, Mercy had taken a leave of absence from her job. She hadn't wanted to, but Doc had thought it best for the boys and her, and Sam had agreed, even adding his two cents. "How do you expect those boys to get used to their new surroundings if you drop them in somebody else's lap every day while you go to work?" he'd asked her one night as they stood together in the parlor after putting the boys to bed. "I make a good livin' and earn plenty to support us all. Maybe once school starts up again, you can go back to work, but your role has changed drastically. You're a mother now."

She'd lifted her head in one fast jerk and frowned at him. Clearly, he'd hit upon a nerve. "I am not their mother," she'd stated firmly, "nor will I ever try to take her place."

"Sorry, wrong choice o' words. But you're their guardian, as am I. And the way I see it, they need as much stability as we can provide."

At that, she'd plopped into a chair next to the fireplace and taken to massaging her temples. He'd remained standing, one hand resting against the mantel, while she'd stared down at her lap, probably battling for the last remnants of her independence. In some ways, he'd pitied her. This was not the life she'd bargained for. But neither was it the life the boys had wanted—not by a long shot. He'd mentally prepared his defense, in case it would come to that, but Mercy had let out a long, deep breath and said, "I know you're right."

She could have knocked him over with a sneeze, but he'd tried not to react; he'd just smiled and given a reassuring nod.

He hadn't paid his mother a visit since moving out of her house, deciding it best to give her time to adjust and, hopefully, settle down some. And so it took him by surprise when he spotted her in town, two weeks after the wedding. He was on his way to May's General Store, both boys in tow, and she was approaching them on the sidewalk, her head down, her flower-bedecked bonnet blinding her to everything but her own toes. He figured she could walk in front of a team of horses and never know what hit her.

"Mother?"

The hat bobbed as she came to a halt and lifted her chin. The first thing he noticed were the dark circles under her eyes. Had she not slept a wink in the past week?

"Samuel? Is that you?" Her shrill voice unsettled a flock of birds perched in a nearby tree and sent them soaring across the street, where they congregated on the rooftop of the Paris Bank and Trust building.

He didn't much feel like hugging her, so he rested his hands on both boys' shoulders. "Have you met John Roy and Joseph?"

She peered down her nose at them, and he noted the lack of warmth in her eyes, not to mention the absence of a smile. "I saw them the night of the…you know. How do you do?" She made no move to shake their hands.

"Boys, this is my mother. Can you say hello?"

"Hello," Joseph answered for both of them, standing taller and jutting out his chin. "We don't gots parents anymore, so Mercy an' Sam took their place."

His heart must have stopped for all of two beats. "We didn't 'take their place,' Joseph," he hastened to reply. "We just…." He looked to his mother, wishing she would offer a word of consolation. Of course, she stood stock-still and silent, whether because she was unable to find the proper words or because she was completely aloof, he couldn't say. "We just want to give you a home to grow up in…a place to feel safe."

"I felt safe in my other house, but it burned down. What if Mercy's burns down, too?"

If he were a regular church attendee, Sam might have had an apt response, something borrowed from a wise preacher. "That's not goin' to happen, Joseph," was all he could say, despite knowing he shouldn't make any such promise. Houses and businesses went up in flames all the time. How did one explain to a six-year-old that the things in which you placed your hope and trust sometimes vanished in a moment? Even adults struggled to come to terms with this fact. If Mercy were here, she would say that God was in control of the universe, even when tragedy struck and hearts shattered, and that those who placed their trust fully in Him would not be disappointed.

Sam glanced at his mother again, for once wishing she would speak. For crying out loud, the boys' parents had perished in a fire, and all she could do was stand there and bite on her lip? He wanted to give her a good shake.

"Do you gots any kitties?" John Roy asked in a quiet, somber tone.

"What's that?" His mother leaned in.

"Kitties. Do you gots any kitties at your house?"

"Oh, cats?" She cast Sam a long look. "No. Well, yes, I suppose there are cats out in the barn. Virgil—er, Mr. Perry always keeps them out there, for the mice, you see. They're not pets, though. No."

"We gots two kitties. They's named Barney and Roscoe. Roscoe's my kitty. Mercy lets him sleep with me."

"Oh, dear." She wrinkled her nose.

Sam might have laughed, had he been more in the mood. His mother detested animals of all types, which was uncanny, considering she lived on a farm that bred cattle for milk and meat, grazed horses and goats, and raised a few chickens for eggs. Of course, Virgil Perry had always manned the farm, taking more ownership of it than even his father had. Sam often wondered if his mother planned to transfer the deed to him someday. He supposed it wouldn't bother him, one way or the other, although he'd never liked Virgil Perry. The fellow had an arrogant air that chewed on Sam's last nerve.

"We got ar kitties at that Gladdie lady's house."

"That—who?" his mother asked.

Sam shook the clogged thoughts from his head. "Gladys Froeling."

"Oh." His mother's forehead crumpled. "Her."

"Mercy's aunt."

"Yes, yes, I know who she is. Good gracious, I've lived in these parts a lot longer than you have."

"Yes, you have, *Mother.*" He turned to the boys. "Well, we'd best move on." He cast his mother one last look. "It was nice seein' you."

As they proceeded past her, she reached out and touched his arm, sending a quivering chill right up his back. She had never been very demonstrative. "When am I going to see you again?"

He lifted both eyebrows. "I thought you didn't want anythin' to do with me."

"Where would you get that idea?"

"You didn't come to my weddin'."

"Well, of course I didn't, and I think you know why. I would like for you to visit, but I made it clear I don't want you bringing...*her.*"

"I see." He issued a brief smile and sighed. "Then, I suppose we won't be seein' much of each other." He turned and urged the boys onward, hastening his steps at the sound of his mother's heels clipping frantically along the wooden planks after him.

"Surely, you don't mean to say you're cutting off all ties," she said to his back. "How could you do such a thing to your own mother? Have you no sense of decency?"

He stopped and turned around. "Decency! You're hardly in a position to lecture me on that."

"What? Why, I never—"

"This hatred for the Evans clan has got t' end, Mother. Perhaps you hold the key to startin' the process. Have you ever thought o' that?"

She clamped her mouth shut and stood there, red-faced, staring him down.

Wanting to put an end to the argument, for the sake of poor John Roy and Joseph, he broke the silence. "Give it some thought, Mother."

She glanced down at the boys. "I wouldn't mind if you brought them."

Even as she said it, a wrinkle formed on her nose, as if the very notion of youngsters on her farm would stir up a nest of hornets. He knew it all stemmed from the loss of his twin brothers, Lloyd and Lewis, who at age two had both come down with scarlet fever. They'd lost the battle only three days apart from each other. Sam, three years old at the time, had been spared, and had no memory of that mournful period. He'd sure heard about it later, though. In some ways, he wondered if she hadn't always resented that he hadn't been the one to contract the disease instead of her beloved twins. She'd always talked about how everyone would dote over them when she took them out in the carriage, dressed in identical outfits and wearing perfect little smiles. She sure had a whole lot more daguerreotypes of them scattered around the house than she did of Sam as a boy, not that he cared.

"Good day, Mother." Taking both boys by the hand, he turned and headed up the street, past the Paris Fish Market and Grandy's Best Meats. This time, she didn't try to stop him, but he could feel her eyes burning holes in his back.

"Was you fightin' with y'r mama?" asked Joseph as they crossed the street at West Wood and Poplar.

Sam released a long-held breath. "I guess it did seem that way, didn't it? I'm sorry you had to be party to that."

"Party?" John Roy raised his head.

"Are we havin' a party?" Joseph asked. "Is that why we's goin' to the store?"

Sam gave a lighthearted chortle, loving their innocence and wishing he could reclaim a little of it. "Well now, I'm sorry to say Mercy didn't send us to the store for party favors, but that's not to say she won't plan a party one o' these days." He couldn't quite picture her hosting anything festive at this particular time. Shoot, it was hard enough wrangling even a tiny smile out of her. He reached inside his pant pocket for the list she'd given him that morning. Looking it over, he noticed, among other items, a ball of twine, baking soda, maple syrup, and stone-ground corn meal. "Nope, no party today, I'm afraid."

"Well, can we at least get us some candy sticks?" Joseph asked. "Ar mama always bought us ar favorite colors when we comed to the store."

Sam's heart took its usual tumble at the mention of their mother. "Well, o' course we can. What do you think I am, a big ol' grouch?"

The boys giggled, and in that moment, Sam thought he would buy out the whole inventory of candy sticks, if it would take away the pain of their loss.

14

After scrubbing the last of the clothes on the washboard, giving them a thorough rinse, and wringing them out, Mercy dropped them into the wicker basket and then, with aching back, hefted the heavy bundle onto her hip and made her final trip to the clothesline. Garments of all sizes, colors, and types—from the boys' underwear to Sam's shirts and trousers to three sets of bedsheets and pillowcases—billowed in the afternoon breeze. Good gracious, what had happened to her quiet existence? Wasn't it only yesterday she'd had the Watsons over for supper, sharing in carefree conversation while the boys entertained them with their antics and animated storytelling? Life had gone from simple to complicated in a span of seconds, and some days she wondered if she would wake up and find that all of it had been a dreadful nightmare. Oh, how she wished for it.

Still, it could be worse. Sam had been nothing but kind, even if she still hardly knew him. During the week, he left for his shop at dawn's first light and didn't return until suppertime; when he was home, he took every opportunity to escape with John Roy and Joseph, whether outside for a game of hide-and-seek or to the store, as now, running errands. It was nice to be able to finish the laundry without being distracted by the boys' constant pleas for

119

attention. She loved them dearly, but assuming their round-the-clock care had turned out to be an overwhelming job.

What had she been thinking, wanting to continue working at the clinic? Doc Trumble had been right to encourage her to take a break, at least for the time being, in order to care for the boys and tend to her household, but she still missed the sense of independence it had given her; the satisfaction of bringing home an income. Moreover, it pained her how quickly he'd hired a replacement—Eloise Hardy, a trained nurse who'd recently moved with her husband from Nashville to Paris to be closer to her ailing parents. Her qualifications far exceeded those required, and she surpassed Mercy in years of experience.

With the sun beating on her shoulders, Mercy took a swipe at her damp brow and set to hanging the last of the wet clothes on the line, glad for the dry ones she'd been able to remove to make more room. For years, she'd used only a portion of the rope suspended in an L shape across her back-yard, and had even pondered taking some of it down, but now she needed an extension. Her heart blossomed with gratitude, for earlier that week, the judge had granted Sam and her full custody of the boys. At the same time, she felt a sting, for her gain was her friends' loss—and their loss was her lament. Would she ever feel whole again? And, more important, would she and Sam find the means for helping the boys heal from their own heartache, never mind that they were young and resilient?

One of the kittens—she still couldn't tell them apart—leaped into the basket of damp laundry. The sight of them romping nearby made her smile, and a kind of thick emotion seeped into her heart. She bent down and touched the downy-soft head. "Whichever you are, Roscoe or Barney, you sure are cute." The kitten rubbed against her and mewed softly, as if to summon his brother, who came bounding toward her over the plush lawn. She went down on her knees and gathered them both up, bringing them to her hot cheeks, where a fresh batch of tears had started coursing downward. "Oh, Lord…oh, Lord" was about all she could manage.

Regaining control, she placed the kittens back on the ground and returned to the chore of hanging clothes. She pinned the last item on the line about the same time Sam and the boys returned in the rig, their loud spurts of laughter renewing her sense of purpose.

Over supper around the dining room table that evening, the boys chattered about the toad they'd caught in the backyard, the pictures they'd drawn in the dirt with sticks, and the pretty rocks and bird feathers they'd found. It was difficult to squeeze in a word edgewise, unless they happened to both stop at the same time for a sip of water, in which case Sam would make a polite comment about her tasty fried chicken and potatoes or remark about the sizzling heat and his eagerness for the arrival of autumn, with its cooler temperatures.

Their conversations thus far had been of little substance, probably because they focused most of their attention on the boys. She appreciated his attentiveness to John Roy and Joseph but imagined he must miss his independence. So much had changed for him, and it still stunned her that he'd willingly given up his bachelor lifestyle to be chained to three people he barely knew.

"Sam got in a fight with his mama today." Joseph's announcement brought Mercy's chewing to an abrupt halt, and she knew her eyes must surely be bulging.

Sam scrunched his brow and set down his water glass. "Not a fight, Joseph." He gazed across the table at Mercy. "We ran into my mother in town today. She wasn't what you'd call overly friendly."

"She tol' Sam to come an' see her," Joseph went on, "but he said he wouldn't go unless you comed, too."

Sam looked startled. "I didn't think you boys were payin' attention."

"We was. Well, I was. I don't think you like your mama very much."

"I like her fine." Sam scratched his whiskery jaw. "Finish what's on your plate, please." Then he looked back at Mercy. "Like I said, she wasn't friendly."

She swallowed and set her fork down. "I'm sorry for the tension I've caused between the two of you. Please don't let me stand in the way of your going to see her. She'll just resent me more if you don't."

"Believe me, you're not standin' in the way." He finished off his last bite of chicken.

Mercy took a sip of water. "She must be so upset over this…arrangement. You never did tell me how she reacted to the news that you were marrying me."

He gave a droll little laugh, and she noted the pleasant ring to it. "Let's just say it would've been helpful if I'd plugged my ears beforehand."

"I don't know how you can joke about it."

"Can we be done now?" John Roy inserted, wiping his mouth with his sleeve.

"Yeah, can we? I'm full," Joseph chimed in. "But not too full to play outside," he added.

Mercy glanced at the boys' plates. Satisfied that they'd eaten enough, she gave a quick nod, and they pushed back in their chairs. "Carry your dishes to the sink first, please."

"Okay," they said in unison. Hands full, they scurried from the dining room. She heard them drop their dishes in the sink with a clatter, then scamper out the back door.

Mercy smiled to herself. "I believe they'd live outside if we let them."

Sam chuckled. "You're right about that. I was the same as a kid." He fiddled with his cloth napkin. "Gettin' back to my mother…I make light of her rudeness because it's better than feelin' sorry for myself. Flora Connors likes to be the one makin' the decisions, somethin' you learned the night of the fire. And when things don't go her way, she spreads her unhappiness far and wide. The feud aside, she didn't appreciate bein' left alone in that big farmhouse, and so she's tried to convince me that her health is failin'. Meanwhile, Doc Trumble says she's in better shape than most women her age."

"She's lonely, then."

"I suppose." He licked the underside of his upper lip contemplatively, while raking his fingers through his untamed blond hair. Mercy couldn't help remarking to herself that his features were more than pleasing. "She's made an art form outta manipulatin' folks. Believe me, after thirty years spent under her roof, I know how she operates."

Realization dawned on Mercy. "I guess marrying me made for the perfect escape."

He squeezed one eye nearly shut and tilted his head to the side. "I guess you could say that, but I also care a lot about those boys. I don't want you thinkin' that gettin' out from under Mother's clutches was the only reason I married you."

"I'm actually glad that you had ulterior motives," Mercy confessed. "At least I don't have to feel guilty for trapping you."

He arched his brows. "Are you kiddin'? I thought you'd be angry."

"Why would I be angry? It's not like I expected you to marry me for love." At the mention of love, her cheeks went as warm as a skillet.

"Love?" He batted the air. "Nah, 'course not."

A span of unexplained silence fell between them, so she searched for a new topic of conversation. "Tell me about your childhood."

"Only if you tell me about yours—and you start."

"Why do I have to start? I asked you."

He grinned. "Ladies first."

She liked his straight-toothed smile. "All right, then." She adjusted her position in her seat, then began divulging all she could recall about her mother—her kind, gentle ways; her patience and munificence; the games they used to play; the household tasks she'd taught her; and her strong faith and desire to show Christ's love.

"It must have been pretty awful for you when she got sick," Sam said. "How old were you?"

"Ten, and I remember it like it was yesterday—the doctor coming and going from the house several times a week; my father and I trying to coax her to eat and drink; her dreadful cough…I think that's when I first started entertaining thoughts of becoming a nurse. I was quite determined to make my mother well again. Unfortunately, my determination didn't save her."

"What did she die from, if I may ask?"

"They called it lung fever. I suppose today they'd say pneumonia."

He shook his head. "I'm sorry for your loss."

"Thank you. Do you think the boys are all right?"

"I'm sure they're fine, but I'll go check on 'em to put your mind at ease." He rose and walked into the kitchen, with its window overlooking the backyard. "They're fine. Playin' on the tree swings."

"I don't think I thanked you for rigging those up," she said when he returned to the dining room. Such a kind, generous soul he had.

Sam smiled and sat down again. "I had to, after seein' how much they enjoyed those swings at your aunt's house." He folded his muscular hands on the table and leaned across it, his eyes fully intent on her. "Okay, now tell me a little bit about your father."

"My father?"

"Yes, what was he like?"

"I imagine you've heard stories."

He cocked his blond head to one side. "A few, but I want to hear 'em from you."

"I'll start by saying he wasn't the most affectionate man. You would think my being the only child would have caused him to dote on me, but I think he always resented not having a son. My mother had four miscarriages before she finally had me. I don't think she was terribly strong, and maybe that was something else that grated on him. Pa liked his booze, too, and it sometimes made him turn a bit gruff and ornery. Don't get me wrong; he loved me, and I never doubted it. He just had a strange way of showing it." She gestured with her hand. "One thing he did was provide for me. Despite his drinking, I have to say he was a hard worker. He paid off the mortgage on this house a year after Ma passed."

Even though she wasn't thirsty, she took a few sips from her water glass before proceeding. "After Ma died, he was very lonely, and it drove him to drink even more, and staying out late, sometimes all night. I used to lie awake and count the stars outside my bedroom window, just waiting for the first sounds of his horse clopping up the drive.

"Pa carried a lot of guilt for Ma's death. He always said he should've tried harder, even though Doc said there wasn't much that could be done for her condition. I'd hear him cry himself to sleep, and so I'd do the same, in my own bedroom. I wish now we could have cried together, but he wasn't the sort of man to share his emotions, even with his own daughter."

Sam's brow creased with concern. "I'm sorry for what you've had to endure."

"Thank you, but I didn't do it alone. God has been my strength through everything—including the loss of my father."

His face blanched. "That was an awful day, wasn't it?"

Her chest heaved. "The worst. How old were you at the time?"

"Let's see…twenty-four, I think. Uncle Clarence and I were slavin' hard at the shop and grumblin' that my father was late returnin' from his lunch break. 'Course, it was nothin' new. He'd been doin' that a lot, comin' to work late, leavin' when he pleased, takin' long breaks durin' the day. Really got my uncle's goat. We'd formed a partnership, the three of us, and my father wasn't holdin' up his end of the agreement.

"Anyway, we heard a bunch of commotion outside, horses gallopin' up the street, and people just hootin' an' hollerin'. We stopped what we were doin' to have a look. Folks were headin' toward town. My uncle asked what was goin' on, and that's when one of Sheriff Marshall's deputies rode up to break the news about the shootin'. I still remember the feelin', the way my heart sank clear to my feet."

"I remember the feeling, too," Mercy said quietly. "I was working at Doc's place when the news came in." Her body gave an unrestrained shudder, and she instinctively rubbed her chilled arms. "How did your mother take the news?"

He pinched the bridge of his nose and frowned. "Strangely. That's about the only way I can describe it. Uncle Clarence and I rode out together to tell her, and all she did was sit down in a chair, put her face in her hands, and shake her head, over and over. Later, after the trial and sentencin' and all that, she fell into what Doc termed a 'nervous fit' and took to her bed for several weeks." He gave his head a shake. "Truth is, I don't think she mourned my father's absence as much as her ruined reputation. Terrible thing to say, but it's how I feel. My parents fought round the clock. They didn't need much of a reason. He always threatened to fire the farm manager, Virgil Perry, just to get a rise out of her. Father hated the guy, but for some reason, he kept him on. Mother felt the same, but he knows that farm inside an' out, so she's left him in charge." He chuckled morosely. "In those days, I'd come home late and leave before dawn, just to avoid my folks' brawls.

"I had big plans back then. I'd arranged to buy a small house over on East Ruff Street, but it didn't pan out. The fellow up and sold it to someone else just before I was about to put the money down. I kept searchin', determined to get out of the house, but then that blasted shootin' took place, and I felt obligated to stay with my mother awhile. Didn't think 'awhile' would turn into six years."

"Until I came to your rescue," Mercy teased.

He chuckled again, but it was lighthearted this time. "And I thank you."

That brought a pause to their conversation, so they sat in silence for a moment, the only sounds the clip-clop of a passing horse, the dining room curtains whispering on the breeze, and an annoying drip coming from the kitchen faucet.

Mercy stared at a fresh gravy stain on her newly washed tablecloth.

To her surprise, Sam reached across the table and laid a hand over her folded ones. "You're still raw from the loss of your friends, aren't you?"

"I'm doing better every day."

"I'm glad for you if that's the case, but don't feel like you have to hide your emotions on my account. If you ever feel like screamin' or cryin' or throwin' a little tantrum, I won't object."

She smiled, eyes still fixed on the stain. "I appreciate that. Come to think of it, I haven't had a chance to throw a real tantrum in a long while."

Without looking up, she heard his lips part in a smile. "Well then, you're due." He pushed back in his chair. "Let's go outside and check on those boys."

"You go. I should clean the dinner dishes, and—"

"The dishes'll keep till later. And I'll help you."

"You will?" She couldn't envision a man washing dishes or drying them, didn't even know if she wanted his help. Growing up, the most she'd seen her pa do in the kitchen was draw water from the spigot for a drink.

There came a crooked grin on Sam's nicely formed mouth. He stood and motioned with his hand. "Come on, Mrs. Connors. Let's get some fresh air."

Mrs. Connors? It was the first time she'd been addressed by that title, and she didn't know how to feel about it.

He followed her through the kitchen, and when he put his hand to the center of her back, a batch of chills altogether unfamiliar chased up her spine.

15

Sunday morning ushered in a thunderstorm, reason enough in Sam's mind to skip church, but Mercy wouldn't hear of it. "We may have had a good reason for staying home the last couple of weeks, our being newly married and all, but I wouldn't feel right missing another service. The boys need to get back into a routine, and Sunday church is a good place to start."

He would have liked to remind her this routine of waking early on Sundays was going to be a challenge for him. However, he had agreed to accompany her to church, and he didn't want to go back on his word so early in the marriage—or ever.

Riding in his rig, they would be exposed to the elements on all sides, even though he'd pulled the canvas top up after hitching up Tucker. Fortunately, the rain dwindled to a drizzle just before they left, and there were enough lightweight blankets for everyone's lap, which helped to keep them dry. Plus, the little country church was only a couple of miles outside of town.

Mercy had a fair-sized barn—nothing like what he was used to, but it had three stalls, enough for housing their two horses, plus an extra stall for storing hay, buckets of grain, and riding gear. Of course, their rigs stood out in the elements and were none the worse for it. It had taken Tucker a few days to make the adjustment, not to mention acquaint himself with Mercy's Appaloosa, Sally. At first, the two had done a lot of nickering back and forth, pawing in the dirt, and Tucker apparently hadn't been at all sure he liked the sights, smells, or sounds of his new quarters. But by day three or four, he'd settled down and started making himself at home.

The church bells chimed quarter to ten as Sam turned the rig into the churchyard with his new family in tow. He immediately scanned the area, looking for a parking spot that wasn't situated in the middle of a big mud puddle. When at last he staked his claim on a patch of high ground, the boys filed out pell-mell and dashed toward the church.

"Boys, wait for us," Sam called. "We'll go in together." He jumped down to the ground and raced around the rig to take Mercy's hand.

The boys screeched to a halt and turned, John Roy's hair mussed at the crown, where he had a curly cowlick, and Joseph's shirttail hanging out of his breeches. Shoulders sagging, they waited for the adults to catch up.

"Never have I seen two boys so eager for church," Sam said to Mercy.

"They enjoy it very much. Truthfully, though, I think it's seeing their friends afterward that has them all excited."

When they reached the boys, she bent to tuck Joseph's shirt back in his pants, then smoothed out his short jacket. Since there was nothing to do for John Roy's curlicue, she straightened his white collar instead, then gave a satisfied smile, pulling back her shoulders and glancing up at Sam. "Shall we go in, then?"

He grinned and swept out a hand. "After you, madam." The threesome went ahead, and as they ascended the cement steps leading to the front door, he scolded himself for admiring Mercy's pretty ankles when she lifted her skirts.

They found a bench about halfway down the aisle and scooted past an elderly couple who had planted themselves on the end. *Confound it*, Sam thought. He'd wanted an aisle seat, just in case he got restless and needed to step outside for some fresh air. It had been a long while since he'd sat through an entire sermon.

Several folks stopped along the way to shake his hand and greet Mercy and the boys. Some of them he recognized from town. The folks at Paris Evangelical Church were a friendly bunch, he'd give them that.

The lively hymn singing lifted his spirits, and Reverend Younker's message took him quite by surprise, in that it actually held his attention. Speaking about a passage in the book of Philippians, the old preacher, who'd married Mercy and him mere weeks ago, exhorted the congregation to shine as lights in the world, bearing the likeness of God before their fellow men. Sam had to ponder that thought. Did people see God in him? He doubted so. How could they, when he'd barely cracked open his Bible in years—not counting the verses Uncle Clarence had instructed him to read in Jeremiah? Had he found true satisfaction in serving the Lord? Not at all. He hadn't taken the time to grow or let God nurture him. How could he possibly know any kind of satisfaction if he never gave God a chance to reveal Himself?

The boys sat between Mercy and him and fidgeted, tracing images with a fingertip on each other's legs or arms while the other tried to guess the picture. Every so often, they would erupt into quiet giggles, which Mercy quickly stifled. Once, she glanced over their heads at Sam and rewarded him with a minuscule smile, the sight of which made his pulse thrum in wild abandon. It was ridiculous, he knew; that his wife had a lovely smile should not have set his heart in motion, nor should the fact that she looked pretty in pale green, or that he liked the way she'd put her hair up, allowing some of it to fall around her temples, framing her face…none of that should have affected him. And yet it did.

At the close of the service, folks filed down the aisle, some of them stopping to talk to Mercy, others offering words of congratulations to both of them on their marriage. He wanted to remind them all of the circumstances surrounding it—tell them they'd married for the boys' sake alone—but he figured it wasn't necessary. There wasn't a soul in town who didn't know they hadn't married for love. After all, he was a Connors; she, an Evans.

As they moved outside, a blast of warm air greeted them, the sun pushing out from behind the clouds. Wafting up on a gentle breeze were the sweet scents of a nearby rosebush, and overhead, the birds delighted in announcing the rain had stopped. Excited children, John Roy and Joseph included, took off, chasing each other around the church perimeter, their pent-up shouts no longer squelched. Not for the first time, Sam marveled at how well the boys had fallen into their new routine. He wondered if and when reality would come crashing in on them.

"Mercy! Wait a moment." Coming from behind was an older woman, tall and spry, her green eyes gleaming like two stars, with white wisps of hair poking out from under her wide-brimmed floral hat. Sam recognized her as one of the "protesters" from their wedding day, and a wave of dread swept through him.

"Why, Aunt Aggie!" Mercy gave the woman a quick hug. "I didn't… I'm surprised to see you here. I thought you attended the Lutheran church."

"Yes, yes, I do," the woman said, stepping back to brush herself off, as if the brief embrace had somehow wrinkled her perfectly pressed suit. "But Reverend Tolford went out of town, and one of our church deacons was preachin' today. I can't abide that man's sermons, don't you know, so long and drawn out…by the time he winds down, I just know my Sunday roast has burnt blacker 'n tar. Not t' mention he's got that awful habit of clearin' his throat at the end of every sentence." She clicked her tongue before raising her gaze to Sam. "Well, hullo there, Samuel Connors. I hope y'r treatin' my niece well."

"Aunt Aggie." Mercy's brow crimped.

Sam grinned. "Ma'am." He offered his hand, and when she extended hers, he took it in both of his. "I'm doin' my very best. Nice to meet you face-to-face." As hard as it was to treat her with civility, he knew it would pay off in dividends. "You're Fred's wife, correct?"

"Indeed. A scoundrel he is, but then, you already knew that."

Indeed was right. Fred Evans never missed an opportunity to fight, and Sam pitied the man who got in his way, especially if he were a Connors. Agatha leaned in. "Your mother's not much better, if I may say so."

"Aunt Aggie," Mercy cut in for the second time, her tone scolding.

"Well, it's true as the gospel, child. Ever since your weddin', she's been creatin' quite a stir amongst the menfolk. Says Mercy here won't allow Samuel t' go visit her, and I says to m'self, 'That don't sound like ar Mercy, her bein' the peacemaker of the family an' all.'"

Sam felt a ball of fury form in his stomach. "You're absolutely right. My mother's spreadin' falsehoods."

Mercy's face wrinkled with concern. "Why, just yesterday, I told Sam he ought to go see her."

Agatha nodded. "I figured as much. I'm comin' to terms with the whole notion o' you two marryin', but my Fred and our boys are still purty peeved."

Tension seized Sam's chest like a balled-up fist. He'd thought that getting through the wedding ceremony would be the worst of it, but it seemed that their relatives—at least some of them—were getting even more riled now that the vows had been said. Would nothing melt the hatred and mend the breach between these two families? He supposed it was something he should pray about.

A few women joined the circle, and the subject changed to the upcoming meeting of the knitting guild, something in which Sam had no interest. Just in time, Carl Redford, a longtime acquaintance from grade school days, wandered over, providing a welcome escape. The two men separated slightly from the group and spent some time catching up, talking about Sam's blacksmithing and Carl's job as a clerk at the local drugstore.

Before long, John Roy and Joseph trotted up, red-faced and breathless. "We goin' soon?" asked John Roy.

Mercy must have overheard, for she stepped away from the circle of women. "Yes, we are, honey. I have a chicken cooking in the oven."

They bid everyone good-bye and headed for their rig and a very patient Tucker, who stomped and whinnied at their approach. All in all, Sam's return to church hadn't been all bad. He was almost looking forward to next Sunday.

⌒

"What in the world?" Sam muttered as they turned into the two-track driveway.

Mercy glanced up, and fury welled within her. On the front porch, her two lovely planters had been overturned, and both wicker chairs had been tipped on their sides. One of the front windows was also broken. She grew impatient for Sam to rein in his horse so she could jump down and investigate. "I don't know, but I'm about to find out."

"Don't go up there without me," he said quietly, so the boys wouldn't overhear. "Might be somebody lurkin' around."

She nodded, but when the rig came to a halt, she couldn't help it; she hefted her skirts, leaped to the ground, and set off on a purposeful march across the yard.

"Wait here, boys, and keep Tucker company," she heard him say. "We'll be right back."

At least two out of three had listened to him. He ought to be pleased about that. Mercy approached the front porch to assess the damage.

Sam checked out the broken window, peering inside. "Looks like somebody heaved a rock. It's lying on the floor, and there's glass everywhere." He glanced back at the rig. "Better get that cleaned up before we let the boys inside. I'll check around back, make sure it's clear, and send them there to play."

Mercy nodded, for the moment unable to speak. Dread twisted an ugly knot in her gut. Who would do such a thing? Hadn't the boys been traumatized enough? While Sam led the boys to the backyard, she righted her poor planters, then used her hand to scoop some of the spilled soil back inside. The flowers had lost a few blossoms, too.

Sam returned a few minutes later. "Those swings should keep 'em occupied awhile," he said.

"Do you think one of our relatives did this?" Mercy asked him quietly.

He lifted one wicker chair, setting it upright again. "I would hate to think that any of our relatives would deliberately damage their own kin's property."

"But you heard Aunt Aggie. Both sides are upset with us."

Sam shook his head. His face read of utter disdain. "I guess I'll pay my mother a visit. I have to find out if she's involved in this."

"Surely, your own mother wouldn't be party to vandalism."

"She wouldn't have been here, no, but she might be at the center of the storm. Your aunt did say she's been stirrin' things up. Sorry to say, I wouldn't put it past her."

Mercy nodded.

"I'll pay the sheriff a visit tomorrow," Sam added. "File a report."

"I suppose that's best."

They ate their lunch in somber silence. Any other day, it would've been delicious, the chicken done to perfection, the carrots and potatoes seasoned just right. Today, however, it went down Mercy's throat with a fight, and she had to keep taking sips of water to settle her stomach. It nettled her to think that Sam's relatives—or, worse, her own—were in some way responsible for the vandalism, and on the Sabbath, no less.

"Who done broke that window?" John Roy asked after a while.

Mercy looked to Sam. "We don't know, exactly," Sam said. "Maybe one of the neighbor boys got a little too rambunctious."

"They should'a comed to church," Joseph chided.

Mercy couldn't help smiling at his naiveté. It helped to lessen the sense of foreboding she felt in her chest.

Sam appeared to have no trouble clearing his plate. He pushed back in his chair and rubbed his hands together. "Well, if you'll excuse me, I'm gonna ride out to my mother's place for a visit."

"Can we come too?" Joseph asked.

Sam smiled ruefully. "Another time, okay?"

"But she invited us!"

"I know she did. And I'll be sure to take you, just not today."

Joseph lowered his face and stuck out his lip. It was the first Mercy had observed him in an all-out pout. "I'm going to need your company," Mercy said, trying to keep her voice light. "We'll think of a game to play."

"In the house, though," Sam inserted briskly, meeting Mercy's eyes. *Stay inside*, he mouthed.

"Aww!" both boys protested.

"Do we hafta?" Joseph whined.

Mercy forced a smile. "Yes, but you can go outside when Sam returns." She bristled at having to stay cooped up on such a nice day, but then, that vow she'd made to love, honor, and obey came back to muddle her head.

She had a lot to learn about this matter of marriage.

16

$\mathcal{S}$am hitched Tucker to a post in front of his mother's house, climbed the porch steps, and knocked at the door. Getting no response, he strolled around to the side yard to search her out. He found her kneeling in the garden, her back to him, pulling weeds. Her tattered straw bonnet covered her gray hair, which she had pulled into her habitual severe knot at the back of her head. Hot rays of sunlight seared his shoulders as he plodded down the flower-strewn path, yet unnoticed—unless he counted Virgil Perry, whom he spotted watching him from the double doors of the barn. Sam waved but got nothing more than a casual nod before the man vanished into the murky shadows. It was milking time, if the sound of bawling cattle from inside was any indication.

His approaching steps must have alerted his mother, for she glanced over her shoulder, gasped, and then rose to her feet, teetering a tad from having stood too fast. Normally, he would have reached out a hand to steady her, but he didn't have the most genial attitude at the moment.

"Well, suffering saints, would you look at what the cat dragged home? Wasn't it just yesterday you said you wouldn't come visiting if you couldn't bring that wife of yours?"

"This is not a cordial visit, Mother. I need to talk to you about somethin'."

"Oh?" She swept a hand across her forehead, leaving a long, dark smudge in its wake. "What other possible reason than cordial could you have for visiting your ailing mother?"

"You're not ailin'."

"Of course I am. Most mornings I have so many aches, I can barely rise from bed. And my chest, why, it's been paining me something fierce. Makes breathing a regular burden."

It took all his energy not to tell her she'd been saying the same things for years, or that he had it on good authority from her doctor himself that she was hale and hearty. A second glance at the barn revealed Virgil watching from the doorway again. "Let's go in the house for a minute."

"Good idea. I'll get us some sweet tea. I'm parched."

"I'm not stayin' long."

"You'll stay long enough for a glass of tea, won't you? I've really missed you, Samuel. It's far too quiet around here with you gone. I still don't understand why you married that girl."

"That 'girl,' as you refer to her, is my wife, and you'll do well to keep your opinions about her to yourself."

She gave a loud wheeze and wiped her hands on her apron, then gazed skyward. "It was right nice of the sun to come out after that morning rain, but did it have to bring such scorching heat?" At least she saw the importance in changing the subject.

"Yeah, it's hot. Let's go inside." *And escape Virgil Perry's piercing stare.* He glanced at the barn once more, then followed her up the path. "What are you doin' workin' on the Lord's Day, anyway? You never used to let me do anything on Sundays—no baseball, no goin' down to the water hole, and certainly no playin' with the neighbor boys."

"Engaging in worldly pleasurable on the Sabbath is one thing, but chores of necessity are something altogether different."

"I see." Of course, he didn't, but now was not the time for arguing over her convictions. He could tell her they were just a bunch of man-made rules that didn't line up with the way true Christians ought to live—with hearts of joy and gratitude, overflowing in love for others. Not that he was a good example, but he knew folks who were—Uncle Clarence, for one. And Mercy.

Yes, she had a willful spirit, and she could react quicker than a swatted fly if something didn't set right with her, but she also had a generous heart. Her love for God and others was evident, and he greatly admired her for it.

He opened the door for his mother, who scooted into the kitchen ahead of him. A cool breeze played with the sheer curtains over the sink. He pulled out a couple of chairs from the round wooden table, seated himself, and watched his mother fill two glasses with sweet tea. She started humming, something she rarely did, unless she wanted to cover up a basket of nerves.

He tapped his fingers on the red and white checked tablecloth and watched as she wiped up a small spill on the counter. He'd wanted to wait till she sat, but his patience grew too thin. "I talked to Agatha Evans today."

With her back to him, his mother went rail-stiff. "Where on earth did you see her?" She gave a half turn.

"At Paris Evangelical Church."

Now she faced him head-on. "You went to church?"

"That was one of the stipulations of our marriage contract, so to speak, my attendin' on a regular basis."

"Humph. You should be going to First Methodist, where your family attends, including your *beloved* Uncle Clarence and Aunt Hester." She always had resented them, and while he'd never quite figured out why, he supposed it boiled down to jealousy. They had a strong marriage, with three children, all of them married with kids of their own, a strong faith in God, a good number of friends, and Sam's utmost respect.

"And anyway, what was Agatha Evans doing at Paris Evangelical? Everyone knows the Evanses are all devout Lutherans—well, except for Agatha's worthless husband, Fred, who hasn't set foot in church since I don't know when. And of course, Mercy Evans considers herself too good for the Lutherans."

He didn't want to discuss the denominational preferences of the Evans family, but her remark made him curious. "How would you know anything about Fred Evans?"

"Oh, piffle." She carried over the glasses of tea, then plunked herself down in the chair. "Doesn't all Paris know the comings and goings of folks?"

"Guess not." He shrugged and took a few gulps of his tea. It did taste awfully good. "Well, I should get on with my reason for comin' here. When we got home from church today, we found that someone had thrown a rock through one of the front windows and made a mess of the front porch, over-turnin' planters and upsettin' the chairs. I plan to stop at Sheriff Marshall's office tomorrow to report the incident."

"That's unfortunate. The vandalism, I mean. But I don't see what it has to do with me."

"Maybe nothin', but Agatha Evans indicated you've been tellin' folks Mercy won't let me visit you."

"Well...." He could almost see her mental wheels spinning. "It *is* because of her you're not coming around every day. You said yourself you wouldn't visit me without her, so, in a sense, it's her fault."

"It's not her fault. It's my decision. If you can't accept her into the family, then I'm goin' to have to limit my visits. Who of our relatives have you been grumblin' to about my marriage, anyway?"

"Oh, for pity's sake, Samuel, you make me sound like some ogre."

"Just answer my question."

"Well, of course, I pay visits to Ella on a regular basis, and Frank and George's wives, Alice and Ida. I don't see much at all of Hester, mind you. Clarence won't allow it."

"I doubt that, Mother. More likely, Aunt Hester prefers not to listen to your gossip. Neither she nor Uncle Clarence shares your hatred for the Evans family."

"I don't gossip. I merely state facts."

He sucked in a cavernous breath and blew it out his nostrils. "You have to stop all the nonsense. Somebody vandalized Mercy's house, and I wouldn't doubt your negative talk, gossip or not, has helped stir the pot."

"What? You can't actually believe your own relatives would be capable of doing such a thing. I'd say, more than likely, it was Mercy's cousins. They're an odious bunch."

He shook his head, realizing the futility in stretching out the matter much further. "We're tryin' to help those boys adjust to life in the wake of their loss. Surely, you can understand that much."

No rejoinder followed. Instead, she took a few more swallows of her tea and gazed over the rim of her glass at something on the wall, perhaps the painting of sheep on a hillside with their shepherd. He could imagine her mind swirling with all manner of ideas on how to entice him to linger at her table.

A knock came on the door, and then Virgil Perry walked in without invitation, his towering presence taking up the otherwise roomy kitchen. Sam never had liked the way the fellow entered his mother's house with a mere knock, rarely, if ever, waiting for her to beckon him in. Virgil had no greeting for him, just a quick, rather cold, glance in his direction. "I'm headin' out to the west field f'r the rest o' the day. Everything all right in here?"

"Of course it's all right, Mr. Perry. I have no idea why you find it necessary to inform me of your comings and goings. Now, go on with you." Sam noted how his mother didn't so much as turn to look at the man. Sam stared at him, willing him to meet his gaze, but he kept his eyes averted. He made a little snuffling sound and walked out, closing the door none too softly.

Sam sat taller to see through the window, and watched him tramp back to the barn. "That man carries some chip on his shoulder. Why do you keep 'im on, anyway? I seem to recall Father wantin' to fire 'im some years back."

"He keeps this farm running fine."

"He gives me the creeps. Always has. Why'd he ask if everythin' was all right? Have you given 'im reason to believe I'd do somethin' stupid?"

"For crying in the sink, of course not. My affairs are none of his business."

"That's what I would think, but he sure does like to act as if he owns this place."

"Pff. He's my hired hand."

"He's a little more than that, Mother. Maybe you've given him too much authority."

"What are my options? You certainly never expressed any interest in taking over the farm. That would've been my one heart's desire, you know, you inheriting this place. It could've been all yours."

"You and Father knew from the start I had no desire to farm. It's never been my passion. A person should be passionate about what he does for a livin'. Why don't you sell this place and move closer to town? It would save you a whole lot of headaches."

Her eyes rounded to saucer-sized circles, as if he'd just committed blasphemy. "This has been my home since your father and I married—just as it was yours for thirty years." She raised her chin and jutted it forward, accentuating the move with a loud sniff. "Still could be, if you hadn't decided to up and leave."

He sighed. Would she never let up? He decided he'd outstayed his visit, so he finished the rest of his tea, set down his empty glass, and rose, the chair legs screeching against the wood. "Please, Mother, no more negative talk concernin' Mercy, all right?"

She gave another loud sniff and raised her chin a notch higher. "I'll do whatever I please, since that is exactly what you did in marrying that woman."

Oh, but she could be a pill when she set her mind to it. He leaned over and kissed her on the forehead. "Good-bye, Mother."

She cast him a pleading look. "When will I see you again? You hardly stayed long enough to call this a visit."

He sighed. "I said what I came to say."

"Surely, there are other things to talk about. I've been so lonely all by myself in this big ol' house." Her practiced, pouty tone grated on his nerves.

"If you'll allow me to bring Mercy along, I'll come visit again some night this week."

She rolled her eyes skyward. "I don't want an Evans on this property."

"She's not an Evans anymore, and you'd do well to accept that."

She firmed her shoulders and shook her head. "Never."

"All right; then, as I said before, I guess we won't be seein' much of each other."

"I told you I wouldn't mind if you brought those boys over sometime."

So, she'd meant it. It crossed his mind that they might well be the necessary vehicle for melting her icy heart. "We'll see. Right now, I've got to get back home to fix the window that someone, whether Connors or Evans, broke. If you happened to get wind of who did the deed, you would let me know, wouldn't you?"

"Humph. I'm not sure how I'd ever come across such information. No one ever tells me anything."

"Uh-huh." *And birds bark.* Flora Connors, family matriarch, had an uncanny ability to stay abreast of the goings-on in the Connors clan. Sadly, he didn't trust her much further than an ant could jump.

⌒

Through the sheer curtain, Flora watched her son ride off. A touch of guilt raced through her veins for her utter stubbornness, but anger quickly took its place. If he thought she intended to give an inch, he had another think coming. Those Evanses were all the same, a hateful, crude, uncharitable bunch, and none of them, not even Samuel's wife, deserved a second look. Yes, Flora's own husband had murdered Oscar, but it couldn't be helped. He'd said loathsome things. No one knew the full story, of course—and no one ever would. Well, with the exception of Virgil Perry, who insisted on reminding her nearly every day of her life. If only she were free to fire him, just as Samuel had suggested. Too bad he practically owned the very shoes she wore.

She thought about the vandalism done to Mercy's house. She would have to ride out to Gilbert's place and remind him, along with his boys, Frank and George, that the Connors clan stuck together. In no way should damage be done that would affect their own kin. Dumb fools. No doubt, they'd been dreaming up their scheme when she'd gone visiting a few nights ago. Yes, she'd been complaining, and rather loudly, that Samuel had left her high and dry; she may have mentioned her desire to teach that new wife of his a lesson for tricking him into marrying her. But not at Samuel's expense, for pity's sake!

When Samuel disappeared around a cluster of trees along the sloped road leading back to town, Flora blew out a breath and moved away from the window. She walked to the screen door that overlooked the side yard, including the path to the barn, and spotted Virgil maneuvering his draft horses down the weedy two-track road to the west field. She resented his presumptuousness in intruding on Samuel and her, and later she would make her feelings known. A lot of good it would do. He had leverage—even more now that Samuel had married.

Life was such a mess right now, and the only way to straighten it out would be to spill the truth.

The *ugly* truth—which would never come out if she had her way.

17

"What's it like, bein' married to a Connors?" Mercy's cousin Amelia, Aunt Gladys's only daughter, asked between bites of lemon cake. They were seated in the kitchen, Mercy near the window, with a view of the boys playing on the tree swings Sam had hung for them. She and Amelia had always been close, perhaps because Gladys was her favorite aunt, and the cousins were of similar age. Amelia had married two years ago and now, at age twenty-seven, was pregnant with her first child, due in February.

"Not as awkward as I thought it would be. His father shot my daddy, but Sam had nothing to do with it. He still feels like a stranger, mind you."

"It takes time to get to know someone through and through." Amelia sipped her beverage between bites, swallowed, and then eyed her with particular interest. "Is he romantic?"

"What?" Mercy nearly choked on the forkful of cake she'd just put in her mouth. Her cheeks went hotter than the August sun. "Heavens, no. I mean, I have no idea. He might be, but I haven't witnessed it. It's not...you know...that kind of marriage."

"You still don't share a bedroom?" Amelia's eyes blew up like green balloons about to pop.

"Mellie, you know we married for convenience alone."

"Yes, but…well, I thought by now you'd…*he'd*—"

"No! He's not like that. He's very…." What was he? "Kind, and…."

"Patient?"

"I suppose."

"So, what you're sayin' is, he hasn't exercised his rights yet?"

"His—? No! Of course not."

"My stars in glory, girl! Norman didn't—"

She raised her hand. "Stop right there, Cousin." Surely, her face showed crimson. There'd been a day when she and Amelia had been comfortable speculating about the things a man and woman did after marriage, but once Amelia had married, all such talk had ceased, to Mercy's relief. Frankly, she didn't *want* to know what went on between husband and wife, leastways not between Amelia and Norm. "May we please change the subject?"

Amelia tossed back her head of golden waves and gave a hearty, yet feminine, laugh. "Oh, oh, you're blushin' red as a tomato, Mercy Evans—make that Mercy *Connors*!" She put a hand to her slightly rounded belly. "You wait and see, darlin'. The day will come when you and Mr. Connors will fall over backward in love, and try convincin' him then that this union is purely for convenience."

"Oh, stop it, you ninny. We are not having another minute of this conversation, you hear?"

"I hear, I hear."

Mercy rose from the table to get a better view out the window.

Amelia sobered. "Sorry, Mercy. You know I'm just joshin' you, don't you?"

She waved her cousin off. "Yes, I know. Just—don't mention it again, if you please. It's plain embarrassing."

"Well, it shouldn't be. Look at my belly, Cousin. You think it's gettin' rounder from pure coincidence?"

Mercy took her eyes off the boys and angled a glance at Amelia. "No, you silly goose. I know all about the birds and the bees, as they say."

Amelia stood to her feet and filled in the gap between them. She put an arm around Mercy's shoulders and squeezed her close. "I want you to be happy, Mercy."

"I'm as happy as I can be, considering the circumstances."

"Yes, well, they aren't the best, I suppose." Together they watched the boys trying to toss a ball back and forth, neither one having the knack yet of throwing or catching, despite Sam's nightly practice sessions with them.

"They sure are sweet boys," Amelia observed. "You're doin' a mighty fine job with them."

Mercy stared out the window. "I don't know. Sometimes I feel like an utter failure. I'll never make them as happy as their parents could."

"Perhaps not, but you can do a better job of it than most. God had His reasons in allowin' that fire, and it's not ours to question but to trust. I'm just glad the boys wound up in your care and not in the hands of strangers."

"Yes, I couldn't have lived with myself if I hadn't fought to the end to keep them with me."

They stood in silence for a moment.

"There hasn't been any more criminal activity around here, has there?" Amelia asked.

"No, nothing."

"Good. Did the sheriff ever find the culprit who broke your window?"

"No, not as far as I know. I think he closed up the case, chalking it up to a petty prank. Apparently, he's asked around town, but with no witnesses and not a single lead, there's not much he can do. I'm beginning to think that it wasn't our relatives, after all, but rather someone who randomly targeted our property. Probably some bored neighbor kids."

"Well, we know right off no Evans would stoop so low. Can't say the same for the Connors clan, though."

"And they would say the same thing about us. It's a toss-up between who's meaner. I'd be lying if I said I trusted every one of our family members."

She felt Amelia's gaze on her face. "Bart an' Davey aren't the best at keepin' the peace, are they?"

Mercy giggled low in her throat. "They gave Uncle Albert and Aunt Gertie a rough go of it growing up, what with all their carousing about town. They were a regular disgrace to the family for a while there, always getting into trouble with the law. I think they've finally settled down, now that they're married and have a couple of kids."

"Let's hope so." Amelia grinned. "I'd guess Bart's not the best husband to Mary. Poor thing. I wouldn't want t' be wearin' her shoes."

Mercy giggled. "He's always been hardnosed, bigheaded, ornery, and… I've plumb run out of adjectives, but I know there must be more."

They shared a laugh before they let their gazes travel back to the two youngsters in the backyard. "Now that I think on it, I s'pose there could be a cousin or two on the Evans side plain mad about you marryin' a Connors," Amelia mused, "especially since one of theirs killed your daddy."

"And then, there is our dear uncle Fred, who carries his own personal grudge against the Connors family. He and Pa were close. I think he died a little himself the day Pa died."

Amelia nodded soberly. "It's true, Cousin."

"Speaking of cousins, did I tell you Wilburta and Frieda paid me a visit while I was in the middle of my husband hunt? Wilburta said that it would be downright shameful, if not sinful, of me to marry Samuel Connors."

Amelia scrunched up her nose and huffed. "Wilburta wouldn't know a fine man if she were married to one. Which she isn't." She and Wilburta had always been at odds with each other, which Mercy found comical, considering they were quite alike in many ways.

"Amelia Clarkston, shame on you. Ellis is a good man."

"He married Wilburta, which makes him a little slow-witted, if you ask me."

Mercy couldn't help but chuckle. "Oh, stop it, silly. I've never had a problem with Wilburta."

"That's because she never picked on you growin' up. She bossed me around somethin' fierce and ran tattlin' to Mama every chance she got. Durned near lost my Christianity over her. How come nobody ever picked on you, Mercy Evans Connors?"

"Probably because they felt sorry for me—losing Ma and all, and then being neglected by Pa."

Amelia gave a knowing nod. "You pretty much raised yourself, when it gets right down to it."

"I suppose you could say that."

"Was Uncle Oscar ever mean to you? In a physical way, I mean?"

"No, nothing like that. He was just quiet and withdrawn. After Ma died, it was like he didn't know what to do with me. Sometimes I think he forgot I existed. As I got older, he tried to make it up to me by buying me things, and he worked extra hard to pay off this house."

"Maybe he had some sort o' premonition of things to come."

"I don't know, Mellie. All I do know is that he saw to it that I'd be well taken care of, and for that, I'm grateful."

"Where did he spend his time when he wasn't workin'?"

"At the saloon, I suppose. He drank a lot."

"I know. Mama told me."

"He often disappeared for long hours and sometimes didn't come home till after I'd gone to bed. Looking back, I suppose I had my lonely times, but I decided early on not to nurse my wounds with self-pity. It's just not who I am."

Amelia picked up some of the dishes and carried them to the sink. "Well, one thing is clear: I ain't complainin' 'bout you marryin' a Connors. I got nothin' against it. Matter of fact, I'm glad Sam Connors offered his hand to you, and I look forward to gettin' to know him better."

As do I. They had been married for almost one month, and she still treated him like a boarder in her home, tiptoeing around him and speaking to him no more than necessary, gladly allowing the boys to dominate the mealtime conversations. And he seemed to do the same. In short, neither of them quite knew what to do with the other. Granted, they'd had a lengthy chat about their childhoods, and they'd tried to piece together the why and wherefore of the vandalism, but those had been rare exceptions. Most of their talks centered on the boys—fitting, she figured, since they were the reason they'd married.

Amelia squeezed her shoulder, calling her back to the present. "If anybody gives you grief, you just sic your cousin Mellie on 'em, you hear?"

Mercy laughed. "I pity anyone who would rile a pregnant woman."

Amelia nodded with mock seriousness. "You an' me both."

⌒

Sam stood at the anvil, using a pair of pliers and a hammer to mold, bend, and pound a red-hot hunk of iron into a circle. He'd been working on wheels for a customer's horse-drawn carriage and had already completed the wooden portion of the wheel that the flattened iron would fit around.

"You tryin' to kill it?"

"What's that?" Sam swiped at his brow with his shirtsleeve.

His uncle nodded at the metal. "You're beatin' it like it was your worst enemy."

"Oh." A close appraisal revealed shoddy work. He growled and thrust the heavy chunk of metal back in the chamber with the tongs, letting it turn to liquid fire before pulling it back out and starting afresh. He chided himself for taking his mind off his task, even for an instant, a careless blunder when working with fire.

"What's on your mind?" Uncle Clarence asked.

"Not much." Sam tossed his tools on the workbench, where they landed with a clunk, and watched the red-hot hunk go black as it cooled.

"Uh-huh. You've been awful quiet the past few days. You still thinkin' on that broken window? Chances are it wasn't a personal vendetta, or you'd've found a note or somethin', don't y' think? Good possibility it won't happen again."

His uncle knew him well. "Sheriff Marshall seems to think it was the work of some rowdy youngsters. Don't know why they'd pick Mercy's house, though. Did I tell you I dropped in on Mother that same afternoon? I wanted to see if she had any clue as to who might've been behind it."

"You mentioned that the next day, but a customer came in, and I never did hear the rest o' the story. You really think one of our relatives did it?"

"Don't know. I'm hopin' not, but I can't shake the suspicion. There are folks on both sides unhappy with us, my mother chiefly. She knows how to stir a pot till it boils, that's for sure."

Clarence sighed. "That woman is a handful, I'll grant you that. My brother tried 'is best to keep 'er happy, but I don't think he really understood what she needed."

Sam nodded. "They were an odd couple. My only recollection o' them ever showin' affection for each other was after my brothers died. I remember walkin' in the kitchen one day and seein' Father holdin' Mother in his arms."

Clarence shook his gray head. "Didn't have much in common."

"No. Not like you an' Aunt Hester."

The man smiled pensively. "Now, there's a woman to feast your eyes on."

Good thing love's blind, Sam thought. While Aunt Hester was certainly loving and sweet-natured, she didn't strike him as the type to turn a man's eye, even in her prime, with her plump figure and slanted-toothed smile.

Love sure was mysterious, and he wondered if he'd ever experience the intrigue firsthand. He liked to think he and Mercy might reach a level of affection at some point, but first they'd have to get better acquainted. So far, she'd come off as guarded, and who could blame her? She was nursing deep emotional wounds from the loss of her friends, and the responsibility of raising their sons weighed heavily on her shoulders. She so wanted to do right by them—as did he. While he hadn't known the Watsons personally, he knew they had loved their boys with every fiber of their beings. He had to figure out a way to earn her trust and give her reasons to smile again.

"The Lord put me an' Hester together some forty years ago and gave us a slew o' great kids. I suspect He had good reason for bringin' you and Mercy together, too. Besides providin' those boys with a safe home, your marriage has brought you back t' church. Don't see how that could be anythin' but good."

Sam had to admit he'd been enjoying Sunday services, had even cracked open his Bible a few times and started rereading certain passages and Bible stories he'd long forgotten.

Uncle Clarence held the large cross-peen sledgehammer head he'd been forging at arm's length, lifting an eyebrow in assessment, and then gave a nod of approval before setting it down. It had been a long day. A rain shower early that afternoon had cooled the temperature, making the working conditions much pleasanter, but sweat droplets still rolled down his face and neck, dampening his shirtfront.

"Shall we call it a night?" Uncle Clarence asked, pulling his apron over his head.

"You'll get no argument from me."

A small grin played on Clarence's mouth, his gray mustache twitching at the corners. "Your wife a good cook?"

"The best." It was true—Mercy's cooking was far better than he could have hoped. Lately, he'd found himself impatient to get home at the end of the day. Mercy would peek out the kitchen doorway with a shy smile as he went upstairs to wash up, and he would be welcomed minutes later by the tantalizing aroma of a savory meal, along with the incessant chatter of two lively boys. It was an altogether foreign feeling, considering he often used to work right through the supper hour, even though he knew full well he'd get a good tongue-lashing from his mother for doing so.

"Nothin' quite like goin' home to a warm woman and a hot meal. And a good snuggle by the fire is a nice benefit in the wintertime."

"Uncle Clarence! I've never heard you talk like that."

"Well, you weren't married before. I reckon I can be a bit more forthright 'bout such things now."

Sam rolled his eyes. "You can still spare me the personal details."

Clarence threw back his head and let a good chortle rumble out of him. "You wait and see, young man. Come winter, you'll know exactly what I'm talkin' about."

He already did, to a degree—except for the part about snuggling by the fire.

18

Standing at the stove, Mercy paused in stirring her creamy potato soup long enough to press one corner of her apron against her damp forehead. It wasn't so much the heat of the day as the steam from the pot that made her perspire. In fact, the weather had been downright pleasant for a Tennessee August. The boys had gone to play and have supper with the Hansen boys, who lived two doors down and were close in age to John Roy and Joseph. Mercy didn't know their mother well, since the family had moved to the neighborhood only six months ago, but she'd spoken to Dora Hansen often enough to feel comfortable accepting her invitation when she'd stopped by that afternoon. The boys' enthusiastic response had further confirmed her decision.

The time alone was more welcome than Mercy had expected, and she'd accomplished a great deal in the boys' absence. She'd even caught herself humming a couple of times, something she hadn't done since before the fire.

Her heart tripped at the sounds of Tucker's hooves and Sam's mellow "Whoa." She dabbed at her forehead again with the hem of her apron and darted to the window in time to see Sam leading Tucker through the barn door. Her first thought was that he and his uncle had closed their shop early, but the wall clock registered 5:30, the time he usually arrived home. She'd been so absorbed in enjoying the solitude, she'd let the time slip away. Why, she hadn't even set the table yet.

It would take him a few minutes to get Tucker settled in his stall, feed and water him and Sally, and stow the tack, but she still scurried about, wanting to have everything in order before he walked through the door. It would be their first meal together without the boys, and she wanted it to go as smooth as butter.

She quickly set the table, using the good china; sliced up a loaf of fresh bread; and removed the kettle of soup from the stove, covering it with a lid to keep the steam in. Then she glanced around, touching her hair as she did. Good gravy! She'd never put it in a proper bun. It was still gathered back in a girlish ponytail. What on earth would Sam think if he saw her in this state? Moreover, what would he say about the boys' absence at the supper table? Both she and Sam were accustomed to letting them fill in all the awkward spaces in conversation. Heavens, would they even have enough to talk about?

Before allowing herself another second to dwell on the matter, she dashed upstairs to tend to her appearance.

⌒

As he usually did when he got home from work, Sam slipped off his sooty boots, set them behind a wicker rocker in a corner of the covered porch, and entered the house in his stockinged feet. Man, the place smelled good—like fresh bread and savory herbs—and his stomach rumbled in approval. He waited for the boys to come bounding down the stairs or sailing around the side of the house from the backyard, whooping their excited salutations, but an uncanny silence welcomed him instead. He then awaited Mercy's silent smile of greeting from the kitchen, but she didn't appear. Where was everybody? He decided to go investigate.

The first thing he noticed when passing through the dining room was the table, set—for two rather than four—with fine china plates, crystal stemware, fancy silverware, and linen napkins with a floral print. In the center of the table was a crystal vase of roses. No boys tonight? Where could they be?

He then heard a board creak overhead. Mercy would have an explanation. Shrugging, he swiveled on his heel and headed for the stairs and his normal routine of washing up before supper.

At the top of the stairwell, he heard faint rustling sounds coming from Mercy's open bedroom door. "How could I have been so careless?" she was saying. "I should have known you'd steal it." He slowed his steps and approached with caution. What he saw nearly stole his final breath. His wife was bent at the waist, to get a better view beneath the bed—giving *him* a better view of her derrière. "You give me back that yarn, you little rascal. Here, now." He folded his arms and settled against the doorframe, fully mesmerized by the sight of her long, black-as-night hair, which he'd never seen unbound, cascading to one side and almost touching the floor.

She lowered herself flat on her stomach and reached an arm under the bed, then slid over, until her head and half of her body disappeared, giving him a satisfying view of her shapely calves, pretty ankles, and bare feet. "Aha! Got you, you little scamp! Now, where is your partner in crime? I know he must have helped you."

Something rubbed against Sam's ankle. He reached down and scooped up the tiny ball of fur—the exact duplicate of his brother, the apparent scamp.

"Lookin' for somethin'?" he asked, as the kitten snuggled against his chest.

He had no idea a woman could move like that—slide out from her hiding place and rise to her feet quicker than a thief leaves town. She let go of the kitten as she righted herself, and the little monster scurried out of the room like a streak of lightning. Sam released his cohort, who chased after him, both vanishing down the hallway.

With her dark eyes almost as big as the ball of blue yarn she held in her hand, she stared at him. "I didn't hear you come upstairs."

He raised one stockinged foot. "I crept," he teased. "You had me a little more than curious about what you were doin', especially when I heard things like, 'You give me that, you rascal.'" Eyes cast at the floor, he noted the trail of blue yarn, stretched under the bed and out the other side, around a chair, through the feet of the small table next to it, and back under the bed. "I see a little varmint made quick work o' that yarn. Were you knittin' somethin'?"

"I *was*, but the scamp unraveled most of my work." She went down on her knees and reached under the bed, presenting him with another nice view. She came back out and, still kneeling, held up what looked like a partial mitten. "I thought I'd knit a pair for both boys, with colder days in the offing. I guess I'll have to start again, thanks to Roscoe or Barney. Or maybe both."

He grinned. "Glad I'm not the only one who can't tell those two creatures apart."

She grabbed hold of the bedstead and pulled herself up. "They're identical, as far as I can tell, from their four white paws to the black tips of their tails."

He chuckled. "I've noticed, although I'll admit I haven't studied either one of 'em to any great extent. There are other things in this house I'd rather spend time lookin' at."

She must have caught him staring at her hair, for she swept it off of her shoulder as her cheeks turned a pinkish hue. "I had intended to put my hair up and change into something more presentable," she murmured.

He scanned her attire—a belted floral dress with a white collar and buttons that trailed halfway down the front. "Don't bother. You look more than presentable in my eyes."

She wrinkled her impertinent little nose. "Oh, forevermore. I look like a poor, bedraggled ragamuffin."

"Then how do I look?" He did a downward assessment of his own shirt, one of the three he'd worn so often to the workplace that it'd developed a few tears and permanent dark stains, despite the apron he always wore to protect himself from flying ash and other debris. His trousers, likewise, had seen many a better day, with their knees worn and pocket stitches frayed.

"You look"—she grinned, exposing a pretty set of sparkling teeth—"not much better than me, I suppose."

They shared a short-lived laugh. Was it their first? He glanced down the hallway. "Where are the boys, by the way?"

"Oh, they accepted an invitation to play with the Hansen boys. Their mother pledged to feed them supper and have them home around seven. You don't mind, I hope."

"Mind?" He blinked. "Mind that I don't have to race outside and throw the ball back and forth, or play chase or hide-and-seek or good guys an' bad guys?"

She tilted her head. "Good guys and bad guys?"

"Of course. Every boy's gotta learn that game. It's done with pretend weapons and lots o' runnin'."

"Pretend weapons?" She raised her eyebrows. "That makes me feel so much better."

He reached over and gave her hair a playful tug. It was even silkier than he'd imagined. "They wouldn't've learned that particular game if it weren't for me, you know."

She took a tiny step back. Had the gentle touch made her uncomfortable?

"They'd be missing out on lots of things if it weren't for you. I appreciate all you do for them."

"No need to mention it, because you know what? Tonight I plan to enjoy a little respite."

"That's what I've been doing all afternoon."

"Save that thought and tell me all you've done over supper."

"All right."

"But give me a few minutes to change and wash up." She started to speak, but he held up a finger. "And don't think for a second you need to do the same. Like I said, you look more than presentable. In fact, you look lovely. I, on the other hand, have been workin' in a dusty shop all day, handlin' iron and old tools, and ridin' my horse."

She sucked in a deep breath, gathering her hair in both fists at the back of her head, then ran one hand the length of it.

"And don't feel like you have to hide this beautiful mane. I rather like it down."

"Oh."

He winked, then turned. "I'll meet you downstairs in a few minutes."

To his utter satisfaction, when they reunited in the dining room, he saw that she hadn't done a thing to her appearance; she'd merely donned a pair of low pumps. He preferred her barefooted, but he didn't want to press his luck. She might very well balk if he made any more requests. They enjoyed a wonderful meal and surprisingly easy conversation, once they'd selected the unlikely topic of blacksmithing. Mercy brought it up and seemed curious, so he gave her a brief overview of the forging process. He liked the way she leaned across the table and seemed to listen, not only with her ears, but with her eyes. He tried to recall the last time anyone had asked him about his profession but came up empty.

"What sort of techniques do you use in this forging process?"

"Oh, I don't know. A lot." He sipped on his water. The potato soup was excellent but steaming hot.

"Like what? Name them." She raised her spoon to her mouth, then gently blew on it. The simple act almost entranced him, and for a second, he questioned his state of mind.

"You can't possibly be interested in this."

"But I am!"

Her brown eyes pulled him in, and he heard his own breath catch. He laughed to cover his reaction. "Well, there's drawin', which just means lengthenin' the metal. Then, there's shrinkin', by which you thicken or shorten it; and bendin', or punchin', meanin' you make a hole in the metal. Lots of terms that probably don't mean a great deal to you, but they're second nature to me."

"I think it's quite fascinating."

He stared across the table at her, studying her face as if seeing it for the first time. "Hmm. Yes, so do I."

"What?"

He jerked back, realizing his blunder. "It's, uh, fascinatin' that *you* find it fascinatin'."

She giggled, and the sound fairly floated through the room, putting him in mind of the gentle breeze wafting in through the open window behind him.

As the meal continued, she recounted, at his insistence, how she'd spent the afternoon: weeding the vegetable garden, sweeping the porch, cleaning her sewing room, sorting through some paperwork, and getting caught up on other things she hadn't found time to do since taking custody of the boys. When he asked her if she missed working for Doc Trumble, she said yes, but not as much as she'd expected to. He asked how she'd been handling her grief lately, and she answered that there were good days and bad days. He nodded and said he understood about that sort of thing, thinking it might be an opportune time to wrap her in a comforting hug, but also deciding that walking around the table to do it might come off as awkward.

They'd just started clearing the table when a knock came to the door.

"That must be Dora Hansen, bringing the boys home," Mercy said.

"I'll get it," Sam offered, seeing that her arms were full of linens.

When he opened the door, a man who looked to be in his seventies stood on the porch. "Evenin'," he said in a pleasant voice, with a smile to accompany the greeting. "Name's Horace Morby. I live a couple o' houses thataway." He tipped his head to the left. "The wife didn't go through the mail till tonight, and when she did, she found somethin' that should've come to you." He extended an envelope to Sam. "You are the blacksmith, ain't y'?"

"Oh, yes. Sorry, Samuel Connors." With a movement that was less than suave, Sam accepted the envelope, giving it a hurried glance before stuffing it in the pocket of his pants. "Thanks for walkin' over. I hope it wasn't too much of an inconvenience."

"Pfff, weren't none a'tall. Wife's always tellin' me I need to walk my supper off most nights. Well, I'll be goin' now." Horace lifted his saggy hat an inch off his head of sparse white hair, then plopped it back in place and gave a quick nod. "An' welcome to the neighborhood. The wife said she would've sent you folks a platter o' cookies if I hadn't eaten 'em all."

"Quite all right. Thanks again."

Before closing the door, Sam glanced up and down the street, expecting to see the boys. Craziest thing. He missed them.

19

"Who was at the door?" Mercy called from the kitchen. She knew it couldn't have been Joseph and John Roy; the house was still so quiet.

"Neighbor," she heard Sam reply. "Fellow by the name of Morris Horby."

"Morris Horby? I've never heard of him."

"Said he lives a couple o' doors down."

"Oh!" Her spurt of laughter couldn't be helped. "You mean Horace Morby."

He didn't seem to catch the humor in his error. "Morris Horby, Horace Morby. At least I was close."

She stepped out of the kitchen, wiping her damp hands on the sides of her skirt. "The Morbys are nice people. What did Mr. Morby want?"

He held up an envelope. "Apparently the mailman delivered a letter to them that should've come here. He was kind enough to bring it over."

"Is it addressed to both of us?"

"Uh, no. It's from one of my cousins, someone I haven't seen or heard from in a very long time. She's…somewhat estranged from the family."

"Really? Would I know her?"

"I'm not sure. She's a bit younger than you, I think, and she moved to Nashville about six years ago. Her name's Persephone Greve. 'Course, her maiden name is Connors. She's my uncle Gilbert and aunt Ella's daughter, the youngest of their brood. I don't think she gets on too well with her parents or brothers. She came along when my aunt was in her forties. I recall my mother sayin' Ella didn't want the baby, but there wasn't much she could do about it. Good chance she resented her, but who knows?"

"Oh, how could a mother resent her own child?" Mercy accentuated her point with a click of the tongue, then creased her brow. "I do remember Persephone, but not well. She was a couple of years behind me in school, so we never played together, but then, I wasn't allowed to associate with the Connorses."

Sam just stood there, studying the letter, with a frown on his face.

"Well, are you going to open that letter or just stare at it?"

"I—sure, I guess."

He kept eyeing the envelope, and it suddenly occurred to her that he might want privacy. "I'll just go finish cleaning up the kitchen," she announced.

He made no argument, so she turned and left the room, wondering if he'd tell her about the contents or keep her in the dark.

Five minutes later, he still hadn't returned to the kitchen, and a strange sense of trepidation came over her.

~

Just as the wall clock struck seven gongs, the boys barged inside the house, more wound up than two spools of thread, completely aflutter about their time at the Hansens'. "We played baseball an' tag, and Mr. Hansen showed us how to dig for worms, so's you can catch big catfish," Joseph explained in one breath. "An' Mrs. Hansen let us help her carry in water from her well. They don't gots a faucet; they gots a big pump handle that y' gotta be real strong to lift up then push back down, over an' over. John Roy wasn't strong enough, but I was."

"Was so!" John Roy cried. "I just din't want t' do it."

"They gots chickens what gives eggs, too," Joseph continued. "Can we get us some chickens, Mercy? Them chickens likes to be held."

"You have kittens to hold," she told him with a smile. "We don't need any more critters around here. And, speaking of the kittens, go hunt them down and put them outside, would you? They probably need to relieve themselves about now."

As both boys scooted off, still full of energy and excitement, Mercy called after them, "Don't wander too far, now. It's almost bath time."

Left alone with Mercy once more, Sam clutched the envelope in his pocket and deliberated for the dozenth time whether he should share its contents with Mercy, despite his cousin's insistence that he keep them a secret. He had no desire to deceive his wife, but he also wanted to use good judgment. What would he accomplish by telling her what his cousin had revealed—and not revealed? It would only cause undue worry. At the same time, secrets between spouses were not healthy, no matter that he and Mercy weren't spouses in the traditional sense. It nettled him that Persephone had put him in this awkward position, and yet perhaps she'd thought she had no choice. Questions circled in his head like a pesky swarm of bees.

"Well." Mercy rubbed her hands together and pivoted her body to face him. Her dark eyes locked with his. "Everything all right?"

He knew she referred to the letter. "Yeah, everything's fine." His chest tightened with the slight untruth.

As dusk settled outside, a persistent goldfinch sang a calming song—*per-chip-er-ee, per-chip-er-ee*—and he imagined her nestling in with her younglings for a warm summer night's sleep. Off in the distance, a couple of dogs barked back and forth. Mercy held her clasped hands at her waist, waiting, he knew, for him to elaborate.

Oh, good glory, what was the point in dragging it out another second? He had no choice but to show her the letter. He yanked the thing from his pocket and held it out.

She looked at it but made no move to take it.

"Here." He shoved it closer. "I want you to read it."

"But…it's not addressed to me."

"Doesn't matter. You're my wife, and you have a right to read it."

"Not if it's private."

"How about I read it to you?"

She hesitated, brow crinkled, lips pursed.

He reached out and snagged her hand. "Come on." He led her into the parlor and lowered himself onto the divan, Mercy settling in next to him. They sat close enough that their thighs touched, sparking a flicker of warmth in his gut. He cleared his throat and chewed over how to preface the letter. "Like I said, I haven't seen or heard from Persephone in a long while—years, probably—so I was more than a little surprised to get this letter."

"Please, if your cousin intended it for you alone, I don't think you should read it to me."

"She did, but it's my right to disregard her wishes. Maybe together we can figure out what's goin' on here."

A tight little gasp came out of her. "What do you mean?"

"Don't worry." He patted her on the knee, something he'd never done, and was surprised she didn't flinch. "Let me read it to you, and then we'll talk." He unfolded the parchment and felt her lean in closer as he began to read.

Dear Cousin Samuel,

It has been a very long time since we talked or even saw each other, not for lack of want on my part but because it is just best for all concerned that I don't return to Paris. I have my reasons.

I understand that you married Mercy Evans. (News travels fast and far, though I learned this not from my parents or siblings but from my childhood friend Adelaide Lawson, who still lives in Paris. We keep in contact, but I confess not even she knows the reason I've never come home.) I'm sure your Mercy is a fine woman, but I fear her last name alone will bring you great strife. I am aware of damage already done to your property.

I have something important to tell you about, but I cannot write it in a letter. For that reason, I ask that you come to Nashville at your earliest convenience. Do not bring anyone with you. In fact, tell no one of your plans to visit me—or even about this letter. The sooner you come, the sooner your questions will be answered.

Hank and I have room to accommodate your overnight stay. I look forward to seeing you. I shall await your reply so that I can prepare for your visit.

Best regards,
Persephone Greve

Sam refolded the letter and looked at Mercy. Her eyes seemed to have taken on a darker, sharper hue than before, perhaps due to the reflection off the flaming lamp on the side table or the sheer intentness with which she'd listened. He heard her breath catch, and he wanted nothing more than to reassure her. But he needed reassurance himself!

"Tell me your thoughts," he said.

"My thoughts?" She met his gaze, her brow crimped with confusion. "I…I don't know what to think. I'm a little mystified."

"That makes two of us, then."

"When will you go see her?"

"I can't go right away. Uncle Clarence and I are swamped with orders. It wouldn't be fair to him."

"Surely, he'd understand. Whatever information your cousin has seems urgent."

"I know, but there are other things to consider—namely, my concern about leavin' you and the boys alone."

"That's really quite funny," she said, actually giggling. "I've been pretty much on my own ever since my ma died, and I had the boys to myself for a few weeks before you moved in. I think we'll survive just fine."

"But your property hadn't been vandalized before, either. I'm worried somethin' else might happen while I'm gone. I think I'll give it a week or so, just to make sure things remain quiet around here. And when I do decide to go, no one but you and Uncle Clarence will know I'm out of town."

"The Lord will take care of us. I'm not worried."

The kitchen door slammed shut, and the boys came pounding down the hall. "Mercy, where are you?" John Roy squealed.

"We're in here," she called.

The boys rounded the corner, then stopped, breathing hard, and peered at them through troubled-looking blue eyes. "We can't find Barney," said Joseph. "He went through the bushes and din't come back out."

"How do you know it was Barney and not Roscoe?" Sam asked.

"'Cause Barney gots more black on one side than Roscoe," John Roy said. "See?" He held up the supposed Roscoe.

"Ah, so that's how you tell." Sam smiled. "Well, I'm sure he'll come back. He's probably just sniffin' things out."

"Dogs sniff things out," Mercy corrected him, with a glance that seemed to question his intelligence. "Cats sneak."

"Oh. Well then, he's probably sneakin' up on somethin'—maybe a mouse."

"Somebody tooked him," said John Roy.

"What would make you think that?"

"'Cause we heard somebody," said Joseph.

An unsettling feeling spread through Sam's stomach. He slid forward on the sofa. "What do you mean, you heard somebody?"

"Barney meowed real loud," John Roy said, "and then we heard somebody run away on the other side of the bushes."

Now Mercy eased forward, her skirts brushing against Sam's leg. "Which side of the yard?"

Joseph pointed to his left. "Over there."

She angled Sam a worried glance to match the boys'. "The shrubs are tall on that side. Old Mr. Ferguson likes his privacy, so he rarely trims them."

"Is he disgruntled?" Sam asked. "I mean, would he…you know?"

Mercy shook her head. "No. No, he's not like that. He enjoys his solitude, but he's a kindly old man. He would never…."

Good thing she'd read his mind. He hadn't wanted to alarm the boys by asking directly if the man would intentionally hurt their pet.

Sam pushed himself up, then winked at the boys. "Think I'll go outside and investigate for myself. How's that sound?"

Mercy nearly beat him to a standing position, brushing the wrinkles out of her skirt. "I'll come with you."

"Uh, no, you won't."

"Why not?"

He turned his back to the boys, lifting his brows at her. "Because one of us should stay with them." This he said through gritted teeth.

She took a baby step back as understanding dawned. "All right, then. I'll get them ready for their bath."

He gave a quick smile, then faced the boys again. "That's a fine idea. Boys, you go on upstairs with Mercy."

"But...." Joseph balked. "What if you can't find Barney?"

"Don't worry, I'll find him."

But he didn't find him, even after prowling around the neighborhood for the next hour, calling the fur ball by name. He looked under neighbors' porches, behind bushes, even up in trees, all the while listening for the tiniest meow, but all he heard were those same barking dogs, the occasional clomp of horses' hooves, and the squeak of a wagon wheel in need of greasing. To say he was perplexed put it lightly. How could a kitten escape so easily, unless—as Joseph had said—someone had taken it? Why anybody would steal a kitten from an innocent kid was beyond him. More baffling—and far more disturbing—was the timing, for how could someone have pulled off a catnapping unless he'd been watching the house, waiting for the opportunity? A shiver ran down Sam's body as he made his way back to the house.

Mercy met him at the door, wringing her hands. "Did you find him?" she whispered frantically.

He looked up the stairs, then back at her. "Where're the boys?"

"Tucked in bed, but Joseph is having none of it. He's up there crying because John Roy is hogging Roscoe, and he doesn't have a kitten to cuddle."

Sam shook his head. "I don't know where Barney could be. I looked everywhere."

"How could one little kitten disappear so quickly? I don't like that Joseph thought he heard footsteps. Do you think he really did, or could it have been his imagination?" There was a distinct tremor in Mercy's voice, and, for the second time that evening, he felt the need to reassure her.

He rested a hand on her shoulder. "I'm sure Barney's fine. He's probably just hidin' somewhere, and he'll show up in the mornin'."

She moved out from under his hand. "In the morning? That little guy is too young to be out at night all alone. He's not big enough to defend himself. We have to find him." She hiked up her skirts and pushed past him, nearly knocking him off balance. He snagged her by the arm, and she whirled around. "Let go. I need to find Barney."

"He's a cat, Mercy. He'll find his way."

"What? How can you say that? He's a helpless little kitten, too small for his instincts to have kicked in yet." She was serious, and the sheen in her eyes said she was also near to tears.

"What're you gonna do?"

"I told you, I'm going out to find him."

"I've just spent the past hour lookin' for him, and I tell you, he's not out there."

"Did you find Barney?" came a small voice from upstairs.

They spun around. Joseph stood at the top of the staircase, gazing down at them, eyes hopeful.

Sam shook his head. "No, buddy, but don't worry yourself. Like I just told Mercy, I'm sure he'll turn up."

In the shadows, Sam could see the boy's face drop just before the bawling erupted. Mercy left Sam's side and hurried up the stairs to enfold him in her arms. All the commotion brought a sleepy-eyed John Roy out of the bedroom, Roscoe tucked under one arm. The sight of his brother's hysteria brought him to tears, as well, and soon, even Mercy had joined the crying chorus. Sam darted up the stairs himself, meeting his little makeshift family at the top and encircling all of them in a tight embrace. "Shh," he whispered. "Shh, it'll be all right. No need to cry."

But he figured they *did* have need to cry, every one of them. They'd already lost so much. Losing poor little Barney was more than any of them could bear right now. And as he stood there, hugging them close, he came to a startling realization.

He loved all three of them.

20

Mercy and the boys cried for the next several minutes, taking turns sucking in gasps and expelling sighs between rounds of tears. Then, Sam gently led them downstairs, talking in low, soothing tones as they descended. He situated them on the couch in the living room, across from the fireplace, with Mercy in the middle, then knelt on one knee in front of them, his large, callused hands resting atop the boys' knees in a fatherly gesture. He didn't try to shush them, as before; he just let them cry, and Mercy noticed that his own eyes appeared slightly damp in the corners.

Mercy sniffled, trying to stanch the flow of her own tears. What in the world must Sam think? It was bad enough that he had two sobbing children to tend to, but a wife who'd also lost control of her faculties? She wouldn't blame him if he visited Judge Corbett tomorrow and asked him to start the annulment proceedings. He'd bitten off more than he'd bargained for when he'd "married" the three of them.

There was a lull in the boys' crying spasms, and Joseph swiped at his nose with the back of his hand and whimpered, "I miss Barney."

"I know you do, son," Sam soothed. "I'll look for him some more after you go back to bed. How's that?"

Whether it was the mention of missing something or the idea of going back to bed, something triggered an all-new eruption from John Roy. "I m-miss Mama an' Papa."

A painful gasp came out of Mercy at the unexpected statement. Sam cupped the boy's head from behind and drew him to his chest, then locked gazes with Mercy. "Of course you do." Her heart split down the center. There it was—the bedrock reason behind their shattered emotions, Barney's disappearance having put a chink in their heavy armor. Till now, they'd held themselves together from day to day with tiny threads of self-restraint, but this latest development had broken down their flimsy resolve and forced reality to the surface. Death had visited them, and none of them had fully dealt with its hammering blow. Fresh tears trailed down Mercy's damp cheeks at the realization that she couldn't comfort the boys in the way they needed when she could barely contain her own anguish. How she thanked God for Sam's strong presence in that moment.

"Papa used to t-tuck us in," cried Joseph.

"And M-Mama readed us s-stories," said John Roy between hiccupping sighs.

"And sang us songs."

John Roy cried louder.

Joseph cut loose a wail that nearly took off the roof. "Why'd they have t' die?"

The question shot out like a bullet, one they'd all been dodging every day since the disaster had struck. Unfortunately, it hit its mark tonight—square in their aching chests.

"I don't know," Sam answered, his tone wavering. "It was their time, I suppose."

Mercy pulled herself together as best she could. "But it wasn't *your* time, and we must look at it that way—that God had a special purpose in bringing Sam to your rescue. God has plans for you, boys, and for all of us, and someday He'll reveal them to each of us." She knew she spoke far above their level of understanding. Heavenly mercies, she spoke above her own. "I don't claim to have the answers, by any means, but this one thing I know: God loves us, and He wants us to trust Him, especially when times are hard."

Her words seemed to have a calming effect, even on her. The four of them spent the next few seconds in sober silence, sniffing and pondering private thoughts, and then Joseph aimed his gaze at Sam. "You was ar angel."

Sam produced a weak smile and tousled the boy's downy hair. "I know you've said that, but, believe me, I'm no angel. I was just at the right place at the right time."

"No." He shook his head stubbornly. "God sent you to save us. Mercy said so."

Now Sam's eyes welled up. He lowered his head and studied the floor for a moment, then raised his gaze to meet Mercy's, blinking away tears. "All right, I'll accept that."

Mercy reached out and touched Sam on the forearm. It was the first she'd felt his firm muscle, and she found it comforting if not intriguing. The only men she'd ever had intentional physical contact with had been patients of Doc Trumble's, and she realized with suddenness what a sheltered existence she lived. "Thank you, Sam," she managed.

"For what?"

"For just…helping us through this."

He smiled and laid his hand on hers, and the warmth of his touch sent a surprising tingle straight up her arm. "At no time do I want any of you to hold back your tears." His voice was firm yet gentle. "If you need to cry, you get it out, you hear? And if you ever need to talk about…that night, well, you just feel free to do it. Everybody understand?"

Still conscious of his hand on hers, Mercy pulled away—lest he detect her quickening pulse—and put it back where it had been, around Joseph's narrow shoulder. She tugged both boys closer. "I think we all feel a little better now, don't we, boys?"

They gave slow, quiet nods.

"A good cry never hurt anybody," said Sam, his steady voice soothing her senses.

Joseph wiped his drippy nose. "Mama tol' us cryin' keeps your head from achin'."

John Roy nodded against Mercy's chest, where her dress fabric stuck to her bosom from having soaked up so many of his tears. "An' from esplodin'."

Despite it all, Mercy chuckled. "Exploding?"

John Roy sat back and blinked bloodshot eyes at her. "If you don't cry, your tears'll fill up your head and make it burst wide open."

She and Sam shared a smile. "That's good to know, isn't it, Sam?"

"Indeed. We don't want any explodin' heads." Sam smiled. "Your mother was very wise to tell you that cryin' can be a good thing."

"'Specially when y'r bleedin'," Joseph put in. "If y'r jus' cryin' 'cause you din't get your way, y'ain't supposed to cry."

Sam grinned. "Well, that's true enough."

The way he rested on his haunches made Mercy question whether he had grown uncomfortable. "Do you want to sit on the couch with us?"

"Nope, I'd rather stay right here and look at each o' you. Have to make sure you're all okay." His gravelly tone planted a tender craving in her heart.

She combed her fingers through John Roy's tangled hair. "Thanks to your kindness, we're feeling a fair piece better now."

He touched her knee, his blue eyes searing a path to her heart. "Glad to hear it."

Joseph sucked in a breath, his cheeks puffing up, then blew it out. "Can we ask Jesus to bring Barney home?"

"Of course we can," Mercy said. "God hears all our prayers, great and small, and answers each one."

"Who's gonna pray, you or Sam?"

"Mercy is," Sam shot out.

John Roy wriggled free of her embrace and scooted off the couch. "We gots to all kneel down, like we do before bed, 'cause God likes it better that way." With hands folded, he demonstrated the posture he and Joseph assumed every night before bedtime prayers, and Joseph followed suit, kneeling next to him.

Mercy smiled gamely at Sam, then slid off the couch and joined the boys on her knees. Sam positioned himself next to her, their sides brushing. With head bent, eyes closed, and palms pressed together, she led them in a simple yet heartfelt prayer, thanking God for His love, care, and protection and then asking for little Barney's safe return.

The four of them moved to the kitchen, where Mercy read aloud a comforting passage from the Bible while the boys—Sam included—enjoyed a bedtime snack of chocolate cookies she'd baked that afternoon, washed down with cold milk. Once Joseph and John Roy had been tucked back in bed for the second time that night, Sam followed Mercy out of the room, gently closed the door behind him, and then led her down the hallway. "How 'bout a cup of tea in the kitchen before I go outside for another look around?"

"That sounds nice."

"Might have to nibble another cookie, too." He winked, and Mercy's stomach flipped.

They sat at the kitchen table, sipping tea, Sam snacking on cookies till the half dozen or so she'd spread on a platter had all but vanished. He stared at the last remaining morsel, knowing he could easily down it in one bite but also knowing he'd regret it later when he awoke with a stomachache, so he decided to let it sit there and continue tempting him instead.

Of course, that lone cookie wasn't the only thing in the room tempting him. Mercy sat across from him, her hair cascading down her shoulders like a waterfall, looking downright lovely, puffy eyes and flushed cheeks and all.

"This has been quite a night," Mercy said with a sigh. "First, that letter from your cousin, then Barney going missing, with the possibility that someone took him, and then our wild hysterics...I'm sorry you had to deal with all that."

He set his cup down and inclined his head at her. "It's my job."

"Your job?"

"I married you for better, for worse, remember? If my family goes a little berserk on me, then so be it. It's my job to take care of you in the good times and bad times alike."

A tiny smile turned up the corners of her mouth. "I imagined you going to the judge tomorrow to start the annulment proceedings."

He laughed and shook his head. "You think I'd toss you all away over a little cryin' spell?"

She tucked a few strands of dark hair behind her ear and studied her teacup. "Well, I...I appreciate your understanding."

A thumping sound at the front door had both of them turning their heads. Sam shoved back his chair, planted his hands on the table, and pushed himself up. "Stay here." He left no room in his tone for negotiating, and she didn't argue.

With purposeful strides, he crossed the dining room and the living room to the front entryway. Reaching the door, he was surprised to see no silhouette through the window. He opened the door, first a crack, then a little wider, sticking his head outside and craning his neck in both directions. That's when he heard a soft meow. On one of the wicker chairs under the window sat a wooden crate with a board resting on top—a makeshift lid, of sorts. A shrill mewing persisted as he stepped onto the porch, approached the crate, and lifted the board. There lay a little ball of fuzz, quivering with fright.

Sam lifted Barney out of the box and began to check him over for wounds, while cooing, in a tone far more effeminate than he would have liked, "What in the world were you doin' in that crate, little fella?" He was relieved to find the kitten unharmed; the only difference was the string tied rather tightly around his neck, with a note attached. Sam loosened the knot, freeing the kitten of his noose. He kept the unread note clutched in his fist.

"My stars in glory, you've found him!" Mercy said, rushing onto the porch.

"Not exactly." Sam handed Barney over to her. "He was left on the porch, in a wooden crate."

"A wooden crate? Who on earth would put him in—what's that you're holding?" she asked, pressing the kitten to her cheek. She drew so close to his side, he felt her breath on his cheek and caught a hint of a pleasant floral scent, whether from her hair or her skin, he couldn't say—although he would have liked to investigate.

"Some kind of note." He began to unfold it.

"What's it say?" She lowered her head to get a better view, effectively blocking his line of vision. At least he could tell, at this close proximity, that the flowery fragrance came from her hair. He wondered what she used to make it smell so luscious. He shook off his tangle of thoughts, then lifted the letter where they both could see it.

Mercy squinted at the scribbled shorthand. "You two had no business marrying," she read aloud, and he was glad she'd taken it upon herself to decipher the almost illegible, mostly misspelled, writing.

"'Connors and Evans blood ain't meant for mixing. Didn't your daddies… learn'—I think that's what it says—'you that long ago? You best get… divorced…'fore trouble mounts. The news'—I suppose he meant *noose*—'around your dumb cat's neck is to warn you that if you don't divorce soon, somebody's going to get hurt.'"

Mercy's mouth gaped wide as she gawked up at Sam, who was equally dumbstruck. She then snatched the paper from his hand to study it. "It looks like a man's handwriting, if you ask me. A man who can't spell worth a cat's tooth." She quirked her brow at him. "What did he mean by 'somebody's going to get hurt'? I don't want to be responsible for any bloodshed. Somebody ought to tell this person there's already been enough sorrow. And why should we have to explain our decision, anyway? Least of all to our loony relatives who don't know what it means to keep their noses where they belong. Don't they know we married for the sake of convenience and not love?"

With every sentence, her voice rose in pitch. Unable to resist, he reached out and cupped her cheek in his hand, which brought an abrupt halt to her flow of words. "For a godly woman, you sure know how to spout off."

She opened her mouth and sucked in a loud breath, then clamped her lips shut. He couldn't help but chuckle at her perplexed expression. "Don't worry, there's nothin' wrong with a little righteous anger. Heck, I just read the other night the account of Jesus tossin' over tables in a show of anger when He caught some people buyin' and sellin' goods in the temple."

He hadn't known her chocolate eyes could get any bigger or rounder, but they certainly did. "You've been reading your Bible?"

He cocked his head and grinned. "I have, and I've been enjoyin' it, I might add—and learnin' a few things along the way. But that's a discussion for another time. For now, I want you to take that kitten upstairs to Joseph. He'll be so relieved to find 'im safe. Just don't tell 'im he came delivered in a crate."

"I wouldn't do that. Will you…are we going to continue this discussion?"

He lifted one brow, tempted to say he'd much rather sample the taste of her lips than talk. But he supposed she wouldn't go for the idea, considering she'd just affirmed the basis for their marriage as convenience, certainly not love. Apparently, her feelings for him in no way compared to the growing ones he had for her.

21

Flora Connors adjusted her hat. The thing was big and heavy, not to mention uncomfortable on such a hot day, but it simply wasn't proper to leave the house without one, so she'd donned it at the last minute, while one of Virgil's hired hands had hitched up the buggy. In her estimation, women these days didn't dress appropriately, particularly when going into town. Many went straight from gardening or doing household chores to shopping and other public activities, a most unappealing, indecent sight.

She sniffed, straightened her back, and lifted her chin high as she pulled the reins to the right, directing her horse onto Blakemore Street and then heading south, toward Wood and the center of Paris. She had a long list of errands, after which she planned on stopping by the blacksmith shop to say hello to Samuel, since he didn't have the decency to pay her a visit. She couldn't believe how inconsiderate he'd become since marrying that Evans woman. She refused to refer to her as a Connors, much less her daughter-in-law, no matter the legitimacy of the union. She would never forgive Samuel for committing such treason against his family.

Flora found a shady spot to park her buggy in front of Paris Bank and Trust. She climbed down, looped the reins around a hitching post, brushed off her bell skirt, and adjusted her hat again. Stepping up onto the wooden sidewalk, she nodded at a couple of Paris citizens as they strolled by, then opened the big, heavy door of the bank and walked inside. Several customers stood in line, single file. Next time, she would come earlier, to avoid the crowds. She draped the long strap of her satchel over her shoulder and released a long sigh.

It must have been a loud sigh, for several heads turned in her direction. One of them, regrettably, belonged to Wilma Whintley.

"Afternoon, Mrs. Connors! Looks like we've got a little wait here. Fortunately, it's not as hot today as yesterday. Must be a storm's brewin'. My gout always acts up when the weather's about to make a drastic change. How are you doin'? You're lookin' mighty fine in that lovely getup. I must say, purple becomes you."

Flora forced a smile. "Thank you, Mrs. Whintley. I'm fine, and you?" She was hardly in the mood for conversing with the likes of Wilma Whintley, a busybody if ever there was one, and she thanked the Lord she didn't have the woman's reputation for incessant blather. As the widow of Ernest Connors, her image was one of courage, strength, and resilience. Through her husband's six years of undeserved incarceration, until his sudden death due to illness, she'd stood by his side, and folks respected her for it. Oh, they might not admit it to her face, but it showed in their expressions. And she didn't need any public association with Wilma Whintley tarnishing her fine image.

"Oh, gracious me, I'm as fine as a silver spoon. Never better. Well, except for this gout, as I mentioned. I presume you're plannin' to attend the community picnic this Saturday, hosted by the Paris Women's Club? It'll be quite the affair, like always."

"Of course. I wouldn't miss it." Flora didn't especially wish to go, but it wouldn't do for her to skip when folks counted on her delicious cakes, cookies, and pies at the baked goods sale. She always received high praise for them.

"I serve on the plannin' committee, you know."

"Isn't that nice." Flora could about imagine how their meetings went, too. Once they finished with business, the gossip would begin. That was reason enough not to join the Paris Women's Club, never mind that she'd been invited only twice. She couldn't abide their worthless chatter. Besides, what if one of them started questioning her about matters she didn't care to address—namely, her husband's sentence? Yes, the courts had closed the books on the case, but she had no doubt folks still talked about it in hushed tones, wondering what really had transpired on that dreadful day. Oh, she kept a number of secrets locked away, secrets of which she alone—and that vile Virgil Perry—had knowledge. No, best all around she stay clear of that talkative, if not nosy, club.

The bank clerk finished with a customer, and those in line took one step forward. Wilma eyed her askance. "Nice havin' your son for a neighbor! You do know my yard backs up to Mercy's, don't you?"

No, she hadn't known. "Well, aren't you the lucky one? I mean—how nice for you."

"Yes, she's a fine young woman, that Mercy. And your son, my, what a handsome feller. Friendly, too, is what I hear. I haven't had much opportunity to talk to him over the fence, mind you, but I see him out back most every evenin', playin' with those darlin' li'l boys. I'm sure you must miss him, but you know what they say—you didn't lose a son; you gained a daughter."

"Is that what they say?" She didn't like the direction this conversation had taken, particularly since it seemed to have attracted the attention of the other bank patrons, and one of them, a man, wore a definite smirk on his face.

"How noble of Sam to rescue those boys from that house fire, and then to marry Mercy so she could take custody of 'em. She sure was devoted to the Watsons. Terrible tragedy, their deaths." The woman wagged her head and frowned, closing her mouth for all of five seconds—probably to catch her breath.

"Yes, wasn't it?" The bigger tragedy was Samuel's marrying an Evans, but she'd keep that thought tucked away. She glanced with impatience at the people ahead of her in line. A small child started fussing, and her mother bent to pick her up, whispering something in her ear that made her giggle.

"Of course, I'm sure you weren't too thrilled by their decision to marry," Wilma went on, "or perhaps you've put that silly feud to rest by now."

Silly feud? How dare she! What did she know about their families' history? The line advanced one step, and Flora began counting the seconds until she could leave the confines of this building—and, better yet, the presence of this intolerable woman.

"Mrs. Connors?"

She glanced up and saw the bank president, Edgar Landry, standing in the doorway to his office. "Won't you come in? We can conduct whatever business you have in the privacy of my office. I'm sure you'll find it more comfortable."

About time! Mr. Landry always treated her with the respect she deserved. Of course, he had all her investments, so he'd better. With great relief, she left the line, not bothering to return Wilma Whintley's farewell.

⌒

Sam's workday buzzed past with nary a minute to stop for a breather. Over the last month, customer orders had piled up, spiking a discussion between him and his uncle about whether to hire an assistant. "It'd be to our benefit," Sam had said just yesterday.

"But we'd have to train 'im," Clarence had pointed out, "and right now we're too swamped to think about it. Now, if my boys had showed some interest in smithin', it might be a different story today, but nope, they're wrapped up in careers o' their own choosin'. I'm fine with it, o' course. Can't live life through my sons."

He thought he detected a bit of regret in his uncle's voice, and why wouldn't he? Just as he, Sam, had shown no interest in farming—much to his mother's lament—his cousins Peter and John had wanted nothing to do with the family business. It made him question who, if anyone, would carry on the work when he was gone. He thought about John Roy and Joseph and wondered if, as they grew a little older, he oughtn't to bring them over to the shop and demonstrate the art of blacksmithing. Might catch their interest.

In light of how busy they were, Sam hated to bring up the matter of his desire to take off a couple of days so he could travel to Nashville to visit the cousin he hadn't seen in years. The more he thought about the letter from Persephone, the more he longed to jump on the next train, if for no other reason than to put his curiosity to rest. Besides, the incident with Barney's going missing and then the peculiar manner in which he'd been returned kept hounding him. He needed to get some answers, and while he couldn't be sure Persephone truly had any, he couldn't ignore the things she'd written. Someone was up to no good, and Persephone just might be able to shed a little light on the matter. Even Mercy had encouraged him to go see her, and when he'd said he still didn't feel comfortable leaving her and the boys alone at night, she'd suggested they could go stay with her aunt Gladys, which had eased his mind a great deal.

His uncle had begun whistling one of his favorite hymns as he paused to inspect one of the dozens of hinges he'd made that afternoon. Sam would be happy with a rate of production half as fast as his uncle's, but he didn't want to sacrifice quality, so he kept working at a comfortable pace. Clarence often reminded him that smithing was an art form of which only time and practice and a wagonload of passion could expand his abilities and improve his skills. "When I was a young buck like you, I didn't have near the finesse that you already have. In a few years' time, you'll be workin' circles 'round me," he'd said. Sam appreciated his vote of confidence but doubted the accuracy of his prediction. Fortunately, he loved the profession, so it wouldn't bother him if his uncle remained a hair better at it than he.

"What's that you're whistlin'?" he asked.

"'Standin' on the Promises,'" he answered, still studying his work.

"Nice tune. What are the words?"

He put the hinge down and rubbed his whiskered jaw. "We sang it at First Methodist last Sunday. Been in my head ever since." He cleared his throat and broke into song, his rich tenor voice carrying through the room and probably out the windows. "Standin', standin', standin' on the promises of Christ my Savior; standin', standin', I'm standin' on the promises of God." As he sang, Clarence waved his arm, as if conducting an orchestra. When he finished, they both cut loose with light laughter.

"You have a nice voice, Uncle. Who'd you inherit your musical talents from, your mother or father?"

"Your grandmother Connors had a fine voice. She stopped using it for God's glory, though."

"What do you mean?"

A deep line etched Clarence's already crumpled brow. He lifted his apron and sopped up the moistness gathered there. "She and Pa grew so embittered over fightin' with the Evans family, she lost all her shine. The song went right outta her."

"What was there to fight about?" Sam was intrigued, but Uncle Clarence had always been tight-lipped about the feud, so he tried to keep his tone blasé.

"What wasn't there? A county judge ruled in our family's favor when it came to property lines and some other issues concernin' livestock, and you'd have thought they'd have let it rest, but no, the fightin' continued, especially after Cornelius Evans—that's Mercy's grandfather—died of sudden dropsy. I don't remember the details, but I know his passin' created an even bigger stir, with the Evanses blamin' Pa—your grandfather—for Corney's premature death. I remember Ma and Pa talkin' some nights into the early-mornin' hours, even raisin' their voices. 'Course, I never did learn all the ins and outs of the bickerin'; and, frankly, I didn't care. Still don't. It seemed so silly to me as a kid, but I guess it mattered to them as adults. Shortly after Corney Evans died, his wife sold the farm, makin' all that fightin' over property lines seem ridiculous. She moved her family to a house in town, and everyone said she took a big loss in the sale. She taught her kids to hate the Connors, and, o' course, your grandparents did the same with regard to them."

"But not you. How come?"

Clarence shook his head and shrugged. "I saw what it did to my parents and siblings. No way was I gonna be party to it. Besides, the Lord had His hand on me from a very young age, and I knew hate could have no place in my heart if I was goin' to serve Him."

Sam considered that. "My reasons were similar to yours, but I don't think they were spiritually driven. I just wanted to take the road opposite the one my mother chose for me. She was always so hard to please, and downright pessimistic, so I determined early on not to be like her."

Clarence chuckled and scratched his head, making several thin gray strands of hair stand on end. "Can't blame you for that. Still, I wouldn't rule out the spiritual aspect. I believe God's been preparin' you from the time you were this high"—he extended his palm at table height—"to marry Mercy. He knew it wouldn't do for you to hold a bunch of antagonism toward her family, or you never would have married 'er. In my opinion, He kept your heart soft."

"You really think so?" The notion that God had been working in his life from an early age gave Sam something else to mull over, even made him more anxious to get home and crack open his Bible for his daily reading.

"I'm sure of it. You asked the Lord into your heart when you were but a boy, and from that day forward, God's kept you safe in His care…even in your strayin' years."

He laughed. "Polite way to put it, Uncle—'strayin' years.'"

Clarence grinned. "I remember you comin' into the shop when you were but a boy to tell your father you'd asked Jesus into your heart. Pardon my sayin' so, but my brother could be quite a dunce. Said you were too young for such decisions. I told him I disagreed, and then I encouraged you, which got your pa's dander up. He didn't like my interferin'."

Sam smiled, conjuring a vague recollection. "I couldn't have been more than seven or eight, and you're right, that man could be a dolt sometimes. Never was the nurturin' sort. Shoot, you treated me more like a son than my own father ever did."

Clarence gave his head a slow shake. "I s'pose I did. Never could abide him treatin' you with anythin' less than kindness. You were a good kid. Shoot, most of my nieces and nephews are good kids, or at least started out that way. It's their parents what went wrong, bringin' 'em up to be so hateful toward the Evans clan."

"You and Aunt Hester did right by your kids."

The older man's chest puffed out with his hefty sigh, and he looped his thumbs behind his suspender straps. "They turned out fine, if I do say so, and I'm proud they're all servin' the Lord. Raise your kids up in the way they ought to go, and when they grow up, they won't depart from it, is what the Bible says. Well, maybe not word for word, but that's the gist of it."

Outside, the trees made a rustling sound as a pleasant cross breeze wafted through the windows and counteracted the heat coming off the shop's ever-glowing furnace. A chipmunk scampered up the oak tree trunk just past the window and took to scolding a blue jay that'd come too close. Sam decided to take advantage of their unscheduled work break and broach a new subject.

"What do you know about my cousin Persephone Greve?"

The question didn't seem to faze Uncle Clarence. "Gil an' Ella's young-est?" He scratched his temple. "I'm sorry to say she's one I failed to get to know as well as some of my other kin. She came along a little later; don't think Gil an' Ella were quite prepared for 'er. Why'd you ask?"

"Oh, I was just curious. I've been thinkin' about goin' to visit her."

Clarence's silver brows shot up. "That so? What brought that on?"

Shoot, he might have known he'd ask. "Just thinkin' about the cousins I don't know very well. She's probably the one I know the least. I guess I'd like to connect with her—and meet her husband. I didn't go to the weddin'."

"Few did. It was a small affair, was what I heard. I'm not even sure Gil an' Ella went. They seem to be estranged from her, which I've never under-stood. It's not somethin' they choose to talk about, though, so I don't bring it up." He left his station and walked to the small wooden icebox in the corner, opened the door, and took out a Mason jar filled with water. He unscrewed the lid, took several swigs, then wiped his mustache. "When you plannin' to go see Persephone?"

Sam let out a long-held breath. "I was thinkin' soon."

Clarence sniffed. "Mercy and the boys goin', too?"

"No, they'll go stay with Mercy's aunt Gladys."

"That's a good idea, considerin' that strange incident with your cat. Never can be sure what folks'll do these days. We live in some crazy times."

"Yes, we sure do."

"Well, I, for one, think it's a good idea, you gettin' to know your long-lost cousin."

"Really?"

"Why not?"

"We've got a lot of orders to fill."

Clarence swatted the air. "Won't hurt folks t' wait a few extra days. They'll get their orders in due time."

"You sure?"

"O' course, I'm sure. Go."

"Well then, I'll probably leave in the next few days, maybe Monday."

"Fine by me. You plannin' on stayin' awhile?"

"No, just overnight."

Relief seeped out when Clarence didn't comment further. Out front, a horse whinnied, and a woman's voice gave a commanding "Whoa."

Sam peeked out the window and saw a familiar horse and buggy parked out front. Scowling, he turned to his uncle. He did not have time for this. "It's my mother."

22

"Mother? What are you doin' here?" Sam stepped outside and closed the shop door behind him.

"Is that any way to greet your mother? Come help me down from this buggy."

"Sorry." He crossed the space between them and lifted his arms to assist her. "How are you?"

She settled herself on the ground and put a hand to her back. "How do you think? My back and neck are aching something fierce. I can barely stand, after riding into town on that hard, bouncy seat. Since you moved, I've had to do all the driving myself."

He braced himself for her usual whining fest. "Why don't you ask Virgil or one of the hired hands to escort you?"

She wrinkled her nose and adjusted the flowery contraption on her head, the fancy leaves and feathery branches doing a fine job of shading her entire face. "I don't like asking Virgil to do me any extra favors, and as for the hired hands, most of them smell like horse dung. I could not abide sitting next to them for a journey of two blocks, much less two miles."

"Like I've said, you ought to sell the farm and move into town. You'd like it much better, I'm sure."

"I can't do that."

"Why not?"

She raised her chin. "I just can't, and that's all there is to it."

"You can't or you won't?"

She gave a loud sniff and looked skyward. "My, it's a hot day, isn't it?"

"Not exceedingly, no."

She fanned her face with her white-gloved hand. "Well, it is when you're standing directly in the sun. Take me over there in the shade." She pointed to the lone wooden bench situated under the large maple tree at the corner of Jackson and Park streets.

"I can't take much longer than a few minutes to visit. Uncle Clarence and I still have a lot to do before closin' up for the day."

"Well, surely he'll understand the importance of you spending time with your mother. After all, I did go out of my way to come and see you."

He might have told her she shouldn't have bothered, but that would be boorish of him. Besides, he did want to discuss something with her. He took hold of her bony elbow and escorted her across the street. She walked with a slight limp, something he hadn't noticed the last time he'd seen her, and the notion that she'd manufactured it just for today rankled him. Was she that starved for attention? He ought to feel sorry for her, but after years of dealing with her theatrics, sympathy for her just didn't come naturally.

They sat down, and he decided to get the niceties out of the way. "You look very lovely today, Mother." It was true, actually. She could be a striking woman when she put her mind to it. Sure, she looked all of her sixty-two years, but she still exuded a classic beauty, with her fine facial features, slender frame, and fashionable garments. Even her hats, big and gaudy though they may be, were in vogue, if the front covers of the latest fashion magazines were any indication. Last winter, she'd put one under his nose while he'd been reading the *Paris Post-Intelligencer* in front of the fireplace. "You see?" she'd said, a finger on the photo. "My hats are very much in style."

"Purple suits you well," he added.

"Humph. You're the second person to tell me that today."

"Is that so? Who else told you?"

"That busybody Wilma Whintley. I saw her in the bank a while ago."

"Ah, Wilma Whintley—or, as Uncle Clarence refers to her, Wilma Windbag."

She actually laughed, although with her gloved hand to her mouth to cover her glee.

"Why don't you smile more, Mother? It becomes you."

"I do smile when inclined, but not for no reason." She looked at her now folded hands in her lap and reclaimed her long face. "I find few things to smile about these days."

"You'd find a great deal to smile about if you got to know Mercy and those little boys we've committed to raise."

She didn't respond but stared off, a melancholy look in her eyes. Probably thinking about the two little boys she'd lost.

Feeling a wave of regret, Sam put an arm over the back of the bench and gave her thin shoulder a squeeze. "You'd be surprised how much they can lighten your spirit. Joseph is smart and talkative, and John Roy is curious and full of energy. Who knows? You might be a balm to each other. They've lost so much, you know—from their parents right down to their toys and the beds they used to sleep on."

"Yes, I know." He thought he detected the slightest softening in her tone. "It's unfortunate. I did tell you to bring them by sometime. I doubt I'd have much to say to them, but they'd probably enjoy it if you showed them around the farm."

"You failed to include Mercy in that invitation."

She sniffed and raised her chin in defiance. "That's because I won't abide an Evans on my property."

"She's not an Evans; she's a Connors."

His mother scoffed. "She will never be a Connors in my book."

He released her shoulder and slid away from her, clasping his hands between his spread legs and leaning forward, elbows resting on his knees. She certainly knew how to dampen the mood.

He waited till his anger settled, then changed topics. "Do you happen to know anything about a relative of ours who might've stolen one of our new kittens?"

"Good heavens, why would anyone do that?"

"You tell me. Whoever it was returned the cat—in a crate, mind you, with a noose around its neck and a threat attached, suggestin' worse things could happen if Mercy and I didn't divorce."

"Sweet blazes! Was the cat dead?"

"No, thank goodness, but I don't like the implications of the note. Somebody's up to no good, and it's gettin' out of hand."

She smoothed an imaginary wrinkle from her skirt. "Well, if you think I had anything to do with it, you can think again."

"Still no idea about who threw the rock through our window?"

He noticed that she didn't answer him as readily this time. "No. I mean, I suppose I did complain to a couple of your cousins about your marriage, but, blessed saints, I never suggested they do you any harm."

"Which cousins?"

"Which? Oh, I don't know. I don't recall."

"Sure you do."

"All right. I was visiting Gilbert and Ella shortly after you and Mercy married, and Frank and George were there with their wives and children. I suppose I stirred the pot a bit."

"You're awfully good at that, Mother—stirring the pot."

"Humph. It's not as if I'm the only one who's unhappy about this ridiculous union. Everyone thinks it's disgraceful. Why, even Mercy's relatives are outraged. Why don't you go inquire of some of them?"

Ignoring her question, he blurted out, "Why'd Persephone distance herself from her whole family?"

Her head jerked up. "Persephone?"

"Your niece."

"Oh, for goodness' sake, I know who she is. It's just that I haven't heard her name mentioned for some time."

"Why'd she leave Paris?"

"She got married. I suppose her husband talked her into it."

"No, she left well before the weddin'."

"Well then, I couldn't tell you. Neither Gilbert nor Ella has much of anything to say about her." She stood, with surprising ease for a woman with a sore back. "It's getting late. I should be returning to the farm."

Sam rose, as well. "You just got here."

"You're the one who told me you couldn't afford much time for visiting. Anyway, I have several food items to put away and chores to tend to when I get home."

He scratched his head and nodded down at her. "Thanks for stoppin' by." He took her by the arm, and as they crossed the street, he noticed that her limp had mysteriously disappeared.

At the hitching post, he unlooped the reins, then helped her into the carriage before handing them up to her.

"Be careful drivin' back," he said, stepping away to give her space to turn the carriage around.

Before tapping the horse with the reins, she glanced down at him with a question in her face. "Whatever made you ask about Persephone?"

He shrugged. "Just curious, I guess."

She nodded, and in her eyes, he thought he detected a wish to say more, but she didn't.

As he watched her drive away, he stood there, thinking how very little he truly knew about his mother.

23

If the hundreds of people milling about Johnson Park were any indication, Mercy would guess the entire population of Paris had turned out for the community picnic. People she hadn't seen in months were there, as were folks she'd never met—young families, older couples strolling hand in hand, women attired in their finest dresses and colorful bonnets, men looking dapper in suits and bowler hats, and children squealing with laughter.

As they walked, Sam made no attempt to hold her hand, but he did keep a possessive, protective hand at the center of her back, a move that both disarmed and charmed her at the same time. The boys ran several steps ahead of them, looking this way and that, nearly bursting with excitement and joy. It was the first Mercy had seen them in such a mirthful mood since the loss of their parents, and she had to believe the crying spell of a few nights ago had accomplished a great deal in releasing their pent-up emotions. It had been a definite turning point for her, as she hadn't cried once since then, or battled any bouts of gloominess. Instead, she'd been making a conscious effort to praise the Lord in everything, to stop questioning His reasons for allowing bad things to happen, and to start trusting Him with all of her heart. She glanced at Sam out of the corner of her eye and silently thanked the Lord for her husband's patience and kindness. His heart seemed a bottomless well of both.

"Mercy! Oh my lands, I'll be a pink-nosed gopher snake, is it really you?"

Mercy stopped and whirled at the sound of the high-pitched female voice. Putting a hand to her brow to shield her eyes from the bright sunlight, she felt her mouth sag open and her eyes pop at the sight of a familiar light-haired, fair-skinned wisp of a woman, holding a little girl who looked to be about a year old. "Joy? Joy Westfall?"

"Yes! Remember me?"

"Remember you! How could I forget my earliest playmate?" The girls had been inseparable in their early years, but Joy had moved away in the summer after sixth grade, around the time Millie's family had come to Paris. Now Mercy gazed at her warm, friendly face, in awe at how little she'd changed. "What are you doing here? Have you moved back to Paris?"

"No, I haven't moved back—yet. I'm visitin' my aunt, who's not doin' too well these days. You know Myrtle Stitt, don't you?"

"Yes, of course. She lives in that little house right next to Paris Evangelical Church."

"That's the one."

"I attend services there, along with my husband and"—suddenly she realized she hadn't made any introductions—"this is Samuel Connors, by the way. Sam, meet Joy Westfall. She's a dear friend from childhood."

Joy smiled. "So, the family dispute's been settled, then?"

Sam chuckled. "Not exactly, but we're workin' on it. I remember the name Westfall…do you have an older brother?"

"I have three brothers, actually—Gordon, Claude, and Willis."

"Ah. Willis is the one I recall. He was around my age."

"All three got hitched and moved far away, much to Mama's despair. My father passed on a couple of years ago, so she's been awful lonely. She's movin' t' South Carolina in November t' live with Claude and his family."

"And where do you live, Joy?" Mercy asked.

"Well, I did live in Indiana, where my—where Annie's, um, father lived, but…let's just say I'm a bit displaced right now. Aunt Myrtle's asked me t' come live with her, but I'm not sure we'd all fit in that little box of a house. I'm thinkin' on it, though. She could use the help, since she's ailin' an' all."

Mercy smiled, her heart aching for Joy's apparent dilemma. "You'd be a great help to her, I'm sure, and she'd love your company."

"I do admit it feels right good to be back."

Joy shifted the little girl to her other hip. By now, John Roy and Joseph were tugging on Sam's sleeves, anxious to be on their way. One could hardly expect five- and six-year-old boys to stand still when there were sack races, relays, balloon tosses, cakewalks, horseshoe competitions, and a myriad of other activities going on around them, not to mention aromas of every description wafting over from the food tables. As if reading her mind, Sam tipped his hat at Joy, then turned to Mercy. "I think I'll take the boys explorin'. What do you say we meet over there by that bench in ten minutes or so?" He gestured at a wooden bench presently occupied by an elderly couple.

"That would be perfect. Joy and I can catch up a bit."

Joy straightened. "Oh, I don't mean t' keep you from your family time."

"No, no, that's fine," said Sam. "You two enjoy your visit. The boys and I will go look around." He grinned and tapped Mercy on the end of her nose. "I'll see you later."

His tone sounded almost intimate, causing a shimmer of joy to shoot up Mercy's spine. He took the boys by the hand, and as they walked away, Joy whispered, "Jumpin' butter beans, Mercy, you've got yourself a good man there."

"That I have." Mercy kept her eyes on the threesome until they melted into the crowd. She gave a slow sigh.

Joy touched her arm. "Aunt Myrtle told me all about your gettin' married and how it come t' be. I was heartbroken to hear about how those boys' parents died." She shook her head. "Such a terrible thing, but at least them sweet little boys got t' stay with you."

Mercy nodded. "Looking back, I suppose it was all part of God's bigger plan. Not that I understand how His plans work, mind you, only that I'm learning to trust Him more."

"Well, I don't know about God's bigger plan. Shoot, I can't say I even believe in God anymore, the way my life's turned out."

"I'm sorry, Joy. I didn't realize things had gone badly for you."

"Oh, they ain't gone all bad. I got my daughter here, and that's what counts most." She tousled the little girl's hair. "Can you say hello, Annie?"

The child gave a toothy smile.

Mercy leaned forward and tweaked her rosy cheek. "Hello there, Annie. Aren't you a pretty little thing?"

Her wispy blonde hair matched her mother's perfectly, and her eyes were the same shade of blue. *My, but they make a striking pair*, Mercy mused. It made her long for a daughter of her own—a foolish notion, considering she and her husband didn't even share a bed. She wondered if they ever would.

"You sure are lookin' pretty, Mercy. Marriage suits you well, I can see."

Mercy felt herself blush. "Thank you, but I was just thinking how lovely *you* look. I don't think you've changed a bit since the last time I saw you."

"Right around then, I'd say. Daddy moved us just after my twelfth birthday."

"You went to Kentucky, right?"

"Yes. He took a coal minin' job, but it wore 'im clear to the bone. He took sick after about six years and lived another three after that. Doctors never did know what kill't him. Mama died a little that day, too. But enough about me! Aunt Myrtle tol' me all about your daddy, an' the awful way he died." She lowered her voice. "I can't help but think it must be a little awkward, you marryin' the very man whose father…."

"I'll admit I didn't see it working at all, at first. Truth told, I didn't want to marry him, but he convinced me it was for the best."

Her eyes brightened. "So, he wooed you, did he?"

"Good gracious, no, nothing like that. What he did was make me see the practical side of things. He saved the boys from the fire, you know."

"Aunt Myrtle told me."

"Well then, there was already a sort of bond with the boys; that, and his desire to get out from under his mother's thumb. I don't think anyone could blame him." She leaned close and whispered, "The woman despises me."

Joy screwed up her face. "I don't know why. You never did anythin' to her."

"It's enough that I'm an Evans. Plus, I 'stole' her son away."

"Oh dear."

The winds swept down and snatched at Mercy's skirt, and she clutched the yellow gingham in her fist. Joy adjusted her straw hat, the brim of which flapped slightly in the breeze. "Well, we really should be gettin' back to Aunt Myrtle's place. I need to make her some lunch and put Annie down for a nap. It was right nice seein' you, Mercy. I hope to run into you again."

Mercy wanted to ask about Annie's father, but if Joy had wanted to talk about him, she would have done so by now. Had she married and divorced, then? Or perhaps never married at all? Mercy knew only that something had caused her life to turn so sour as to make her doubt God. To Mercy's recollection, Joy had been raised by God-fearing parents. "Perhaps you'll come to church tomorrow," Mercy suggested. "It is right next door, after all."

"Oh, good glory, no. I wouldn't want to cause them walls t' cave in."

"But—"

Annie threw her head back and let out a yowl. Joy frowned. "Best get this little one back to Aunt Myrtle's 'fore she throws a fit. She's windin' up for one right now." She leaned forward and kissed Mercy on the cheek. "I hope our paths cross again soon."

"Stop by my house if you get a chance," Mercy called to Joy as her childhood friend hurried off, her somewhat tattered, colorless skirt whipping in the wind. Annie peered back at her over her mother's slender shoulder, and Mercy waved and smiled. The girl wagged a pudgy hand in response.

Mercy turned, spotting her family seated on the bench where they'd agreed to meet. The boys were swinging their legs, licking candy sticks, and talking to Sam. About the same time she started toward them, Sam glanced up and met her eyes.

He was leaving on the morning train to visit his cousin in Nashville, and the reminder brought an unexpected ache somewhere in the region of her heart. It had suddenly occurred to her that she would miss him. Day by day, little by little, he'd been stealing pieces of her heart, and she hadn't recognized it until now.

24

By mid-afternoon, the boys had played most every game, participated in every possible race for children their age, and sampled just about every delectable treat they'd laid eyes on. It seemed the ladies of Paris had been cooking for weeks, if the platters of cookies, candies, cakes, and pies could be counted as proof. Mercy had done her part, contributing several loaves of bread, a beautiful triple-layer chocolate cake, and some jars of strawberry preserves. Each treat cost a few coins, the Paris Women's Club donating the proceeds to charity, and Sam felt as if his pockets were emptying faster than a jackrabbit could shoot across a field.

His stomach felt near to bursting after partaking of the tasty buffet and then indulging in several sweets right along with the boys. Mercy, too, said she'd eaten enough to last her clear into next week. They'd laughed, talked, and enjoyed each other's company as they strolled around Johnson Park, stopping every so often to chat with friends old and new, while the boys joined in a game of tag with some kids they recognized from the neighborhood, then played on the park's seesaws and swings.

Earlier, Sam had seen his mother from a distance. It appeared she'd come with her sister, Sam's aunt Mable, and her husband, Henry. Sam had intended to go say hello to them, and take his bride and the boys along, but his aunt and uncle had left before lunchtime, and he'd lost track of his mother. Now, he located her on the other side of the park, near a cluster of parked buggies, speaking in a rather animated fashion to a woman he didn't recognize from this distance. The woman was accompanied by several others. His mother waved her arms about as she talked, looking downright cross. At one point, she raised her index finger and pointed it directly at the woman, who mirrored the gesture.

Sam nudged Mercy in the side. She'd been watching the boys as they frolicked with their friends.

"Hm?" She turned to him.

"See my mother over there?"

She scanned the area. "Yes."

"Do you recognize the people she's talkin' to?"

Mercy squinted. "That looks like…Aunt Aggie. Look, there are my cousins on the sidelines, including her son Clyde and his wife, Effie. Oh, and there's Davey and Bart, my uncle Albert's boys."

"Oh, great, look who's joinin' 'em."

"Who?" She blinked, trying to focus. "Is that George? And Frank? Your mother's bodyguards?"

"You got that right. Looks like we could be in for a little trouble."

"Oh, no." Mercy started toward them, but Sam snatched her by the arm and pulled her back.

"Let's give it a minute or so and see how this plays out. We don't want our presence makin' matters worse."

"That's true." She cast a hurried glance at the boys. "Maybe we should just go home. I don't want John Roy and Joseph exposed to some kind of loud clash with our relatives."

"Nor do I, but let's just wait a bit." He saw that a few inquisitive citizens had started gathering around the assemblage of Evans and Connors folk. "Ugh. Just what we *don't* need—a batch of nosy people eggin' 'em on."

Moments later, another man entered the scene. "That's my uncle Fred," Mercy whispered. "Aunt Aggie's husband. He can be pretty tetchy when rubbed the wrong way." Fred sidled up to his wife and joined in the discussion.

"Oh, boy."

"What do you suppose they're talking about?" Mercy asked.

"We can only imagine. My mother's mad about somethin', but that's nothin' new. She looks like a boilin' kettle whose top is about to blow."

Mercy giggled. "Uncle Fred and Aunt Aggie aren't any better. Saints above, I've heard those two go at each other a few times. When I was about ten, I saw Aunt Aggie throw a frying pan at Uncle Fred. He ducked just in time, and the pan hit the wall and broke a picture. Then Aunt Aggie started scolding Fred for moving."

That evoked a chuckle from Sam.

Just then, something truly incendiary must have been spoken—perhaps a scathing insult or a vile accusation—for the voices rose in volume, and fists started flying. The crowd surrounding the conflict swelled faster than a four-alarm fire, forming a human ring that blocked Sam and Mercy's view. The next thing they knew, someone screamed, and then several shouts erupted, as a dust cloud arose from the burgeoning circle.

Sam turned worried eyes on Mercy. "Stay with the boys," he told her. "I've gotta get over there." And he took off at a run.

❧

"Did you really have to get right in the middle of it?" Mercy dipped a cloth in warm, soapy water, preparing to tend Sam's swollen eye, his bloodied nose, and his lower lip, which had already doubled in size since the fight. It had ended half an hour ago, with a single gunshot fired skyward from Sheriff Marshall's pistol. With the aid of eyewitnesses, the sheriff had rounded up the key participants and hauled them off to jail, and then he'd declared the community picnic over, demanding that everyone pack up and head home.

Fortunately, the festivities had already begun to wind down, or Mercy would have felt even worse. As it was, she felt partially responsible for the ruckus, since the spat had reportedly centered on her wedding. Sam's mother had been lucky enough to escape jail, sent home with a reprimand instead. Mercy so wished the sheriff would lock her up for a few days, just to teach her a lesson; but then, he would have to do the same with Aunt Aggie.

Mercy didn't know whether to be mad at Sam for joining in the fight or relieved that things hadn't gone worse for him. He could have landed himself on one of Doc Trumble's cots again, perhaps even sharing a room with her cousin Bart, who'd been knocked backward into a tree trunk and suffered a head wound requiring several stitches. Now, wouldn't that have been a dandy fix?

"And sit still," Mercy said, dabbing at his head. "I'm trying to get the bleeding to stop."

"I am sittin' still."

"No, you're squirming."

"I'm not squirmin'. And, for your information, I didn't get right in the middle of it. I got pulled in."

"Couldn't you have resisted?"

"When your cousin Bart threw a punch at my face, I had no choice but to deliver him a good blow in return. A man's got to defend himself."

"No choice? I think not."

"Even the Bible says 'an eye for an eye,'" he muttered through his swollen lip.

"I see you failed to read further," Mercy retorted. "It goes on to say, '*Whosoever smiteth thee on thy right cheek, turn to him the other also.*' A couple verses further down, it says, '*Ye have heard that it was said, Thou shalt love thy neighbor, and hate thine enemy: but I say unto you, Love your enemies, and pray for them that persecute you; that ye may be sons of your Father which is in heaven.*' That is the Christian way, Samuel Connors."

"You've got those verses memorized?"

Mercy laughed. "You have no idea how many times I've recited that passage to myself over the years. Memorizing it came easy."

"So, you're sayin' I was supposed to stand there and let your cousins beat me senseless?"

"No, silly, you were supposed to get yourself out of there and leave the whole mess to Sheriff Marshall to sort through."

"There were people gettin' hurt. I had to help defend 'em."

"Your family, you mean. You had to defend your family against my family. Is that what you're saying?"

"No, I—I don't know exactly what I'm sayin'. Oh, I hate this feud."

"No more than I."

"I don't want it comin' between us."

She continued dabbing at his wounds, unsure how to respond to his comment. His breath, warm and feathery, brushed over her as she worked, and she was keenly aware of his blue eyes examining her at close range. She swiveled her body to avoid his gaze, dropped the cloth into the bowl of soapy water on the table, and then wrung it out again. "A Christian seeks to exist peacefully with his enemies," she said, applying pressure with the cloth against a cut above his eyebrow that refused to stop oozing blood.

He jerked when she hit a tender spot, and she didn't bother apologizing. She'd suggested on the way home that he go see Doc Trumble, but, of course, he wouldn't, his excuse being that Doc already had his hands full. For once, she thanked the Lord she no longer worked at the clinic. Injuries from senseless brawls were her least favorite ailment to treat, even though she knew not to show any bias when assisting the sick and wounded.

"It was nice of Dora Hansen to offer to watch the boys for a while," he said, breaking into her thoughts. "What did they say about the fight?"

"Thank goodness, they weren't even aware of it. Dora noticed it right off and came over to tell me she'd take them home, as her family had just finished packing up to leave. The boys were so excited for the chance to go home with the Hansens, they missed all the racket, and since Dora's husband had parked his rig on the opposite side of the park, they had no reason to look over there. They will, however, see your face as soon as they walk in the house. What do you plan to tell them?"

"I guess I'll tell 'em I messed with the wrong people."

"Be prepared for a bunch of questions." She stepped back to study his wounds. "That's about as much as I can do for you, except I think I'll put a bandage on that cut above your eyebrow. How did you get that?"

"Compliments of Cousin Bart."

Mercy grimaced. "I suppose you're responsible for his falling backward."

He looked only a little sheepish. "He made me mad, doggone it."

She shook her head, making a tsking sound with her tongue, and reached for the bowl. "I'll go empty this and get the bandages." Before she could pick it up, he caught her by the wrist and turned her to face him, coiling his free hand around her other wrist. She inhaled sharply at the contact, and a shiver of awareness climbed up her back, her heart hammering hard against her chest. Slowly, he drew her closer, in between his knees, and then closed his legs, so that his thighs held her captive. It would have been easy to flee, but her feet stayed planted in place.

"I'm sorry for makin' matters worse," he said softly.

"I didn't say you made matters worse."

He nodded. "Well, if it's any consolation, I didn't go over there with the intention o' fightin'. I wanted to do what I could to stop it. But I guess you're right; I should have left the whole matter in the sheriff's hands, even though it took 'im a good six or seven minutes to reach the scene. I'm just glad nobody else pulled out a gun. I saw a few who had 'em at the ready."

She sucked in a breath. "The Lord knows we don't need any more bloodshed. Does anybody know how this ruckus actually began? And is it true that our marriage sparked it?"

"To an extent, from what I gathered. I don't even want to know what they said about us, but I'm assumin' the conversation between my mother and your aunt was the kindlin' for the fire, and then folks started losin' their wits and throwin' punches for no good reason." Sam sighed. "Oh, Mercy. What're we gonna do with them?"

She smiled. "It's what they're going to do with us that has me more worried."

In a quick and fluid move, before she had a chance to resist, he pulled her onto his lap, and her pulse started thrumming in her throat. Why, she couldn't remember the last man whose lap she'd sat on—her pa's, probably, when she'd been a little girl. Sweet dancing Moses, what to do with her racing heart?

"Has anyone ever told you you're as temptin' as a bowl full o' candy?"

A nervous giggle rolled out of her. "Good glory, no!"

"Glad to hear it. I wanted to be the first."

With their faces almost touching, Mercy swallowed, realizing she'd run out of words. Matter of fact, her mind had emptied of everything, including the whole incident at the park. All of her concentration was required for the act of taking a normal breath. *Heaven help me, what's happening? Is he going to…? No, he wouldn't. But then….*

He used a finger to tip up her chin. "Mercy?"

"Yes?" Her voice had a quivering quality she'd never heard before.

"Have you ever been kissed?"

"W-well, yes. You kissed me at our wedding, remember?"

"That wasn't a real kiss."

"It wasn't?" She bit her lip to stifle her inner excitement.

"No, I'm talkin' about a real kiss. Has anyone ever given you a…you know…romantic kiss?"

"I'm embarrassed to answer that."

"Don't be."

"Then…I'll admit no one has, but if you're thinking about kissing me now, well, I don't know if we should. I mean, I thought this marriage was supposed to be just an arrangement."

"It *is* just an arrangement." She didn't know why his response disappointed her. What had she hoped he'd say—that he wanted to change that?

"Oh."

"But that doesn't mean we can't kiss, does it?"

"I don't know. Aren't there rules about that?"

He tilted his head and narrowed his eyes, as if deep in thought. "I should think we could make up our own rules, startin' with kissin'. Let's say that kissin' is officially okay within a marriage in name only."

"Just kissing?" She wanted to make sure to get it straight in her mind.

He gave one quick nod. "Yep, just kissin'. Nothin' beyond that."

She considered him for a moment while one of his thumbs caressed her wrist, making her pulse quicken the more. Trying to appear as though it didn't affect her, she shrugged. "I suppose that'd be fine." She snagged a quick breath and lifted her chin a tad higher. "Go ahead, then."

Without hesitation, he leaned forward, and for a moment, they tried to decide which direction to approach from and where to put their noses. It was awkward and amusing at the same time. Her breathing sounded funny, coming out all rough and uneven, and it mortified her that he probably heard it. At first, their lips just barely touched, and the contact made her pull back. "Oh, your lip. It must hurt."

Even with the swelling, he managed that crooked smile she'd come to love, and raised his hands to cup her face. "I'll take that chance." He drew her closer, till the tips of their noses touched, and a tingling sensation raced clear to her twitching toes.

Their lips met for all of three seconds before she drew back again and looked at him, even more breathless than before. "Wow," she whispered.

He chuckled. "That was nothin'."

"There's more?"

This time, he put his arms fully around her, then planted his mouth against hers in a practiced manner—as if he'd kissed a hundred girls before her—and the kiss lingered as their bodies brushed, and she swayed from left to right, experiencing textures and tastes she hadn't known existed. At first, the kiss was almost timorous, two mouths sampling each other. But then it grew in strength, like waves on a sandy shore, as they played at the kiss, her timid hands coming up to splay across his muscled back, her lips teasing his, trying new angles.

She pressed her palms more tightly to his back and settled herself more snugly against his chest, marveling at their differences—she soft, smooth, and pliable, and he hard, rough, and substantial. That knowledge, while not audibly shared, intensified the kiss, and a kind of eagerness she'd never known fired up inside her. *Oh Lord, my husband has turned me into a ball of mush* was the thought that came to her. *Is there any help for me?*

A gentle parting, a searching of eyes, and then a sinking into each other's mouths once more answered that question. Nope, no help. From this point forward, she would forever know a deep, persistent longing.

This wondrous exploring of mouths ended all too quickly, and when he pulled away to gauge her face, she was certain he saw a pink hue that hadn't been there earlier. He grinned, looking rather self-satisfied. "That, my dear, is a kiss."

25

To avoid having to explain the roughed-up condition of his face, Sam had retreated to his bedroom before the boys returned from the Hansens' and even feigned sleep when they knocked on his door. He'd overheard Mercy explaining that he wanted to get some sleep before his trip. It was a shame that he hadn't gotten to wish them good night or rehash the day's events with them, but he figured it was worth keeping them ignorant of his participation in the brawl at the community picnic. Some example he was turning out to be! Hopefully his wounds would fade sufficiently by the time he returned from Nashville on Tuesday. He'd at least had a chance to wake the boys in the early hours, when their room was still dark, and kiss them both on the forehead before heading for the train station.

He'd also kissed Mercy good-bye, although the exchange had in no way compared to the passionate kisses they'd shared the night before. He'd feared that if he kissed her like that again, he wouldn't make it to the train station on time. Good grief, what had gotten into him? The woman had him so entwined around her little finger, he couldn't figure out how to free himself—not that he felt like trying. Still, she'd made it clear she wanted theirs to remain a marriage in name only, so he'd have to keep it that way—even if it killed him.

After making several brief stops along the way to drop off and pick up passengers, the pulsing locomotive hissed to a stop in Nashville a little after ten in the morning. Sam wondered if he'd recognize his cousin Persephone, or if she'd even be waiting for him at the station. He'd sent her a letter, thanking her for the invitation and announcing his plans to arrive on Sunday morning, also assuring her that she needn't pick him up till after church—assuming she and Hank attended. He didn't want to put her out, so he'd offered to stay in a hotel, if that would make matters easier. She hadn't responded to his letter, but then, he hadn't expected her to, since she would have received it just yesterday, or maybe the day before. In retrospect, he probably should've waited to hear back from her, but she'd been so insistent on his coming right away, he'd assumed she wouldn't mind. Besides, after yesterday's fracas, he was even more interested to hear what she had to say on the subject of the feud.

When the train stopped, he straightened his starched collar, tightened the knot in his tie, and buttoned his suit jacket, then ran his fingers through his hair and plopped his hat on his head. He was glad he'd gone to the barbershop a few days ago, taking the boys with him for a long-overdue haircut. His bruised, battered face had gotten him plenty of suspicious stares from fellow passengers; he didn't need scruffy hair, to boot, or Persephone might very well send him straight back to Paris.

He took up his leather bag, hefted the wide strap over one shoulder, and eased his way into the crowded aisle. Behind him, a child whined that he was hungry, and his mother assured him Grandmother would have breakfast waiting. "Will she have pancakes?" "It's a good possibility." "Will Grandpa let me drive his tractor?" "I'm sure he will if you ask nicely."

Sam smiled at the exchange as they moved along at a snail's pace. He lowered his head to look out the window at the platform, where a multitude of folks stood waiting, either to greet incoming passengers with hugs or handshakes or to embark on their own journey. Like the lad behind him, Sam's stomach rattled from hunger. If Persephone didn't meet him at the platform, the first item on his agenda would be locating a diner.

Gripping the steel handle by the door, he climbed down to solid ground and scanned the crowd. No one looked remotely familiar, so he made his way to the sidewalk, then strolled down the platform till he had passed the locomotive, giving him a full view of the town. There, he took in the scents, sounds, and sights of his new surroundings. He hadn't been to Nashville for three or four years, and he noticed a few changes: some newly erected buildings, freshly laid brick streets, and electric wires strung overhead to illuminate the place at night—something Paris still lacked. For a Sunday morning, the place was bustling with activity. There were many people milling about, some standing on street corners, smoking, and others darting across the road, dodging streetcars and horse traffic. Church bells clanged noisily nearby, and a whistle pierced the air as another train chugged into the station, four tracks over. In that moment, Sam decided he much preferred the quieter atmosphere and slower pace of Paris.

With the conductor's raspy pronouncement of "All aboard," the platform crowd thinned a bit as folks embarked. Sam started for the station, thinking he would grab some coffee and a bite to eat. If Persephone didn't show up by then, he'd hire a driver to drop him at the Greves'. He probably should have planned on that from the start. He reached inside his jacket pocket, feeling around for the envelope printed with their address.

"Samuel Connors?"

Startled, Sam turned in the direction of the deep male voice. Approaching him was a tall, dapper-looking fellow dressed in a brown tweed suit, shiny leather shoes, and a bowler hat. If it hadn't been for his pleasant smile, Sam might have assumed the fellow to be pretentious and stuffy.

"Yes?"

The man extended a hand. "Hank Greve. I thought it might be you, the way you were standing there, looking a bit displaced."

"Yes, yes! Nice to meet you." Sam shook his hand.

"Persephone sends her regrets for not coming to the station. She's in a motherly way, and she's suffering from a bit of a weak stomach this morning."

"Oh, I don't mind. I can find a hotel, if that would be better."

"No, Persephone would have my hide if I didn't bring you home straightaway. She's eager to see you."

Sam noticed the man eyeing his bruised face. "Uh, I got in a bit of a scuffle yesterday." He rubbed his swollen jaw. "It looks a lot worse than it really is."

"Well, that's a relief. I'd hate to see the other guy."

He scratched his head just above his temple and gave a sheepish grin. "'Fraid he spent the night at the local medical clinic, but don't worry—you're safe with me. I promise, I was only defendin' myself. I'll tell you and Persephone all about it later."

"I'll be interested to hear about that. By the way, she showed me the letter she sent you, and I told her it was high time she unloaded that weight. Good golly, nobody should have to carry around a secret like that for… what's it been, a dozen years?"

Sam shook his head. "That's the main reason I'm here. She said she had things she wanted to tell me that she couldn't put in a letter."

"She certainly does. Come on, then; my carriage is this way. We'll have to cut across to the other side. Watch your step around all this horse dung. The street cleaners don't come out on Sundays till mid-afternoon. Sorry about the stench. Between that and the suffocating train smoke…well, welcome to Nashville."

Sam chuckled. "I understand."

"You must be famished. Persephone's prepared us a late breakfast, although she had to pause and dash outside. Apparently, it's the bacon that gets to her."

"Oh." Sam allowed himself to imagine, for the briefest moment, Mercy carrying a child—his child—how she'd look with a pregnant belly. Of course, it made for a foolish notion, since the terms of their marriage didn't account for that sort of thing. "Congratulations, by the way," Sam put in. "Is this your first?"

"Yes, indeed. We're a little beside ourselves with enthusiasm. She's not due to deliver till spring, so we're in for quite a wait. It'll be my folks' first grandchild, and they're more than a little excited themselves." Hank gestured to the right, toward a cluster of horses hitched to rigs of assorted sizes. "Persephone's parents don't know, of course. I'm not certain she'll clue them in. They aren't on the best of terms, as I'm sure you're aware."

"Yes, I've heard." Sam transferred his bag to the other shoulder.

"Can I take that for you?"

"No, thank you. I'll manage."

"My carriage is just ahead. It's a short ride to our home."

Sam found his cousin-in-law a likable sort, genial and easygoing. "I'm anxious to see Persephone. It's been years."

"I'm sure you two will have much to talk about. We want to hear all about your new wife, of course. Persephone remembers her, but with that feud and all…well, you know how it goes."

Did he ever. It wouldn't be long now, and maybe—just maybe—Persephone would shed enough light on this ridiculous vendetta to give him a brand-new perspective.

~

Flora descended the church steps, the hot, moist noonday air making sweat droplets form on her brow that would've rolled down her face, had she not had her lace handkerchief at the ready.

"My, my, it's so muggy today," said Matilda Howard, the preacher's wife. "Feels like we might be in for a good drenchin', if those low clouds are tellin' the right story."

Flora put on her best smile for the plump woman. "You're certainly right about that, Mrs. Howard. It's just plain sticky today, but it didn't put a damper on the reverend's fine message, that's for sure." Of course, his sermon had been duller than an old kitchen knife.

"Why, thank you! I'll tell him you said so."

Flora pressed her handkerchief to her forehead.

"My, that was quite the hullabaloo at the community picnic."

"Pardon?" Flora pretended not to hear Mrs. Howard, with whom she had no desire to discuss the events of yesterday. All she wanted to do was tell her to climb to the top of Blue Ridge and jump off.

"I said, that was quite a hullabaloo at the picnic," Mrs. Howard repeated, glancing at Flora from beneath her feather-strewn hat brim. "It's a sad thing indeed that it had t' end on such a sour note."

Flora forced a smile. "Oh, I believe the events of the day had mostly concluded."

"I suppose so, but—"

"I best be getting home, Mrs. Howard. I'm expecting guests for lunch. Good day, now."

Of course, she wasn't expecting a soul for Sunday dinner, but she needed an escape. She made a beeline for her wagon, ignoring the scowls sent from various clusters of her family members still milling about the churchyard. Hadn't she gotten her fair share of menacing glares during the service? She knew they were put out with her over yesterday's fiasco, but why they faulted her for starting it was anyone's guess. If somebody was to blame, it should be that old biddy Agatha Evans, who'd waltzed right up to Flora to announce that her own pie had placed first, while Flora's wasn't even a finalist—as if she'd needed enlightening.

She supposed it hadn't been wise to tell Agatha, in front of God and everybody within earshot, to go bury herself—and to take her pie with her. Insults had been flung back and forth, until someone had struck the first blow—Connors or Evans, Flora knew not. And so it had begun, the infamous altercation that had landed men from both families in either a cell in the sheriff's office or a cot at Doc Trumble's clinic.

Reaching her rig, she loosened the reins from the hitching rail and then walked around her horse to the front, preparing to climb up. She'd planted her foot on the bottom step when a deep, rattly voice called out, "Mornin', Mrs. Connors. Saw your Samuel boardin' the early train. Looked to be the Nashville line."

Bringing her foot back down, she turned and saw old Mr. and Mrs. VanKuiken hobbling toward their wagon, arm in arm. "That so?" she asked.

"Yep," Mr. VanKuiken confirmed. "I was out for my mornin' stroll. I only see'd him from a distance, but it was 'im, sure 'nough, all spiffed up in his Sunday-go-to-meetin' attire. Guess he weren't headin' f'r church, though. He away on business?"

She bit her lip, doing her best to appear unaffected. "I really couldn't say, Mr. VanKuiken. It's not as if I have any bearing on his comings and goings."

"No, no, I s'pose you don't, now that he's married an' all." He tipped his hat at her. "Well, you have yourself a fine day, ma'am."

"And you folks, as well." She put on a smile and watched them pass. Apparently, they hadn't been at the picnic yesterday, or Mr. VanKuiken surely would have brought up the ruckus.

On her drive home, a few drops of rain started to fall, dampening her mood the more. What business did Samuel have in Nashville? Just then, she seemed to recall him inquiring about his cousin Persephone, who, if she wasn't mistaken, lived there. Why on earth would he want to go visit her? She didn't know; but suddenly, it became a most urgent matter that she find out.

⌀

"What we goin' t' eat?" John Roy asked, the second that Aunt Gladys opened the door to usher them all inside.

"John Roy, mind your manners," Mercy chided him gently. "Remember, we're guests in Aunt Gladdie's house."

"Heavens to Betsy, you're family, each one o' you!" Aunt Gladys exclaimed. "And for your information, we're havin' beef an' potatoes. Can't you smell it?"

Mercy inhaled. "It smells wonderful. Why is it that everybody else's cooking always smells better that your own?"

Aunt Gladys laughed as she waddled toward the kitchen. The boys bent down to untie their shoes, then pulled them off and set them in two neat pairs against the wall, just as Mercy had taught them to do. The notion that they were beginning to settle into a routine with her and Sam made her so grateful. Not that she wouldn't have given anything to have her friends back, but she was thankful they were adjusting to their new reality.

In light of the way the picnic had concluded, she'd decided to join her aunt, uncle, and several other relatives for the service at Paris Lutheran Church. With Sam gone, it just felt safer that way. Besides, he himself had suggested it. Still, she had to admit to feeling a bit misplaced in Aunt Gladys's church.

Sam had told her he'd miss her and the boys, making her expect something more than the parting peck he'd given her—nothing compared to the gloriously sweet kisses they'd shared last night. It made her wonder if he'd enjoyed them as much as she—and whether he'd ever kiss her with such abandon again. After all, he'd made it clear he wanted to maintain a marriage in name only.

Gladys peeked around the corner while tying on her apron. "Won't be too long 'fore we eat, darlin's. Everybody make y'rselves at home. Matter o' fact, why don't y'all go upstairs and unpack? You can freshen up in the washroom, if you like."

"We'll do that, Aunt Gladdie, and then I'll come right back down to help you get things ready."

"Oh, ain't much to do, really. Table's already set—I did that before church—and the meal's almost done. You just go on now and get settled in."

They enjoyed friendly chatter during the meal, both Gladys and Mercy making a point to avoid the topic of yesterday's clash of fists in the boys' presence. Thankfully, no one had brought it up with Mercy after church, for she wouldn't have known how to respond. She felt just as much in the dark as everyone else about what had transpired between Aunt Aggie and Flora Connors. Only one thing was certain: Tempers had flared and sparks had flown.

After a dessert of apple pie to round out the yummy dinner, the boys carried their plates to the sink and then, with Mercy's permission, headed outside to play on the swings. It was such a pleasant day, now that the rain had passed and the sun had come out.

If only she could crawl out of this hopeless pit of loneliness and longing for her husband.

26

*O*ver a late breakfast, Sam relayed the most recent family news to a curious Persephone. Of course, her first question had to do with the brawl on Saturday, the evidence on Sam's face prompting plenty of questions. She expressed sadness that the feud had escalated, and he thought she might elaborate—perhaps decide it was time to share her "secret"—but she remained mum on that, instead changing the topic to his marriage and the events leading up to it. She asked all manner of questions about Joseph and John Roy. After that, she inquired about the latest happenings around Paris.

All in good time, he told himself. Perhaps she was having second thoughts about sharing the real reason she'd invited him to Nashville. He could respect that. Either way, he found himself doing most of the talking, answering her myriad of questions. He noticed that she made no mention of her parents, Gilbert and Ella, nor did she inquire after her brothers, Frank and George.

After breakfast, Persephone stood and began clearing the table, telling Sam and Hank to stay put. So, the two got to know each other better. Hank had grown up the son of a preacher in Rochester, New York, and the family had moved to Nashville when his father accepted a position at a

213

Presbyterian church. It was there that he'd met Persephone. She'd left home at seventeen, with nothing but a few dollars in her pocket. After five days of searching for work, hungry and destitute, she'd somehow found herself on the front steps of his father's church. His parents had taken her in for a few weeks, until they'd found her a home with a kindly older couple whose children had grown. She'd taken a job at a neighborhood grocery, and her employer, finding she was clever with numbers and quick to learn, soon put her in charge of the books. She'd started attending the Presbyterian church, where she surrendered her life to God. Not long after, she grew a heart for children and started teaching Sunday school.

"From the moment my parents took her in, I knew I'd marry her someday," Hank said. "She didn't have much to say to me, early on; truth is, she admitted later to not even liking me much. Of course, I eventually won her over with my charm." He laughed. "I just couldn't keep my eyes off of her. Here she was, a young woman who'd left home for lack of acceptance, and she was more mature and loving than any well-adjusted woman I'd ever met. My parents loved her, too, mostly because of her effect on my church attendance." He winked. "My motives for wanting to go were a bit different from what they would have preferred, but I eventually got my spiritual life straightened out, thanks to Persephone's example."

Ten minutes later, Persephone rejoined them but almost immediately excused herself again, clapping a hand over her mouth and dashing out the back door.

Hank shrugged. "Like I said, she's been doing this off and on. We've started keeping a pail right next to the bed, for when…you know, she can't make it outside in time."

"Maybe you should go check on her," Sam suggested.

The fellow gave a nervous grin. "You don't mind?"

"No, 'course not. Please, go."

Hank nodded and pushed back in his chair, then hurried out the back door, leaving Sam alone at the dining room table, sipping his coffee and studying the pictures on the wall. *I eventually got my spiritual life straightened out.* Sam chewed on the phrase as he sat there, tapping his fingers on the side of his coffee mug. He was glad he'd stuffed his Bible in his satchel and meant to take time to read from it before bed tonight.

Around mid-afternoon, Persephone emerged from her bedroom, claiming to feel better, but about the time they all prepared to embark on a sightseeing tour around town, she took sick once again. Later, while skimming through a book in the living room and listening to poor Persephone retch up what few bites of supper she'd managed to eat, Sam acknowledged that this trip hadn't quite lived up to his expectations. Something compelled him to pray about it. "I know You've brought me here for a reason, Lord," he whispered. "Please show me how to trust You fully. I believe Persephone holds a secret that might help end the feud—or at least give it meanin'. So, if You want me to learn this secret, please give Persephone the wherewithal to share it. Above all, Lord, Your will be done." It might have been the most heartfelt prayer he'd uttered, and it was certainly the first time he'd offered his request right back to God in surrender, and the realization brought him a deep, surpassing sense of calm.

When he awoke the next morning, somewhat confused about his surroundings, Sam blinked several times to clear his sleepy head, as the first powerful rays of sunlight cast their golden glow through the window in the little room he'd been assigned. He'd slept as well as could be expected, for someone who'd spent the night on an unfamiliar, lumpy bed, with an open window letting in all the sounds of nighttime—barking dogs and yowling cats, the clip-clop of horses' hooves, the chugging of trains passing through town, and the occasional hoot of an owl. Each noise was nothing new; he'd heard them all on the hot summer eves in Paris, when the air was still and the windows open. But they somehow reverberated in a whole new way in Nashville, making him lonesome, missing Mercy and the boys.

He stretched his arms skyward, then breathed in deep and threw off the lightweight blanket and sheet. Sitting up, he lowered his feet to the floor, and his right heel brushed against something. He bent over and retrieved his Bible. Just before snuffing out the kerosene lamp and drifting off to sleep the night before, he'd read until he couldn't keep his eyes open, stopping midway through the thirteenth chapter of 1 Corinthians. The last thing he recalled reading was something about love not seeking its own way or being provoked. The passage had made him think about the feud, and how it ultimately stemmed from someone not getting his own way. Selfishness—that's what the whole thing boiled down to; that, and utter lack of love and kindness.

Somewhat refreshed, he stood and stretched again, then padded barefoot across the room to the washstand, glancing at his reflection in the mirror. He groaned. The bruises had started to turn a sickening shade of green, and the cut above his eye remained red and puffy.

At breakfast, Persephone looked like a different person, even had a healthy glow about her. "I'm so sorry about yesterday," she said for at least the tenth time, sitting across the table from him in the dining room, nibbling on dry toast and taking small sips of steaming tea.

He waved his wrist. "No need to apologize, Persephone. Really. I've enjoyed gettin' to know your fine husband." Talking with Hank on the front porch the evening before, Sam had learned that he had a contract with the Tennessee Central Railway Company to transport passengers between the station and local places, such as hotels and steamboat landings, via the horse-drawn omnibus. This he did four days out of seven. When he wasn't working, he attended class at the Peabody College for Teachers, aiming to earn his teaching certificate by the end of next year and, after that, put out his feelers for a job at a country school. "I'm a small-town boy at heart," he'd said with a low chuckle. "'Course, Persephone would love to go back to Paris someday—but that is not to be."

Persephone fingered the rim of her cup and smiled, and Sam recognized for the first time her Connors smile and nose. She was a real beauty, with her golden locks tied back in a bun, a few stray strands falling around her face, framing her high cheekbones.

"He is a fine man, my Hank. He was sorry he needed to work today, but he's trying to put in some extra time, in hopes that his boss will show a little leniency, should the baby decide to come on a day he's assigned to work. We'll have to wait and see how that goes."

Sam nodded. "And what about you? Hank said you're still keepin' books for Appleton's Grocery Store. Guess I wasn't aware you'd keep workin' in… your…um, condition."

She tossed back her head and laughed, the sound putting him in mind of church bells—and his aunt Ella. He still wondered what had caused the rift in their relationship.

"My 'condition,' as you put it, is not all that delicate. I have my days, but those are becoming fewer and farther between. Yesterday was rather out of the ordinary. As for my job, I don't work on Mondays, anyway, and I told Mr. Appleton not to expect me tomorrow until after your departure."

"I was hopin' to catch a ride with Hank when he heads for work, so I should be off pretty early."

"I'm sure that will work perfectly."

They both sipped their beverages, and then Sam spoke again. "You have a laugh much like your mother's." Her blue eyes took on a darker hue. "I'm sorry. Should I not have mentioned her?"

She set her cup down, then gathered the crumbs from her toast into a neat little pile on the white tablecloth. "No, of course not. It's just…I'm disheartened every time I think of her, and the way we parted. It was more my father who chased me off, but Mama had to go along with him. I've written her a few times, but her replies have always been brief. I'd like to mend the broken fences, especially once the baby comes, but I think it will take a miracle."

Sam hesitated. "Why is that, if I may ask? I know you left home as a young girl. Hank told me the whole story of how you landed on the steps of his father's church."

"Ah, so he told you about that, did he?" Her eyes regained some of their usual twinkle. "I suppose he also told you how he loved me at first sight, while I could barely stand him."

He chuckled. "Somethin' along those lines, yes. He said his family took you in for a time, until you moved in with an older couple."

"Yes, the Thompsons, such lovely people. Hank and I visit them as often as we can." She fixed her gaze on something over his shoulder. "Hank has a wonderful family. I absolutely adore them." She smiled down at her stomach. "This baby will have the best grandparents."

"And what about your parents? Don't you want them to know their grandchild?"

Moistness collected in the corners of her eyes. He had some sort of dadburned power for making females cry. He reached clumsily across the table and touched her arm. "Don't bother answerin' that."

She sniffed and straightened her shoulders. "It's fine. Gosh, I should have known I'd get emotional." She giggled and wiped her eyes. "To answer your question, yes, I'd like our baby to grow up knowing both sets of grandparents. But Mama and I, we've never gotten on too well. She had me at forty-three, and it was no secret she considered me a surprise—an unwanted one. I was more of an annoyance to Papa. He'd raised boys and didn't know what to do with me, I think. He didn't really want me out in the barn, and I wasn't much use to him in the house, except to help Mama prepare his meals and to hand him his evening paper." She pursed her lips. "I can't say I recall one decent conversation with my father, unless you count the scoldings he doled out on a regular basis. I couldn't please that man to save my life."

A wave of empathy came over Sam. He'd grown up feeling much the same—unwanted and ignored. But this was not about him, and so he kept the observation to himself. He tried to phrase his words with care, not wanting to push for fear she'd stop talking.

"So, when you reached an appropriate age, you decided t' take off?"

She nodded and started fumbling with a cloth napkin, staring at her fingers as she worked the fabric. "There was a pivotal moment when I made that decision. Something happened that just affirmed my need to leave. I know you're curious…after all, it's why I asked you to come here in the first place. High time I got on with it, right?"

27

$\mathcal{S}$am held his breath. He couldn't find his tongue, so he just gazed across the table at Persephone, hands crossed in front of him, willing her to continue.

"At the dinner table one night, I raised some questions about the feud between our family and the Evanses. I'd been curious for years and needed answers. And for the first time, Papa actually told us how it all got started, with the property dispute in the early 1830s, which sparked decades of fighting—everything from barn burnings to fistfights, such as the one you found yourself tangled up in the other day."

Sam touched his jaw and found it still tender and somewhat swollen. "Yeah, I knew all that. Keep goin'."

"Well, in the summer of eighty-four, everything came to a head with the fatal argument between Uncle Ernest and Oscar Evans, and I'd always wondered what had caused it. Papa told us that, according to a witness at the trial, Oscar Evans accused your father of deliberately fashioning ill-fitting shoes for his horse, causing the animal to go lame and, ultimately, to die. Other accusations were flung back and forth, and then, allegedly, Oscar made some incendiary remarks about your mother."

A sickening sensation churned in Sam's gut. "My mother?" So far, no other part of Persephone's account had come as a surprise. He'd sat through most of the court hearings and heard almost every testimony. "That's news to me, Oscar mentionin' my mother in the dispute. I wonder what he said, and why it didn't come out in court."

"Papa said it came from a disreputable source—old Solomon Turner, Iris Brockwell's caretaker."

"Why should Solomon Turner be considered disreputable?"

Her gaze rested steady on him. "Let's be honest, Samuel—who is going to listen to a former slave? It's unfortunate but true. Apparently, Judge Corbett ruled his word unreliable, thereby disallowing it in court."

Anger welled up in him like hot lava. "That's outrageous."

"Of course it is. Anyway, more than one witness testified that a drunken Oscar Evans took the first swing at your father, and that your father swung back but missed. Then Oscar took another swing and hit your father's jaw. That's where the self-defense plea started, even though Oscar was not in possession of a gun. Papa says that Mr. Turner, who'd been standing behind a crate of onions in front of Joe's Market, reported overhearing Oscar slander Aunt Flora. Papa wouldn't tell me what was said, only that it was a pack of lies. At any rate, that's when your father drew his gun, and Oscar rushed at him…and was shot. Witnesses reported that Uncle Ernest blew the smoke from the muzzle of his gun with a gleeful smile when Oscar went down."

"I recall that detail from the trial." It had sickened him then, and it sickened him now.

"Of course, you know the rest of the story—how the jury handed down a guilty verdict for first-degree murder, given the fact that he could have walked away but didn't." She gazed down at her lap, her lips pressed together in a straight line.

Sam sat in silence, wanting her to proceed.

She entwined her fidgety fingers, clasping her hands, and briefly fixed her eyes on the ceiling before meeting his gaze once again. "Now comes the part that prompted me to leave home, once and for all."

"I'm listenin'."

"I told my family about something I'd witnessed at your house when I was ten years old. I'd never told a living soul, but for some reason, after hearing Papa talk about the feud that night, I decided I couldn't guard the secret another second."

Sam's brow was creased so deeply, it almost pained him.

"Mama had sent me to deliver a basket of eggs to your house. It was a hot day in June, and I remember arriving in a sweat after the mile-long walk and wanting nothing more than a drink of cold water. I didn't see anyone around, other than the foreman, working on a wheel of his rig over by the barn. He didn't see me, as his back was turned in my direction.

"I walked up the porch steps and knocked on the door, but no one answered. I waited several seconds, then knocked again—still no one. I was just going to leave the eggs on the porch, but then I figured they ought to go in the icebox, and besides, there was the matter of my thirst. I didn't think Aunt Flora would mind if I put the eggs away and then got myself a drink of water.

"As soon as I stepped inside, I heard laughter coming from upstairs. I recognized your mother's voice and thought I would say hello, so I laid the eggs on a table near the door and walked up the staircase. What I saw next...." She stopped, unclasped her hands, then quickly squeezed them together again, swallowing hard. "It was a shock, to say the least."

Sam didn't realize till that moment that his heart had started racing. He swallowed, too, but a lump in his throat made it painful. "What, exactly, did you see?"

Persephone kept her eyes lowered. "I stopped outside your parents' bedroom door and peeked inside, and saw Aunt Flora...kissing a bare-chested man. And it wasn't Uncle Ernest."

"What?" Now, instead of racing, Sam's heart stopped. "Not my father?"

She met his gaze, nodding solemnly. "I jumped back from the door, but they didn't hear me, so engrossed they were in what they were doing. I don't know why, but something compelled me to sneak another peek. This time, I recognized the man. It was Oscar Evans."

In one fluid move, Sam jumped out of his chair, knocking it against the wall with a loud racket. Fingers splayed across the tabletop, he glared at Persephone with such intensity that she looked away again. "What are you sayin'?" The anger in his voice shocked even him, so it was no wonder Persephone lurched back, her eyes widening to boulder-sized spheres.

She blinked, regaining her composure. "I believe your mother and Oscar Evans were having an affair."

"That's impossible!" he bellowed. "She—she hated him! He was her mortal enemy. I don't see how it could have possibly been him."

"But it was, Samuel." She kept her voice low and calm. "I had seen him pass by our house when I was outside hanging clothes on the line. I knew his horse…and, Samuel, that same horse was grazing in the barnyard at your house that day. I remember, because his horse was dappled; your parents kept only chestnuts and sorrels."

Sam completely lost all ability to speak—even breathe, for that matter. He turned and bent to right his chair, then stood there, gripping the back of it and staring down at his cousin. Then, scratching the back of his head, at last he found his tongue. "So, you told your parents?"

"No! I couldn't. It seemed too vile a thing to speak of, one of those things you want to hide deep in your soul and pretend you didn't witness. And that is exactly what I did, for years—until that night at the dinner table. I was sixteen, and I'd carried the secret so long, it had eaten a huge hole in me. Anytime we had a family gathering, I wanted to confront Aunt Flora. And when I heard family members lashing out with utter distaste for the Evans family, I'd glance at her and watch her nod in agreement, with her face all twisted into a frown that seemed genuine to everyone but me.

"Don't ask me why I chose that particular night to reveal the truth to my family. I just couldn't keep it in another moment." She blinked somberly. "How I wish I had."

He told himself to breathe, and so he sucked in a cavernous breath through his nostrils, still gripping tight to the back of the chair, needing to steady himself as visions of his mother and Oscar Evans galloped through his head. "What happened?"

Persephone looked down at her lap. "They accused me of making it up—said I was looking for attention. Papa banged his fist on the table, calling me a spineless liar; Mama leaped up and rushed out of the room; and my brothers both shrieked vicious things at me. Frank raised his hand, and I believe he would have hit me, had Papa not commanded him to sit back down. They all defended Aunt Flora, insisting she would never do anything of the sort, that she and Uncle Ernest had a perfect marriage, and on and on.

"Oh, Samuel, it was dreadful. After that night, no one would speak to me—not even Mama. I became invisible, most likely at Father's orders. I couldn't believe they gave no credence whatever to my story, but I suppose I should have expected as much. They didn't think I had the capacity to keep quiet about something like that for so many years. If you want the truth, I think they hated the idea of letting go of the feud. The very notion of the tables turning on their reasons for its existence fed their fury the more, only now they focused it on me, as well, and they wanted me gone.

"So, right after my seventeenth birthday, I packed my bags, left a note on the kitchen table, and walked out the door, taking what little money I had to my name, and headed for Nashville, with no specific plan, just a belief that I would find work in a city that size.

"I did send Mama a few notes, the first to let her know where I was, and then a few other bits of correspondence. In her replies, she never once asked me to return; in fact, she said Papa wouldn't hear of it." She paused. "I've kept up with Adelaide Lawson. She wrote me about the vandalism done to Mercy's property shortly after you married."

Sam nodded. "It was unusual, for sure. Someone upended the porch furniture and two planters, and shattered a window, to boot."

Persephone shook her head. "I hope you weren't home at the time."

"No, thank the good Lord. Happened on a Sunday mornin', while we were at church."

"A Sunday morning, you say?"

"Yep."

"Did you report it to the authorities?"

"Yeah, but the sheriff doesn't have any leads, far as I know."

Persephone chewed her lip pensively. "Do you know if he's questioned my brothers?"

"Frank and George? I don't know. Why do you ask?"

Persephone sighed. "Because I have a hunch they're the ones who did the deed. They rarely attend church—at least, they never used to come with us—and in their adolescent years, they spent many a Sunday morning playing pranks on various neighbors. Turning things upside down, from potted plants to doghouses, was their signature."

"My own cousins?" Sam seethed like a boiling pot. At present, he did not have a scrap of godly love for his messed-up family. "They should have known it was too late to change my mind about Mercy after I'd said 'I do.' What's wrong with those idiots? Did they actually think vandalizin' our property would accomplish anything?"

"I know you're angry, and rightfully so, but please try not to do anything rash until you pray about this matter."

Pray? He couldn't even think straight, let alone pray with all this rage surging through his veins.

⌒

Joseph and John Roy couldn't stop bouncing around as they waited at the train station for Sam's return on Tuesday. They'd been gingerly hopping over cracks on the platform, trying to avoid touching them, as if doing so would scald the bottoms of their shoes.

"Will Sam be on this train?" Joseph asked.

"He surely will," Mercy answered, her own heart jumping with anticipation for getting that first glimpse of her husband. Yes, she wanted to know what, if anything, he'd learned regarding the feud. More than that, she could hardly wait to receive his kiss of assurance that he'd missed her as much as she'd missed him. It had been fun and even relaxing to spend time with Aunt Gladdie, but it would be good to get back to her cozy home and play at being a family again, even if it was the unconventional sort.

Overcast skies threatened rain, and when the train came chugging in, the acrid smoke it expelled meshed perfectly with the drab clouds. Brakes screeched as the big locomotive huffed to a stop, and Joseph and John Roy, typical boys, stood in awe at the sight, as if they hadn't already seen dozens of trains in their short lifetime.

Joseph gave an enthusiastic squeal when the passengers started disembarking. "What door is he gonna come out of?"

"I don't know, darling." Gracious, one would think they hadn't seen him in weeks. Yet she could hardly fault their excitement, considering how her own heart pitter-pattered.

"There he is!" John Roy had spotted him first.

"Where?" Joseph wanted to know.

It took a minute for Mercy to locate him, and by the time she did, both boys had set off on a run. They reached him simultaneously, and when Sam bent to scoop them up in his arms, her heart welled up with a mixture of love, relief, excitement, and perhaps a bit of apprehension. How would he react upon seeing her? She approached slowly, wanting to observe the tender hug he bestowed on the boys. But when his eyes met hers over the boys' heads, and he smiled, suddenly all seemed right with the world.

The ride back to the house was filled with the boys' nonstop chatter, each wanting to outdo the other with tales from their stay with Aunt Gladdie. Mercy barely got in one word, and Sam didn't even try; he just held the reins and kept his eyes on the road, every so often glancing back at the boys to nod and smile, and doing the same with Mercy. He'd embraced her, as well, but she'd immediately sensed something different in him—a certain reserve that put her on edge. To her further disappointment, his kiss had amounted to little more than a peck on the cheek. Had his absence provided him time to evaluate their relationship, perhaps causing him to regret the passionate kisses of the week before?

Once home, the boys piled out of the wagon first, leaping to the ground like little jackrabbits. As usual, Mercy waited in her seat for Sam's assistance. After snagging hold of his satchel, he jumped down and met her on her side, reaching up to help her climb down. She had hoped for two hands at her waist, and maybe a little twirl to make her skirts flare, but no. He merely supported her descent, then turned without a word and walked to the porch, the boys trailing right behind him, still squealing and squawking.

Lunch consisted of sandwiches and soup, and the boys continued their chatter through most of it.

"I should probably go to the shop," Sam said after downing his final spoonful of soup. "Uncle Clarence will be happy to see me."

I'm happy to see you, she wanted to say, but didn't. "Yes, I'm sure he will."

After Mercy excused the boys, they sailed upstairs for their baseballs and handcrafted bats, gifts from a kindly citizen after the fire. They'd forgotten to take them to Aunt Gladys's house and were eager to resume playing with them, hopeful that a few other boys from around the neighborhood would want to join them for a game, even though neither had quite mastered the rules.

When the door shut with a loud *thwack*, Mercy gave a jolt, whether from the noise or her tense nerves, she couldn't say. "Are you going to tell me about your visit with Persephone?"

"What? Yes, o' course, but I better get to work first." He stood and pushed his chair in. "Don't wait on me for supper, Mercy. I need to pay my mother a visit, and I'm not sure what time I'll get back. You don't mind, do you?"

He planned to visit his mother? "No, that's fine," she managed. No way would she let him see her disappointment.

"I just need to talk to her about…some things."

She cleared her throat. "What sort of things, if I may ask?"

"We'll talk later, okay?" He came around the table and planted a light kiss on her head. "Thanks for lunch."

Rather than respond, she sat in the quiet as he crossed the room and slipped out the back door with nary a second glance. Her heart sank clear to her toes.

What on earth had surfaced in Nashville?

28

Sam didn't give Virgil Perry so much as a slight nod when the fellow tipped his hat at him from the barnyard. Nor did he bother to knock. "Mother!" he bellowed, slamming the door behind him. He marched across the braided rug in the entryway to the base of the staircase, his boots echoing through the house with every step on the wood floor, which always shone to perfection. Too bad his mother's life didn't reflect the same sheen. Tarnished—that's what she was. Tarnished, tainted, and two-faced. Well, the jig was up, the charade over, and he meant to tell her so—after he got to the bottom of this mess.

"Mother!"

She appeared at the top of the stairs, an open book in hand. "Well, for heaven's sake, what is all this racket? You don't have to scream. Should I ask you to go back out and come back in after you've settled down? By the way, it's nice to see you, as well."

"Stop with the nonsense and come downstairs," he ordered.

"What? Don't speak to me in that tone."

"I'll speak to you as I wish, Mother. You and I have some serious things to discuss."

"Well, I never! Of course, I'll come downstairs, but not until you apologize for using that angry voice with me."

He bit back a curse word. "Sorry. Now come down here. *Please.*" He tacked on the last word begrudgingly, but only to get her moving.

She huffed. "I suppose that will have to do. Would you like some tea or coffee?"

"No."

"No? You must be really upset, if you won't take my coffee. I have fresh-baked cookies, too."

Though tempted, he had no wish to play into her ploy of hospitality. When she reached the bottom stair, he pointed at the divan. "Sit," he commanded her.

"Oh, my mother's gizzard, your face!" she gasped. "Was that a result of that terrible fight at the picnic?"

"Yes, and don't bother makin' a fuss over it or tryin' to say you had nothin' to do with that—that circus."

She set her book on the coffee table and lowered herself onto the couch, her jaw set in its usual stubborn fashion, her mouth unsmiling. "Well then, did you come to tell me about your little jaunt to Nashville?"

That tripped him up a bit. "What? Who told you I'd gone?"

"Oh, just someone who saw you at the train station on Sunday morning. It doesn't matter. What was your purpose in going?"

"I went to visit my cousin Persephone."

She looked only slightly discomfited by that tidbit. "What in the world prompted you to do that?"

He took a seat across from her but didn't settle back. Instead, he sat forward, feet firmly planted on the floor, elbows resting on his spread knees, hands loosely clasped. "She invited me, and I accepted."

"What would possess her to do that? You barely knew each other growing up."

"She had somethin' to tell me, Mother. Somethin' very important."

"Oh?" She licked her firm lips, and he noticed the harsh lines that wrinkled them, put there by years of frowning. "I'm most interested to hear about it."

He gave a bitter chuckle. "I doubt you'll be once you hear it. I'll just come out with it: I know about your affair with Oscar Evans."

Had he told her his father's ghost stood right behind her, she could not have taken on a whiter hue to her face. Every drop of blood seemed to have drained from her head, moved down her body, and gone right out the toes of her black patent leather shoes. She broke into a sweat, which prompted her to press a handkerchief to her forehead, but it was not enough to ward off the dead faint that followed.

~

Dizzy, sweaty, and disoriented, Flora crawled her way back to consciousness, but the memory of Samuel's dread confession brought on another dizzy spell. How could he possibly know? How had he discovered it? No one knew, certainly not her niece. Why, it had happened so long ago, Flora barely recalled it herself. Even as the thought surfaced, she knew it for a lie. Not a day went by that she didn't think about it—all thanks to Virgil Perry.

"Mother?" The voice at her ear and then the cool damp cloth to her forehead brought her around. She wanted to awaken, but only if it meant what she'd just experienced had been nothing more than a bad dream.

Reality crushed her hopes when she looked and saw Samuel staring down at her with unsympathetic eyes. "Can you sit up now?" Nothing in his tone denoted concern. If anything, her faint had been an inconvenience, for she heard the irritation in his voice.

"Y-yes." She could not bring herself to look him in the eye, so she focused on her lap instead, pressing her palms to the cushion to brace herself, her queasy stomach complicating matters. "H-how did you find out?" She hated that asking the question amounted to an admission of guilt.

"Persephone told me."

"What? But...how could she possibly—"

"She saw you kissin' 'im—in your bedroom, of all places. She was just a little girl at the time, but her memory of that day is as clear as if she saw it yesterday. It's part of the reason she wound up leavin' Paris. Some six years after witnessin' it, she finally decided to break the secret to her family. They refused to believe her and ultimately drove her out."

Persephone had caught them in the act? Flora was mortified. She thought she'd been so careful.

"I really can't believe you did that, Mother," Sam said, his voice dripping with disgust. "It's the picture o' hypocrisy. I can't imagine what will happen when the rest of the family finds out."

A thundering head forced her to lie back down. She hated to show such weakness, but all of her strength had drained out of her, stripping her down to the bone. A tiny, unexpected moan arose from somewhere deep within, and she shielded her face with her arm, as if doing so would also mask her shame. "Are you…going to make the announcement?"

"No. It's not my place."

A particle of relief ran through her. "Good."

"That would be your job."

"What?" Another groan escaped, and she sneaked a peek at him from under her arm. "I couldn't possibly do that."

"You can and you will. You have a lot of wrongs to make right." His voice carried the stiff sternness of a parent censuring a young child.

She swallowed hard, still hiding her face under the fleshy part of her arm. "It's no one's business what happened those many years ago, Samuel."

"My foot it's not!" His shrieking retort gave her a jolt. "How can you say a thing like that? It's everyone's business. Criminy, it's the whole town's business at this point!"

She peeked out from behind her arm and saw him rubbing the back of his neck, his posture rigid and unforgiving. She had an urge to reach out her hand to him, even though she knew he wouldn't take it. He hated her. And how could she blame him? She'd been a terrible mother.

She gathered air into her lungs, then forced herself to sit up once more. Sweat beaded her forehead again, so she took a couple of swipes at it with the damp cloth Samuel had given her. "It wasn't an actual affair," she said quietly.

Samuel glared at her. "You kissed a man you weren't married to. I think that counts as an affair."

"I didn't—I mean, we didn't…you know…sleep together."

"Stop it, Mother. I don't want to know the details of how far you did or didn't go. The whole notion of your even kissin' someone other than Father sickens me."

"What about the notion of your father kissing another woman?"

His shoulders slumped, and he stared at her through disbelieving eyes. "He never would've done that."

She sat a little taller. "The last time your father kissed me was just after the twins died. He tried to comfort me in my loss, but I refused it. I didn't know how to deal with the pain, so I lashed out—at him, at you...at everyone, I suppose. In my grief, I let him slip right out from under me, and slip out he did. He started paying visits to MaryLou Hardwick."

In the span of two seconds, Samuel's face went from whitish to ruby red. "You're tellin' me my father visited a prostitute?"

"If you need confirmation, I have substantiating evidence."

He eyed her warily. "Like what, exactly?"

"I have a letter. Shall I get it?"

He leaned back in the chair, hands gripping the armrests so hard that his fingers turned white as chalk. His blue eyes, deep as the still ocean, took on a darker hue under his thick, tawny brows. My, she'd raised a handsome boy. She hated to see his features contorted by grief, but it was high time he knew the truth.

"We've gone this far," she ventured. "May as well tell you the whole sordid story."

"I told you, I don't want the details."

She rose to her feet. "You may not want the details, Samuel, but now that you know the truth, *I* need to share them. I'm afraid of what will happen to me if I don't."

29

$\mathcal{E}$very nerve in Mercy's body seemed to stand at attention as she paced the floor and wrung her hands, her stomach aflutter. Yes, Sam had said he intended to pay his mother a visit after work, so she hadn't really expected to see him at the supper table, but now the clock read seven thirty, and she'd started fretting that something wasn't right. Not normally one to worry, she took in a few gulps of air to relax herself, then walked to the window for the hundredth time. The boys were in the living room, keeping busy with a large box of wooden blocks. In the last hour, Mercy had needed to step in and settle several minor disputes about who was in charge of their little building project. They rarely argued, and she figured their feisty temperaments were mostly the result of Sam's three-day absence. They'd come to love him very much, evidenced by the way they'd hurtled into his arms at the train station.

He'd acted so strange ever since their reunion that morning, highly distracted, as if he were hiding some deep agitation. What had he learned from his cousin, and how would it affect their relationship? Perhaps the secret concerned Mercy, and his cousin had urged him to seek a quick divorce. Maybe he'd gone to consult a lawyer after working a few hours and visiting his mother—if he'd done those things at all! She recalled his quick little peck on the cheek, and when allowing herself to analyze it, decided it amounted to little more than a friendly, brotherly kiss. Oh, bother! Why on earth had she given in to those heavenly kisses, only to have to come crashing back to reality? They'd agreed on a marriage of convenience, and that's exactly what they had—unless he'd already filed for divorce, in which case the marriage would come to a screeching end.

My, but she could weave a tale when she gave her imagination free rein, and the longer she waited for his return, the wilder the scenario became, until she'd worked herself into a regular whirlwind of emotions. When eight thirty rolled around, she tucked the boys into bed, her worry transforming into outright anger. How dare he make her wait like this! What did he take her for, an old rug he could walk all over?

When she finally heard the door creak open, she checked the clock. Ten minutes after nine. In her newfound anger, she'd taken up a ball of yarn, determined to finish the blanket she'd been working on for what seemed like years. She heard him kick off his boots and sigh.

It took all her willpower not to look up when he entered the room. "You can put the paperwork right there on the table," she said, eyes fixed on the two needles swooping and looping at lightning speed. "After I've had a chance to look it over, I'll sign it, most likely in the morning. Should make for fascinating bedtime reading."

"What?" His voice sounded low and croaky, not to mention weary.

"The papers. I said to put them on the table."

"What papers are you referrin' to?"

She huffed a heavy breath. "Don't pretend you don't know what I'm talking about."

She heard him scratch his head. "I've never seen you knit so fast."

"Well, feast your eyes, then." She cast him the briefest glimpse, not missing a single stitch, and when their eyes connected, she noticed that one of his remained puffy and bruised, but the cut above his eyebrow was healing nicely. She worked faster, winding the yarn around the needle several times, as the pattern called for, then knitting the next stitch with it.

"What're you makin'?"

She sniffed. "A blanket. I've been working at it off and on for months."

"I see. For those cold Tennessee winter nights, I s'pose."

"I suppose."

"I'm sorry I'm so late."

"You might have let me know."

"I did tell you I was goin' out to my mother's."

She knit faster and faster. *Yarn forward and over needle; yarn forward and around needle; through the back loop; together; slip, slip, slip, knit three; slip, slip, purl.* Two big hands covered hers, forcing her to stop. Her shoulders slumped as her fingers stilled. *Here it comes,* she thought. *"Mercy, I want a divorce."*

"Wait on the LORD: Be strong, and let thine heart take courage." Yes, she'd been comforted by Psalm 27 just that morning, but it felt like a million years ago.

He released her hands and stood up straight. "Lay your knittin' aside, Mercy. We have a lot to talk about."

Still unable to bring herself to look at him, she stuffed her needlework in the burlap bag at her feet. "The papers being the number one item, I suspect," she muttered.

His stockinged feet were firmly planted smack in front of her. "What papers?"

"The divorce papers. You may as well come out with it."

"Divorce...what? I don't want a divorce, Mercy. What made you think a thing like that?"

Relief flooded her veins like warm water rippling down a narrow valley. Still, she wouldn't rejoice just yet. She dared glance up at him. "Well, you'd been gone for hours. What was I to think? You got home, ate a quick bite, and then left in such a rush...."

"Mercy—"

She batted at the air. "It's fine, really. I don't know what I was thinking, expecting anything more from a marriage of convenience."

"Come here." He bent down, took her hands in his, and helped her up. Right away, his arms encircled her, his chin resting on her head.

With hesitation, she wrapped her arms around his broad back, not because she wanted to but because it would've been awkward to leave them dangling at her sides.

"You're somethin' else when you get riled." She could almost *hear* his grin, and she didn't appreciate that he found the whole matter amusing.

"I'm sorry," he added. "Will you accept my apology?"

"It depends."

"On what?"

"Your giving me a good reason why you chose your mother's company over ours."

He set her back from him and tipped her chin up with the tip of his finger. "Rest assured that I would have much preferred bein' with you and the boys tonight. I've missed you, Mercy. It's been three very long, tirin' days."

His eyes were pools of sincerity, and she felt a stab of guilt for having been so angry at him. Still, she wouldn't rest until she knew the secret. She set her gaze on him, immediately distracted by a tuft of hair curling above his forehead. Oh, but she wanted to test its texture. Gracious, what she wouldn't do for that sort of freedom. "I...I missed you, too. And the boys kept counting the days till your return. I will confess, though, they had a great deal of fun at Aunt Gladdie's. She kept them busy helping her in the kitchen, and Mr. Gleason proved a patient tutor, teaching them to milk cows, for one thing. Of course, he pushed them on the swings for hours. The man's a gentle giant."

His hands moved up her arms, then slid down to her waist. A prickle of delight teased her belly. Without warning, he bent and touched his lips to hers, and her calm quickly shattered with an urgent need for more. *More.* Standing on tiptoe, she melded her lips to his, tightened her arms around his back, and listened to the song welling up in her veins.

I'm in love. Oh, Lord, I'm so hopelessly in love!

⟡

Sam ended their kisses while he still had a smidgeon of willpower. Another minute, and he'd be sweeping her up, carrying her to her bed, and claiming his husbandly rights! They'd agreed to kisses only, and he meant to keep his word, if it was the last thing he did. Besides, he had important news to tell her, and he needed his wits intact.

Flustered, he swept a hand through his hair, then gave his head a slight shake. "You're gettin' way too good at this kissin' game, young lady."

"Then why did you stop?" Her voice trembled with disappointment.

A dry chuckle rolled out of him. "Because it was the smart thing to do. Come on, let's sit down over here." He took her by the hand and led her across the room to the divan. "We need to talk."

For the next several minutes, he summarized his visit with Persephone and Hank, doing away with all the preliminaries. Then he drew in a breath, wondering if he had the guts to go on but also knowing he had no choice. He angled his body toward her and took both her hands in his, fixing his gaze on her gorgeous, guileless face. "Now brace yourself, Mercy. I've got somethin' to tell you that'll shock you clear to your toes."

A wave of alarm saturated her expression. "What is it?"

"My mother had an affair," he whispered. "With your father."

He waited for the angry scream, the leaping up from the sofa, and the instant tears of denial. Instead, she stared at him, unspeaking, her face unreadable, her eyes searing.

"Did you hear me?"

She blinked three times. "I think I did, but…I'm not sure I heard *right*."

He massaged the tops of her hands with his thumbs. "Unfortunately, you did."

She gave her head several quick shakes. "What?"

He let spill all that Persephone had told him, and in the telling, he watched her face show a myriad of expressions, everything from piqued interest to bewilderment, from doubt to utter disbelief, and finally to full-out shock. He fought the impulse to just stop, to shield her from all he'd learned, but he knew he couldn't do that. He'd heard the truth, and she deserved to know it, too. She started to cry, so he held her, but then she pushed back, wiped her eyes, and asked him to retell certain portions of Persephone's story, which he was glad to do.

With the information finally settled in her brain, she gave a little sniffle and adjusted her position, tucking a bare foot beneath her. Her bent knee made contact with his, but she didn't react; she just let it rest there. She looked briefly at her clasped hands, then met his gaze again. "So, you confronted your mother. How did she take that?"

"She fainted."

She covered her mouth, so that all he saw were her big, bloodshot brown eyes.

"Don't worry," he added hastily. "She's fine now. But knowin' I'd found out about the affair nearly threw her over the cliff."

"I don't understand how the two of them...I mean, weren't they supposed to be archenemies? What would draw them together?"

"I wondered the same, so this is where it all gets very interestin'...and disheartenin' at the same time. You recall I had twin brothers who died of scarlet fever when they were two." She nodded a few times and leaned in. "I was just three, so I don't really remember. What I do recall is how I became invisible to my mother after their deaths. She withdrew into a shell of her own makin' and refused to come out. I'm not sure she ever has. What you see with her is a big pretense. She tries to appear all put together and in control, but it's just a façade.

"Accordin' to Mother, my father tried to console her after my brothers died, but it didn't help; she just got angry with him. She couldn't understand how he could go on with life. Lookin' back, I suppose he wasn't much better off; he just showed his grief in different ways, mostly by keepin' his distance. Over time, they lost the ability to care for each other, speakin' less an' less, till the only reason they communicated was to fight about one thing or another.

"In those days, Mother didn't have much use for me, either. I know, you'd think she would've looked at me and said, 'I lost the twins, but I still have one son to care for,' but it didn't go like that. Some days, it was like she could barely tolerate the sight of me. She loved the attention those twins brought, everyone always swoonin' and cooin' over 'em, so when they died, that left her sort of stranded with me, and she never quite figured out how to handle havin' only one child.

"Anyway, Mother said the marriage basically died in those years of grievin'. Father worked long hours in the shop, then went to the saloon, often stayin' out past midnight. I guess I wondered where he went but not enough to ask. Besides, I didn't want him bitin' off my head. By then, I'd learned to manage on my own, and I preferred to keep my distance. I figured the less I knew, the better off I'd be.

"One day—this would've been a couple o' years after your mother died—my mother was puttin' away the laundry, and she found an envelope hidden under some clothes in one o' Father's bureau drawers. The seal was broken, so she pulled out the contents and read what she could only term a love letter."

"A love letter to your father?" Mercy's voice had a gravelly tinge. "Who wrote it?"

"Do you happen to know the name MaryLou Hardwick?"

Her eyelids fluttered, perhaps with veiled curiosity. "Paris's lady of the night? Yes, faintly, but she left town several years ago."

"Yep, after my father paid her a large sum to disappear."

"Your father? I don't understand."

"Apparently, MaryLou and my father carried on an affair lastin' four years. In the letter, she professed her love for him, and begged my father to get a divorce.

"Mother said that after he read this, she flew into a rage. She packed all my father's things and set them on the porch. Of course, when he got home, he wanted to save face, promised her he'd stop seein' MaryLou, if she would only let him stay. I'm not sure what all transpired between 'em, but she ended up givin' him another chance, and things between them smoothed out for a time. Before long, though, he started comin' home late again, and she knew he was seein' MaryLou.

"One afternoon, Mother was drivin' the buggy home from town when one o' the wheels fell off and landed her in a ravine. I recall the incident. I was fifteen. She told us an older gentleman had come along, tended to her bruises, used his horses to pull her wagon out, and fixed her wheel right there. As you've probably guessed by now, that 'older gentleman' was none other than your father. They had an immediate attraction, my mother said, despite the longstanding feud between their families. They started talkin' 'bout how lonely they both were, and before she knew it, they were meetin' on the sly."

Mercy rubbed her forehead. "I would have been eleven. I told you how my father spent a lot of time away from home, but I figured he was either working or drinking at the saloon. It didn't seem suspicious to me, but then, how would I have known what signs to look for? I do know he was lonely, but an affair with your mother? I can hardly believe it. Especially consider-ing the awful things he said about the Connors clan."

Sam nodded. "My parents always railed on your family, maybe even more so after Mother's affair wound down. Accordin' to her, it lasted only a few months. Once my father found out, it didn't take long for the relation-ship to unravel."

"How did he come to learn about it?"

He gave a sarcastic smile. "Their trusty foreman, Virgil Perry, spilled the beans. Mother had no clue Virgil had been spyin'. He gathered what he called 'incriminatin' evidence' and blackmailed my parents. As long as they paid up, he vowed to keep his mouth shut. And that arrangement continues to this day. I told my mother she has exactly two weeks to tell the truth, to her relatives and yours, before I inform Virgil his little jig is up. If I tell him too soon, he'll beat Mother to the punch, and, knowin' Virgil Perry, the story will get the wrong slant...not that Mother's version will be much better.

"At any rate, Mother says both affairs, hers and Father's, ended abruptly, and that's when Father withdrew a good sum of money from the bank and sent MaryLou packin'. As for Oscar, Mother said he got fightin' mad at Ernest for bringin' the whole thing to a halt. He claimed to have genuine feel-ings for Mother, but she told him she couldn't, in good conscience, continue seein' him, not after Father found out. After that, Oscar started sendin' my father scathin' letters, callin' 'im a two-timin' husband nowhere near good enough for my mother, and threatenin' to tell the town about his escapades with MaryLou. This went on for years, until it finally met its end in that fate-ful showdown in eighty-four.

"Mother and I didn't talk about this, but Persephone told me Solomon Turner saw the whole thing. He would have testified, but the judge refused, claimin' he was an unreliable witness."

"I never heard anything about that."

"I never did, either, but I plan to pay Mr. Turner a visit tomorrow."

"Do you think that's wise? He's getting up in years. Maybe he'd just as soon forget what he saw and heard."

"I'll go easy on 'im. I also plan to call on my cousins Frank and George, Persephone's brothers. If her hunch is right, they're the ones responsible for breakin' our window."

"Are you sure? Why would your own cousins…?"

"Exactly."

"Were they also responsible for Barney's disappearance?"

"Persephone wasn't sure."

Mercy sat in stunned silence while they both pondered private thoughts, the room fallen so still, Sam could hear Barney and Roscoe's breathing from a chair across the room, where the two lay tangled in a big black-and-white ball.

"My parents never patched up their relationship," Sam went on, "but they kept up the façade of a happy marriage, Mother puttin' on a big show for the public during the trial. She had me fooled.

"When my father died, I think her so-called grief stemmed more from guilt than anythin' else. My mother is a walkin' mess, and I plan to disown her, just as soon as I can put this whole business behind me. The way I figure it, the sooner everybody discovers the reason this feud has gone on for so long, and realizes how ridiculous it is to keep it alive, the quicker I can be done with her."

Mercy crossed her arms over her chest, rubbing her upper arms, as if to dispel a chill. "You sound so cold. Do you really plan to disown your mother?"

"I certainly don't want any kind of relationship with her."

"She'll die a lonely old woman."

"If so, it's her own fault."

"Don't let a seed of bitterness take root in your soul, Sam. Once you start fueling it with fury, it'll grow faster than a weed. You don't want that to happen. Look what bitterness did to your mother."

He loved Mercy, but he didn't need her preaching at him. Not now, not ever.

30

Mercy lay staring at murky shadows on the ceiling. Sam had left before dawn, before she'd had a chance to brew a pot of coffee or fry up an egg. He hadn't even rapped on her door to say good-bye; he'd just slipped quietly down the stairs and disappeared into the early-morning dark, the owls still hooting, an occasional dog howling at the fading moon. It made her wonder if he'd slept at all. Perchance he'd lain awake all night, reviewing their conversation from the night before, then grown too restless to remain in bed. She prayed he would consider her caution not to let bitterness overtake him, for she knew how detrimental it could be. She'd seen it firsthand, when her ma died and her pa looked for someone to blame, making God his target.

Obviously, the events of the last few days had changed Sam on certain levels. She didn't see that spark in his eye, that jovial, teasing spirit, or that gentle, caring manner. Oh, he'd been nothing but kind to her, but more guarded. Even his kisses had been short-lived, if they'd happened at all, before they'd bidden each other good night. He'd spent little time with the boys yesterday, and she wondered what today would bring, especially if he followed through with his plans to visit his cousins as well as Solomon Turner.

Frankly, the whole thing had changed her, too, but she refused to allow the disheartening news to chop away at her soul. Her father's name had never been spotless, but this new revelation would drag it further into the mud and ultimately draw attention to her, whether in the form of sympathy or spite. Either way, she would do her best to keep her head high, her spirits uplifted, and her faith in God strong as ever. She could only pray Sam would do the same. If she'd learned anything about life, it was that when adversity struck, a person had one of two choices: focus on the Father in faith and extend forgiveness, or look inward and find bitterness and blame. She didn't want to put herself in the second category. She'd seen too many examples of people it had ruined.

After she'd read from her Bible and then gotten on her knees in prayer, a sense of peace and refreshment came over her. Things would work out. She didn't know how, exactly; she just knew that when one fully surrendered to God, He had a way of making it work for the good of those concerned. Just as she had done after losing her precious friends to the fire, she chose to claim her favorite Bible verse, Romans 8:28: *"And we know that to them that love God all things work together for good, even to them that are called according to his purpose."* God *would* work everything out for good—He had promised to!

Aunt Gladys stopped by around eleven o'clock, after picking up a few supplies in town. "Just thought I'd stop in t' tell y' my house is too quiet since you children deserted me," she said to Mercy when she opened the door.

The boys ran to greet her, squealing, so she bent at the waist with open arms to enfold them in a hug. "Gracious me, you'd think you didn't just see me yesterday mornin'."

Joseph snagged her by the hand and pulled her toward the living room. "Come see our great big fort, Aunt Gladdie."

The woman glanced over her shoulder and caught Mercy's eye.

Mercy grinned. "They've been working on it all morning, Auntie." She followed the threesome into the living room, where the boys had fashioned a hideout of bedsheets and an oversized quilt spread across several dining room chairs.

"My, oh my," Gladys said, clapping a hand to her mouth. "This is quite a fort."

"We's protectin' ar town," said John Roy, "'cause there's enemies surroundin' us."

"Well, I suspect they'll skedaddle once they get wind o' you fierce fellas. Never can be too careful."

"Who are the enemies you're guarding us from?" Mercy asked.

"We don't know their names, but they cause lots o' trouble, an' they always want to fight and be mean," Joseph explained. "Everybody in the town's ascared o' them, so we have t' keep people safe."

Aunt Gladys slid Mercy another quick glance. "Well, you keep on protectin' us, and we'll all feel a lot safer."

As the boys resumed their play, Aunt Gladys slipped an arm around Mercy and led her out of the room. "Seems like them boys have heard talk 'bout all the feudin'."

"I suppose they've overheard some things, even though Sam and I have done our best not to say anything in front of them," Mercy conceded. "They found out about the fight at the picnic from some neighbor boys. It couldn't be helped."

"How are you doin' with all of it, sweetie?"

"Oh, just fine." Of course, her answer came off a tad sarcastic. "Would you like a cup of tea?"

"You know I would. Shall I help you?"

"Nope, you go make yourself comfortable in the other room, and I'll be right with you."

When she returned, she found her aunt seated next to the hearth, perusing a piece of paper. The woman glanced up, then went back to her reading.

"What's that?" Mercy asked, setting a cup and saucer on the round table next to her.

Aunt Gladys held it out, and Mercy's heart dropped. "Oh, that."

"You told me somebody snatched Barney an' returned 'im in a crate with a note, but you never actually showed me the note."

"No, I didn't think it was necessary." Mercy sat down in a chair. "I'd completely forgotten about sticking it between the pages of that book."

With scrunched brow, Gladys went back to studying the wrinkled paper. "Humph. Interestin'."

"What's that?"

"I recognize the handwritin'."

"You do? Whose is it?"

"It's my brother Fred's awful scrawl. I'd know it anywhere. And t' top matters off, he can't spell t' save his sorry life, so that makes it the more obvious to me he wrote it."

"Uncle Fred? Aunt Gladdie, are you sure? Would he really do a thing like that?"

"O' course he would, the old coot." She cut loose a low growl. "Just as soon as I leave here, I'm goin' out to their place t' give him a piece o' my mind."

"But…it's not yours to worry about. I don't want you—"

Gladys raised her palm in a halting manner. "Don't say another word, darlin'. I can handle my brother. In fact, I'd prefer to."

Mercy took a sip of tea, then lowered her cup and saucer gingerly to her lap. "Thank you, Auntie. Saves me from having to confront him."

Gladys waved an arm. "Don't you worry your little self about confrontin' your uncle Fred, or anybody, for that matter. You got enough stuff t' fret over. I'm about as mad as a hornet right now, and I shall take pleasure in doin' the honors."

Mercy drew in a deep, unsteady breath. If her aunt thought she was angry now, Mercy wondered how she'd react when she learned about her other brother's affair with Flora Connors.

⁓

Flora could barely drag herself out of bed in the morning, the way her stomach churned and her head pounded. Never had life looked so glum or insufferable. What did she have left? She'd lost her son, and soon she'd lose the rest of her family. What would her relatives say when she exposed her long-held secret? How could she possibly go through with it? She wasn't sure, but if she didn't, Samuel would spill the beans, and then folks would think even less of her. Oh, why had she been so foolish, giving in to her lustful desires those many years ago? Yes, she'd been lonely, and Ernest had started the whole business when he'd taken up with that tart MaryLou, but that hadn't given her license to commit the same wrong. At least she hadn't taken it to same degree. Still, as Samuel had said, the kisses alone were betrayal enough. Looking back, she knew she might have gone further, were it not for Ernest finding out. She'd liked Oscar Evans, until he'd turned on her for refusing to leave Ernest. And when he'd started sending threatening notes, why, everything had gotten plain ugly. In truth, he'd started losing his mind, and his excessive drinking hadn't helped the situation.

To save face, Ernest had insisted they try to go back to as normal a life as they both could manage, and while it hadn't been easy, they'd much preferred that to having their reputations tarnished. Oh, such a mess they'd made—*she'd* made—by living a lie for so many years.

Too weary to even get dressed, she found herself still in her nightclothes at ten, standing at the stove and preparing to boil a kettle of water for tea, when Virgil rapped at the door and then let himself right into the house. She'd intended to ask Samuel to fix the broken lock, but the way things were between them now, she couldn't expect him to do her any favors. She whirled around. "How many times do I have to tell you to stop coming into my house uninvited? You know I don't approve of that."

His grin came straight from the devil himself. "At least I knocked. Give me credit for that much."

"Pfff. Get out."

Ignoring the order, as usual, he sauntered right past her, opened a cabinet door, and peered inside, moving a few cans and jars around. Anything to get her ire up. She decided not to react; she merely left the stove and walked to the table to stand behind a chair, gripping its back and wishing she were strong enough to pick it up and heave it across the room, hitting him square in the back. That would knock him off his feet.

Without removing a thing, he closed the cabinet door, swiveled his body around, and leaned against the counter, his flabby arms crossed in front of him. "Sam sure stayed a long time yesterday. What'd he want?"

"If that were any of your business, I'd tell you, but it's not."

His upper lip curled back in one corner, revealing yellowed teeth. "Thought you two weren't on speakin' terms."

"Don't you have work to do?"

He chuckled. "Don't you owe me some money?"

"I already paid you what you're due this month."

"I'm due for a raise, that's what I'm due."

Her chest ballooned with a heavy intake of air. "I can't afford to give you one cent more, Mr. Perry. Now, kindly get out of my house."

He pushed away from the counter, his smirk firmly in place, and headed in her direction. She tightened her grasp on the chair. "Don't come near me."

She'd always managed to hold her own with Virgil Perry; she was his bread and butter, and he knew it. Still, he did give her the creeps when he drew too close, with his oversized frame and unshaven face. The air between them smelled of hate and revulsion, but it also reeked of body odor, and she wanted him gone.

"What's the matter, li'l lady? You seem a mite tense this mornin'."

She would not back down. She raised her chin a notch. "I'm as calm as can be."

"Is that so?" He glanced down at her hands. "Then why do your knuckles look like the blood's been washed right out of 'em?"

She let go of the chair and dropped her hands to her sides. "You have work to do, Mr. Perry. Go tend to it."

His chuckle grew tenfold, turning into a bitter-sounding cackle. "All right, all right." He touched the end of her nose with a cold finger, and she lurched back. "Now, don't you forget about that raise you owe me."

"I don't owe you a penny extra, you scum-sucking, beetle-faced rat."

He laughed all the way to the door. "We'll see about that, boss lady. We'll just wait and see."

When the door closed behind him, she pulled out the chair and dropped into it, elbows propped on the table, face buried in her hands, as if in deep prayer. That's when it occurred to her that she didn't know the first thing about prayer—at least, not the genuine type. It also occurred that the sooner she swallowed her pride and told folks about the affair, the sooner she could get Virgil Perry off her property.

31

When Sam knocked on the door at the home of his cousin Frank, Frank's wife, Alice, opened it and gave him a look of surprised delight. "Why, Samuel! What brings you here? Good gracious, I see your face took a bit of a bangin' in that ridiculous fight last Saturday, but I must say you look a fair piece better'n Frank. Is this a friendly call?"

"Depends. I'm lookin' for Frank. Is he around?"

"He is, actually. He an' George are in the kitchen, gettin' some refreshment before headin' back out to the fields. Want I should get 'im?" She started to turn.

"No, wait! They're both here?" Could luck have swung any better in his favor? Or perhaps it wasn't luck at all but divine intervention. He let that novel thought ruminate for a moment.

"Yes, it's nearin' harvest, so they team up this time o' year."

Now that she mentioned it, he did recall that. Had he taken up farming, he might well have been sitting at that table himself. He often contemplated whether his choice to take another direction career-wise had affected his relationships with his cousins. None of them ever seemed much interested in spending time with him, and why would they? They had little in common, when it came right down to it. "Well, I'll be. That'll save me a trip. Thanks, Alice."

He didn't miss the tight little gasp that escaped her mouth when he strolled right past her, uninvited. His cousins looked up when he sauntered through the archway. Alice was right; Frank hadn't managed to dodge as many fists as he had, and the same went for the black-eyed George. Both men scooted back in their chairs and stood, big grins on their faces. "Well, would you lookie what the cat dragged in," Frank boomed. "Alice, get this fine man a cup o' coffee or a bottle o' brew. What's y'r preference, Cousin?"

Sam raised his hand. "No thanks to both, Alice. This isn't a social call, and besides, I haven't imbibed since marryin'."

George raised his eyebrows. "She got you in chains, does she?"

"Not at all, but I'm not here to talk about my wife—or the boys we're raisin' together."

The men took their seats again, and Frank gestured to an empty chair. "Have a seat, then."

"Don't need to. Just came to say my piece, and then I'll be on my way," he said in dull monotone.

Frank gave a nervous chuckle. "Go ahead, then."

"I'm here to tell you I'm stayin' married to Mercy, and if any more intentional damage is done to our home—say, broken windows or upturned planters—I'll be sure to point Sheriff Marshall in the right direction." Frank opened his mouth, but Sam halted him with his hand. "Don't even think of interruptin' me, you monkey-faced clown, and don't try to tell me you fellas aren't the ones responsible for the vandalism—on a Sunday mornin', no less, when you should've been in church. I ought to slap you both silly."

Stepping up to the table, he splayed both hands atop it and leaned over, eyeing them at close range. He noticed with satisfaction the way they scooted back in their seats. "And another thing. This feud between our family and the Evans clan is about to end—real fast. You'll soon know what I mean. And when you do, take heed that you put blame where blame is due—and not on my wife or me. You hear?" When neither acknowledged his question—both just sitting there, with their jaws dropped to their knees—he repeated himself with almost alarming emphasis. "I said, do you hear me?"

To this, they gave several fast nods. He straightened with a chilly smile. "Glad to hear we're all of one accord." Never having bothered to take off his hat, he adjusted it on his head. "Lookin' forward to seein' you ladies on better terms next time." He turned and walked out, leaving three speechless cousins in his wake.

Sam squeezed his heels into Tucker's sides to urge him along to his next stop, Brockwell Manor, which stood in regal splendor at the end of a long, straight, pebbled driveway. It was the residence of Iris Brockwell, a stubborn, feisty widow in her late seventies, whose late husband had amassed a great fortune providing legal counsel to the Louisville and Nashville railroad lines. He didn't know much more about Mrs. Brockwell, but his main interest wasn't with her; it was with her personal butler and longtime friend, Solomon Turner.

As he rode, Sam planned in his head how he would broach the subject of the fight with Solomon Turner, hoping to discover what the man had overheard on that fateful day in 1884. That morning, he'd told Uncle Clarence what he'd learned at Persephone's and sworn him to secrecy, with the caveat that he could tell Aunt Hester. While his uncle's initial reaction had been anger, he'd quickly cooled down, saying it was in the past and there was no point dwelling on it. "May as well move forward with forgiveness and put the feud behind us," he'd said. *Easier said than done.* Sam doubted his relatives or Mercy's would ever quite forget, either. Even Sam couldn't quite embrace that perspective, and he didn't know when or if he ever would. His mother had really done it this time, and it would take a miracle to find it in his heart to let the matter go.

Sam gave the door knocker three taps. Several moments later, the door opened, and there stood Solomon Turner, a large but unassuming man, impeccably dressed in a dark suit and tie, his short goatee and mustache neatly trimmed. He greeted Sam with a formal nod and a slight bow of his gray head. "Help y', suh?"

Sam quickly removed his hat. "Good afternoon, Mr. Turner. I'm Samuel Connors. Don't know if you remember me, but—"

"Why, Mistah Connors, o' course I do." Beneath his trimmed mustache, he gave a big grin that showed his teeth, bright white except for one gold on top, which glimmered in the light. "Din't recognize you at first, I'm afeared, but now that I see y' at close range and without that hat, why, sure I know you. What can I do f'r you, suh? If you were needin' t' see Missus Brockwell, she's takin' her mid-afternoon doze."

"That's fine. Actually, you're the one I wanted to talk to."

"Oh?" Only the faintest hint of concern skipped across the man's dark, ruddy cheeks. He glanced behind him, then stepped out into the warm breeze and closed the oversized entry door behind him, its latch giving a quiet, controlled click. He gestured at the array of wicker chairs and settees arranged on the wide veranda. "Would y' care t' sit, suh?"

"That'd be fine, Mr. Turner."

They each took a seat, Sam in a stationary chair, Solomon in a rocker, which squeaked back and forth. "Fine day."

"Yes, it is."

How to begin? He decided to just get on with it. "Mr. Turner, I've heard from several sources that you witnessed the murder of Oscar Evans, but the judge wouldn't hear your testimony in court. Is that true?"

"Well, suh, yes, it is. Them prosecutors questioned me, but when they tells Judge Corbett who their chief witness is, he says he won't allow no blackie in his courtroom. He done used a worse word than that, suh, but I ain't goin' t' repeat it."

Sam gave his head a remorseful shake. "I'm sorry you had to endure that, Mr. Turner. It was plain ignorant of him. I don't mean to stir up any trouble, but I was hopin' you could tell me what you saw and heard…just for my own enlightenment."

The man looked out over the rolling hills surrounding the property. "Don't know how much you want t' know, suh."

Sam cleared his throat. "All of it, if you don't mind."

"I'd have to dig down deep in my ol' thinker. It ain't what it used t' be."

"Take your time, Mr. Turner."

"Well, from what I recall, I was jus' comin' outta Joe's Market when I overheared a good deal o' arguin' in the alleyway. I stood there, outta sight, too afeared t' move. Thought about walkin' back inside, but then sumthin' just made me stay put. I ain't the nosy sort, Mistah Connors, but that argument didn't sound like no ordinary row, if you know what I'm sayin'."

Sam nodded, fingering the rim of his battered Stetson. "What were they sayin'?"

"Don't know as I should tell y', suh. It might not set too well."

"It's okay. I've heard quite a bit already; I just need some confirmation."

"Well, suh, I hear Mistah Evans confess t' havin' a affair with yo' mama some years before. He tol' yo' pappy he still loved her and it'd be in 'is best interest t' release her for a divorce, and yo' pappy, he says that ain't happenin'. He start yellin' and screamin' obscenities an' sech. I do believe Mistah Evans had gone too heavy on the sauce, the way he was slurrin' 'is speech. Might be he was clear outta his head. Weren't many folks out that day, 'cause it was so blamed hot, you could'a fried bacon on a brick. There was those two across the street, but ain't no way them fellas could'a heard as much as me. 'Course, it's them two what took the witness stand, but it's all fine, 'cause the jury done found yo' pappy guilty anyway."

His words proved a lot to take in, and Sam spent a few moments digesting them. "Thank you, Mr. Turner," he finally said. "Thank you for takin' the time to talk to me. I just needed to hear your side of things. It gives me a new perspective on that day." He put his hat back on and then stood.

Solomon started to rise, as well.

"Don't get up on my account."

"No, I ain't, suh. I best get busy on Cook's grocery list. It was nice seein' y' again, even if the circumstances coulda been better. How's that new wife o' yours and them poor kids? I saw 'em the night of the fire. It sho' was a cryin' shame, them losin' their folks, but they's safe now. Thank the Lord you rescued 'em."

"We're makin' do—thanks. I'm just grateful I was at the right place at the right time."

"The Lord saw to that, Mistah Connors. Yes, He sho' 'nough did."

Sam nodded. "Thanks again. I'll be on my way now."

After mounting Tucker, Sam kicked him into a canter. A dazzling sun reached down its blistering rays and pierced his shoulders like fiery fingers, yet his inner core shivered with newfound coldness toward his mother.

Don't let a seed of bitterness take root in your soul, Sam. Once you start fueling it with fury, it'll grow faster than a weed.

Mercy's words pounded in his head, but he pushed them aside.

Too late, he thought. *It's already growin'.*

32

As autumn approached, Mercy looked forward to a break from the heat. She also hoped the change in seasons might bring about a change in spirits around the house. With the start-up of school, Joseph now spent his days away from home, which put John Roy in a downcast mood and her in a lonesome one. On top of that, she'd had to invent new ways to keep John Roy entertained, so accustomed was he to following his older brother around like a pup on a leash.

The send-off had made Mercy heartsick, for it should have been Herb and Millie's honor to see their older son off to school for the first time. Instead, she and John Roy had been the ones to walk him the few short blocks to the two-story building on Poplar that served children in grades one through eight. Sam had tried to comfort her, but his words, while gentle and soothing, had lacked genuine understanding. After all, what did he—or she, for that matter—really know about the boys' deepest needs? Ill equipped, that's what they were, and some days barely treading water. Add to that Sam's cynical view of his mother's shenanigans—no matter that her father had played just as big a role, if not bigger, in the whole fiasco—and their little household stood in need of a transformation.

Perhaps that explained why she found herself taking a walk to Paris Evangelical Church, where she planned to meet with Reverend Younker to talk through some of her concerns. Something told her the kind old gentleman with infinite amounts of godly wisdom would have just the right words. She was grateful to her cousin Amelia for offering to watch John Roy for the day. The boy had been ecstatic, for he'd learned on a visit earlier that week that Amelia and her husband, Norman, had a big farm with animals galore and wide-open spaces to explore. Norm had graciously allowed John Roy to ride with him on his field wagon and help with a few simple chores, later telling Mercy he'd enjoyed the taste of what life would be like with a child, with Amelia and him expecting their first in February.

The sun baked Mercy's back and shoulders, and she regretted not riding Sally to the church. The poor old girl didn't get as much use or attention as she had before Tucker had come on the scene, and Mercy worried she might feel neglected. But she'd decided she could use the exercise herself. Besides, walking would give her more time to ponder how many details of the sordid affair to divulge to Reverend Younker. She had every confidence he would keep her secret safe for as long as necessary—which wouldn't be much longer, seeing as Flora had called a family meeting. It was scheduled to take place in her home tomorrow evening, and Sam had said he planned to go, not so much to support his mother as to act as referee, should the news spark a squall right there in her living room.

When the little white clapboard church came into view, Mercy took a calming breath. The sight of the simple structure, with its bare windows, weathered bell tower, and shroud of ancient shade trees and overgrown shrubs, always lent a measure of comfort. Even more reassuring was the interior, with its rows of backless benches, central potbelly stove, narrow platform at the front, and wooden altar, where she'd knelt as a fourteen-year-old to invite the Lord Jesus Christ into her heart. She breathed a prayer of thanks, followed by a plea for courage, as she turned off the dusty road onto the dirt driveway.

A few houses dotted the cozy neighborhood, all small and boxy, with tiny front porches. On either side of the church were two residences, one of them the parsonage—a two-story with a wide veranda—and the other a tiny abode belonging to the elderly Myrtle Stitt. More than once, Mercy had thought about her conversation with Joy Westfall and wondered if she were still visiting her ailing aunt. Perhaps, after her appointment with the preacher, Mercy would venture over to find out.

"Well, hello there," came a deep, mellow voice. Reverend Younker stood, shoulders a little stooped, on the church steps, holding one of the double doors open wide.

"Hello, Reverend. I hope I haven't kept you waiting." Her yellow skirt flared in an updraft, so she pressed it down with both palms before mounting the steps.

"No, no. I've been praying and preparing for Sunday morning's message." While not as spry as he'd once been, the elderly fellow still had energy aplenty for serving the Lord and delivering a fine sermon every week. Even so, Mercy wondered just how much longer he'd stand behind that pulpit before relinquishing it to someone else. She'd heard murmurings of his retirement but couldn't bear to think about it. "You walked all the way from town?" he asked as she stepped through the door.

"Yes. It was lovely." Inside the sanctuary, a cool breeze drifted through the open windows. She removed her straw hat, glad she'd remembered to grab it off the hook. "My, it feels wonderful in here."

"Yes, doesn't it? All thanks to those towering oaks outside. Let's find a seat, shall we?" He led her up the aisle, stopping at the pew the Ammerson family occupied every Sunday.

Mercy slid along the bench, set her straw hat beside her, crossed her legs at the ankles, and folded her hands in her lap, ignoring the little lump that formed in her throat at having to spill her feelings.

Small talk filled up the first few minutes of their time together, but soon the pastor wanted to address her purpose in coming. Mercy began by telling him about her frustrations with caring for the boys, her fears that she and Sam weren't "doing it right," the crying spell from several weeks back, when the cat had gone missing, and her concerns that perhaps the boys were bottling up feelings they didn't know how to express. Of course, she carefully avoided any talk about her marriage—until the reverend asked point-blank how she and Sam were doing as a couple.

Her heart did a crazy little flip. "We're still getting to know each other, I suppose."

"Perfectly understandable." He nodded. "These things take time, even with couples who court months before saying their vows. As you grow more intimate with each other, you'll find yourselves revealing the hidden things, and before you realize it, you'll know each other quite thoroughly. It's how a relationship matures. But, as I said, it all takes time and patience."

Heat sprang to her cheeks at the word "intimacy." Sam had kept their kisses few and far between, mostly good-night pecks, and she feared he'd started growing tired of her. But she wasn't about to broach that subject with the preacher—much less tell him they still didn't share a bedroom.

Instead, she confided in him how the knowledge of Sam's mother's affair with her father had seemed to steal a portion of Sam's joy. She asked what she might do to help restore it, so that things could return to the way they were before.

To her surprise, Reverend Younker didn't so much as flinch at the wretched story. Rather, he gently patted her hands. "Unfortunately, my dear, there is nothing you can do to restore Samuel's joy. That is something he must choose for himself, through faith in Christ. Bitterness can fester over time, though, so we shall pray it doesn't come to that."

"That is precisely what I told him."

He gave a tender smile. "And take care that you keep your words free of a preaching tone. Giving him orders he is powerless to fulfill in his own strength will only drive a wedge between the two of you. Your best defense is prayer. After years in ministry, I am utterly convinced of this one thing: God hears the pleas of a praying wife."

They talked a bit longer, and then the reverend offered to pray for her. Tears formed behind her eyes, but she blinked them back, and when she stood, a sense of peace that all would be well rushed over her.

As Reverend Younker walked her to the front, she turned to him, unable to stifle her curiosity. "You didn't seem shocked when I told you about Flora Connors and my father."

He paused and scratched the back of his balding head. "I'll be honest, Mercy…I learned of this attraction years ago."

Her head jerked up in surprise.

"I never mentioned it to anyone except my Thelma, but I spotted the two of them in town one day, concealed between two buildings and having a discussion that looked…rather intimate. I briefly considered interfering but decided against it, thinking I should keep my nose where it belonged. Now I realize I should have made it my business, as a man of the cloth. While your father was a widower, Flora Connors was very much a married woman, even if there was another woman who desperately wished she weren't."

Mercy blinked, putting the pieces together. "You knew about MaryLou Hardwick?"

He nodded. "Before leaving town, Miss Hardwick came to see me and spilled the entire story—how she'd fallen in love with Ernest Connors, even begged him to divorce Flora. She wondered if there was any hope for her soul, after all the destruction she'd caused. And right over there"—he tilted his head toward the back of the church—"I introduced her to Jesus Christ. She didn't even bother walking to the altar, just tearfully dropped to her knees by the bench. She walked back out the door a changed woman. That was the last time I saw Miss Hardwick, but three years ago, she sent us a letter, saying she'd settled in West Virginia and found a Christian man who loved her, despite her past. They were to be married that spring." He smiled. "It's just one more example of how God can take an ugly circumstance, turn it around, and make it work for His honor and glory."

Mercy grinned. "Romans eight, verse twenty-eight. '*And we know that to them that love God all things work together for good, even to them that are called according to his purpose.*' It's been my favorite Bible verse for as long as I can recall."

His smile broadened. "You are a fine woman, Mercy Connors, and I'm confident all things will work together for good in your little household. Keep your faith alive, young lady."

He opened the heavy door, and she looked up at him once more. "Thank you, Reverend. I feel so much better already."

"It was my pleasure."

She stepped over the threshold, then quickly turned again, catching him just before he closed the door. "I wanted to ask you, do you happen to know if Myrtle Stitt's niece is still visiting?"

He glanced toward the little house. "She surely is, but they've left town for a few days. Myrtle very much wanted to see a few of her relatives before…well, before she passes on. I don't know just how much time she has left on this earth, but she's making the most of every moment. Thelma and I have been checking in on her, and the neighborhood ladies have been generous in providing meals. It's a mighty fine thing, her and Joy reuniting."

"Is Joy…is she married?"

"Not that I know of, no. Don't know much about her background."

"Nor do I." She paused in the sunshine, rejoicing in its warmth, yet knowing she would arrive home drenched with sweat. A cool bath would be the perfect remedy. "Well, thank you again, Reverend. Please give your wife my greetings."

With that, she set off up the dusty track carved out by hundreds of wagon wheels, thinking about the men in her life whom she deeply loved—well, one man, actually, and two sweet little boys.

⌒

Before going downstairs for supper, Sam stood at the mirror and combed his hair back, but to no avail; his wavy strands, more unruly than usual in this muggy weather, flopped back over his forehead in disarray.

The sounds of the boys bickering in the living room and Mercy puttering around the kitchen—and issuing an occasional reprimand—rose through the floor register. Since the start of school, the dynamics between the boys had changed, with Joseph showing a more grown-up side, and John Roy desperately trying to keep the pace. Joseph had even grown a full inch since early summer, according to the little pencil marks on the kitchen wall, and John Roy, who'd grown barely half an inch, didn't like it one bit. He'd claimed Mercy hadn't measured right and had insisted on a redo—which, of course, had changed nothing.

Sam smiled to himself. The pair was something else. His wife was something else, too, and he'd found it necessary to keep curtailing their kisses, for lack of trust in his ability to control his desires. Good gravy, but that sassy lady had hooked him good!

Delectable aromas of fruit pie, vegetable stew, and fresh-baked bread wafted up through the floor register, overwhelming his senses. What he wouldn't do to stay home tonight rather than go to his mother's house and face all his relatives, especially when she dropped the big bomb. He prayed for a good outcome but didn't hold out much hope.

He had to eat in a hurry, something he regretted but couldn't help. Lately, he hadn't been spending enough time with the boys, having to work extra hours to keep up with the abundance of orders from retailers and private buyers. He hoped the new fellow Uncle Clarence had hired would help ease their load. So far, he'd proved a good worker, and his prior experience at a shop in northern Indiana surely couldn't hurt.

He folded his napkin and laid it on the edge of the table, scooted back in his chair, and stood. "Excellent supper, Mercy, but I'm gonna have to excuse myself so I can get over to my mother's place."

"I know," she said, in a whisper that drowned in the boys' groans of disapproval.

"Why?" John Roy dragged the word out so that it ended on a low, whining note, his sad eyes looking ready to drop a few tears.

Sam gave a sympathetic smile and walked around the table to pat the boy on the head. "I'm really sorry. I'll try to make it home before you go to bed, so I can tuck you in. And I promise we'll have some playtime tomorrow night."

"We better!" John Roy set down his fork, folded his arms across his chest, and dropped his chin.

"Don't be a baby," Joseph scolded.

"He's not," Sam said. "He misses our playtime, and I don't blame 'im." He crouched down to the boys' level. "I think he's been missin' you too, Joseph."

"No, I ain't," John Roy blurted out, his arms still locked in front of him.

Sam ignored the remark. "There've been a lot of changes lately, and we all have to work together to get through them. Can we do that?" Sam cast Mercy a glance he hoped communicated his need for help.

She read it correctly, and reached out and touched John Roy's arm. "Sam will spend time with you tomorrow. Has he ever broken a promise?"

Sam held his breath as he waited for a reply, but it came only in the form of two heads moving from side to side. It would have to do. "There, see? I'll be back later. And I'll devote this Saturday to the family, how about that?"

The statement brought both boys to life, and when he glanced at Mercy, he found her eyes as bright as black diamonds, and he knew a sense of relief. He hadn't paid her nearly enough attention, either, what with his morose moods of late. *Lord, how I need Your divine touch.* The silent plea put a hungry spot at the core of his heart, and he vowed to seek the Lord's presence with more diligence in the days to come.

Mercy walked Sam to the door. "I'll be praying for you tonight," she whispered. "I'm asking that the Lord will lay it on your relatives' hearts to show forgiveness and mercy."

He tilted his head to the side and lifted her chin with a curved finger. "I think I know why your parents named you Mercy. You have a heart full of it. They must've had some sort o' premonition of what you'd grow to become."

She gave a timid smile, then lowered her gaze, her dark, feathery lashes sweeping down to cover her midnight eyes. He bent and touched his lips to both lids. "I'll see you later."

When he walked out, he sensed her watching as he untied Tucker's lead from the post in the front yard. He mounted up and directed Tucker down the drive, glancing back when they reached the road. Sure enough, there she stood in the open doorway, her body silhouetted by the hall light. He waved, and the silhouette waved back.

Folks started arriving at his mother's at seven on the dot. His family was a punctual lot—he could at least give them that much. Arriving simultaneously were his uncle Clarence and aunt Hester, along with their sons, Peter and John, and their daughter, Sarah. Sam noted that his cousins' spouses were not in attendance; undoubtedly they'd stayed home with their children. *Good.* He'd hoped they'd all have the sense to leave their kids at home, considering they'd heard that his mother had urgent news to impart.

On their tails came his other aunt and uncle on the Connors side, Gilbert and Ella, and their sons, Frank and George; again, the wives must have stayed home with the children. The only one missing was Persephone—the one relative Sam would have taken great pleasure in seeing. Just before he'd left for the train station after their visit in Nashville, she'd wrapped him in a hug and told him not to be a stranger, insisting he return soon with Mercy and the boys. He'd promised he would. When he'd turned to leave, she'd stopped him with a hand to his arm. "Would you tell my family I love them?" she'd asked, with tears welling in her eyes. "And one more thing…would you tell Mama she's about to be a grandma again?" With a lump in his own throat, he'd told her it would be his pleasure. He hadn't yet had the opportunity to deliver the message, and he figured what better time than tonight?

His mother was a basket of frayed nerves by the time everyone had gotten situated in the living room, some of them seated in chairs, the more agile ones—himself included—occupying spots on the floor. A small part of his heart reached out to his mother, but it didn't quite stretch wide enough to lend any support. *This is her problem,* he told himself, *and her business to dig her way through it in whatever way she can.* He didn't necessarily relish the hard, icy emotions frosting over his insides, but he didn't think they would thaw out anytime soon.

A hush came over the room as every pair of eyes fell on his mother. She gave a half smile, and for the first time, Sam noticed her chin quavering. This announcement wouldn't come rolling off her tongue, by any means. He cleared his throat. "Um, thank you all for comin'." He hadn't intended to speak, but when all heads turned in his direction, expressions either fraught with concern or simply curious, he decided to stand up. He rubbed his hands together, praying silently for the right words. "As you know, my mother has somethin' she wants to tell all of you…somethin' important."

Several heads bobbed up and down.

"What is it, Flora?" asked Aunt Ella. "For heaven's sake, are y' dyin' or somethin'?"

"Mother!" This from George, one of his mother's most beloved nephews. "Just talk to us, Aunt Flora. We're all here to listen."

"That's right, Auntie. It can't be all that bad," said Frank, tied with George as his mother's favorite relative. Both seemed always at her beck and call whenever she had a mind to wreak havoc on a member of the Evans clan. In fact, Sam wouldn't be a bit surprised if she'd known all along about the part they'd played in breaking Mercy's window. She could deny it till she was blue, but he wouldn't buy it, no sir. What little trust he'd once had in her had burnt away like the last cut of kindling in a roaring fire.

His gaze rested steady on her. "Go ahead, Mother. Your family's waitin'."

Not one to cry, she actually wiped away a single tear, prompting the entire room to gasp in shock, then fall completely silent. "Samuel is right.

I have something to tell all of you." Her voice trembled. "And it's not going to be simple or painless. It involves this…this lifelong feud with the Evans folk."

Several people started murmuring.

"What about those pieces o' horse dung?" Frank asked, sitting straighter, his spine looking as if it'd been fused to a steel rod.

When everything in him wanted to strangle his cousin for his crassness, Sam remained oddly calm. "Let my mother continue."

She looked to him for something—strength? courage?—but all he could give her was a nod. She opened her mouth and let the dreaded tale unfold.

And unfold it did, to the dismay of everyone present. Creased brows, dropped jaws, confused faces turned angry, and arms flung wide in shock were just a few of the reactions when she exposed her long-held secret.

To her credit, she didn't try to hide the truth about falling prey to Oscar Evans' advances, and she even admitted to having enjoyed the attention. When someone asked how she could have done that to Ernest, she hung her head and stared at the balled-up handkerchief clutched in her fist. Sam had to give her additional credit for not dragging his father's name through the mud, but then, he figured she had her reasons. Revealing his own four-year affair would shine a different light on things, making folks detest her all the more for driving him to it. She could only take so much of the blame. This way, it sounded as if Sam's father had pined for her till the day he died—and that two men rather than one found her attractive.

Sam decided to let the matter go. As long as she came clean about her own actions, he really didn't care whether the family ever found out about his father's escapades with Miss Hardwick. What possible good could come from complicating the story with more dirt?

33

Flora pushed down the awful urge to retch in plain sight of everyone. She'd never seen such foul-looking faces or experienced such outright disapproval and wrath, especially from her husband's family. At least her sister, Mable, still claimed to love her, even though it'd been clear something had changed between them the instant Flora had confessed her secret several days prior. She never would have told her at all, if she hadn't thought the news would leak from another source.

She'd hoped—foolishly, it seemed—for a little commiseration from Clarence and Samuel, the two men who had known Ernest best. But neither of them offered a word of support, so she plowed through the whole tale, sharing almost every sordid detail. Did they think it was easy confessing one's sinful past in front of God and everyone? Surely, she deserved some tiny morsel of mercy. But her family seemed to disagree.

She forged ahead with her final words of the evening. "I make this…this confession tonight…to tell you that this feud…well, it has to stop."

"An' why's that?" Frank asked, rising to his feet. "Your tale don't make me hate them people any less."

"What is it you base your hate on, Cousin?" All eyes fell to Samuel, and Flora felt momentary relief from the piercing stares. "And, to clarify things,

265

this is no tale. It really happened, and it knocks the foundation out from under this feud. It started as an argument over property lines, but all o' that is long past. The only remainin' bone o' contention is Mother's infidelity with Oscar Evans, and he and my father are both dead. What on earth is there left to fight over?"

"They hate us just as much," George put in. "What's to keep them from continuin' the fight?"

Samuel glanced at Flora before responding. "My mother sent a written confession to Gladys Froeling, with a request that she hold a family meetin' of her own, at which she was to read the confession aloud. It is Mother's hope, and mine, that Mrs. Froeling will encourage her relatives to drop the whole matter."

Flora kept her eyes down, mostly to avoid her family's accusing glares. She had yet to apologize for her actions, and while she supposed she ought to, she didn't feel any genuine remorse. Truth told, she wouldn't have even called this meeting if Samuel hadn't insisted on it. Why did Persephone have to intrude where she didn't belong? Speaking of letters, she ought to send her one. *Darling Niece Persephone, Thanks for all the trouble you rained upon your family. Love, Your adoring aunt Flora.*

"Do you have anythin' else you want to say to the family, Mother?"

"What?" She raised her head at Samuel's prodding question. "Well, yes, I suppose I do. I…I'm very sorry for all the confusion I've caused."

"Confusion?" George blurted out. "Confusion, Aunt Flora? Don't you mean deceit? Don't you mean grotesque lies?"

Her heart thudded. "I never actually li—"

"O' course you did!" Gilbert shouted. "You been lyin' for years, makin' us believe you hated the Evans family, stirrin' up whatever nest you could to bring down a mountain o' trouble. Admit it, Flora—y'r nothin' but a fraud."

Flora gasped and covered her mouth with her handkerchief.

"Now, Gil," Clarence started in his level tone, "there's no cause to get all riled—"

"O' course there's cause!" Ella got to her feet, though none too quickly, with all the extra flesh she carried in her midsection. "Here, you been comin' to my house all these years, talkin' bad 'bout them Evans folk, and you was almost one of 'em y'rself, by goin' out on poor Ernest with—with *Oscar Evans*, of all people!"

"Poor Ernest" nothing! But Flora wasn't about to reveal his own misdeeds. She didn't want her family knowing he'd been unfaithful to her. How would that make her look? Why, they'd immediately blame her for failing to give him everything he needed. She bit down hard on her lip to keep from spouting back, then swiped at another insufferable tear. She couldn't recall the last time she'd allowed herself to cry. It'd been years, to be sure.

"You stood by him at the trial like a loyal wife," George sneered. "You was probably mournin' the loss of Oscar more'n you was worried 'bout your husband's ordeal."

Several gasps arose around the room.

"All right, that's enough," Samuel announced, holding up a hand and forcing a calmer atmosphere. Flora could not have been more grateful. "I think it's time you all went home and sorted through this thing on your own. Yellin' at each other won't accomplish anything."

"That's right," said Hester. "Let's all take our leave." Hester had always been kind to Flora, but never overly so. Even now, her sister-in-law avoided looking at her; she merely rose with the rest of the family and made her way to the door. Clarence's family had always kept mostly to themselves, maintaining peace at all costs. If she'd ever needed support, Gilbert and Ella were the ones she'd turned to. Now, she had no one. Her own sister had put distance between them, and in a few days, Mable would catch a train with Henry to spend three months visiting his brothers and sisters out West. What on earth was Flora to do?

Everyone, including Samuel, filed out wordlessly, closing the door with a click that gave her a jolt. Immediately an overwhelming sadness tackled her senses and nearly bowled her over. Still, she would not cry any more than the two tears she'd already shed—no, sir, not even in the privacy of her own home. She was Flora Connors, after all—resilient and unruffled.

◞

Sam walked into the cool evening air, listening to the unbridled fuming of a number of his relatives as they headed down the sloped yard toward the hitching posts. The night sky twinkled with the first stars, and a full moon rose over the treetops.

Uncle Clarence helped Aunt Hester climb aboard the wagon, then swiveled on his heel to face Sam. "Well, I'd say that went over as well as it could have." He tipped his head toward Gilbert and Ella, who stood in a circle with their kids, yammering away.

"I'm just glad your own family is more subdued." He gave his uncle a pat on the arm. "Thanks for makin' the trip."

Pete leaned down from the wagon. "You call on me if you have need of anything, you hear?"

"Thanks, Pete." Sam nodded. "I appreciate that."

His uncle released a slow sigh. "Well, we best get movin'. I'll be seein' y' in the mornin', bright an' early."

Sam slapped him on the back, then watched him climb aboard the rig. Once settled next to his wife, he inclined his head at Sam. "It'd be best if you could find it in y'r heart to forgive your mother."

Sam restrained himself from rolling his eyes. "I'd prefer we not talk about that just yet."

"He's right, Clarence." Aunt Hester swatted her husband's arm. "Leave 'im be."

Uncle Clarence wagged his head, then maneuvered his wagon toward the gravel road, the vehicle pitching and swaying on the bumpy path.

Once they vanished from view, Sam set his gaze on Uncle Gilbert and his bunch, still clustered together, their mouths all flapping at once. Hopefully the piece of news he had yet to share would silence them, at least for a little while.

"Thanks again for comin' out," he said, breaking into their private prattle.

They all lifted their heads and gawked at him, as if he had no business interrupting. Uncle Gilbert grumbled under his breath.

"What's that, Uncle?"

"I said, we'd have been better off stayin' home."

"Maybe so, but then you'd have found out another way. This sort of news won't stay contained."

"Pfff. It's plain disgustin', is what it is."

"Yeah, an' disheartenin', too," Frank said. "I always had great respect for Aunt Flora. Now I ain't so sure."

Sam didn't know how a fellow could respect someone who encouraged constant bickering between two families. His mother had been at the center of almost every dispute. What a fraud. "I'm not about to disagree with either of you, but I didn't come over here to discuss my mother when she's not here to defend herself. I do have somethin' to tell you, though."

Aunt Ella cocked her gray head to the side. "What else could there possibly be to tell?"

"I went to see Persephone a couple of weeks ago."

Uncle Gilbert's head shot up. "What'd you do that f'r?"

"She invited me. Said she had somethin' important to tell me. She'd heard I'd married Mercy, and she wanted me to know the real reason we've been fightin' with the Evans clan for so long. If it hadn't been for Persephone, who knows how long we would've been at each other's throats?"

"So, she wasn't lyin' when she told us she seen them two kissin'," Frank said quietly.

"No, she wasn't," Sam affirmed.

"You kicked her out, Pa," George said.

Uncle Gilbert looked down and scuffed at the ground with his shoe. "Yeah."

"Maybe it's about time you go make things right with her," Frank tacked on.

Uncle Gilbert sneered. "Listen to you, Mr. I-Never-Make-No-Mistakes."

"Hush up, both o' you," Aunt Ella ordered. She looked at Sam, her eyes softer. "You said she's well?"

Sam nodded. "She is. She found herself an excellent man in Hank Greve."

"I ain't convinced 'bout that," his uncle groused.

"Then I guess you'll have to find out for yourself one o' these days." Sam shrugged. "You should know that Persephone misses you and said she'd like to have you back in her life at some point—when you're ready, o' course." He paused. "She's expectin' a baby."

Aunt Ella gasped, covering her mouth with her hand.

For the first time since his mother's announcement, they all stood mute, gawking.

Frank spoke first. "My little sister's gonna have a baby?"

"She sure is," Sam affirmed. "She looks right fine, too."

"Is she feelin' well?" Aunt Ella asked, her eyes moist with tears.

"Uh, most of the time." He smiled to himself, recalling how sick she'd been that first day of his visit.

"Thank you for passin' on the message, Samuel." She glanced at Uncle Gilbert. "Even if my husband refuses to join me, I have some apologizin' to do to my daughter."

Uncle Gilbert's head jerked up. "I didn't say nothin' 'bout refusin' to go."

"You didn't have to."

The family bid Sam good-bye, then climbed into Uncle Gilbert's wagon, keeping up their quibbling as they pulled away from the house. As he'd done with Clarence and his clan, Sam watched until they'd disappeared around a bend in the road. He inhaled until his lungs burned with fullness, then slowly let his breath back out, feeling a bit of tension fly out, too. He didn't know whether to thank the Lord that the ordeal had ended or repent for not showing more compassion while his mother had stumbled and stammered through her pathetic, remorseless profession. Her apology had come out sounding insincere, if not forced. He shook his head several times, then bent to retrieve a small stone and threw it, his target any tree in the thicket behind the house. Until she demonstrated true regret for her actions, he didn't hold out much hope for having any sort of relationship with her.

"She'll die a lonely old woman," Mercy had said.

Well, so be it.

He turned on his heel and headed back toward the house, kicking up dust with every step. Across the yard, he spotted Virgil Perry's large frame leaning in the doorway of the barn, a stogie sticking out the side of his mouth, the light of a kerosene lamp behind him outlining his bulk. He kept his head angled down, the brim of his hat low, to avoid acknowledging Sam.

Seeing him reminded Sam of his one remaining job. He adjusted his hat and turned toward the barn. "Evenin', Mr. Perry," he said, taking care not to put a drop of warmth in his tone.

Virgil lifted his head and feigned surprise. "Well, hullo there, Samuel."
He tipped his hat at him. "I see the Connors folk had a big shindig tonight.
Didn't last too long, though."

"Nope, it didn't."

The man shifted his weight. He knew something was up. "Everythin' all
right?" He blew out a puff of smoke.

"Nope."

Silence prevailed for five long heartbeats, while two sets of eyes bored
deep into each other. "Say y'r piece," Virgil finally stated, unmoving.

"I intend to. It'll only take a moment of your time. You ready?"

The fellow's lip curled up in the corner as he made slits of his piercing
eyes. "Yeah."

"Two words: You're fired."

Virgil gave a humorless smile but failed to hide the little twitch in his
shoulder. "You can't do that. Your mother calls the shots."

"Sorry, in this case, I'm callin' 'em. I'm tellin' you y' got till tomorrow
mornin', eight o'clock at the latest, to get your sorry backside off this property." He returned the cold smile. "And don't be thinkin' 'bout comin' back
here with some fancy lawyer. It won't do you any good, seein' as the sheriff's
already onto you—as is Judge Corbett. Yeah, I paid each o' them a little call a
couple o' days ago. Mother informed me of the bribes, Perry. The game's over,
and the deep, dark, ugly secret's out, so you got nothin', you hear me? It's over."

Virgil stared, unspeaking, and raised a hand to scratch his stubbly jaw.
"I don't know what you're talkin' 'bout."

"Uh-huh." It took all his strength not to knock the fellow off his feet.
"Get this through your thick, bony head, then. You're lucky you're not
headed for the state pen. Blackmail's a crime, Perry. I thought you were
smart enough to know that. Apparently not. Now, the good news is, we're
not pressin' charges—not at this point. You cause us any trouble, though,
an' you're history."

For the first time, Virgil showed his nerves when he licked his lips and
swallowed, his Adam's apple jumping like a fish at a mayfly. He dropped his
cigar and ground it out with his boot. "I'll pack my gear."

Sam took great care to keep his voice calm and steady. "That's good,
Virgil. That's real good." He started to head for the house, then paused and

said over his shoulder. "I'd skedaddle real fast, if I were you. Might want to start makin' tracks before dawn. Never can tell what Sheriff Marshall's thinkin'."

When he turned again, he heard the man do a fast shuffle.

34

$\mathcal{S}$am had not gone out to see his mother even once since the family gathering, and Mercy feared the wall would one day grow too thick and high to ever come down. Moreover, she didn't like that he refused to talk about it, always clamming up whenever she suggested he at least try to make amends. Oh, but it was hard following the reverend's advice when it came to holding her preaching to a minimum. Yes, his mother might die a lonely old lady, but she didn't want to watch Sam evolve into a grumpy, coldhearted old man.

Aunt Gladys had been kind enough to host a family gathering at which she read aloud Flora Connors' confession and apology for her moral failure with Oscar Evans. Mercy had declined attending, not wishing to hear her father's name soiled even further. She certainly didn't condone his actions even one particle, but hearing the matter rehashed with her relatives didn't sound appealing.

According to Aunt Gladdie, the evening had gone as well as could have been expected—and that was all the summary Mercy had needed to know that the upheaval had been every bit as tense as it'd been at Flora's place, from the sound of Sam's report. Her aunt had also decided to deal with Uncle Fred and his catnapping prank in front of an audience. Apparently, while her family had thought nothing of involving themselves in a fistfight with the Connorses, bringing innocent children into the melee didn't sit well with anyone. Mercy had actually laughed when her aunt had relayed the family's censure of Fred for pulling such a dirty trick on two innocent children who'd just lost their parents. "You nabbed their kitten?" Aunt Aggie had shrieked. "I always knew you was a low-down fool, Fredrick Evans, but I didn't take you for a snake in the grass!" After she'd spouted off, she'd picked up a large volume from Aunt Gladdie's bookshelf and cracked it over his head.

Of course, Mercy had yet to receive any sort of apology from Uncle Fred. Frankly, she didn't expect one. Besides, it was the boys he owed it to, and she certainly didn't want him bringing the matter up with them. Best all around to put the whole thing behind them.

It was a sparkling Saturday, and Sam had taken the boys to play at a nearby park that had exactly one rusty slide, two swings, and a rickety bench. What it really had of value, though, was wide-open space, big enough for running long distances, hitting fly balls, and practicing batting techniques. Sam had invited Mercy along, even coaxed her to come, but she'd declined, claiming she had a list of household chores needing attention—bureau drawers to sort through and organize, floors to mop, and baking to do. None of it was extremely urgent, but she wanted the boys to have Sam all to themselves. They needed it, and she figured he did, as well.

Before long, delightful smells filled the kitchen: fresh-baked cookies cooling on a rack, a loaf of bread just out of the oven, and chicken noodle soup simmering in a pot on the stove. Those scents, mixed with the sweet peace that filled her soul after an hour of Bible reading and prayer, gave her a fresh outlook on her future. One verse in particular from the gospel of Matthew kept echoing in her mind: *"Let your light shine before men, that they may see your good works, and glorify your Father which is in heaven."* She had no notion as to why this verse, which she'd read dozens of times over the years, now held such special meaning, but she intended to take it to heart. "I will not let my light go out, Lord," she prayed aloud as she dusted a side table in the parlor, knowing even as she said it how very weak she could be when it came to keeping her promises to Him. *"'I can do all things in him that strengtheneth me,'"* she quickly recited.

Footsteps sounded on the porch around three thirty, so she naturally assumed Sam and the boys had returned, albeit a little earlier than expected. As usual, her heart gave a little extra thud at the anticipation of seeing her husband. Their relationship had not deteriorated in the least, but it hadn't progressed, either, and she couldn't imagine what to do to change it. She was nearing the conclusion that perhaps it was exactly as Sam wanted it—purely platonic.

A loud knock followed. Apparently the boys weren't back. She laid down her knitting, walked to the door, and peeked through the curtain. The caller was a shabbily dressed man she didn't recognize. A tiny lump of worry settled in her chest. She opened the door and peeked out. "Yes?"

"Hello, ma'am. My name's Ruford Medker. I'm a hired hand over at Flora Connors' place." The mucky-looking man finger-combed his shaggy brown hair, which hung well below his shirt collar and looked as if it hadn't seen a drop of water or a speck of soap in a month of Sundays. Even worse than his appearance was his stench.

Mercy made an effort not to wrinkle her nose. "Is there something I can do for you?"

"Is your husband around?"

"No, I'm afraid he's out at the moment, but I'm expecting him home within the hour."

"Oh, drat."

"Is something wrong?"

"Durn certain. His mother done took a bad fall down 'er steps, and she ain't lookin' good. I took her to Doc Trumble's, and he sent me here to come git 'er son."

She gasped. "Could you—would you drive me over there? Please?"

"You bet."

"Just—I'll be right with you." She raced into the kitchen to remove the pot of soup from the stove, then ran in search of pen and paper. Finding both, she quickly scrawled a note to Sam, laid it on the table, and then raced out the door. Mr. Medker stood beside his wagon, but she didn't wait for his assistance; she just hoisted her skirts and climbed aboard with little effort. On the way to Doc's, she prayed for Flora Connors. *Please, God…please, God. No more tragedy, Lord.*

The only thing that played back in answer were those words from Matthew: *Let your light so shine. Let your light so shine.*

Doc met them at the door. "Ah, you're here. I'm glad to see you, Mercy. Mrs. Hardy left early today, so I'm rather stranded," he rambled. "Where is Sam?"

"He's at the park with the boys. I didn't want to wait. I left him a note, so he should be here shortly."

"Good, good."

She followed her former boss down the familiar hall, ignoring the tiny pang of regret for leaving the job she'd loved, even though she knew she'd done exactly what she'd needed to. The malodorous Mr. Medker followed after. She'd wanted to send him packing, for fear he would stink up the whole place, but she knew he needed to learn of his employer's condition.

"How is she, Doc?" she finally asked.

"We'll talk in a moment," he said in a hushed tone.

In spite of her experience treating problems and ailments of all types, her first glimpse at the woman caused a shudder to course through her body. "Good gracious!" She turned to Mr. Medker and whispered, "How many stairs did she fall down?"

"The whole flight, far as I know."

"How did you find her?" Mercy asked.

"I was in the side yard an' heard her groanin' through the open windows. I stepped up to the house an' peeked inside, and that's when I seen 'er, layin' on the floor at the foot o' the stairs." He scrunched his face into a tortured grimace. "She was layin' in a big pool o' blood."

A tiny tear escaped Mercy's eye, trickling in a straight path down her cheek and falling on the front of her dress. "Does she have any broken bones?" she asked Doc.

"As a matter of fact…." He lifted the blanket at the corner to reveal two bandaged arms. "Two broken wrists."

"Oh, dear. She won't like that. Was she awake when she arrived?"

"She was awake, all right," said Mr. Medker. "She done bawled the whole way over. I never heard such carryin' on. Soon's we got here, though, she fell into that stupor."

"I'd venture it's partly due to shock from her injuries, and partly the hefty dose of laudanum I gave her to calm her down," Doc said. "Mr. Medker's right about her being all distraught. Frankly, I'd never before witnessed Flora Connors in a tearful state."

Mercy reached for the woman's forehead and pushed away a section of gray hair matted with blood. "This is quite a goose egg."

Doc nodded. "I fear she's had a slight concussion."

Mercy bent down, relieved to hear steady breathing. "She'll be fine, then."

"It'll be a long recuperation, I'd guess. I'll keep her here for a few days."

"Naturally."

"After that...." Doc's gaze lifted. "She's going to need constant care."

"We'll see to it, Doc."

Doc eyed her. "She has other family."

"All of whom are very upset with her at present."

"Yes, so I've heard."

Mr. Medker stepped out of the room, and Mercy took advantage of his absence to suck in several deep breaths. If Doc had noticed his odor, he didn't mention it, nor would he. In his line of work, he'd breathed in every stench known to man, and she sometimes wondered if he'd lost his sense of smell because of it.

"Do you have other patients in beds?"

"Just one. He'll go home tomorrow."

Mercy nodded. "I'll sit with Mrs. Connors."

"Are you sure?"

"Yes. Someone should be with her, in case she wakes up."

"You want me to tell that Medker fellow to go on back to the farm, then?"

"Yes, please."

He started to walk out.

"Doc," she said, halting him.

He twisted around. "Yes?"

"Did you smell him?"

"Who?"

She laughed. "Never mind."

⁓

Sam couldn't drive the wagon fast enough. John Roy and Joseph whooped and told him to speed up. He tried to keep his eye on them and the road at the same time, reminding them to stay seated and hold on tight. They had no idea what the rush was about, only that they were on the ride of their life. He'd read Mercy's note in such a hurry that he'd had little time to process it. Apparently, his mother had been hurt, but that was the extent of what he knew. *Lord, please don't let me be too late.*

When they arrived at Doc Trumble's office, he jumped down from the rig, then reached up and snagged hold of both boys at once.

"What's we doin' here?" John Roy asked.

"My mother's been in an accident," Sam explained, setting both boys on the ground. "I need to find out what's going on. Can I trust you two to behave yourselves?"

"We're always good," Joseph announced, drawing his shoulders back.

"No, we ain't," said John Roy.

"Shh, don't bicker." Sam's tone was testy. He took a breath to settle his nerves. "Come on." He ushered the boys into the too-quiet, dimly lit office. The waiting room was empty, since business hours ended at noon on Saturdays. "Follow me," he said, leading them down the hall.

"Is Mercy here?" asked Joseph.

"Yes, somewhere."

"Mercy?" yelled John Roy.

"Shh." Sam clamped a hand over the boy's mouth, just as Mercy poked her head out a doorway at the end of the corridor.

"There you are," she said, meeting them halfway. She wrapped Sam in a quick embrace, then stepped back, her face wearing a smile that didn't manage to mask her concern. "Your mother fell down a flight of stairs," she said quietly. "She's…pretty banged up."

"Is she gonna be all right?"

"Doc thinks so. He and Mrs. Trumble have gone out for some supper, so we're the only ones here, except for another patient across the hall from your mother." She glanced down at the sandy-headed boys and put a finger to her smiling lips. "You'll have to be extra quiet for the people who are feeling poorly. Can you do that?"

They stood taller. "You bet!" said Joseph.

"Good. Then, I'm going to ask you to go sit down in the waiting room while I take Sam back to see his mother."

"Can't we come too?" Joseph whined.

"Not quite yet. I want to take Sam back there first."

They shrugged their shoulders, then turned and walked back down the hall in the direction of the front room.

"Okay, then," Mercy whispered to Sam. "Follow me."

"Wait. How does she…you know, look?"

She pressed her lips together, and a muscle ticked in her jaw. "She broke both wrists, for one thing, and has a probable concussion and bruises aplenty. She's sleeping right now. Doc gave her a bigger than usual dosage of laudanum." She paused and met his eyes. "Are you ready to go in?"

He swallowed and took his time answering. The truth was, he wasn't sure he wanted to see his mother. "Yeah, I guess."

Sam lagged a few feet behind Mercy, every stride making the lump in his throat grow a little bigger. He didn't know what to make of his emotions. One minute, he couldn't stand his mother; the next moment, he panicked at the thought of losing her.

Mercy had discussed every part of her but her face. Even if she had, nothing could have prepared him for what he saw—the puffy, blackened cheek; the bloodied temple with a golf-ball-sized lump; the split lower lip. Moreover, with her eyes closed as they were, she looked near death. He almost wanted to lean over her mouth to make sure she was breathing. "I've never seen her so still and…well, vulnerable."

"She's in a deep sleep." Standing beside him, Mercy lent Sam a strength he hadn't known he lacked. As if sensing his weakness, she put her arm around him and squeezed. "She'll look worlds better when she wakes up. You'll see."

Unexpected moisture collected in his eyes, and he coughed to cover it. Mercy glanced up and noticed his emotion. "Sam."

With his thumb and forefinger, he squeezed the bridge of his nose, keeping his gaze lowered. "I guess I don't want to lose her."

"Of course you don't, sweetheart. She's your mother."

"She hasn't been a very good one." He didn't miss the endearment—*sweetheart*—and it only served to weaken his resolve the more.

"Well, no one's perfect."

He sniffed, feeling like a fool for blubbering. The last time he'd shed a tear had been upon hearing the news of his father's death in prison—and that had been in the privacy of his bedroom. "She's never even told me she loved me."

"She does, I'm sure of it."

They lowered themselves into the two wooden chairs near his mother's bed. Sam clasped his hands between his knees. "Do you think we should let the boys come in? I worry about them sittin' out there alone."

"I think it will be fine. Later, you can take them home. I plan to sit with your mother all night."

"No, I should do that. She's my mother, after all."

She hesitated. "Are you sure?"

His throat contracted. "Yeah, I'm sure."

35

$\mathcal{M}$ale voices, sounding close yet a thousand miles away, tugged at Flora's senses, and she willed herself to awaken. Foggy…so foggy. That was the only word she could draw upon to describe the condition of her brain right now. Furthermore, she couldn't place her surroundings, as the bed she lay on had an extra-hard mattress, the blanket tucked beneath her chin was stiff and scratchy, and the overall *feel* of the place was crisp and sterile.

Pain sliced her side, and a moan came out of her.

"Flora, can you hear me?" said the male voice. "She's coming out of it, Sam. Flora? It's Doc Trumble."

Samuel? Doc? What had happened to land her at Doc Trumble's place? She tried to lift her arms, perhaps to throw off the blanket and sit up, but they were weighted down with something—maybe even tied. A pain shot clear up to her left shoulder, and another moan escaped.

"You took quite a fall, Flora," the doctor said. "Do you recall it? Can you open your eyes?"

Wanting to open them and doing so were two different things. In fact, it took everything in her even to keep from falling back into sweet oblivion. Still, she had to try.

I took a fall? Slowly it came back, in tiny pieces: carrying a box of books down from upstairs, losing her balance on the first step, careening downward, rolling, twisting, cracking against something, and then an immediate jolt of pain to every part of her body. How could she have been so careless? Could she do nothing right? A clumsy fool, that's what she was!

With all her will and might, she opened her eyes to mere slits. Hovering in front of her was Doc's bearded face with those beady green eyes, and behind him stood Samuel, his body leaning forward, his expression unreadable. Oh, how he must hate her, all the more now for bringing this trouble upon him. He always accused her of doing things to get attention, and she would admit that she sometimes did, but not this time. She attempted to open her mouth, but the effort proved too great, and instead she drifted back into her deep, dark place of slumber.

~

Sam sat staring at his mother. Just yesterday, he wouldn't have imagined himself missing sleep to sit at her bedside. He didn't hate her, but he also didn't care much for her. Perhaps he loved her but didn't like her, if that made sense. She stirred, a tiny whiffling sound escaping her lips, so he sat forward. She'd been doing a lot of this over the past two hours, so he didn't hold out much hope that this time would be any different. But then her eyelids fluttered open, and she stared at the ceiling.

"Mother?"

Ever so slowly, she angled her head in his direction. He stood up, so that she wouldn't have to crane her neck, and loomed over her. "How are you feelin'?"

"Samuel? What's happened?"

"You fell down the stairs. One of your hired hands found you in the foyer."

"Oh, yes. I remember."

"You remember? How did it happen?" He saw her move beneath her blanket, and he feared she had escaping on her mind. "Don't try to sit up. Doc says you broke both wrists. He had to set them in plaster o' Paris bandages."

"I've broken my…my wrists? How could that be?"

"You fell down the stairs."

"I know, but…my wrists? When did I do this?"

"Today."

Her eyes glazed over. "Don't hate me for doing it." She pushed the words out as if each one weighed a hundred pounds.

"Why would I?"

"It was so stupid of me." Her eyes closed. "I sometimes do things…for…attention." This she whispered in spurts.

It was a hideous thought, her falling down the stairs on purpose. Was she capable of such a repulsive act? Was she that desperate? He swallowed hard. "Did you do this for attention?"

"Samuel." She cracked open her eyes, then closed them again. "Don't…leave…me. Lonely…come h-o-o-o-me."

"Mother, surely, you didn't do this on purpose." He leaned closer, but she drifted off again, her breathing deep and steady. Doc had expected her to sleep all night, waking only for brief intervals. He'd told Sam to go home and come back tomorrow, but he hadn't wanted to leave her alone. His stomach roiled and his hands turned clammy. What had she meant? In her delirium, had she just confessed to intentionally falling down the stairs? He pressed his hands against the sides of his head and gritted his teeth, wishing he could toss out the ugly mental images of her tumbling down the stairs—*on purpose.*

Rage and turmoil swam in his brain until his temples throbbed. He had to get out of here, had to get away from her. He stood, threw her a parting glance, and stormed out.

⁓

"Mercy. Wake up, Mercy."

As if wrapped in a huge, sticky web, Mercy fought her way to the present, threw off her covers, and jumped to her feet. "What? What's going on? Where are the boys? Is the house on fire?"

Callused hands wrapped around her upper arms and gave a gentle squeeze. "Shh, no. It's me. Sam."

She came awake with suddenness, staring into Sam's probing eyes, his big Stetson sitting on his head at an angle. Realizing her lack of modesty, she whirled around to reach for the housecoat that usually hung on her bedpost. Remembering that she'd put it in the laundry box yesterday, she rushed to her wardrobe in search of something with which to cover herself. "What are you doing in here?" she asked in a panic.

"Settle down, would you? I just want to talk. Sorry I woke you."

"Okay, but…." The memory of his mother's accident came rushing back with a thud. "Your mother! Is she all right? What's happened?" Finding no suitable covering, she hugged herself.

"She did it."

"She did what?"

"She threw herself down the stairs on purpose. She's always feigned sickness for attention, and now she's caused herself an actual injury."

"No, Sam. Not even your mother would do a thing like that. It could have killed her."

"She would, and she did. She said as much."

"She woke up?"

Sam plopped down at the foot of her bed. Since the room was mostly dark, save for the moon's glow outside the window, Mercy deemed it safe to be seen in her thin nightgown. Surely, Sam couldn't make out her features; and even if he did, a husband was allowed to look, for goodness' sake. Besides, he'd come in her room to talk, nothing more. So, she approached the bed and sat down next to him, the mattress springs squawking under her.

"Tell me what she said."

"She mostly mumbled, but I made it out just fine. She said she does things for attention, and then she asked me not to hate her…said what she did was stupid. Said she was lonely and wanted me to come home."

Mercy's gut churned. "Maybe tomorrow she'll be more lucid and can clarify what she meant. I doubt—I mean, I can't imagine—"

"You don't know my mother," he cut in.

"No, I don't. But I soon will. She's coming here whenever Doc says she's well enough to leave."

His head jerked up. "Are you kiddin'? She'd create nothin' but upheaval."

"She can't go home, Sam. With two broken wrists, she won't be able to take care of herself."

"Then somebody else can do it."

"You're her only child, which makes us the responsible party. She'll come here."

He leaped from the bed. "She will not."

She followed suit, and two stubborn sets of eyes locked gazes. "Of course she will. I've already told Doc. It's the right thing to do, Sam, and you know it."

"You'd be stuck carin' for her while I go to work every day."

"I'm a nurse. I can handle her."

"Oh, really? How do you plan to go about handlin' her? That woman is too much for even the most experienced. She'll give you a terrible time, and I can't have that."

"The Lord will give me strength when the time comes. He's promised in His Word that His grace is sufficient to meet all our needs, and that His strength is made perfect in our weakness. All day long, the same verse has been echoing in my head. *'Let your light shine before men, that they may see your good works, and glorify your Father which is in heaven.'* I'm convinced the Lord wants to use me, and He wants to use you, as well, if you can just learn to forgive."

He opened his mouth to speak, but who could argue with the Word of God? He clamped it shut again. On instinct, she reached up and cupped his cheek. "You must learn to forgive her, Sam. If you don't, you'll never experience the abundant life God wants to give you. There is freedom in letting go of the things that bind you."

He frowned and leaned away from her hand. "I'm not bound by anything."

"Of course you are. The bitterness you harbor against your mother for the way she raised you, and now for this latest finding—her affair with my father—it's got you all tied up in knots."

"No, it doesn't."

"Yes, it does."

He breathed in a great gulp of air and grew solemn. "I'd prefer you not preachin' at me, Mercy."

"I'm not preaching. I'm stating a few simple facts." The reverend's advice echoed in her mind: *"Take care to avoid a preaching tone....Your best defense is prayer."* "But if you took it as such, I apologize."

He looked into her face, then took one of her hands in both of his and squeezed. Then, slowly, he bent and kissed her cheek, a feather-light sensation that only made her long for more. She turned her face up in invitation and closed her eyes, but he didn't take the bait. Dratted man!

"We'll talk about this more at breakfast."

She opened her eyes. "I've already determined it's the only thing to do."

"We'll see. Go back to bed." His voice bordered on brisk. Was that it, then? No more kisses? She wanted to scream at him to notice her in her sleeping gown, but his dour mood must have put blinders on him. He turned and headed for the door. Out of frustration, she stomped her foot. "You are a—a belch-breathing stinkweed, Samuel Connors."

That stopped him like a glue trap. "A *what?*" He swiveled around and stared at her, his brawny silhouette blocking the doorway.

She gulped. "You heard me."

He gave one long blink, then looked her up and down. She swallowed what felt like a prickly cactus, knowing she'd stepped over the line with her comment. Step by agonizing step, he swaggered back to her, removing his hat and tossing it on the bed. "Watch what you call me, Mercy, or I may kiss you to the point of no return. Is that what you want, wife of convenience?"

Lord help her, but she couldn't breathe. "What?"

"Don't think for a second you don't tempt me. I'm a full-blooded male who's been mindin' his manners far too long."

She truly had stepped over that line—way over it. "I merely meant—"

He tipped her chin up so that she had no choice but to meet his gaze, their breathing coming out in stops and starts, her racing heart thudding in her ears and making her shiver in the dusky dark.

"Cold?"

"No."

"Scared, then?"

She jerked back and squared her shoulders. "Of course not." Of course, she was! Scared spitless, actually.

His hands clasped her upper arms, firmly yet gently. She shivered again as he drew her close, blanketing her in a warm, tight embrace that soldered their bodies together.

He'd kissed her plenty of times before, but this kiss…ah, this one didn't feel like the others. He didn't simply kiss this time. No, he lavished, then lingered, then drew away by slow degrees before starting the process all over again, deepening, growing, and multiplying the whole experience until she fell into an almost trancelike state, dizzy, breathless, and sated. *I love you, Samuel Connors. I love you, love you, love you.* But she couldn't bring herself to voice the words, as he had yet to utter them aloud to her. Did he feel the same? She wanted desperately to know, yet was even more desperately afraid to ask.

The kiss ended with all due reluctance, and with Sam's nose buried in the curve of her neck. "I've gotta go get a little sleep, or I'll be good for nothin' tomorrow."

"Yes," she managed. *You could sleep here,* she might have said, but her dryer-than-sand throat wouldn't allow the words to come out.

Before turning to go, he pinned her with tired blue eyes. "I don't want my mother livin' with us."

There was no point in arguing further at three in the morning. "Like you said, we'll talk more at breakfast."

He touched the skin beneath her chin, looking like he had something more to say—or do—but then he dropped his hand and walked out.

36

All that week, Flora fussed and stewed at having to be fed, needing help with her private ablutions, and depending on someone else, either Mrs. Trumble, Mrs. Hardy, or Mercy Evans, to give her a drink of water. Yes, Mercy Evans waited on her, arriving early in the morning to feed her breakfast and give her a sponge bath, leaving after lunch to tend to her own chores at home, and returning later to feed her supper. The second and third nights, Mercy stayed there, sleeping on a cot in the next room, in case Flora needed something in the middle of the night.

Flora insisted again and again that she ought to go home, but the girl refused, claiming she didn't mind at all, that Sam was home with the boys and would gladly get Joseph off to school and take John Roy to her aunt Gladys's house. Had Flora's other relatives any shred of compassion, they would have stepped forward, but they were all still mad as hornets at her, and of course her sister and brother-in-law had left town just before the accident.

What a fine fix she'd put herself in, making that brainless misstep at the top of the stairs and tumbling clear to the bottom. Worse, Samuel refused to visit her, claiming she'd done the silly thing on purpose. Good grief, who would purposely throw herself down a flight of stairs? Apparently, she would, according to her son—which made her wonder if his wife thought the same. At the very least, Mercy had to despise her for the affair with her father. But if she did, she didn't let on. In fact, if anything, she treated her with too much kindness—the sort that made Flora uncomfortable. No one else—not even her own relatives, whose good deeds were done with the unspoken understanding that she would return the favor—had treated her in this manner. Apparently, Mercy had learned, in her years of working with Doc Trumble, to treat everyone with a generous spirit, whether she liked the individual or not. It was the only way Flora could make sense of her behavior.

She really didn't understand this girl her son had married. She was like no one she'd ever met, always humming one tune or another; seemingly content to spend her days seated in the straight-backed chair next to Flora's bed, knitting, sewing, or reading her Bible. Occasionally, she shared a passage with Flora and asked her what she thought about it. Naturally, Flora never had anything to say; she could count on one hand the number of times she'd opened her own Bible. The thing was still like new, its fine leather cover soft and pliable, its pages wrinkle free and clean as fresh-fallen snow. Oh, she believed in God, of course. What good person didn't? And she faithfully attended church without fail. Again, what good person didn't? Beyond that, she couldn't claim to know much of anything about spiritual matters. She'd never seen the importance.

Right at seven thirty, the girl came through the door. "Good morning, Mrs. Connors. How are you feeling?"

"Peachy," she replied, unable to produce a smile. All she wanted to do was go home, home to her quiet house and quiet farm, where no one but a few hired hands hung around. With Virgil Perry gone, she rather liked the idea of living out her days in peaceful solitude. Who needed Samuel? Let him stay away, for all she cared; let him believe his cockeyed notion that she'd fallen down the stairs on purpose. She missed him, yes, but if he planned on throwing her accusatory glares for the rest of her life, then he could just keep his distance. Even as she thought it, she knew she wanted a relationship with her son. Rebuilding it would be the trick.

"Peachy is good. I'm feeling peachy myself. Plus, I have some good news."

Flora rolled her eyes at the overoptimistic young lady. "Oh? What's that?"

"Doc says you can leave today. He'll be coming in soon to talk to you and give you a thorough looking over."

"Really?" For the first time in a long while, Flora's chest fluttered with excitement. She tried to sit up, but the pain in her wrists kept her from completing the task. It annoyed her that every little thing she might attempt would require the use of her hands—hands that proved worthless. May as well cut the silly things off, for all the good they did her. At least the rest of her had healed quite nicely: her bruised hip less painful, the bump on her head all but gone, the cuts and scrapes she'd suffered from smacking against the stairs mostly mended, and the headaches caused by the concussion subsided.

"Yes, but…well, there's something else."

Worry curdled in her stomach. "May as well come out with it."

"You can't go home. Doc Trumble says you're unable to care for yourself."

"Well, that's ridiculous. Of course, I can take care of myself. You've spoiled me, but once I get home, I'll figure out a way to make it work."

"I hardly think that's possible, Mrs. Connors. Look at your arms. They are completely bandaged up to your elbows, and when you try to use them for support, you wince in pain. Why, you can't even use your fingers without putting a strain on your wrists. It's simply not going to work. In time, you'll go back home, but not till you're ready and able."

The nerve! "Who appointed you my boss, young lady? I don't need you telling me what I can and can't do. I'll manage just fine." She knew she'd used a harsher tone than necessary, but she couldn't help it. What was the matter with her? Mercy had been nothing but sweet to her, and how had she treated her? With ornery, obstinate snobbishness. People thought she didn't see herself as she truly was, but she looked in the mirror every day, and she knew every ugly secret hiding beneath the brusque exterior.

Mercy brushed right over her words. "You won't be able to bathe, clean your teeth, cook your meals, feed yourself, dress or undress, make your bed, or do any other household chores. Good heavens, you know as well as I you can't even use the privy without help." Mercy sighed, her shoulders slumping. "You can't go home, Mrs. Connors, and that's the simple truth."

Heat rose up her face, not so much from embarrassment as from sheer frustration at having to admit she was right. "All right, then. What on earth do you propose?"

Mercy gave a little backward glance, and in walked Samuel. The sight of him made Flora's heart take a tiny plunge. "You're comin' home with us, Mother," he announced, as matter-of-factly as if he were telling her today's weather forecast. "And there'll be no argument."

꘏

At Mercy's request—order, rather—Sam had moved the sofa out of the front parlor, then gone out and purchased a cot to put there, in his mother's makeshift bedroom. Mercy had fixed it up to look as such, hauling in a small, unused dresser and setting a vase of flowers atop it, along with a bowl and pitcher, and making up the bed with a set of frilly sheets, a warm, pastel blue blanket, and a floral bedspread she'd purchased at the general store. He'd poked his head in the door earlier that week and said, "She'll be here only a little while, Mercy. You're makin' this out to look like a permanent affair."

She'd smoothed out a tiny wrinkle in the bedspread, then turned and waltzed past him with a pretty smile. "'*Let your light shine before men, that they may see your good works, and glorify your Father which is in heaven.*'" She'd been reciting it so often, he'd learned it himself and had started mouthing it along with her.

Now, here they were, jouncing up East Wood Street toward home, his mother seated between him and Mercy on the wagon seat, her bandaged wrists resting in her lap. Mercy did enough chattering for all three of them, and he was thankful for it, as he didn't much feel like conversing, so absorbed was he in thought. How would his mother fit into their daily routine? Would the boys drive her batty? Would she drive them batty? How long before they all, including Mercy, had their fill of her? Doc had said it would be a good three weeks before he could remove the bandages and check to see how the bones were healing. He remained optimistic about her full recovery, but it was the getting there that worried Sam.

They pulled into the drive, and Sam waited for his mother to make some negative remark—the yard could stand a few more bushes; the roof looks like it's sagging a bit on one side; the driveway needs new gravel; the paint is starting to peel from the siding near the peak. But all she said was, "Very lovely house." He breathed a sigh of relief.

The boys barreled out of the house. "Sam! Mercy! You're home!" They bounded down the porch steps and ran across the yard to the wagon, their eyes as round as plates and as full of curiosity about the passenger, as if they'd just found a strange object from another world and wanted to learn all they could about it. To date, most of what they'd heard regarding Flora Connors had been negative, despite Sam and Mercy's efforts to keep their voices down when speaking about her. Surely, the boys must consider her the worst of ogres.

Gladys made her way down the steps, her hand shielding her eyes from the noonday sun. "Hello, Flora. I trust y'r feelin' better after that nasty fall."

Sam held his breath as his mother's gaze shifted to the woman.

"Hello, Gladys. Yes, I'm feeling quite good, thank you, although tired." His breath came out in a whoosh as another wave of shock shot through him. He threw Mercy a quick glance over his mother's head, and she smiled back at him.

He turned his attention to John Roy and Joseph. "Boys, you remember my mother."

They tilted their heads back and scrunched up their faces.

"Kinda," answered Joseph.

"Is she gonna live with us?" asked John Roy.

Flora chuckled. "Goodness, no. I'll be out of your hair before you know it."

"Outta ar hair?" asked John Roy.

"She means she won't be stayin' long," said Sam.

Intending to park the rig later, he twisted the reins around the brake handle and jumped down, then reached up to assist his mother. The move proved awkward with her bandaged arms, but they managed, and he didn't miss the wince she made when she landed a bit too hard on her feet. He felt bad for not having gotten a better grasp on her. "Sorry, Mother."

"For what? I'm fine, thank you." She brushed at her skirts with her bulkily bandaged hands and then walked without assistance up to the house.

"Goodness gracious! Them is big bandages," Joseph said, his expression one of awe.

Sam blinked in disbelief when his mother actually smiled. "Yes, aren't they? You can give them a closer look when we get inside, if you like."

"Would I ever!" the boy exclaimed.

"Me, too!" John Roy chimed in.

It took only a few minutes to get his mother settled. Clearly, she wasn't ready for any kind of house tour, judging by the weary pallor of her face. Sam entertained the boys while the women discussed a number of items Flora might need Sam to fetch for her from the farm, Mercy making a list. When done, she handed it to Sam, then insisted Flora be left alone to rest. Wonder of wonders, she uttered not a word of resistance.

Reaching his mother's house, Sam had to admit she kept the place with care, the two-story edifice looking regal with its stately columns and well-manicured shrubs. An unfamiliar wagon parked by the barn piqued his curiosity, but he figured it must belong to one of the hired hands. Since Virgil Perry's departure, he'd been trying to decide how to proceed with the farm—whether to promote one of the hired hands or to seek out someone new. Since he had no real interest in the place, trying to determine the better course gave him a regular headache.

He jumped down, and as he tethered Tucker to a post in front of the porch, a man emerged from the barn. Sam recognized him as Curtsall Brown, a neighbor whose property bordered the Connors' land.

"Afternoon, Samuel. You remember me, I hope." Mr. Brown hurried his steps and extended a hand.

"Yes, sir." Sam tipped his hat at him, then shook his hand, curious as to what had brought the fellow to his mother's place. "Good to see you."

As if reading his mind, Brown gestured behind him. "Been talkin' to one of the hands. Orville Todd, to be exact."

"Oh?"

"I'll get right to the point. First, I heard about your mother's fall and want to extend my sympathies."

"Well, thank you. Appreciate it."

"Second, I heard about the firin' of Virgil Perry. You want my opinion, I never did trust that man."

Sam grinned and wiped his sweaty palms on his pants. "That makes two of us."

"And, third, I'd like to buy your family's farm."

"Really?" That bit of news nearly knocked him over. "Well, you'd have to discuss that with my mother."

"I understand that, and I will, but I figured since you were here, I'd broach the subject with you, maybe give you somethin' to ponder. I'm prepared to pay fair value for the house and land. My son and his wife and family are moving back to Paris. They been down in Georgia, where her folks is located, but they want to come north again. They'd live in the house, and my son would operate the farm, although it'd be in my name. We'd work out all the details later. Might be you could mention this to your mother...when the timin' seems right, I mean. I know how stubborn that woman can be."

Sam let go a mild chuckle. "You got her pegged. I'll talk to her about it when the opportunity presents itself. Right now's not a good time. Frankly, I like the idea, but whether she will remains to be seen. She's mighty attached to this place."

The fellow removed his hat and scratched his scruffy head of hair, then plunked it back in place. "I know she is, but she can't work it like my son would be able to do. You recall Jeb."

"Yes, sir, I do. He's a few years older than me, so we never connected much on a personal level. I remember him for bein' a fine farmer, though, and a hard worker."

They talked a few minutes longer, and the more they spoke, the more Sam was convinced that his mother would be wise to jump on the offer. The Browns were good people, diligent and loyal. They'd take the farm into the next generation.

After bidding the man good-bye, Sam entered the house through the front door. The familiar place held an unfamiliar eeriness about it, especially when he saw the bloodstains on the floor at the base of the stairs. Someone had wiped them up, but not very thoroughly, and the box his mother had been carrying when she'd fallen lay empty, with an array of books strewn about it. Even though it had been several days, Ruford Medker had pretty much left everything just as he'd found it the day of the accident.

His mother would have a fit if she learned that things still lay in disarray. Moreover, she'd loathe the thought of blood having seeped into the wood cracks to dry there. He was no kind of housekeeper, but he'd have to see what he could do to at least clean up the bloodstains. Sam set the box to rights, then started picking up the books and arranging them inside. They looked mostly the same—leather-bound, with titles in gilded lettering up the spines. When he picked up a smaller volume with a tattered clothbound cover of faded blue paisley print, and no title of any kind, he couldn't resist investigating. On the first page was written, in his mother's hand, "1863–1890." The first entry was simple: *February 14, 1863 – Heart broken beyond fixing. Lloyd and Lewis gone. All my joy and happiness went with them.*

Sam gave a hurried glance at the door, as if expecting someone to come bolting through it to admonish him for reading something so private. And yet the pull to read more tugged at him harder than the obligation to lay it down. He glanced at dates that spanned the next few months and the scrawled messages of gloom, all of which said almost the same thing, over and over. *Miss my precious cherubs. Life will never be the same. No use in living. Can't find it in me to smile. Ernest tries to talk to me, but I don't want to converse.*

He skipped a few more pages, taking him to the first anniversary of his brothers' deaths, and read several more entries. *Cloudy and dreary today, just like my heart. Ernest has grown distant. I don't blame him. Samuel has grown taller.*

Samuel has grown taller. That was it? She'd had nothing more to say about her then four-year-old son? Try as he might, he couldn't dredge up any memories from that time, nor did he want to. He sat down on the bottom step and went back to skimming pages, all of which repeated the same message of despair. Jumping ahead, he landed on 1876, the year of his mother's affair with Oscar Evans. His eyes darted busily from page to page, looking for a clue. Finally, he found an odd entry that read, *Can't sleep. A guilty conscience devours. Soon there won't be anything left of me.* A few pages later, *Ernest despises me, and why shouldn't he?* Then, on the next page, *Ernest is seeing her again. Must see what I can do to win him back. No love between us, only our reputations to think about. Poor Ernest.*

The entry made no sense. She hated his father, and yet she'd written, "Poor Ernest"?

Impatient to learn more, his eyes raced over the pages. The scrawled entries ran the gamut.

I ended it with O., but he won't let it go. He wanted more from me, but I couldn't give it—not in good conscience. We're through. He must come to terms with it.

A bit further, he read, *Samuel is so tall and handsome now. I'm filled with regret that I don't know my son.*

Then, *Ernest gave her money to leave town. She's gone, but she took his heart with her. Poor Ernest is lost without her. It's better this way. What would folks say if he up and married her? We have to think of the family name.*

And then, *Ernest and I will stick it out.*

Weeks and sometimes months separated subsequent entries—spans of time when her head must have been swimming with thoughts and emotions she could have recorded but didn't. Sam flipped ahead, searching for the day of the shooting, dreading yet desperate to know what had gone through her mind. But when he came to the place where the date would have fit, she'd entered nothing. Disappointment flooded him. Only one entry existed from the time of the trial, and all it said was, *Very tired. When will this end? Ernest is going to jail. Life is over. So much of this is my fault.*

He thumbed through the pages until he reached the date of his father's death. *Ernest died today. Dropsy is what the prison doctor said. I pray he didn't suffer.* That was it. His eyes trailed further down. *Ernest's funeral today. Feeling numb. No one here to comfort me, but it's all right. I don't deserve consolation. Have come to hate the Evans clan more than ever, because of what they represent to me. If only O. had stayed away. Might have made things work with Ernest. Might have convinced him to love me instead of her. Too late for calling back the past. Bitter and depressed. Life is worthless.*

Regretting having read this much, Sam decided to scan only a few more entries before boxing up the book for good. He skipped to more recent times. *June 15, 1890 – Samuel entered a burning house and saved two little boys. How did he turn out so good, so brave?* She'd considered him brave? Why hadn't she said so? *Removed him from the home of Mercy Evans. She looks so much like her father. I don't like the reminder. Didn't love him, but I admit I cared too much for him. It was wrong, so wrong. Felt good to know he found me attractive.*

The next entry she hadn't dated. *Fear I am losing Samuel. Can't blame him for hating me; I have been a terrible mother. If only I could turn back the clock and start again.*

Then came another. *Family hates me. I've spilled the truth. It is over. No more lies or secrets. Relieved in some ways, scared in others. So alone. Glad Virgil is gone. Grateful to Samuel for handling that. Like a rock lifted from my chest.*

She'd dated her final entry. *October 12, 1890 – Chilly today. House so quiet. No one to talk to, but can't blame folks for staying away. I'm not very lovable. Plan to clean the attic this week. Life will get better. Must find a way. Refuse to quit.*

Sam closed the book, heaved a loud breath, and slouched against the stairs, staring up at the ceiling. If nothing else, her final entry proved two things: first, his mother had not purposely thrown herself down the stairs; and, second, he was a self-centered, brutish clod, so bent on punishing her for the years she'd overlooked him that he'd failed to notice how much she loved him. If his mother hated herself, he hated who he'd become even more.

Mercy had been right—he was a belch-breathing stinkweed!

Right there, in the silence of the front hall, he went down on bent knee and confessed his sins, tears of repentance coursing down his face, his heart aching with regret, and, on the horizon, freedom in Christ bounding toward him like a song on wings.

37

Sam was different. Mercy couldn't put her finger on it, but he had changed in the past week—quite drastically, in fact. And she found she liked the new Sam. Gone was his morose mood, even with his mother under the same roof, and even despite her somewhat cantankerous attitude about having to be waited on from morning till night. He'd been spending more time with the boys after work, keeping the suppertime conversations pleasant and nonconfrontational, and infusing the household with new, unnamed energy that helped to keep the atmosphere cheerful. As for their passionate kisses, they had yet to reoccur—their contact was limited to mere pecks. She imagined, even hoped, his mother's presence was to blame. Of course, it was possible he'd reached a pivotal point at which he had to make a decision about the marriage—all or nothing—and he didn't want to kiss her fully again until he'd chosen. Oh, how she prayed he'd want to keep the marriage alive.

Flora had showed obvious improvement in the days since leaving Doc's office. She could feed herself again, finally able to hold a fork and grip a cup. She'd also regained enough mobility to tend to her personal business, and Mercy found it almost humorous, the way she made a point of announcing when she was headed for the privy, adding, "And, no, I don't need help." It had become a joke among the rest of them, the boys included, whenever they too walked to the outhouse. "And, no, I don't need help," they'd say before heading out the back door. Even Flora had learned to laugh at the joke. It was so rare to eke as much as a smile out of her, so an actual spurt of laughter brought Mercy enormous satisfaction.

Flora had also taken an interest in reading, so Mercy provided her with plenty of material to pass her time, mainly copies of the *Ladies Home Journal*. Flora had even taken to reading to Joseph and John Roy from the *Golden Days for Boys and Girls* periodicals, and the boys loved gathering close to her on the divan, even if Flora didn't reciprocate the snuggles. After a while, Mercy noticed a softening in her eyes when they scooted up next to her.

She also noticed Flora reading from her Bible, which she'd started leaving within reach on the coffee table. One quiet afternoon, with Joseph at school, Sam at work, and John Roy sprawled on the rug for a rare nap, Barney and Roscoe curled up beside him, Mercy saw Flora with her nose buried in the Good Book. Not wanting to interrupt her reading, Mercy offered to make her a cup of tea. Flora accepted, and when Mercy returned with the steaming beverage, Flora lowered the Book to her lap and deftly clamped the cup between her bandaged hands. Mercy was about to return to the kitchen when Flora's voice halted her.

"It's been a source of comfort…your Bible."

It was the first time, in Mercy's recollection, that Flora had initiated conversation, and she silently prayed for the wisdom to say the right thing. She sat down in a chair by the hearth. "It always brings me joy and comfort, too."

Flora lowered her gaze and picked at a lint ball on her skirt. "I didn't say anything about joy. It's been a long time since I felt that particular emotion."

Help me, Lord. "Why do you think that is, Mrs. Connors?"

"First off, would you kindly start calling me Flora? I am your mother-in-law, after all."

Finally, she'd acknowledged the relationship. Mercy gave a light giggle. "I'd be honored to call you that. I just wasn't sure of my place. I didn't want to offend you."

Flora actually smiled. "I can understand why you'd worry about that. I'm such an old grump."

"No, you're not." Of course, she was, but Mercy thought it best not to agree with her. "Never mind that. Why is your life absent of joy?"

"What is there to be joyful about? I've lost my husband, my family, and, presently, my independence. Suffering saints, my own son only talks to me out of a sense of obligation."

"I don't think that's the case—about your son. Yes, you've had a rocky relationship, but there's always hope. As for your family, they'll come around, you'll see. Just give it time. I think you're feeling a little depressed right now, with all that's happened to you, and haven't we all felt like that a time or two?"

Flora raised her eyebrows. "You? Depressed?"

Mercy tossed back her head and laughed with abandon. "Your expressions are priceless, Mrs.—er, Flora. I should start writing them down."

The corners of the woman's mouth lifted slightly. "I could say the same for you, Mercy."

It was the first time Flora had addressed her by name, and Mercy's soul took to humming "God Moves in a Mysterious Way."

"Maybe so, but to answer your question, yes, *me*. I'm far from perfect, but when I place my full trust in Jesus, I find myself dwelling less on the things that sadden me and more on the joy that comes from serving Him. When I find myself overwhelmed, unsure, or plain heartsick, I make a habit of saying, 'Jesus, help me.' That three-word prayer brings such sweet assurance, for when we cry out, making ourselves vulnerable to our heavenly Father, it's like lovely music to His ears. Think of it—the God of the universe, our Creator, is nearer to us than a drop of dew on the morning grass."

She had no idea where *that* had come from—she'd never been known for flowery talk—so she cringed to imagine what Flora must think. She braced herself for the harsh words that were sure to come.

There was a long silence, and then Flora cleared her throat. "That was... quite profound, if I do say so."

Profound? Mercy couldn't recall one profound thing she'd said in her life. She attributed it to her earlier prayer for wisdom. "Well, it's true," she went on. "God doesn't want us living in sad, lonely states. He wants to fill our hearts with joy. That's not to say we won't have periods of sadness or despair; but when those times come upon us, we don't have to remain defeated and without hope." She gestured to the Bible in Flora's lap. "May I?"

Flora nodded, so Mercy rose and lifted the Book. Sitting back down, she leafed through the pages until she reached Psalm 3. "Here's one of my favorite verses, if you don't mind."

"No, not at all. Please, read it to me—and any others you consider favorites."

She couldn't believe her luck. But then, it had nothing whatever to do with luck and everything to do with God's perfect timing. "All right, then, here it is. *'But thou, O LORD, art a shield about me; my glory, and the lifter up of mine head.'* That is to say that when you're feeling especially disheartened, He is right there with you, ready to lift you up and bring encouragement." Without waiting for a response, she hastened to the next verse God put upon her heart, finding it faster than she thought possible. "Here's another verse, this one from Psalm forty-two. *'Why art thou cast down, O my soul? And why art thou disquieted within me? Hope thou in God: for I shall yet praise him for the health of his countenance.'* Did you catch that? His countenance is our health. In other words, God's smile is the reason we smile."

Rather than present Mercy with her usual sour face, Flora actually grinned, showing her pearly teeth. "Well, isn't that something? You've given me much to think about, Mercy. Thank you."

"Thank you"? Her heart could barely contain those two simple words, the very first ones of gratitude the woman had uttered. Miracles seemed to be pouring in from every direction.

"You're welcome." She stood and handed the Bible back to Flora, then hesitated, wondering if she'd outstayed her welcome.

Flora must have sensed her indecision, for she motioned at the chair. "Sit, please. I have something to say."

Mercy did as told, again silently praying for God's will to be done in all things. After straightening her gingham skirt, she clasped her hands in her lap and straightened her posture, as if awaiting a lecture from the president of the board of education.

"Nothing really untoward, other than kissing, ever happened between your father and me."

If a bolt of lightning had stretched its hot fingers through the roof and pierced her in the side, she could not have been more shocked. "I—you didn't have to tell me that."

"I know."

"What's done is done, and I hold no grudges."

"That's very generous of you, but you should still know the truth, so there won't be any question. I liked your father very much, but I appreciated his attention more than anything else. It wasn't what you'd term love—at least from my side. Ernest had started doling out less and less affection after our twins died, and even less than that when he found someone else. I was plain lonely, and Oscar came along and filled the void. I'm not saying it was right. I just want you to know that it never went beyond a few kisses. Now, I'll tell you he wanted to pursue the relationship, make it into more than it was, but I refused. He even told me he loved me, but I never uttered the words back to him. After that, things started going very sour, and my life went even more topsy-turvy. Your father...he was very lonely, and there were no other women in all of Paris he cared about chasing after. Truth is he found me a challenge, and that challenge kept him busy and his mind occupied."

"Sam told me everything from that night he went out to confront you."

"Good. There should be no secrets between husbands and wives. That's what came between Ernest and me...that, and my inability to cope with my grief over the loss of our sons. After they died, I didn't treat Samuel the way he deserved. I still had him to dote on, but I couldn't see past my own selfish needs to reach out to him. I will carry that guilt with me for the rest of my life."

"You needn't. God will take it away, if you will just confess to Him, as well as ask Sam to forgive you."

Flora looked at her lap, entwined the eight fingers that hung out the ends of her bandages, and then glanced up and smiled. "Has anyone ever told you you'd make a mighty fine lady evangelist?"

Mercy smiled. "I'm no evangelist, and God knows it. I'm just a woman who loves Him and wants everyone to share in the same joy He's brought to me."

"You have been aptly named, my dear."

"*My dear*"? Her soul kept up its humming. "It's funny you should say that, since Sam said it to me just the other day."

Flora's head bobbed up and down. "Then you should know it's true. But, back to what we were discussing…since Samuel told you of our talk, have you anything further you want to ask about what happened between your father and me?"

Mercy shook her head. "I would love to put the whole thing to rest, and in truth, I don't need, or even desire, to know another thing. That is between you and God."

The woman's shoulders slumped, as if weary from a long day of work. She dabbed at the corners of her eyes, where moisture had collected. "Then, may I ask you to…forgive me…for bringing so much grief upon you and Samuel?"

As if springing from the blocks in a footrace, Mercy leaped from her chair and went to Flora. In one fluid move, the women embraced, Flora's hug a bit more awkward, with her arms bound up as they were, but Mercy's making up for it. She clung to her tightly, with tears running down her face, and wept the more when Flora's wall of emotion shattered and her own tears gushed like waves upon a shore.

⌒

One woman in tears was more than Sam could handle, but two pushed him over the cliff. When he and Joseph came through the door, disturbing not only the women's private moment but also rousing John Roy from a nap, he wanted nothing more than to walk back outside and return later.

"Samuel," his mother said.

Mercy released her and sat back, wiping her red, swollen eyes.

"Mercy and I…well, we've been doing a great deal of talking."

Mercy sniffed and started to laugh. "And crying."

"Yes, and that," his mother said.

Joseph cast a worried look at Sam, and poor John Roy just sat on the floor in a stupor-like state.

"Is everythin' all right?" Sam dared ask.

"Everything is better than all right," his mother said, eyes brimming. In all his days, he could count on one hand the times he'd witnessed her in tears. "I've settled some things with Mercy, and, frankly, I'd like to do the same with you, if that's all right. I know you just got home, but would you mind sitting down so we can talk?"

Lately, he'd been picking up Joseph from school, taking him home, and then returning to the shop for a few hours. Uncle Clarence would wonder what was keeping him. On the other hand, he'd mentioned that he might call it quits for the day and come in extra early the next morning. Either choice would meet with his uncle's approval.

"Yes, I could do that."

"What's you goin' t' talk about?" Joseph asked.

Mercy rose and held her arms out to the curious boy. "Come on, sweetie. Let's go out to the kitchen and check the cookie jar, shall we?"

"Cookies?" Joseph said, his voice turned chipper.

"If you'd like," she said, urging him forward and then reaching a hand toward John Roy. "You too, sleepyhead. Let's hear what your brother did at school today." She snagged hold of his lazily uplifted hand and tugged him up. Just before the threesome left the room, Mercy slipped Sam a knowing smile, then blew him a kiss, and his world tilted with dizzying pleasure.

⁓

Flora could not stop the flow of tears. The dam had broken, and it seemed she would never regain control of her emotions. She confessed to Sam the mistakes she'd made while raising him, and then she asked his forgiveness for the mess she'd made of life, for him and for their family. He gave it so readily, a fresh set of tears burst forth, unrelenting and unashamed. His arms around her only made her cry the more, for she couldn't recall the last time they'd embraced, or when she'd experienced such coursing warmth, relief, and happiness—and all at the same time. Was this the joy of which Mercy had spoken?

"I have never told you what a fine son you were, Samuel—and are—but I'm telling you now."

"Mother, it's not necessary."

"But it is. After the twins died, I neglected you. In my heart, I knew the Lord had spared your life, but something in me felt unworthy to be your mother. If I couldn't save the twins, how could I possibly be assured of saving you? I knew that if I lost you, too, my heart would stop beating. In some pathetically sick way, I believe I thought that devoting myself wholly to you would be your doom. I had failed to keep two of my sons alive; what was to keep me from failing you, as well? Fear overtook me, and I couldn't allow myself to love you in the way you deserved. I was too terrified of suffering another great loss. And, oddly, I lost you anyway…not in the physical sense, but in every other way." She frowned, trying to make sense of her explanation, which was unfolding to her as she gave it utterance. "Your father was not much better, Samuel, so let me apologize for him while I'm at it. I know he loved you, but he didn't know how to express it. Neither of us did, I'm afraid. But now…now, Samuel, I want to tell you I love you. I do. Oh, Samuel, I do."

Sam held her close. "Mother, I've got a confession o' my own, and I'm afraid it'll make you want to take back at least a portion o' that apology."

Rather than pull back, she kept her head resting wearily on his broad, hard chest. "What is it?"

"The other day, when I went out to the house to collect the items you wanted, I happened upon the box of things you were carryin' down from the attic when you fell…specifically, your diary. I'm sorry, but I read bits and pieces of it."

She was amazed that she didn't even bristle at the news, but it wasn't as if she had anything to hide. Her dark secrets were already out in the open. "Did you learn anything new?"

"Not really." He sounded tentative. Probably afraid of her, poor dear. "Well, one thing."

She leaned back to study him. "What was that?"

He swallowed, his Adam's apple bobbing. "I know you didn't throw yourself down those stairs. I misunderstood something you said, and it was plain foolish of me to accuse you o' that. Forgive me?"

"Pfff, there's nothing to forgive. Lord knows I've been guilty of faking illness to gain your attention."

This drew a good chuckle out of him, but he quickly sobered. "I have another confession."

She sat up, somehow gathering her strength. "I'm listening."

"After readin' your diary, I got down on my knees and confessed my sinful state to the Lord, asked Him to forgive me for not servin' Him as I should. And you know what? He did. Since that day, I've been free from guilt."

The tears started again. "Oh, Samuel, I need to do the same."

He smiled. "Well then, what are we waitin' for?"

Together, they bowed their heads, and Samuel led them in a prayer. She immediately realized her prayer to her heavenly Father had opened up a brand-new world to her—one of sunshine and not gloom, one of hope and not despair, and one of mercy and not blame.

38

Flora returned to her home exactly two weeks after leaving Doc's office, one full week earlier than he'd advised, but her days of rest and recuperation, not to mention her stubborn resolve and her newfound faith, had done wonders to heal and restore her—physically, as well as emotionally and spiritually. Even Doc had noticed a difference in her countenance when she'd gone in for another evaluation, accompanied by Mercy and Sam. "Flora Connors, I do declare, you've gotten younger and prettier, if an old married doctor can be so bold. What's happened to you?"

She'd smiled. "If you want the truth, I've been reborn, Doctor."

"Is that so?"

"The Lord forgave my sins, of which there were many."

"Well, I'll be, Flora. Religion looks good on you."

"It's not religion, Doctor; it's faith in Jesus."

Mercy didn't quite know where the good doctor stood with God, but at least he hadn't disputed Flora's faith. He'd removed the bandages and announced that the bones were healing nicely, then estimated that complete recovery would require another three to four weeks. Then he'd reset both arms, telling her with a hint of teasing not to even think about carrying something down a staircase. As for housework, he'd issued strict orders not to do anything that would cause strain. "If you feel the slightest twinge, you're overdoing it," he'd said, "and you'll pay later by way of incorrectly healed bones and eventual arthritis."

After hearing Doc's assessment, Sam and Mercy had pleaded with Flora to stay with them for the remainder of the recovery period. She'd refused, claiming they needed to concentrate on each other again, that she would rest better in her own surroundings, and that, with Gladys Froeling's promise of three weekly visits to prepare meals and help with chores, she'd survive just fine. To Sam and Mercy's utter shock, the unlikely pair had become fast friends. Gladys had even suggested that she and Flora study the Bible and memorize verses together, and Flora had happily accepted the challenge. Why, if ever there'd been a miracle of vast proportions, this was it!

Sam had spoken to his mother several times about the prospect of selling her farm. Before, she'd always balked at the notion, but the last time she'd hedged. "It's the only house I've ever lived in, apart from my childhood home, but I'll pray about it," she'd said, adding, "Oh, it feels good to say I'll pray about it! I've never said that before."

An hour after Sam had raised the subject, she'd broached it again. "If I were to sell the farm, where would I move?" Sam had suggested she buy something smaller and more manageable, closer to town, convenient for shopping, and Mercy had expressed eagerness in helping her look for a suitable property. Later that day, he'd taken Mercy aside and whispered, "Things may be getting better between my mother and me, but that doesn't mean I want her livin' next door, so please don't look at any houses on our street." Mercy had laughed so hard, she'd gotten a stitch in her side.

It was a crisp, clear Saturday morning when Sam and Mercy took Flora home. The boys had hugged her good-bye, then gone next door to spend the day with the Hansen boys. When they arrived at the house, Flora inspected every nook and corner, paying special attention to the place where she'd landed at the bottom of the stairs. Not a trace of blood could be seen, and everything stood in perfect order, all thanks to Aunt Gladdie, who'd rounded up a few relatives—her daughter, Amelia; Aunt Aggie; and Mercy's cousins Wilburta and Frieda—and made sure that not a speck of dust remained. They'd even restocked the pantry shelves and prepared a few small meals, waiting with preparation instructions in the icebox. Flora nearly wept with gratitude.

Her own family had been slow to come around, with the exception of Sam's aunt Hester, who never had been one for holding grudges. She'd told Flora to be patient, saying the family had been asking about her and would pay a call in due time.

"It's fine," Flora had said. "Now that I'm a Christian, I probably need to make a more sincere apology. I don't think they believed me the first time." This she'd said somewhat in jest, but Mercy believed she'd make the effort to right things with her relatives. After all, Flora had said, the Connors folk were known for sticking together. If that meant a bigger effort on her part, then so be it.

They hugged Flora good-bye, promising to return in two days. On the ride home, Sam directed Tucker on a detour. "Where are we going?" Mercy asked, pulling her woolen scarf a little tighter around her neck.

He turned to her with a devilish grin. "Have you noticed it's just the two of us for the first time in three weeks?"

"Mmm, yes, I did notice that. But what does that have to do with the route you're taking?"

His grin went a little crooked. "Oh, I don't know, maybe I want to show you somethin'. It's a little silly, but nonetheless...."

"Silly? I like the sound of that."

He looped a powerful arm around her shoulders and drew her to him. "That's because you're quite experienced in silliness."

"Hey! Watch it, mister."

He laughed and took the reins again, and they drove through the Tennessee hills, passing trees just changing from verdant greens to oranges, reds, and yellowish hues. The winds ruffled the boughs, shaking loose more leaves to join the ones already covering the ground like a multicolored quilt.

Soon they bumped along a narrow trail she didn't recognize. The wagon tipped and swayed, and she had to keep her arm looped around Sam's to keep from pitching forward. Up ahead, she spotted a small, broken-down shack and a ramshackle barn surrounded by weeds, the land around both seeming completely unkempt.

"What is this place?" she asked.

He pulled the brake, bringing the wagon to a halt, then tossed the reins over the handle. "This, my dear, is where it all began. It's where my great-grandparents first set up camp when they arrived from England. They bought this big patch of land"—he moved his arm in a semicircle—"and raised a couple o' kids here, my grandpa Connors, for one."

Atop the highest peak of the barn roof, an eagle was perched. The bird watched them with big, probing eyes, probably wondering who would dare infringe on his hunting territory.

"How did you find this place? And who owns it now?"

"I've known about it since I was just a kid. My father drove me out here once, and somethin' kept drawin' me back to it. No one's lived here for years. Last people who did moved to North Carolina. Whether they still own it is a mystery to me." A few empty bottles and pieces of garbage strewn about indicated someone used it as a hideout.

"What made your great-grandparents sell?"

"When their family grew, they decided to buy a larger piece o' property five miles north. Before my great-grandfather died, he deeded the new property over to my grandfather. *Your* grandfather owned the acreage bordering on *my* grandfather's land, and that's when the dispute took root over where the actual borders lay. I figure if my great-grandfather had never sold this spot o' land we're sittin' on, there never would've been a feud. But then, you and I might not have ended up together, either. In fact, our lives would've been completely different. It goes back to that verse in Romans about God makin' everythin' work out for good to those who love the Lord and are called accordin' to His purpose. He truly does cause the bad situations in life to turn around for our good when we fully trust Him. I didn't tell you this, but that day I went to my mother's to gather up a few items for her, I settled things with the Lord. You were right about the danger of fuelin' a root of bitterness with fury. I didn't want that to happen to me, so I surrendered my anger to God."

Mercy's soul took wings like an eagle's. "Oh, Sam, I'm so happy to hear you say that. I knew something had happened to change you. And you're right—God does work even in the ugliest of circumstances when we trust Him. It took an appalling tragedy—namely, the loss of my best friends—to bring the boys into my life and, through them, you. I never would have dreamed that anything good could come of that catastrophe, but the truth is, I know Millie and Herb would've wanted me to raise John Roy and Joseph, and having you to help has made the transition so much sweeter and smoother."

"So, you don't regret windin' up with me?"

"What? No, of course not." She hesitated. "Do you regret winding up with me?"

He swept his arms around her and kissed her cheek. "Not a chance. Come on, I have somethin' else to show you."

"What?"

He jumped off the wagon and reached up for her with outstretched arms. She went into them, delighting in how he lifted her at the waist, whirled her around, and set her down, all as if she weighed nothing. He took her hand and led her through the tall grass. They stopped by a big oak tree, and he gave it a thorough looking over, until he put his finger on a specific spot. "There! See it?"

She stepped in for a closer look and identified an ancient carving—a heart with letters inside. Squinting, she made it out. "It says 'S. C.,' and there's a plus sign under it. It's not finished." She looked at Sam. "Sam Connors?"

He nodded. "I was sixteen, and I had a crush on somebody. But it was ridiculous, not to mention impossible, so I left the rest of it blank."

"Who was the girl?" Curiosity had her mind whirling. "Should I be jealous?" The very notion of him caring for another woman did strange things to her heart.

He laughed. "I told you it was ridiculous—back then, anyway. So, no, you've got no reason to be jealous."

"What made it so ridiculous?"

"The girl. She was only twelve, and quite beyond reach."

Her head snapped up, and her heart thudded heavily. Could it be? "What are you saying?"

He chuckled and brushed his knuckles over her cheeks. "That girl was you, Mercy. You. I saw you every day when you passed by on your way home from school. You were always walkin' with some skinny little blonde."

She sucked in a loud breath. "That was Joy Westfall—you met her at the picnic."

"Yes, I remember."

"Oh, my goodness. Surely, you didn't notice me way back then."

"I did. You were the prettiest little brunette I'd ever seen. I'd watch you from the window, and, once in a while, I'd even come outside, pretendin' I needed to make a trip to the outhouse, just so I could feast my eyes a while longer."

"But, why didn't you…you know, pursue me when I got older?"

"Why? Because our families were at such odds. I figured I'd be the last person on earth you'd ever accept a date from, so, why bother even askin'?"

She grimaced. "And when you suggested we marry, I was utterly opposed to it."

"It took a bit of convincin'."

"I couldn't see it workin' between us, not because of who your family was as much as I couldn't see myself married to the man whose father shot my pa. Forgive me?"

"No need to, honey. It's all in the past." He reached into his back pocket and produced a jackknife. "I think it's time I finish this carvin', don't you?"

"Oh, Sam." She giggled. "Really?"

"Watch me."

He leaned against the tree and with great care carved out the letters M.E.C. beneath the plus sign. Once done, they both stood back to admire it. "Let's come back in ten years and check it again," she said.

He put an arm around her shoulder and tugged her close. "Sounds like a good plan. We'll bring the whole family—meanin' our five or so kids, includin' John Roy and Joseph, o' course."

A tiny gasp escaped her lips, and she angled him a shy glance. "Really?"

He kissed the top of her head. "Yes, really. But, for that to happen, I guess we'd have to do away with our arrangement."

Her pulse skipped. "Arrangement?"

"It's a little hard to make kids in a marriage where only kissin' is allowed."

"Oh." Now her pulse did more than skip; it accelerated. She looked up into his eyes.

He cupped her face with his work-roughened hands. "I love you, Mercy. Always have, always will."

Overwhelmed with emotion, she let a single tear fall untended. "I love you too, Sam, now and forever."

The murmured declarations made them stare at each other, their gazes still locked like two puzzle pieces. "Come here, brown eyes," he finally whispered. Like heat lightning, she moved into his warm embrace, their lips meeting in reckless abandon. Crushed together, they kept kissing, until he suddenly broke away and gazed into her eyes with renewed intensity. "We'll start tonight."

She felt her brows lift under the wisp of hair that had fallen over her eyes. "We'll start what?" She thought she knew, but she wanted to hear him say it.

He pushed her hair back with both hands as if to free her face for his adoring gaze. "Workin' on those five kids."

"One at a time, I hope," she said with a nervous laugh.

"O' course. More fun that way."

Despite the cooling breezes, warmth crept up her face. "Oh, Sam, I—"

He cut her off with another kiss. As it lengthened, they both grew breathless. At last, he pulled away. "Let's go home," he whispered.

Home. The word touched a sweet chord in her heart.

She pressed her palm to his hard chest. "I love that you consider Oscar Evans' house your home."

He lifted her chin. "Doesn't bother me one bit. Home is where you are, honey."

Questions for Discussion

1. Mercy has lost her two best friends through tragic circumstances, and God seems to speak into her spirit with the words: *I will refresh you, My child. Keep your eyes on Me, your Maker and Provider.* When all seems lost, have you ever sensed the Spirit of God speaking to you in such a manner? If you are comfortable doing so, share that experience.

2. There is a great deal of animosity between the Evans and Connors clans. What is your best recourse when caught in the middle of a spat you want nothing to do with, but certain parties try to drag you into anyway?

3. Mercy prays about the man God wants her to marry, but she finds it difficult to determine His leading. Have you been in the position of having to make a tough decision without sensing God's clear direction? What do you do in a case such as that, especially when time is of the essence?

4. When Mercy is going through a particularly difficult time, she silently cries out to God, "Lord, what am I to do? Please give me a sign." *Wait and trust,* He seems to answer. How difficult is it to wait on God and walk in faith when life holds nothing but confusion?

5. When the kitten comes up missing, a discussion arises about how God wants us to trust Him through the hard times. If you feel comfortable in sharing, tell about a specific time in your life when you had little choice but to trust God through the circumstance.

6. Sam quotes Jeremiah 29:11 to Mercy while trying to convince her that marrying him fits best with God's plan. Read the passage for yourself and see how it applies to your own life.

7. When mourning the loss of her friends, Mercy draws a conclusion that God didn't *cause* the tragic house fire, but He *did* allow it. When bad things happen to good people, are you tempted to blame God? Share a specific situation, if you're comfortable doing so.

8. While staying at his cousin Persephone's house, Sam reads from his Bible, and one passage in particular stands out to him: *"Love...seeketh not its own, is not provoked..."* (1 Corinthians 13:5). He relates this verse to the family feud and deduces that it all stems from selfishness. Would you agree that most arguments originate from that motivation—selfishness? Can you give an example?

9. In counseling Mercy, the reverend refers to Romans 8:28, which states, *"And we know that to them that love God all things work together for good, even to them that are called according to his purpose."* Have you found this particular verse to ring true in your own life? Explain.

10. In the end, Sam found it in his heart to forgive his mother for the wrongs she committed. How important is it to rid oneself of long-held bitterness toward another? Do you think it's always possible?

A Preview of

Threads of Joy

Tennessee Dreams ~ Book 2
Coming Fall 2014

1

1892 · *Paris, Tennessee*

𝒯he last shovelful of dirt went into the hole surrounding the stake bearing the beige handmade sign on which was painted, in bright-red letters, *The Perfect Fit Tailoring Shop*. Joy Westfall stomped on the mound, pressing it into place, to better anchor the sign. Proud of her achievement, she stepped back to assess her work. She might have been less hasty with the lettering, but she was a seamstress, not an artist. Still, it wasn't bad, standing tall and rather pompous-looking in the center of her yard. It would have been nice to hire out the work, but she wasn't made of money any more than she was born to fly. Come warmer weather, she'd plant some petunias and pansies around the base of the sign, but for now, it would do just fine.

She drew her coat collar closer to ward off the biting wind. Yesterday, beautiful sunshine and mild temperatures had seemed to promise a warming trend, with the certainty of spring in the offing. As if an affirmation of that guarantee, she'd even spotted a good number of busy robins with bulging bellies. Now, however, sinister black clouds loomed overhead, boding something altogether different—though she knew not what.

Next door, at Paris Evangelical Church, a hundred voices or more sang the final stanza of "Onward, Christian Soldiers." Joy knew it was the last because she'd counted, and they never skipped verses. Across the yard, her beloved daughter, three-and-a-half-year-old Annie, sang along as she dug in the dirt with a wooden spoon, never mind that she didn't know the words. "Oh, for Christmas Shoulders" is what she actually bellowed, but Joy didn't have the heart to correct her.

She'd never set foot inside the little white clapboard church, with the red shingled roof and door to match, even though the church property bordered her own. On the other side of the church stood the parsonage, a simple, two-story structure, painted white, with a cozy covered front porch that wrapped halfway around the house. The neat little yard backed up to the church cemetery, where dozens of etched stones and crooked crosses poked up from ancient graves. On occasion, Joy found herself strolling through the grassy lot, reading gravestones, while Annie crouched to gather wildflowers.

Joy sorely missed the elderly Reverend and Mrs. Younker. They'd been fine neighbors, and she longed for those chats she used to have with the preacher's wife across the churchyard when they both went out to their gardens to pull weeds or check on their vegetables. The woman always asked after Annie and made a point to drop over every now and again with a plate of fresh-baked muffins or a loaf of bread still warm from the oven. Naturally, Joy would reciprocate, with a fruit pie or a chocolate layer cake. The reverend had liked to say that if it weren't for his wife's fine cooking and Joy's magnificent desserts, he'd be trim as any twenty-year-old. As it was, the old fellow wheezed with every step and had obvious trouble keeping his belly bulge contained in his pants.

Joy had long known that retirement lurked on the horizon; she just hadn't wanted to see it come to fruition. Not that she'd ever listened to one of the reverend's sermons, unless she counted the times she'd sat rocking on her tiny front porch on a hot summer Sunday and heard snippets through the church's wide-open windows.

Her parents had raised her to go to church, even though church attendance was more a ritual than anything, but a sordid past now kept her from it altogether. Women with sordid pasts didn't go to church, did they? Shoot, women with sordid pasts didn't even have many friends to speak of. Perhaps that was why she missed the Younkers so much. They'd always treated her with utmost kindness and respect, never condemning her for failing to attend church. Why, the reverend had even said she needn't come to church at all to experience the Lord's forgiveness; she could kneel right down in her own living room, if she had a mind to—but she didn't. Not yet, anyway.

She knew that the Reverend and Mrs. Younker worried over her soul, for they'd promised to pray for her and Annie every day going forward. She still recalled the day she and had Annie stood on her front stoop, waving their hands like two flags, as the couple drove off, their wagon chock-full of trunks containing their earthly possessions, and headed south to live nearer their three grown children.

Joy dabbed at the silly dampness collecting in the corners of her eyes. My, one would think she'd gone soft as a down pillow. She pulled up her skirts and approached her daughter. "Time to go inside, dumplin'. It's gettin' plenty cold out here."

"Aww. Me an' Dorothy wants t' keep playin'."

Lately, it seemed that Annie's invisible friend always played some role in her playtime. "I know, but I got t' check on my soup, and I ain't leavin' you outside by yourself. 'Sides, it's feelin' like somethin' might be brewin' in the air."

The fair-haired child squinted up at her. "Brewin'—what's that?"

Joy reached down a hand to pull her daughter up—and got a palm full of mud for her efforts. "It means the weather could be takin' a bad turn." They mounted the steps together and entered the little house. She would have to stoke the fire to warm up the space. Good gracious, she'd thought she was done using the chimney for the season, but apparently, she'd been premature in hoping it. Mother Nature often played dirty tricks on gullible folks.

Before closing the door behind her, she let her eyes meander to the little church, where she caught a glimpse of the new preacher in his black suit and satin tie, stepping out of the door and taking his place at the top of the steps, in preparation for bidding his church family a good week. He was a fine-looking man, to be sure, with his dark hair; deep, cavernous eyes; broad shoulders, and towering physique—too darned handsome for a preacher, in her estimation. Glory, no man of the cloth ought to have such striking features. It was a wonder the female parishioners even listened to a word he said; for all she knew, they didn't. They certainly did swarm him like a band of bees. Why, word had it that the congregation had multiplied many times over in the past months, mostly due to the spinsters who traveled from miles around for a chance to meet the new minister—the handsome, unmarried, thirty-something minister. Disgraceful, that's what it was. Imagine going to church just to set your eyes on a tall, dark, and handsome preacher.

She latched her door with a louder-than-necessary click. It would be a hot day in the Arctic before she ever stooped so low.

⁓

Lucas Jennings sucked in a breath and prepared for the onslaught of female visitors who were sure to introduce themselves at the end of the service, based on his experience every Sunday since he'd started here. He'd seen at least half a dozen unfamiliar female faces this morning. There would be some batting eyelashes, a curtsy or two, and several white-gloved hands reaching out to give his hand an extra long squeeze, each woman hopeful to catch his eye in a special way. He had been ministering at Paris Evangelical Church since October—a full five months—and was sure he'd met every available woman in Henry County and beyond. He knew it would do him well to marry, so he could get on with the business of doing the work to which God had called him—preaching the gospel and serving the needs of others—but he wasn't about to let that hasten his wedding day. No, when he married, it would be for love alone, and only with the woman whom he knew beyond a doubt God had ordained for him to marry—one with saintly intentions who would serve alongside him in humility of spirit and with a passion to reach the lost sheep of the world—well, maybe not the world, but at least Paris, Tennessee.

So far, Kate Ryerson might fit the bill. One of his parishioners had introduced them at a dinner she'd hosted, having invited both of them with the secret purpose of matchmaking. At first, he'd been put off by the trickery, but he'd found Kate quite pleasant and had followed up with several outings after their initial meeting. So far, he hadn't found in her a single fault—unless it was her over-zealousness for speeding up the relationship process. She was twenty-nine, and she'd hinted more than once that she wasn't getting any younger. From what he knew of her, she came from a good, hardworking, God-fearing family, had a heart for the Lord, and exuded warm, friendly personality. Best, she didn't attend Paris Evangelical Church. Not that he wouldn't welcome her attendance at some point; but, presently, he wanted to keep their budding relationship private. He did not need the likes of Mrs. Grassmeyer or some other busybody spreading gossip about his personal life with the rest of the congregation. Good grief, he had a job to do—one that demanded an investment of heart and soul. The fewer the distractions, the better!

An unusually cold blast of air accosted him as he stepped out onto the concrete landing. Just last Sunday, he'd stood in the dazzling, seventy-plus-degree sunshine to shake the hands of his parishioners; today, he shivered. He decided to go back inside, but before he could reach the latch to pull the door shut, he noticed a sign in the neighbor lady's yard that hadn't been there yesterday. He narrowed his eyes, trying to make out what it said, but he couldn't quite decipher the letters. No doubt, it had something to do with that sewing business she operated from her home. He gave his head a little toss. She was a strange one, that woman—pretty as any picture, as was her little girl, but distant as the rocky shores of the Pacific. Why, he'd never so much as gotten a simple wave out of her when he happened to spot her across the churchyard. It wasn't as if he wanted or needed her friendship, but he wasn't accustomed to people—women, in particular—completely ignoring him when all he wanted to do was say hello.

"You best close that door, Reverend. You'll turn us into pillars of ice." This came from Alan Potter, one of the church elders who'd served on the pastoral search committee that had hired him.

Lucas reined in his thoughts and shut the door against the frigid winds.

"You'd never believe it was short-sleeve weather just a couple o' days ago," remarked Mrs. Potter, a pleasant woman with a pear-shaped body whose gray hair was pulled back into a bun so severe that it nearly ironed the wrinkles right out of her face. She had a big, toothy smile that made up for the dour look.

"'Bout the time y' think spring's arrived, we get hit with a cold streak," Mrs. Mortimer supplied, crowding in for the first handshake of the morning. "Can't complain, though. Ain't had but half an inch o' snow all winter."

Lucas smiled down at the petite older woman, who would have had to rise up on tiptoe to make five feet. She had a curved spine, which told him she'd seen taller days. He extended his hand as a queue formed behind her. "You're right as can be, Mrs. Mortimer. Your Tennessee winter was a welcome reprieve for this Michigander. I'm used to digging out from snowdrifts two and three feet deep. I'll take that half inch and be happy with it."

She nodded, drawing her coat collar up close around her neck. "Fine sermon, by the way," she said, almost as an afterthought.

"Thank you, ma'am." Lucas knew his sermons weren't anything to brag about. Following up a seasoned preacher like Reverend Younker, PEC's beloved pastor of twenty-some-odd years, proved a tall order to fill. This was only Lucas's second assignment, his first post having petered out altogether when the small, aging congregation in St. Ignace, Michigan, reached a point at which nearly everyone was too old and feeble to leave home. The small Methodist church had essentially died right along with its parishioners. When he'd read in the *Evangelical Brethren Herald* about a pulpit opening down in Paris, Tennessee, he'd sent his credentials to the powers that be, along with a written essay detailing his Christian testimony, and the next thing he knew, he was hopping a train to a warmer climate and a larger congregation made up of varied ages. Why, they'd even provided him with a parsonage and an actual salary—meager, to be sure, but enough to survive on. Not only that, but if money did get tight before his monthly stipend arrived, the Lord always laid it on someone's heart to stop by with a covered casserole and some sort of delectable dessert. In his opinion, it couldn't get much better than that.

Three women approached him together, their smiles as big as half-moons, their eyes gleaming with undisguised interest. All three had their hair done up in braids that wrapped around the tops of their heads like crowns. Their plaid dresses had that hand-sewn look. Nothing wrong with that, but the ill-fitting garments clung to their rotund frames in a none-too-flattering way.

"Morning, ladies," Lucas greeted them. "Nice to see you in church today."

They all beamed, the plumpest of the three revealing a large gap between her top front teeth. She snatched his hand and refused to let it go, propelling it up and down like she would a pump handle—and, from the strength of her handshake, he suspected she was used to operating one. "What a fine sermon, Reverend Jennings. Me and m' sisters been meanin' t' come visit y'r church ever since we heard about y—"

The sister standing closer to her elbowed her with gusto, knocking her off balance.

"What she means t' say is, we heard you was a mighty fine speaker, so we thought we'd come hear f'r ourselves, and I'll say this—folks sure was right...about your preachin', that is."

Lucas forced a polite smile. "Why, thank you kindly."

"We're the Harding sisters. You mighta heard of us," said the third. "We live a fair piece from here, but the drive over didn't bother us none."

Lucas had no idea why he might have heard of them, but he let the remark pass. He managed to wrench free of the biggest woman's clutch, then clasped his hands behind him and dipped his head. "Mighty nice to meet you, uh,..."

"Oh, forgive ar manners, Reverend. I'm Erlene," said the one with the firm handshake. She nodded to her left. "This here's Elaine." And to her right, she gestured at the third. "And this is Arlene."

Erlene, Elaine, and Arlene. Nice. Lucas would never remember who was who, but then, perhaps he wouldn't need to, if they didn't return. He judged them all to be close in age, probably in their mid- to late thirties. "Well, I thank you ladies for making the drive out. Mighty nice meeting you." Out of sheer politeness, he focused on the folks next in line, Mr. and Mrs. Milford, and then the Bransons and the Shelhamers. In due time, the sisters made their way to the door, a few thoughtful parishioners greeting them on their way out and inviting them back.

He couldn't help but hope he'd seen the last of the Harding sisters, much as he knew it wrong to think ill of them. *Lord,* he wondered, *will this weekly parade of women ever slow down?* But, even as he silently asked the question, he spotted yet two more women he'd never seen before, standing at the end of the procession, no doubt hanging back so as to be assured of gaining his full attention.

"Fine sermon, Reverend Jennings." This from Sam Connors, the local blacksmith. His pretty wife, Mercy, stood next to him, an arm around each of their two boys. By the look of her midsection, she would spit out a baby most any day, not that he knew anything about the birthing process. He liked the couple and had enjoyed himself the times they'd invited him over for Sunday supper. What he wouldn't give for a handsome family like theirs. Truly, the Lord had blessed them.

Could Kate Ryerson be the woman God had set aside for him? She seemed to have it all—faith, values, eloquence, and a love for God...all qualities any preacher would deem beneficial in a wife. And they did enjoy each other's company, laughing at many of the same things as they took the occasional evening stroll in her neighborhood. One thing lacked, however, and it had been just this morning, while he got ready for church, that he'd identified what that was: love. He *liked* her plenty, but he wasn't *in love* with her...not yet, anyway. They'd shared a few kisses, but each of them had left him dissatisfied. Perhaps the Lord would see to it that his feelings for her increased. He knew that she had strong feelings for him, the way she'd started hinting at marriage after a mere handful of dates.

"We'd love to have you over for supper again," said Mercy, dragging Lucas back to the present. He berated himself for dwelling on other matters when a line of congregants were still waiting to shake his hand.

"That would be wonderful, but I'm the one who should be inviting you." He wasn't sure why he'd said that. No way could he prepare a meal for an entire family. It was hard enough frying up an egg for one.

"No need to return any favors." She gave her rounded belly a circular rub. "I'm always making more than our family can eat, anyway. One of these days, I'll send Sam over with a spur-of-the-moment invite."

"I'm all for spontaneity."

After a bit more conversation, the family bade him good-bye. Soon, the line dwindled, until all that remained were Lucas and the two women visitors.

"Hello, Reverend," the shorter one cooed. She batted her long eyelashes and tossed back her curled locks with a whisk of her manicured hand. "Let me introduce myself."

Come, Lord Jesus. Come quickly.

About the Author

*B*orn and raised in west Michigan, Sharlene attended Spring Arbor University. Upon graduating with an education degree in 1971, she taught second grade for two years, then accepted an invitation to travel internationally for a year with a singing ensemble. In 1975, she married her childhood sweetheart. Together they raised two lovely, wonderful daughters, both of whom are now happily married and enjoying their own families. Retired in 2003 after thirty-one years of teaching, "Shar" loves to read, sing, travel, and spend time with her family—in particular, her wonderful, adorable grandchildren!

A Christian for forty-five-plus years and a lover of the English language, Shar has always enjoyed dabbling in writing—poetry, fiction, various essays, and freelancing for periodicals and newspapers. Her favorite genre, however, has always been romance. She remembers well writing short stories in high school and watching them circulate from girl to girl during government class. "Psst," someone would whisper from two rows over, when the teacher had his back to the class, "pass me the next page."

In recent years, Shar felt God's call upon her heart to take her writing pleasures a step further and in 2006 signed a contract for her first faith-based novel, launching her writing career with the contemporary romance *Through Every Storm*. With a dozen of her books now gracing store shelves nationwide, she daily gives God all the praise and glory for her accomplishments.

Through Every Storm was Shar's first novel to be published by Whitaker House, and in 2007, the American Christian Fiction Writers (ACFW) named it a finalist for Book of the Year. The acclaimed Little Hickman Creek series consists of *Loving Liza Jane* (Road to Romance Reviewer's Choice Award); *Sarah, My Beloved* (third place, Inspirational Readers' Choice Award 2008); and *Courting Emma* (third place, Inspirational Reader's Choice Award 2009). Shar's popular series the Daughters of Jacob Kane comprises *Hannah Grace* (second place, Inspirational Reader's Choice Award 2010), *Maggie Rose*, and *Abbie Ann* (third place, Inspirational Reader's Choice Award 2011). After that came River of Hope, composed of *Livvie's Song*, *Ellie's Haven*, and *Sofia's Secret*. *Heart of Mercy* is the first in her latest series, Tennessee Dreams.

Shar has done numerous countrywide book signings, television and radio appearances, and interviews. She loves to speak for women's organizations, libraries, church groups, women's retreats, and banquets. She is involved in Apples of Gold, a mentoring program for young wives and mothers, and is active in her church, as well as two weekly Bible studies. She and her husband, Cecil, live in Spring Lake, Michigan, with their beautiful white collie, Peyton.

I love to hear from my readers. Please feel free to contact me at sharlenemaclaren@yahoo.com. If you have a specific prayer request, you may rest assured I will add you to my prayer list! There is power in prayer! I love you, my precious readers.